Praise for *Clockwork Lies: Iron Wind*

"When it really gets going, the action sweeps the reader up. There is an eventful train journey, a dangerous mission and plenty of suspense. If you add the aerial visuals and technology this is a very rewarding read."
  —Daniel Cann, fantasybookreview.co.uk

"*Clockwork Lies: Iron Wind* is a fun steampunk adventure with plenty of action and political intrigue. Expect frightening airship rides, train wrecks, secret tunnels, coded messages, terrorists, daring rescues, gun smuggling, and computer hackers."
  —Kat Hooper, *Fantasy Literature*

"The story is also layered in political strife and war, deception and betrayal and love."
  —*Requiem For More Books*

"I am looking forward to seeing where the author heads with the third book of this trilogy."
  —Lyns, *Goodreads*

"Definitely a good starting point for anyone wanting to make the foray into steampunk."
  —Ebony, *Goodreads*

"Loved this book as much as the first. Lighter on the romance - but you could see the love the main characters had for each other - and heavy on the intrigue and world building."
  —Annette, *Goodreads*

· ✳ ·

The Clockwork Heart Trilogy

Book One
CLOCKWORK HEART

Book Two
CLOCKWORK LIES: IRON WIND

Book Three
CLOCKWORK SECRETS: HEAVY FIRE

HEAVY FIRE
CLOCKWORK
SECRETS

DRU PAGLIASSOTTI

EDGE SCIENCE FICTION AND FANTASY PUBLISHING
AN IMPRINT OF HADES PUBLICATIONS, INC.

CALGARY

Clockwork Secrets: Heavy Fire
Copyright © 2014 by Dru Pagliassotti

Edge Science Fiction and Fantasy Publishing
An Imprint of Hades Publications Inc.
P.O. Box 1714, Calgary, Alberta, T2P 2L7, Canada

In-house editing by Ella Beaumont
Interior design by Janice Blaine
Cover Illustration by Timothy Lantz

ISBN: 978-1-77053-054-6

EDGE Science Fiction and Fantasy Publishing and Hades Publications, Inc. acknowledges the ongoing support of the Alberta Foundation for the Arts and the Canada Council for the Arts for our publishing programme.

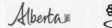 

Library and Archives Canada Cataloguing in Publication
Pagliassotti, Dru, author
Clockwork secrets : heavy fire / Dru Pagliassotti.
-- First edition.
Issued in print and electronic formats.

ISBN: 978-1-77053-054-6
(e-book ISBN: 978-1-77053-055-3)

I. Title.
PS3616.A33775C58 2014   813'.6   C2014-903415-6

FIRST EDITION
(J-20140629)
Printed in Canada
www.edgewebsite.com

DEDICATION

To Dad and Nancy.

CHAPTER ONE

THE RIFLES' PERCUSSION rang in Taya's ears and a cloud of acrid gunpowder drifted through the air. Blood trickled over the snow-powdered courtyard.

She wished she were home.

"There, Ambassador." *Il Re* Quintilio Agosti waved a hand toward the bodies. "I trust you will assure your decaturs that Alzana has brought its traitorous officers to justice."

Cristof's silk-covered fingers tightened on Taya's arm.

A year ago, watching men being executed would have made Taya sick. Now what made her sick was its pointlessness. Nobody in the small prison courtyard believed that the dead men had masterminded the invasion, and nobody believed their deaths would prevent a war between Alzana and Ondinium. The two nations enacted their thousand-year-old script like creaking automata in a traveling stage show, each line and gesture predetermined.

"Are we finished here, Your Majesty?" she asked, her words tasting like ash.

A small smile played beneath Agosti's well-groomed beard. He knew she was disgusted, and he took pleasure from the knowledge. It was the only pleasure he'd get from their assembly. Cristof's emotions were unreadable beneath his ivory mask, and Lieutenant Amcathra and his lictors would be content to stand in the snow for hours if it meant watching more Alzanans die.

"Would the ambassador like to see more?" Agosti countered. "I could arrange to have other criminals brought before the firing squad, if it would amuse him."

Taya tensed. Cristof tapped her forearm.

Enough.

"The ambassador has seen enough," she said, her voice tight. "These executions *weren't* among our demands."

"But they were necessary, nevertheless." The king's expression remained complacent. "A lesson, if you will."

For whom? Taya wondered. She glanced past the king toward the sullen-looking group of aristocrats who'd accompanied them, her gaze inexorably drawn to the cold, hostile glare of Lady Fosca Mazzoletti.

Fosca noted Taya's inspection and her lips pulled back in a grim, humorless smile. There was no way the woman could know that Lieutenant Amcathra had killed her twin brother, Gaio, to save Taya and Cristof, but it was clear that she suspected something. Taya looked away, pulling her heavy fur cloak closer around her shoulders. The other nobles' cold, flat expressions offered no relief. Even the soldiers in the execution squad seemed resentful as they shouldered their rifles.

King Agosti's middle-aged daughter, Rosa, and his sixteen-year-old granddaughter, Liliana, huddled a little apart from the rest of the group. His thirteen-year-old grandson, Pio, studied the corpses with morbid fascination. The young *principe* was still in school, but the brass buttons and military cut of his coat indicated that he'd eventually follow his oldest sister into the army. That sister, Major Pietra Agosti, hadn't attended the execution; she was away with her company. Meanwhile, the king's youngest grandson, Silvio, lay in bed with a cold.

Il Re Agosti glanced at the sky. "It's starting to snow again. If the ambassador doesn't wish to see more, we should return to the palace."

Cristof's fingers moved. *King meet me after.*

"Thank you, Your Majesty." Taya said. "The ambassador hopes to resume our talks this evening. We have much left to discuss."

"Yes, we do, but surely we wouldn't want to disturb our digestion with business." The king patted her arm with careless intimacy. "We'll resume our talks tomorrow."

Say Council end talk soon.

"As you wish," she said, hiding her distaste. "However, the ambassador wishes to remind you that the Council will grow impatient if we don't reach an agreement soon. The decaturs acquiesced to this truce at your request, Your Majesty, but their deadline is almost upon us."

"Indeed, indeed." The king laughed, but no amusement reached his eyes. He leaned closer. "Now that my enemies know where I stand, we should be able to proceed more expeditiously."

Taya reviewed his words twice before deciding that they weren't a threat. Not to her, anyway. She reassessed the hostile expressions on the Family leaders' faces.

What? Cristof inquired.

"The ambassador is pleased to hear that, Your Majesty," she said, shooting her husband a neutral look. "We look forward to discussing the situation with you tomorrow morning."

"Splendid." The king's expression collapsed into a sneer as he turned and regarded his entourage. "Sergeant! We are finished."

The sergeant barked orders. His men saluted the king and marched off, leaving the corpses behind.

"Ambassador." *Il Re* Agosti gestured to the line of towering steam-powered carriages waiting on the parkway before turning to his family.

Taya repeated the king's comment to Cristof as they began their slow walk across the snow-covered cobblestones. Lieutenant Amcathra remained beside them as his seven lictors ran ahead.

You trust him? Cristof tapped as they reached the carriages. The lictors were scrutinizing the steam engine's dials and checking their readouts against a chart. *Il Re* Agosti considered the tall, smoke-bellowing carriages standout symbols of Alzanan's modernity, but Amcathra monitored their operation with open suspicion.

"No, not really," Taya said, waiting for the lictors to let them enter. The Alzanans were already climbing ladders up to their Family carriages. The royal carriage was particularly tall and ornate, painted silver and sky-blue and surrounded by flamboyantly uniformed Alzanan soldiers standing at attention.

"Today's demonstration may have been intended to intimidate dissenters," Amcathra speculated, his rifle cradled in the crook of one arm. "Several of the executed officers belonged to Families in attendance."

Cristof's fingers moved. *Dangerous.*

"He says that sounds dangerous."

"Indeed." Amcathra inspected the chart and allowed his lictors to lean a ladder against the coach's towering eight-foot-tall wheels. "Exalted."

Taya helped Cristof climb and slid into the cabin beside him. Amcathra closed the door as his lictors secured the ladder beneath the vehicle.

Taya drew the curtains and untied Cristof's blank-featured ivory mask. She smiled at her husband's thin, careworn features and pale gray eyes and brushed a wayward strand of black hair away from his forehead. When he wasn't wearing his glasses, the new scars around his left eye were clearly visible.

"How are you feeling?"

"Less pleased than I ought to be, considering there are five fewer Alzanan officers in the world." He rubbed his face against a silk-covered shoulder. The coach jerked into motion, shaking and rumbling over the cobblestones. "What about you?"

"I'm all right." Her smile faded. "I must be getting used to violence."

"I'm sorry."

"I hope the king is finally planning to settle down to our negotiations," she said, avoiding the compassion in her husband's eyes. "I'm ready to leave Alzana."

"One way or the other, we'll be gone soon." He rested a fabric-draped hand over his ivory mask as she set it in his lap. "It's late winter, and the Council will want to attack by spring. We need to be back in Ondinium before that."

"You're assuming we'll fail."

"Did you think we'd succeed?" His crooked smile was humorless. "These negotiations are just a delaying tactic, love. Alzana is rushing to outfit whatever other dirigibles it has in hiding and the Council is rushing to pull more... more *machines* out of storage. This war's inevitable; you and I are just the intermission entertainment."

"Well, our work wasn't entirely in vain," Taya said, trying to cheer them both up. "The other nations have agreed to remain neutral, and I don't think they would have if their ambassadors hadn't met you in Mareaux. Showing them a face instead of a mask made a difference; they aren't as intimidated by Ondinium as they used to be."

"No, nobody would call me intimidating," Cristof agreed. She made a face at him. He raised an eyebrow. "Anyway, you're the one who's done all—"

The coach swayed as something struck the front panel with a sharp report.

"Ambush!" Amcathra roared.

Taya leaned over her husband and tore open the curtains, heedless of propriety. They were paralleling the Capitoli River on the statue-lined Grand Avenue that divided the civic sprawl from the wealthy Family estates. She didn't see anything suspicious, but Amcathra's heavy boots thudded on the roof as he barked commands to his lictors.

"Taya!" Cristof exclaimed. She abandoned the windows to help him pull off his incapacitating public robe. The heavy garment and his ivory mask dropped to the carriage floor. "Where are my glasses?"

"In my reticule."

He grabbed her velvet purse as she returned to the windows and lifted the pane, twisting her head out. A group of black-clad men on horseback was charging down the wide avenue toward them, shouting and brandishing pistols. Each man bore a black stripe running down the side of his face.

"Lictors!"

"What?" Cristof slid his glasses on. The carriage stopped as Amcathra's lictors fell in around its towering wheels, aiming their rifles at the horsemen.

"We're being attacked by lictors!"

"Impossible!" Cristof looked over her shoulder. "The Council—"

He was interrupted by a barrage of gunfire. Taya flinched and Cristof pulled her down between the seats, wrapping his arms around her. Screams, shouts, and shots filled the air. Then Lieutenant Amcathra yanked the carriage door open, balancing on a tall wheel as he hooked the long ladder to its rings.

"Get down," he snapped.

Taya pushed Cristof in front of her. He stumbled over his crumpled robe and discarded mask, shot her a dark look, and clambered down the ladder. Taya grabbed his mask by its strings and followed.

"Other side," Amcathra ordered, stepping from the wheel to the ladder and sliding down its vertical rails. Cristof started to say something and the lictor grabbed him by the shoulder. "*Now!*"

Cristof pulled up his inner robes, revealing the black trousers he'd worn beneath for warmth, and ducked under the carriage. Taya hiked up her skirt, wishing *she* had trousers underneath instead of lace-trimmed drawers, and followed suit. She crouched beside the wheel, squinting through the gunpowder smoke. King

Agosti's soldiers had run forward to meet the attackers. The avenue looked like a battlefield where the riders and royal guards clashed, but Amcathra's lictors remained still, holding their fire.

"They can't be lictors," Cristof muttered next to her ear. "The Council would never do something so stupid."

"Exalted." Amcathra appeared from beneath the coach and handed Cristof a needle pistol, then pulled a bone-handled knife from his boot and held it out. "Icarus?"

Taya hesitated, then handed Cristof his mask.

"Don't lose that," she ordered, taking the knife. "You'll need it later."

"I think this diplomatic mission is over," he said tautly, tying the mask inside his robe. He raised his voice over another barrage of gunfire. "Are those really lictors, Janos?"

"It is unlikely. Few lictors ride."

"Don't you know for sure?" Taya demanded.

"The Council does not tell me all of its plans." The lieutenant turned to the nearest lictor. "Jager, find a safe route into the city."

"Yes, sir!" The woman saluted and tapped the three nearest lictors, jerking her head toward the river. They slung their rifles over their shoulders and jogged off.

Amcathra grabbed the carriage's towering wheel and pulled himself back up to the roof. He lay flat, swinging his rifle around. A horseman broke through the melee, aiming his pistol at the carriage. Amcathra fired and the attacker pitched over the back of his steed, but more assailants were approaching on foot and on horseback. Their lictors opened fire. Taya cringed as one of them jerked and crumpled, his rifle clattering on the stone road, but several of the attackers dropped, too, sliding out of their saddles as their horses bounded away from the fighting.

Cristof ducked out from under the coach and knelt by one of the fallen riders, running his hand across the man's castemark. Black greasepaint smeared his fingers.

"They're not real!" he bellowed. "Janos, it's a frame!"

Amcathra didn't answer, but Taya saw the lictor next to her bare her teeth as she snapped off a shot. The lictate didn't appreciate imposters.

A high-pitched scream rose behind them. Attackers had swarmed the king's carriage, shattering the windows and tearing open the door. Taya grabbed Cristof's sleeve.

"Look!"

"Who cares?"

"Cris!" The king's daughter and grandchildren were pulled out of the tall carriage and thrown to the ground. They landed hard, *Principe* Pio clutching his wrist with an anguished howl. *Principessa* Liliana scrambled to him as their mother Rosa pulled herself to her knees. Their royal guards were nowhere to be seen. "They're attacking the children!"

Taya drew Amcathra's knife and ran toward them. Her husband muttered under his breath, then grabbed the fake lictor's pistol and followed, a firearm in each hand.

Il Re Agosti was hauled out of the carriage next, struggling and shouting. His disaffected aristocrats surrounded him as he lay sprawled on the ground, kicking him in the ribs and jeering. With a shriek, Rosa threw herself at the nearest assailant, trying to pull him away from her father. Ducking her blows, an Alzanan aristocrat turned and shot her in the stomach.

Wails of horror arose from Agosti's grandchildren. Cristof skidded to a halt and fired.

Steel needles tore into the shooter's chest. The man staggered back and collapsed, the mob parting in alarm. Cristof shot again, holding down the trigger and sweeping the needle gun from left to right. A spray of slender metal spikes drove the well-dressed attackers back. Several lost their nerve and ran. Taya sprinted for the king.

"Ambassador!" Lady Fosca Mazzoletti shoved herself forward, wielding a gold-chased, long-barreled pistol. She aimed it at Taya. "Put down your gun or I'll shoot her."

Taya hurled her knife at the woman's face. Fosca's eyes widened. She twisted away from the blade only to find Taya grabbing her wrist and forcing her pistol upward.

"I am *not* going to be a hostage again!" Taya spat. The two of them grappled, their feet sliding over the snow-covered street. Somebody grabbed Taya's shoulder, but a moment later she heard a loud bang and the attacker collapsed next to her. Fosca used the distraction to claw her face.

Jerking her head back, Taya kicked Fosca's knee. The taller woman shifted her weight, throwing Taya off-balance as she muscled her gun closer to Taya's face. Taya struggled to stay upright. She heard an exchange of gunfire and Cristof shouting her name, but the rest of his words were lost in the uproar around her.

Suddenly *Principessa* Liliana landed on Fosca Mazzoletti's back, screaming and pulling at the noblewoman's hair. The gun went off and Taya jerked back, deafened. The girl's fist tangled on a golden chain around Fosca's neck and pulled it taut. The aristocrat dropped her gun and reached into her sleeve, pulling out a stiletto.

The chain broke, leaving the *principessa* off-balance, holding the necklace and a handful of dark hair. Fosca grimaced, stabbing backward and missing. Taya took the opening to swing her elbow against the side of the woman's temple.

"Let's go!" one of the Alzanans shouted, running up and grabbing Fosca Mazzoletti's shoulder. "Agosti's dead and the lictors are coming!"

"Kill the girl," Fosca snapped, clutching the side of her head.

The Alzanan raised his pistol. Taya tackled the girl to the ground, flinching as the pistol's hammer fell on an empty chamber. A rifle fired and the Alzanan collapsed into an ungainly heap in the street not far from where Taya lay huddled. A horse thundered past, its hooves throwing snow and mud over Taya's face. She pressed the *principessa*'s head down next to hers, listening to gunfire.

"It's all right," she whispered in Alzanan. "It's all right." All she could see was the snow beneath her cheek and the bleeding bodies sprawled around her, and all she could feel was the girl's rapid breathing — or was it sobbing? — under her arm. At any moment she expected Fosca Mazzoletti to put a bullet into the back of her head.

"Icarus!" Someone was shouting in Ondinan. "Are you hurt?"

Taya looked up. Fosca had fled and one of their lictors, Helvi, was kneeling beside her. Cristof stood a few feet away, his concern melting into relief as he saw her move.

"Let's go." Helvi swung her rifle around. Taya pulled herself to her feet and held out a hand for the *principessa*. Blood spattered the girl's face and dress.

"You'd better come with us," Taya said in Alzanan.

"Pio...." *Principessa* Liliana's face was white with shock as she lifted herself up, her gaze fixed behind them. Taya turned.

The girl's little brother had been shot in the head; his skull a bloody, shattered mess. Taya's stomach heaved. Not far away, their mother lay in a huddled heap, her stomach soaked with blood. And behind her lay *Il Re* Quintilio Agosti himself, slashed and shot and beaten to death by his angry vassals, a number of whom now lay dead or dying around their victim. Cristof and Helvi had clearly done all they could to avenge the doomed family.

"Oh, Lady." Taya grabbed the *principessa*'s hand and drew her up, wrapping an arm around the girl's narrow shoulders. "I'm so sorry. Come away."

"No— please!"

"It's all right— we'll keep you safe. I promise."

"Taya, we need to go." Cristof had pulled a dead Alzanan's coat over his silk robes and scrounged new percussion pistols from the fallen. With his long black hair falling out of its ornate pins and clasps and his wave-shaped castemarks starkly visible on his naked cheekbones, he looked like the Oporphyr Council's worst protocol nightmare.

"Just a minute." Taya released the girl and ran forward, sweeping up Amcathra's boot knife and looking one more time for any sign of Fosca Mazzoletti. Seeing no sign of the noblewoman, she turned and took *Principessa* Liliana's arm once more. Cristof and the lictors fell in around them, firing at anybody who came too close. The *principessa* was pale with shock.

Lieutenant Amcathra was working on their steam carriage's boiler while one of his men covered him, keeping the false lictors at bay. Amcathra pointed a gloved hand toward the three-foot-high wall that divided the avenue from the snow-covered expanse that led to the Capitoli River. Two of the four lictors he'd sent out earlier stood at the top of the riverbank, their rifles at the ready.

"Follow them, Exalted," he shouted over the gunfire, screams, and pounding hooves.

"Agosti's dead," Cristof reported, also raising his voice. "So's his daughter and grandson. We have *Principessa* Liliana with us."

"Who killed him?"

"The Families— I think Fosca Mazzoletti was in charge."

"Is she dead?"

"I missed."

"Too bad." Amcathra pointed again. "Go."

They climbed over the short wall and ran toward the river. Taya risked a glance over her shoulder and saw royal soldiers and fake lictors shooting each other while bloodstained aristocrats and frightened commoners fled. Wounded humans and horses screamed with pain in the middle of the chaos.

Then the Ondinium steam carriage lurched into motion, barreling into the carriage in front of it. Lieutenant Amcathra and the other lictor vaulted over the wall, holding their rifles in both hands, and charged toward them. The false lictors ducked around the mechanical collision to continue firing at them. Taya winced as bullets whistled past her ears and one of the lictors next to her cried out.

"Down!" Amcathra bellowed. "Get down!"

Taya threw herself and the *principessa* flat. Cristof and the lictors sprawled next to them.

Two heartbeats passed. Taya was about to look up when an explosion thundered around them. She only had a second to register fresh screams before a second explosion followed. Something heavy and searing hit her calf. She shrieked and yanked her leg beneath her, reaching down to make sure her skirt wasn't on fire.

"Taya!" She looked up. Cristof was on his knees, reaching for her across the *principessa*. "Are you all right?"

"I think so." Her skirt was scorched and a steaming, twisted chunk of metal lay next to her, but her skin had only been scalded. "*Principessa*?"

The Alzanan girl mutely lifted herself to all fours, then to her knees. She seemed alive and unharmed. One of the lictors wasn't, though— Taya could tell that from Helvi's grim expression as she leaned over her castemate's body.

Behind them, fire crackled across Grand Avenue. The walls and statues close to the carriage had been blown into rubble, and body parts lay scattered along the street partially obscured by a haze of smoke.

Lieutenant Amcathra and the other lictor joined them.

"We must go."

"Cael's dead," Helvi reported. "Shot in the back."

"Bright, carry him," Amcathra ordered. Helvi took the man's rifle as Amcathra's companion grabbed the corpse and hoisted it over his shoulder.

"What did you do with Jordan and Hind?" Helvi asked, standing.

"Their bodies were inside the carriage."

Taya paled. If that was Amcathra's idea of a cremation....

"Go." Amcathra jerked his head toward the river. "*Run*."

The lictors led them away at a jog. They followed the Capitoli River for several minutes and then, when it was clear the Alzanan rebels had lost track of them in the smoke and chaos, they cut back to a narrow pedestrian access tunnel that ran below Grand Avenue. Jager and another lictor huddled inside, guarding each end.

"Sir, this leads into the city, but there are people all over," Jager reported, her eyes flickering to Cael's body and then back again. They heard another explosion; a third carriage had blown its boiler.

Amcathra turned. "*Principessa* Liliana Agosti."

The young Alzanan shrank against the wall.

"*Principessa*, the Families are in rebellion," Amcathra continued in Alzanan. "Do you have any allies whom you can trust to keep you safe?"

The girl shook her head, wide-eyed.

"Please think again. It is in our best interest to deliver you safely to Family Agosti loyalist— you are the only Agosti left who can attest that we did not kill the king."

Lady! He was right, Taya realized. The princess's testimony could salvage this diplomatic disaster. But tears filled the girl's eyes and spilled down her cheeks.

"She's in shock." Taya patted the girl's arm. "Let's find someplace to hide, and then we'll figure out what to do."

Amcathra looked displeased, but he turned and began giving orders. His lictors smudged mud and blood onto their faces to hide their stripes and opened their jackets and shirts to disguise their uniforms. Cristof wiped ash across the castemarks over his cheekbones. He wanted to remove his telltale robes and go bare-chested under his pilfered coat, but Taya and Amcathra both vetoed the idea, unwilling to risk his health in the middle of winter.

"You know that Mazzoletti — or whoever was behind this coup — has done a marvelous job of framing us," Cristof said as he buttoned his coat to his neck. "We're going to be shot on sight."

"Anybody who inspects the bodies will discover that they are not real lictors," Amcathra said.

"But what about— ah." Cristof nodded toward Cael's corpse. "That's why you're not letting them collect our fallen."

"Correct."

"It won't make a difference. Nobody will get a chance to touch the bodies, and most will believe whatever the rebels tell them."

"Cris." Taya touched his arm. "What about Jayce and the rest of our staff? They're still in the palace."

"I'm sorry, Taya." He clasped her hand between his palms.

She recoiled. "We can't just *leave* them!"

"There's nothing else we can do."

"But— but they'll be killed!" She stared at him in disbelief. They had come to the palace with a staff of six, including their tailor Jayce, who was her best friend Cassi's nephew and a friend in his own right. She and Jayce had survived poisoning and a train crash together, but now....

"I'm sure the Alzanans will keep them alive as bargaining chips," Cristof said, striving to sound confident. Taya looked away. Maybe so, but Ondinium's decaturs viewed their nation as a giant machine and its citizens easily replaceable cogs and springs. They would never pay ransom for a group of lower-caste diplomatic staff.

She didn't know what she was going to say to Cassi if she ever got back to Ondinium.

CHAPTER TWO

BY MIDNIGHT THE small band of refugees found itself in a narrow alley that stank of urine and rotting garbage. The capital was in an uproar, and they'd hidden in the narrow, winding back alleys of its poorest quarter all day.

Principessa Liliana remained with them, her eyes red and her face streaked with soot and tears. Two lictors kept watch on either side of the alley as the rest crouched in a circle of dim light cast from a small window overhead. Cael's corpse lay several feet away.

Taya counted out the handful of coins that they had between them. Nobody had expected to need money at the execution, and they couldn't pawn Cristof's or the *principessa*'s jewelry while they were wanted.

"Well, we have enough for a day," she said. "I'll go buy us something to eat."

"You can't," Cristof protested. "You've been the face of Ondinium since we arrived— people will recognize you even without a castemark."

"I could disguise myself."

"How?"

Taya looked at her dirty skirts. "Well… I hate to say it, but right now I could probably pass as a prostitute."

Cristof gave her a disbelieving stare.

"That would be a reasonable disguise for a woman in this neighborhood at this time of night," Amcathra agreed.

"Janos, I am *not* sending my *wife* into the streets as a— a streetwalker!"

Taya crossed her arms and glowered at him.

"Well, it's not as if—"

"It will not work, Icarus." *Principessa* Liliana's voice startled them all. "Your accent will give you away."

Taya paused, surprised. She hadn't realized the *principessa* spoke Ondinan. She took a deep breath, remembering that she might be talking to the last surviving member of the royal family.

"Is it that obvious, Your Royal Highness?" she asked, formally.

The girl nodded.

That was disappointing. Taya had thought her Alzanan was pretty fluent; it wasn't as accented as the *principessa*'s Ondinan, anyway. She blew out an impatient breath and ran a mud-streaked hand through her hair. Castemarks, accents, clothing... for the first time, Ondinium's singularities struck her as more drawback than distinction.

"I know a place we could hide, if we can get there," Cristof said after a moment. "It's a little risky, and Janos, I'll have to ask you not to write it up in any report you may file...."

"Where is this place, Exalted?" His voice was laden with suspicion.

"Um..." Cristof pushed up his glasses and shot Taya an apprehensive glance. "Well...."

Taya groaned. "You planned a meeting with *him*? *Here*?"

"We didn't *plan* it; we only discussed the possibility."

"'Him'?" Amcathra's expression darkened. "Your brother is here, consorting with Alzanans?"

"He's not consorting. He publishes some books here, that's all."

Principessa Liliana looked up with curiosity.

"The Council was under the impression that your brother lived in Mareaux," Amcathra growled. "That is where you set up his secret bank account."

"If it's so secret," Cristof muttered, "why does everybody know about it?"

The lictor waited.

"Al lives on the border and publishes his political rants here under a pseudonym. It's ridiculous stuff; completely unacceptable in Ondinium and probably not publishable in Mareaux, either— but Alzanans love radical free-thinkers, especially disaffected Ondiniums. Apparently he's developed a following. Anyway, he suggested we rendezvous with his publisher if I found the time while I was here."

"How were you going to find the time?" Taya demanded. "And when were you going to tell *me* about it?"

"*If* I had found the time, I would have told you before I went."
Cristof took her hand. "Really. All he said was that he'd be in the
capital while we were here and that I could contact him through
his publisher. We didn't make any arrangements beyond that."

"This is a very bad plan," Amcathra declared.

"Well, what's *yours*? The last I heard, the Alzanan government
had invested a lot of time and effort into expanding its telegraphic
network. I'm sure the army's monitoring the roads and railroad
tracks from here to the border. We'll need inside help if we want
to escape— or even *eat*, apparently."

"The Council and I anticipated the possibility of an emergency
evacuation. I will get us out of Alzana."

"How?"

"By ship. However, we must meet it at the coast."

"We're on the opposite side of the city right now. But I'll bet
Alister could get us to the coast."

"Your brother is a saboteur and a murderer," the lictor stated.

"He wouldn't murder *me*."

"He's framed you for murder once already," Taya reminded
him. "And he threw you off the Great Engine. *And* he tried to
shoot you."

Cristof scowled. "He wasn't thinking straight."

"I will carry a message to your brother's publisher," *Principessa*
Liliana volunteered. Taya hesitated and saw her reservations reflected
in Cristof's and Amcathra's expressions.

"You are being hunted, *Principessa*," Lieutenant Amcathra
demurred. "The rebels do not want you alive, either."

"I know." The *principessa* pushed her long, curling black hair
out of her face, avoiding the lictor's eyes. "I *know*. I know I am in
danger. I know—" her voice broke. "I know my family is dead.
I know I have no choice except to take my chances with you. I
know all of that better than *any* of you."

"I'm sorry," Taya whispered.

"The ambassador is correct," the girl continued, stubbornly.
"You will not be able to escape to the coast without assistance. I
am not— I am not very familiar with the city, but at least I *belong*
here. I will deliver your message for you, for my own safety as
well as for yours."

"Your accent is no more suitable to this neighborhood than
ours, *Principessa*," Amcathra objected. "It is that of an aristocrat."

The girl's shoulders hunched. "Then I will say as little as possible."

"Do you understand what is happening out there, Your Royal Highness?" Cristof asked, gently.

"A revolution," the girl replied. She opened her fist to reveal Fosca Mazzoletti's broken necklace. "Those Families killed Mama and Pio. They killed my grandfather, the king."

"And they're framing us for it."

She met his eyes. "I do not know how it is done in Ondinium, Exalted Forlore, but in Alzana, they owe me a blood debt."

"Does that mean you are declaring a vendetta, *Principessa*?" Amcathra pressed. The girl nodded. The lictor turned to Cristof with an air of satisfaction. "Exalted, I recommend we support *Principessa* Agosti's vendetta."

"Does that mean we have to help her kill her enemies?"

"And re-establish her Family's presence on the throne."

Cristof slowly nodded. "We're not in any position to fight your enemies just now, Your Royal Highness, but as Ondinium's ambassador, I am willing to support your attempt to see justice done."

"I accept your support," *Principessa* Liliana replied, closing her hand over the broken necklace again. "My allies are Family Agosti's allies."

Taya ran a hand through her short hair, wondering why everybody in the group but her seemed to think that killing people was a good idea.

"First things first," she said, turning their attention back to the problem at hand. "The *principessa* can't go out into the streets wearing all that jewelry."

Principessa Liliana handed her the broken necklace and slipped off her own jewels, dropping them into Taya's reticule. They set aside her fur-lined coat and turned their attention to her dress, transforming it from a *principessa*'s day gown to something more suitably ratty and hard-used. The *principessa* used one of the torn and muddy ribbons they'd removed from her skirt to tie back her thick hair.

"Her bodice should be lower," Amcathra said. Taya shot him a scandalized look. "It is a matter of disguise, Icarus. Prostitutes display more cleavage."

"Do they?" Taya scowled. "Maybe she's disguising herself as a chambermaid, not a prostitute."

"In this neighborhood?"

"I will do it, Icarus." The young *principessa* blushed and tugged down the top of her dress. Taya glared at Amcathra and Cristof, but the two men were taking great pains not to glance at the girl's chest.

Good.

"Do you have the address, Exalted?" *Principessa* Liliana asked, sounding as nervous as she looked. Cristof slipped a hand into the pocket of his pilfered coat, then looked down at it with bemusement.

"Er, no. You'll need to find Muraro Press and tell the owner to contact Alessio Scordato. Tell him … hmm … tell him that Viridinion wants to see him."

"Too obvious," Taya objected. "Even if the publisher doesn't know his history, that name's clearly Ondinium. Here, Your Royal Highness, give him this." She reached into her reticule and fished out the watch Cristof had made for her.

"Taya, no!"

"Alister will return it."

"No. Don't. Use mine."

"But…"

"Hide it well, *Principessa*," Cristof said, handing his pocket-watch to Liliana. "Don't get pick-pocketed."

The girl slipped the watch into her bodice.

"Muraro Press. Alessio Scordato," the girl repeated, standing. "All right."

Amcathra cleared his throat. The *principessa* flinched.

"If…" he gave Taya a sidelong look. "If you tied her outer skirt higher, you would enhance her disguise."

"Why do you know so much about prostitutes, Lieutenant?"

"I have supervised undercover agents before," he replied with a long-suffering air. "The *principessa* is more likely to be harassed if she appears to be a respectable woman lost in the wrong part of town than if she fits the local demographic."

"Give her one of your pistols," Taya said, turning to her husband. She was liking this plan less and less. Cristof's amusement at her interchange with Amcathra faded and he held out the weapon.

"Here, Your Royal Highness. Do you know how to use it?"

While Cristof taught *Principessa* Liliana how to use a gun, Taya tied the girl's skirt a few inches higher and looked at Amcathra, silently daring him to make any more suggestions. He remained silent.

At last the *principessa* was ready to leave, the pistol wrapped in a rag.

"I will return as soon as I can, Exalted," she said, clutching the bundle close to her chest. She glanced around at all of them. "Be careful."

"And you, *Principessa*," Taya murmured with trepidation, slipping her fingers into Cristof's hand for comfort.

· ✷ ·

They retreated deeper into the alley. The lictors sat by the wall with their rifles on their knees, keeping watch. Taya and Cristof huddled together against the winter chill, unable to sleep.

"Ah, here it is. I thought I felt something break." Cristof fished the two halves of his ivory exalted's mask from his public robe and tugged them free of their strings. Taya took them and rested the broken edges together. A large splinter of ivory was missing.

"I don't think it can be repaired," she said, a lump rising in her throat.

"Neither do I." Cristof tugged them from her fingers and threw them behind him, into the trash that had collected in the corners of the alley. "Good riddance."

"I guess we're really at war now," Taya said, quietly. Cristof pulled her closer.

Avoiding war had been unlikely, anyway. Eight hundred and seventy-four Ondiniums had been killed in the Glasgar bombing. The decaturs had reacted swiftly and decisively — every Alzanan had been kicked out of the country, even those who'd lived there for years, and every immigrant and Ondinium of first- to third-generation Demican descent had been required to take a special loyalty test or leave. The Council had tightened its censorship of the press and its restrictions on free assembly, shutting down the nation's most radical publications and organizations. It had also called for an international summit on aerial warfare, a hypocritical move given that it was simultaneously readying its own top-secret fleet of ancient imperial ornithopters. Deep inside Ondinium Mountain, the Great Engine had ground away day and night, spitting out economic forecasts and military simulations.

Taya had hidden from the chaos. Her silence about what had happened in the skies beyond Glasgar had been required by the Official Secrets Act, but it had also been an easy way to avoid admitting the terrible things she'd done there.

"What are you thinking about?" she whispered, trying to avoid her own dark memories.

"What I'm going to say to Alister when we finally meet face-to-face."

"Oh."

"I've imagined it a hundred times, and what I've wanted to say has always changed with my mood." He forced a smile. "I never imagined I'd be asking him for help."

"He'll give it to you."

His smile faltered. "The way I helped him, maybe. Blinded, outcaste, and exiled."

Taya clasped his hand, feeling the scar tissue where a jagged piece of glass had pierced it in the train wreck.

"He wanted to live. You gave him that."

"I wonder how he feels about it now."

"He's doing well enough— a published author with a personal following."

"I suppose." Cristof closed his eyes and leaned his head against the dirty brick wall. "I don't think the Council is going to help us, Taya."

"Since when has it *ever* helped us?" She studied his face, saddened by the scars around his left eye and the new lines that furrowed his forehead and bracketed his mouth. Working as Ondinium's only exalted ambassador had thrust him from one peril to another, and the strain had visibly aged him. "We'll be all right. As long as we're together, we'll be all right."

His lips quirked up as he opened his eyes again.

"Have I told you recently that I love you?"

"Not recently, no."

"I need to work on that."

"Yes, you do." She kissed him. "And the feeling's mutual."

Dawn was approaching when a canvas-covered wagon came to a noisy halt at the mouth of the alley. Amcathra raised his rifle, then lowered it when *Principessa* Liliana appeared, looking around fearfully.

"Hello? Are you still there?" she whispered. "We're here to take you to Muraro Press."

The scent of machine oil and ink washed over the small group as it entered the Muraro publishing house. A small, thin Alzanan with a rat-tail mustache greeted them, his eyes widening as he took in the lictors' stern faces and ready weapons.

"No, no, say nothing," he burst out in Alzanan before anyone could speak. "I see nothing, I hear nothing— I demand complete deniability, *complete*, do you understand?"

"We understand," Taya assured him. "We're here to see...." she frowned. What was Alister calling himself, again?

"Alessio Scordato, yes, I have sent for him. He — You — I was never *told* about any of this, I never *knew* about any of this, and I am leaving as soon as he comes and forgetting this entire morning."

"Thank you, sir."

"Here. Follow me. Sit here. Right here." He led them through the large room, which held several steam-powered presses, to a circle of uncomfortable-looking chairs drawn together around a desk. "*Stay.*"

"You seem a little nervous for a man who publishes radical political tracts," Cristof remarked. Amcathra nodded to his lictors and they spread out, pacing through the rest of the printing press floor with their rifles held at the ready.

"I am a *publisher*, not a *traitor*. Scordato never told me he was associating with *assassins*!"

"Nobody here is an assassin," *Principessa* Liliana objected. "The Ondiniums have done nothing wrong!"

"I didn't hear that! Mister Scordato told me nothing about any of this, *nothing*. I am *very* unhappy with him, I assure you, *very* unhappy." The small man hurried after the lieutenant.

"He's very jumpy," Cristof observed. "*Very* jumpy."

"Stop that," Taya chided, taking one of the chairs. She looked at the bedraggled *principessa*. "You didn't tell him who you were, did you?"

"Of course not, Icarus. I do not know which Family he serves."

"The room appears secure," Lieutenant Amcathra reported, rejoining them. *Principessa* Liliana self-consciously tugged up her bodice. "The publisher has gone to his office and closed the door. Bright is watching him. The rest of us will guard the windows and doors. I regret that there is no food here, but we can make tea."

"Thank you," Cristof said. The lictor nodded and left.

"Did you have any trouble getting here?" Taya asked the girl. "Did anyone bother you?"

The *principessa* shook her head. "I ignored the men who whistled and walked as fast as I could. A street sweeper told me that Muraro Press was on this avenue."

"I'm glad you're safe."

The girl nodded, looking away and biting her lip.

About an hour later, the workyard door opened again. Cristof shifted the pistol in his lap, flicking off the safety.

Tap, tap, tap.

Alister came into sight, his hand on the arm of a pretty young woman in a Mareaux dress. Taya drew in a sharp breath, more disturbed at seeing him again than she had expected.

Her brother-in-law was tall and well-built, with smooth copper skin and a strong, handsome face. His long black hair was braided back and he wore clean but simple garments covered by a knee-length, rust-colored overcoat. A neatly folded black blindfold covered the scarred ruin of his eyes but left bare the jagged slashes tattooed across his castemarks. He carried a leather satchel slung over one shoulder and a slender chestnut cane in one hand.

His guide stopped, studying the three of them with wary eyes. "We are here," she said in accented Ondinan. "Lictors guard the door. Your brother and the icarus are present. I do not know who the third woman is. She is young and wearing a torn dress."

"Al...." Cristof stood, swallowing hard as he set his pistol down.

"Cris." Alister's lips turned up in a wry smile. "Are you what smells so bad in here?"

"Quite possibly. I spent the night in an alley." Cristof's feet seemed frozen in place. "It's good to see you again."

"I wish I could say the same."

Cristof closed his eyes. "I'm sorry."

"I think this is yours?" Alister held out his brother's golden pocketwatch. Cristof reluctantly stepped forward and took it from him, opening his mouth to say something, but the blind exalted had already shifted. "Taya? My silver-winged hawk? Are you there?"

Taya stood.

"I'm here, Alister. How are you?"

"As you see." He smiled, his blind face turning toward her. "How is your leg?"

"All healed. Thank you for the information you sent in Mareaux. If we hadn't gotten it—" she stopped. It might not be a good idea to let *Principessa* Liliana know that Alister had been instrumental in uncovering the Alzanan invasion. "Things would have been much different."

Alister cocked his head, registering her shift in tone.

"Who else is here with us, Taya?"

"*Principessa* Liliana, *Il Re* Agosti's granddaughter."

"Ah...." Alister made a formal Alzanan bow. "I am honored, *Principessa*."

The gesture startled Taya; Alister had been so casually authoritative as a decatur that she had never imagined him deferring to foreign royalty. Then again, he had always been excessively polite toward women of any rank.

"Mister... Scordato." *Principessa* Liliana hesitated over the name. "Do you have any news about my Family?"

"Yes," Cristof jumped in, "what do you know about the rebellion? Er, do you want to sit down?"

The Mareaux girl led Alister to a chair.

"Thank you. This is Florianne, my landlady's daughter. She's been kind enough to serve as my assistant since I moved to Mareaux."

Florianne murmured an inaudible greeting and took the last chair. She was clean and pleasant-looking; not beautiful, Taya thought, but Alister had always valued utility over looks. That's why he'd dated her, once.

"My Family...." the *principessa* insisted, still standing. Alister slid his satchel onto his lap and pulled out a folded paper.

"Florianne bought this on our way over, Your Royal Highness." He held it out. "The news hawks were shouting that Ondinium's ambassador had slaughtered the royal family and attacked the palace. I must say, Cris, that was rather enterprising of you."

"We were framed, of course," Cristof said, irritably. *Principessa* Liliana took the broadsheet. The print was poorly set and the headline took up half the front page. "The rebels faked a set of lictors' stripes."

"Florianne made me hide my castemarks on the way over." Alister laid a hand on the scarf that hung loosely around his neck. "I'll have to cut my visit to Alzana short unless I can convince the authorities that I'm a traitor. I don't suppose you know who's behind the coup?"

"I was hoping you might."

"Have you met Fosca Mazzoletti?"

"Yes." Taya leaned forward. "She was giving orders by the king's carriage."

"If she isn't behind the uprising, you can be sure she's close to those who are."

"How do you know her?" Amcathra demanded, materializing behind them. Alister twitched, one hand tightening on his cane.

"Hello, Lieutenant Amcathra."

"How do you know Fosca Mazzoletti?"

"She's chatted with me a few times. She wanted to know how much I resented the nation that had mutilated and exiled me. I thought she might be a useful contact someday, so I let her believe I was extremely bitter about it. I suppose it's time to renew our acquaintance."

Amcathra gave the exile a baleful look.

"How do we know you are not working for her now?"

Alister's smile held a tightness that hadn't been there before his blinding.

"Because you are still here, Lieutenant."

"Janos...." Cristof shook his head at the lieutenant, who took a begrudging step backward. "I trust you, Al. He's just doing his job."

"As he was when he escorted me to my blinding," Alister said, his voice strained. "Forgive me if I bear some resentment toward your guard dog, Cris."

"I was there, too, you know. Both times."

"You didn't have a rifle trained on me."

"Please..." Taya intervened. "Alister, we need your help."

He made a visible effort to lower his shoulders and raise his head. "To escape Alzana, I assume."

"We need to get out of the capital," Cristof said. "And a few miles north up the coast, if we can. Will you help?"

"How many of you are there?"

"Ten. Eleven, with the corpse." Cristof hesitated. "Twelve or thirteen if you want to join us."

Alister gave another thin, humorless smile. "I don't think the Council would welcome me back."

"We could drop you off in Mareaux."

"No. We'll manage." Alister tapped his fingers on the top of his cane. "I think I can get you out. It will take some time to arrange, though. Gilberto will keep you safe until I return. By the way, have you heard any news about Allied Metals & Extraction?"

"The company was recently forced to halt production," Cristof said.

"I certainly hope so. It seems that some of their personnel are now working for Alzanan employers willing to pay for Ondinium expertise."

"The Council will find that interesting. Patrice Corundel?"

"She's found herself an Alzanan patron. Are you wearing your wings, Taya?"

"No." Taya was confused by the sudden change of subject. "The Council wouldn't let me bring them to Alzana."

"What a pity." Alister stood, slinging his satchel over his shoulder and touching the tip of his cane to the floor. "I'll return as soon as I can. Florianne?"

"Yes." The girl guided Alister's hand to her forearm and led him away. Taya listened to Alister's cane gently tap the steam presses as they left. When the door closed behind them, she turned to her husband.

"He seems well. All things considered."

"I— I couldn't talk to him." Cristof raked a hand through his hair, looking shaken. "I couldn't say anything that mattered."

"You'll see him again. Talk to him then."

He shook his head, frustrated.

Principessa Liliana looked up from the newspaper.

"My brother escaped," she said, softly. "Silvio."

Silvio… Taya placed the name. The young prince with the cold.

"How?" she asked.

"The paper says that he heard the shots and ran away. He hid for hours until the guards found him."

"They must have been loyalists," Amcathra observed. "Your brother was fortunate, *Principessa*. It will be more difficult for the rebels to kill him now and blame his death on us."

"Can we get him out of the palace?" the *principessa* asked. Taya shot the lictor a hopeful look. If they rescued Silvio, they could rescue Jayce and the rest of their staff.

"No. He is safer with Agosti loyalists, and we are safer out of Alzana."

"But I can't just leave him there!" The girl's wail was echoed in Taya's heart.

"What does the paper say about your sister?"

"Pietra? Nothing. Do you think she is in danger, too?"

"Has she ever expressed any interest in taking the throne?"

Taya recoiled and Cristof's eyebrows rose. *Principessa* Liliana needed a moment longer to grasp the lictor's meaning, and then she shot to her feet, the newspaper falling to the floor.

"No! Never! She would *never* do something like this!"

"You are certain?"

"Of course I am certain!"

"Then yes, she is in danger, too."

The *principessa* sank back into her chair. "We must warn her."

"Do you know where she is stationed?"

"No...."

Amcathra waited. She looked away.

"I think it would be best for all of you to get some sleep," he said at last. "We may be waiting here for some time."

Chapter Three

ALISTER AND FLORIANNE returned later in the day with a horse-drawn wagon full of empty crates. They pulled the wagon into the publisher's loading bay.

"What is this?" Cristof ran a finger over the strange characters burned into one of the crates. "It looks... Cabisi?"

"Quite possibly," Alister said. "The Alzanan government has been carrying out quite a bit of trade with Cabiel recently."

"What are they buying?"

"I understand there is a strong demand among the larger Families for Cabisi weaponry."

"I didn't know they *sold* weaponry."

"The Cabisi Thassalocracy is at least as technologically advanced as Ondinium— and it is far more willing to sell its technology to outsiders."

"I'll tell the Council we should look into the matter."

"That would be prudent. Now, if you would, I have a boat standing by at the docks that will carry these crates down the coast for a small fee with no questions asked. I need you inside and quiet."

"A boat!" Taya brightened. She'd always wanted to see the ocean.

Amcathra took charge. "The icarus and the exalted will travel together. Helvi and the *principessa*. Dayvet and Titus. Emel and Jager. I will remain alone, and the body will also be crated separately."

"Cael," one of the lictors muttered under his breath. Taya knew Amcathra practiced the Demican tradition of avoiding a dead man's name until after his cremation, but after glancing at the lieutenant's expression, she decided not to explain on his behalf. She was about to climb into the wagon when she saw the young *principessa*'s face.

"Maybe *Principessa* Agosti and I should travel together," she sighed. She would prefer to be with Cristof, especially if she were going to be stuck in a small, dark space for any length of time, but the *principessa* still hadn't recovered from the sight of fake lictors shooting at them.

Amcathra calmly reassigned everyone, keeping himself and the corpse separate again.

"I've heard more news, by the way," Alister said, standing motionless in the middle of the workyard as Florianne helped the group into their crates. "You've been officially accused of the murders, and your staff has been arrested as accomplices."

Taya squeezed her eyes shut, whispering a prayer to the Lady.

Alister continued. "In addition, it seems you are holding the *principessa* hostage."

"That's ridiculous," Cristof scoffed.

"That's clever," Alister corrected, moving his head in his brother's direction. "If she tries to exonerate you, her enemies will argue that she's speaking under duress. Of course, if they catch her, they'll undoubtedly kill her and blame you for her death, as well."

"Have you heard anything about Silvio and Pietra?" *Principessa* Liliana asked, her voice shaking.

"Nothing new, Your Royal Highness."

"If I could get to one of them...."

"After you're safe," Cristof said.

"Just a minute!" The girl turned to Taya. "Please, Icarus, give me your purse."

Taya handed it over. The *principessa* pulled out a golden bracelet and handed it to Florianne, who took it with a startled curtsey.

"If— if you see any of my Family," she said, softly, "give them this. Mother gave it to me years ago. Let them know that I am alive."

"I shall. But if you please, *Principessa*...." Florianne held up the lid to the crate. Taya and Liliana ducked and held their ears as the lid was nailed shut. Outside, Amcathra continued to give orders.

"This is a nightmare," *Principessa* Liliana breathed in Alzanan, handing the reticule back to Taya. "I can't believe any of this is happening."

"I understand." Taya squirmed and reminded herself to breathe steadily. *There's plenty of air in here.* "Sometimes the whole world seems to be spinning out of control, and all you can do is trust the Lady and try to survive."

"But you seem so calm!"

"Do I?" Clearly the girl couldn't sense Taya's intense discomfort at being trapped inside a box. "Well, Cris and I have been through a lot lately. I guess we've learned to keep moving forward in a crisis."

"...I'm sorry you aren't with your husband, Icarus."

"It's all right."

"It's just that... lictors scare me. Especially your lieutenant. I don't think he likes me."

"I'm sure you're imagining things, Your Royal Highness." Or not. Amcathra had never had much love for Alzanans, and he'd lost classmates and colleagues in the Glasgar bombing. "He's actually very trustworthy."

"But he looks so brutal! That scar..."

"On his forehead? He got that in a train crash."

"I thought it was from a fight."

"No, *Principessa*. The scars on Cristof's face and hand are from the crash, too."

"...I'm sorry."

"Cris was standing next to a window when the train rolled. He... he was badly hurt. Amcathra saved his life. Saved both our lives, actually."

"Then you've known him a long time."

"*I* haven't known him that long. He and Cris have been friends for several years, though."

"He seems very formal for a friend."

"I agree, but we can't break him of the habit."

"You can call me Liliana, if you want."

"Are you sure?" Taya couldn't see the girl's expression in the darkness. "I mean, you're a *principessa*, and I'm just an icarus, and our countries are at war."

"But *we* are not at war, are we?"

"No." Taya smiled. "So please call me Taya."

"Thank you." The girl shifted again. "Do you... do you have any brothers or sisters, Taya?"

Taya heard a tremor in the girl's voice. She took a deep breath and began telling Liliana about her life, hoping to distract them both as the wagon began to move.

Much later they heard a tapping on the top of the crate and someone's sharp "shhhhh." They fell silent, straining to hear what was going on outside. The wagon had reached the harbor, judging from the shrieking of gulls and the scent of salt water. Taya's desire to get out was almost physical in intensity.

The transfer from wagon to vessel went smoothly, although Taya had to brace her hands against the sides of the crate to keep from slipping around as it was moved. Soon they were on their way again, bobbing up and down and listening to water slapping the sides of the boat. The constant motion made Taya nauseous. She pressed her face against the side of the crate, seeking fresh air. The sailors' voices were close but indistinct. Once she heard something thrown overboard with a resounding splash. She tensed, but nothing else happened. Fearful anticipation of being thrown into the ocean kept her nervous for the rest of the journey until the boat came to a shuddering halt.

The crate rocked a few times, and Florianne said something indistinguishable. Alister's voice rose as he spoke in Alzanan.

"Try to avoid dropping them, if you please. My cargo wouldn't do well in salt water."

"Handsomely, boys, handsomely," someone else said in the same language. The crate swung up into the air and hit the ground with a thump, jostling Taya and Liliana against each other.

"That's all, then?" the same strange voice asked.

"Yes, thank you. Florianne, my dear, would you...?"

"For your trouble, sirs."

A chorus of thanks, and then Taya heard splashing and calls to steady the boat and mind the oars, dammit.

A considerable amount of time later, someone tapped on the top of the crate.

"They're gone, and we're going to let you out," Alister said. "Watch your heads."

A crowbar worked its way under the lid and slowly pried the nails out of the wood. Taya gratefully sucked in a lungful of fresh salt air as the lid popped off, revealing Florianne's exertion-flushed face. The Mareaux girl turned to work on the second crate as Taya and Liliana crawled out onto a rocky beach.

"What fell into the water?" Taya inquired, raising her voice to be heard over the loud crashing sound around her. She looked around, searching for the source of the noise. Her eyes fastened with wonder on the endless expanse of water that stretched beyond them.

"The corpse," Alister said, looking mildly surprised. "That's why it was stored separately." He stood on the rocky shore with the tip of his chestnut cane resting lightly by his feet, looking comfortable despite his blindness.

Shocked, Taya turned back to Alister. "You mean Cael? Does Amcathra know you dumped his body overboard?"

"Your lieutenant is the one who told me to do it." Alister shook his head. "I don't blame him for keeping our dead out of Alzanan hands, given the circumstances, but burial at sea strikes me as a thoroughly distasteful prospect."

"Me, too." Taya shuddered, hoping such a dismal fate wouldn't affect Cael's rebirth. She looked around for her husband. "Why didn't you let Cris out first?"

"Ladies first, Taya. And you before my brother, always."

"He's an exalted! *And* the one who's been supporting you— I certainly wouldn't have given you anything."

Alister's lips curled up in a tight expression that was very different from the easy smile he used to affect.

"My fierce little hawk. As unforgiving as ever. Has my brother been treating you well? Have you softened that mechanical heart of his?"

"We're doing fine," she said, instinctively reaching for her reticule and wrapping her fingers around the shape of the pocketwatch inside. The heart-shaped gem in its face was Cristof's quiet, self-deprecating joke. Maybe that was why he hadn't wanted his brother to see it. "He's a good person."

Alister cocked his head.

"'A good person.' Not exactly a ringing declaration of love. Is something wrong between you?"

Taya flushed.

"No, and what's between us is none of your business." She turned and walked away, impatiently yanking up her skirts to keep them from dragging over the rocks.

Then she stopped, her attention riveted anew by the vast, heaving ocean.

That is *what's making all the noise!* It was the water crashing against the rocky shore, sending giant plumes of white into the sky. Waves, she thought, gazing at them in wonder, waves hitting the shore with a regular cadence like the beat of a heart or the ticking of a watch.

She'd read about surf, but she'd never expected it to be so loud.

"Does it ever stop?" she asked, turning to Liliana. The *principessa* had collapsed onto the rocks, gazing despondently at the water.

"What?"

She raised her voice again. "The water? Does it ever stop pumping?"

Liliana gave her a curious look.

"Have you not ever seen the ocean before?"

"No, never. I mean, I've read about it, and I've seen paintings, but Ondinium's surrounded by mountains." Taya sought the horizon and wondered what lay beyond it. "I've always wanted to see the ocean for myself."

"Well, here it is." Liliana brushed a strand of seaweed from her skirt. "And no, it never stops."

"Amazing."

"Taya?" Cristof picked his way through the jagged rocks, shaking his long black hair out of his face. "How are you, *Principessa*?"

"Look," Taya said, throwing her arms out. "Liliana says it never stops pumping!"

He shot a quick, curious look at the *principessa*, then smiled crookedly and wrapped his arms around Taya's waist, pulling her against him.

"Like a giant, very wet engine," he observed next to her ear.

"That's just what I was thinking!"

"Too bad it only pumps saltwater. Can't think of any good use for it."

"The ocean has uses— fish live in it. And shells! Where are the seashells, Liliana? Do they live in the water or on the shore?"

"You will not find any interesting shells here." The girl watched them with a small, melancholy smile. "All of the pretty shells are farther south."

"Mother-of-pearl is a shell, isn't it?"

"That's what they say," Cristof agreed. "But I bought my watch faces pre-cut. I don't know what the stuff looks like in nature."

"Exalted. Icarus." Amcathra's voice carried over the surf. "We have a problem."

"What's new?" Cristof whispered in Taya's ear with resignation. They returned hand-in-hand. The lictors had spread out, stretching and checking their rifles. Liliana followed and hovered on the outskirts of the small assembly.

"Your brother has not delivered us to our destination," Amcathra said, giving Alister a hard look. Taya looked up for the first time and realized that there were no buildings on the rocky, pale cliff behind them.

Cristof slid his hand from hers. "Where are we, Al?"

"The sailors refused to drop me off at the lighthouse because the Alzanan military has set up an outpost there. This is as close as they would come."

"You knew nothing of this?" Amcathra pressed. Alister sighed.

"I don't *live* here, Lieutenant; I publish here. I thought I was doing rather well just finding a set of smugglers willing to take us this far. Believe me, if I were going to betray you, I wouldn't have put myself through this much personal discomfort."

"All right— enough." Cristof raised a hand to forestall Amcathra's response. "Janos, do we have a backup plan?"

"No." Amcathra's eyes were hooded as he considered the problem. "Ondinium has agents on shore who will have signaled to the ship that the exalted is in trouble. It is supposed to check the rendezvous point for four nights before leaving."

"What are *you* going to do, Alister?" Taya inquired. "Are you coming with us, after all?"

"No. There's a path up the cliff about a mile south. From there I'll take the coastal road back to the capital."

"You're going to walk?"

"I'm blind, not crippled." His voice was sharp.

"I— I know, but it's a long way...." Taya's voice trailed off.

"The walk is not difficult," Florianne assured her.

"Are you sure you won't be arrested?" Cristof pressed.

"Your concern is heartwarming, Cris." Alister's tone was dry. "But keep in mind that *you're* the one who's wanted for regicide."

"That doesn't mean I don't worry about you," the exalted mumbled, looking away and folding his arms over his narrow chest. "I went through a lot of trouble to keep you alive, you know."

Alister's lips tilted upward as he turned his blindfolded face toward his brother.

"I have done my best to protect your investment. In turn, I expect you to protect our little hawk here."

"She's the one who protects *me*, most of the time."

"I wouldn't brag about that, Cris," Alister retorted.

"Are we ready to go, Exalted?" Amcathra asked, cutting off Cristof's irked reply. The lictor didn't bother to hide his impatience.

"I think we are," Cristof said, glowering at his younger brother.

"Good-bye, Taya," Alister said. "Good-bye, Cris."

Cristof hesitated, poised to step forward, then jerked away with an irritable lift of one shoulder.

"Good-bye, Al. Florianne. I'll write as soon as I can."

"This way." Amcathra began walking, and the group fell in behind him, murmuring farewells. A few minutes later when Taya looked over her shoulder, Alister and Florianne were still standing next to the jumble of open crates, silently facing the water.

CHAPTER FOUR

THE BEACH BECAME steeper and rockier as they walked. Taya tucked in her skirts and used both hands to steady herself as she clambered over the jagged, slippery boulders. By the third time she'd slipped and fallen, she was reconsidering her love for the ocean. Ocean water was cold and dark, and slimy strands of seaweed clung to her skirts. *The ocean is nice to* look *at*, she decided, *but being* in *the ocean is another matter entirely*. She hoped sailing would be more comfortable.

By midday they reached a wooden fence. Three signs nailed along its length read "Government Property — No Trespassing" in Alzanan. No guards watched it, and the rocky beach continued beyond its uneven posts and rails.

"Looks like a good stopping point." Cristof perched on a boulder and inspected the shredded remnants of his silk slippers. His trousers and the bottom half of his robes were as wet and stained as Taya's skirts. Liliana crouched on another boulder, looking cold and near tears. The lictors gathered loosely around them, rifles at the ready. The exalted looked at Amcathra. "Now what?"

"Jager and I will scout ahead."

"Won't there be a patrol?" Cristof asked.

"It is possible. Stay close to the cliff and wait for me. Bright, you have the exalted. Helvi, the *principessa*. Emel, the icarus. Dayvet, Titus, on watch."

"Yes, sir," the lictors replied in a ragged chorus.

"Bring us back something to eat," Cristof said as Amcathra started climbing over the fence.

"Hide," the lictor ordered, unamused.

"I wish you hadn't mentioned eating," Taya grumbled as they dutifully trudged to the base of the cliff. "I didn't have any lunch yesterday; I was afraid the execution might make me sick."

"There must be something we can eat on a beach." Cristof looked dubiously at the cold water. "I saw starfish clinging to the rocks a little way back. Are starfish edible, *Principessa*?"

"I believe some people eat them." Liliana looked disgusted. "But they're hard and they have slimy suckers."

"They're hard?" Cristof stopped. "They didn't *look* hard. Are they safe to touch?"

"Cris— *later*," Taya said, recognizing the look on his face. Her husband was about to go plunging back down to the water, trying to find one of the wretched things. "Let's not get captured by the Alzanan army because you're squatting on the beach poking at sea creatures."

He blinked, then reluctantly nodded.

"I suppose you're right." He cast her a sidelong look through his glasses. "Just remember that you turned down a starfish dinner."

"Complete with raw, slimy suckers. Yum."

They traded wry smiles. Liliana frowned.

"I don't understand why you aren't more worried," she snapped as they climbed around a steep pile of fallen rocks. "Our lives are in danger."

"Oh, this isn't so bad," Cristof protested, a little out of breath. "I still have a gun, my wife, and my best friend. Not to mention six other lictors and an Alzanan *principessa*. Other than a platter of starfish hors d'oeuvres, what more could I ask?"

"You are insane," Liliana declared.

"It runs in the family," he agreed.

"The Alzanans are maintaining a minimal patrol along the top of the cliff and have nobody guarding the beach," Amcathra reported later. "They appear to be watching for vessels approaching from the ocean. The lighthouse is approximately an hour's walk away and is surrounded by new construction. I could only see roofs over the edge of the cliff, but the new buildings are very large and very high. They have been painted a mottled gray and white."

"Hangars?" Cristof guessed.

"That is my assumption. They are well-positioned to protect the coast and the capital but far enough from the city to avoid being seen by most travelers. The lighthouse would provide a useful landing beacon. I can only assume that the paint choice is intended to hide the buildings from icarii scouts."

"I didn't know we had hangars here," Liliana said in a small voice. "I would have told you if I'd known."

"You had no reason to know," Taya assured her. A sixteen-year-old, even in a royal family, was unlikely to be privy to her country's military secrets. Still.... "Do you know how many dirigibles there are?"

"No," the girl said, downcast. "I didn't even know we had dirigibles until I heard about the invasion."

"Do *you* think your grandfather ordered the attack?" Cristof asked, his attention drawn to the young woman. She averted her eyes from his intense gaze.

"He said he didn't."

"It doesn't matter anymore." Taya put a hand on Liliana's shoulder and shook her head at the two men. "The question is, can our rescue ship get past the outpost to reach us? I assume it's disguised as a Mareaux trader or something else that can pass unchallenged through Alzanan waters."

Amcathra gave her an odd look.

"Icarus. It is not a *naval* ship."

Taya dropped her hand. Next to her, Cristof groaned.

"But — if — how can it be *here*?" she demanded.

"The *Firebrand* has been patrolling the coast since we arrived."

"The decaturs let it leave Ondinium?" She couldn't believe it.

Next to her, Cristof pulled off his glasses and pinched the arch of his nose. "I see the Council is playing its usual game of secrets and lies. I really wish you wouldn't participate, Janos. I'd like to think I can trust you."

Amcathra stiffened.

"I have little voice in the Council's decisions, Exalted. And in this case, its secret is to our advantage."

Taya's mind was in whirl. If an ornithopter had been patrolling the coast for several days, then it had undoubtedly spotted the hangars by the lighthouse. In fact, it had probably made a very good map of all of the coastal defenses near Alzana's capital.

Which suggested that the *Firebrand* wasn't really there as a diplomatic safety net. It was a war vessel preparing for battle. Her jaw tightened. She was going to have words with Decatur Evadare Constante when they returned to the capital.

"To return to Taya's question," Cristof said, his expression as grim as hers, "is the outpost on alert?"

"I saw telegraphy poles along the cliff's edge," Amcathra said. "We must assume the entire nation is on alert."

"If I went up there to talk to them...." Liliana hesitated. "Do you think they'd believe me?"

"They think we kidnapped you." Taya looked at the girl's torn and salt-stiffened clothes, disheveled hair, and dirt-covered hands and feet. "And treated you pretty badly in the process, too."

"But if I explained that it was all a mistake...."

"Do the officers in charge of this outpost belong to one of the rebel Families?" Amcathra asked.

"I don't know."

"Then you would be putting yourself at significant risk by going there."

"What are *we* going to do?" Cristof asked. "Wait here or cross the fence?"

"I do not recommend crossing the fence. The Alzanans have mined the beach and tide pools with steel jaw traps. I have been attempting to think of a means by which we could signal the ship after dark. I am open to suggestions."

"Can't you fire your guns?" Liliana asked.

"Air rifles give off no light and little sound."

"Oh."

"We could use something reflective," Cristof murmured, "but that's only useful if there's a source of light to reflect. The light-house beacon won't shine in this direction, and we don't have any incendiary matches. Do we have flint and steel?"

"I have a steel boot knife," Amcathra replied, "but I am not carrying any flint."

"What about all these rocks around us?" Taya asked. "Are they flint?"

"Would you recognize flint if you saw it?" Cristof countered.

"I know what it looks like," one of the lictors — Dayvet — volunteered. "I'll look."

"Please continue considering alternative solutions," Amcathra said, nodding to the lictor.

"Like what?" Cristof grumbled as Dayvet left. "Wave my hands and cast a magic spell?"

"If we knew the ship was close, we could jump up and down and shout," Taya suggested. "It wouldn't be subtle, but...."

"That would only work in daylight or if the engines were not running."

She sighed.

Dayvet returned a half-hour later, empty-handed. None of the other lictors had come up with a clever solution to the problem, either. With no better alternatives, the small group settled down in the dubious shelter of boulders and shrubs.

"So, Lieutenant." Taya squatted next to Amcathra. "I notice that you seem to rely a lot on Jager."

The lictor gave her a suspicious look.

"She is the most highly ranked of my lictors."

"She seems very competent. Good-looking, too. Have you—"

"You are exhausted, Icarus, and quite possibly hallucinating. I suggest you get some rest."

"But—"

"Please do not waste your time or mine pursuing this line of speculation any further."

Taya sighed and walked back to her husband. The damp air was getting cold. She sat and leaned against his shoulder.

"How are you?" she asked, softly.

"Absolutely miserable. You?"

"About the same." She squeezed his scarred left hand, running her fingers over his gold wedding band. "I saw you limping."

"Blisters and cuts. If I'd known I'd be fleeing for my life, I would have worn a pair of sturdy boots. You'd think we would have learned by now. How are your shoes holding up?"

"They're not. Am I sunburnt?"

"It's that fair skin of yours."

"I hate it."

"I don't." He smiled. "But next time we go to the beach, we'll bring hats."

"And poke starfish."

"Sounds like fun."

They laced their fingers together and lapsed into silence.

· ✱ ·

The sky grew dark and a cold fog rolled in over the water. Taya groaned as she stretched her stiff legs.

"Well, the fog will hide the *Firebrand* as long as it stays over the ocean," she said, shivering. "But they'll need lights to avoid the cliff; the Alzanans will spot them."

"I'll wake up Janos." Cristof stood. Taya heard Liliana sleepily ask a question as he passed, and Cristof replied. Around them the lictors shifted, the two on watch leaning over to awaken those who still slumbered.

Ten minutes later, the shivering group picked its way back to the water's edge and sat back-to-back, searching the horizon. Taya's stomach growled, although the constant noise of the surf kept anyone else from hearing it. She had no idea how much time had passed before she realized she was seeing something blink in the distance. She shook herself and focused.

"Do you see that?" she whispered.

"It's on the beach," one of the lictors murmured. "Can't be the ship."

"Smugglers?" Cristof suggested.

"It is a request to approach the signaler," Amcathra said at last.

"It's a Firebrand?" Taya asked, relieved.

"Yes." He stood. "Follow me."

When they drew close to the light, Amcathra halted. Taya bumped into him and he turned, steadying her with one hand. Liliana blundered into her back, and then Cristof into hers.

"Wait here." Amcathra walked the rest of the way alone. A few minutes later the light lowered and he stepped in front of it, gesturing. They all hurried to join the signaler, who bowed to Cristof and then snapped the lantern's hood down.

"Where's the ship?" Cristof whispered in the sudden darkness.

"Offshore, Exalted," the signaler replied, equally quietly. "We have to be careful. The Alzanans launched a dirigible at sunset. Gave us a turn, but we were far enough away that it didn't spot us."

"We didn't see anything," Taya protested.

"It must have been on the other side of the point," Cristof said. "Where was it headed?"

"Out to sea, Exalted. We waited for it to disappear into the fog before we finished our glide in. Lieutenant Imbrex said if we couldn't get to the rendezvous point, neither could you, so she gambled you might spot a light farther down the coast. I climbed out about a mile downshore and hiked here. Ship'll come in on my signal."

"Does the Alzanan outpost have anti-airvessel weapons?" Cristof asked.

"Cannon."

"And our ship? Is it armed?"

"Yes, Exalted. Lieutenant Imbrex was briefing the gunnery crews when I left."

"Janos…." Cristof's brow furrowed.

"The *Firebrand*'s weapons are intended for ship-to-ship combat, Exalted."

"Then you won't fire at the outpost."

"The Council *has* given permission for ornithopter crews to defend their ship from attack, Exalted. Any attack."

"Even from the ground?" Cristof was outraged. "Does the rest of the caste know that the Council has permitted this— this blatant violation of the nation's most important ethical standards?"

Liliana touched Taya's sleeve.

"What are they saying?" she whispered in Alzanan. "They're speaking too fast for me."

"The ship will pick us up soon," Taya whispered back, trying not to reveal her distress at Amcathra's news, "but there may be a firefight."

"You aren't— you aren't going to attack us, are you?"

"We won't *attack* any land-based targets, I promise." She turned to the others, interrupting the fiercely whispered argument between Cristof and Amcathra. "Lieutenant, try to avoid killing anyone."

"It is too late for that, Icarus. We killed a number of people in our escape from the ambush."

"Well, we don't have to kill anyone *now*!"

"I have taken an oath to do whatever is necessary to keep the exalted safe."

Cristof gave an irritable hiss. Taya laid a restraining hand on her husband's arm.

"All right," she said to the lictor, "but let's try to keep the moral high ground in this conflict."

"When Mister Pitio signals the *Firebrand*," Amcathra continued after an awkward moment, "Lieutenant Imbrex will fire the engines and head toward us. When she arrives, she will drop ladders. We must climb aboard as quickly as possible."

When everyone nodded, the signaler unhooded his lantern and slid its aperture open then shut in a repeating pattern.

A small light appeared within the fog over the ocean. As it drew nearer and larger, Taya heard the rumble of engines and creaking of metal wings. Bright carbon-arc searchlights snapped on and swept the beach, making everyone squint. Their lictors stared in amazement, their rifles sagging forgotten in their hands.

Liliana said something that Taya couldn't hear as the ondium ship's raked-back, predatory prow became visible through the fog. The *Firebrand* made a slow, wide turn, bringing it parallel to the cliffs as its wings angled to stop its forward motion. Crew members ran along the deck as the ornithopter passed the waiting group by several yards before coming to a stop, its giant wings nearly scraping the cliff face.

Liliana shook Taya's arm.

"What is that?" she demanded over the pounding engine. "How does it float like that? Where is its balloon?"

"It doesn't have one. It's built out of ondium."

"But— that's impossible. Ondinium doesn't have any flying ships!"

"It did when it was an empire. The *Firebrand* is a thousand years old." The *Firebrand*'s beautiful, etched ondium hull was a thousand years old, anyway. Its steam engine and operating machinery were state-of-the-art, as were its cannon. The Virtuous Reclamation had forbidden Ondinium to build any new flying vessels, but it hadn't specifically forbidden the nation from maintaining and upgrading the vessels it already had. For centuries the Oporphyr Council had been secretly exploiting that little legal loophole.

Rope ladders tumbled over the ship's rails. Amcathra firmly escorted Cristof to the first, and Taya put Liliana's hands on the next. The girl climbed several rungs and then shrieked as the ladder spun. Taya waved to the aviators leaning over the rails and they hauled the terrified *principessa* up to the deck.

Taya ascended after her husband. Hands grabbed her arms and helped her over the rail, where she found Cristof and Liliana being ushered out of the way as crew members drew up the rest of the group. Amcathra's lictors were as overwhelmed as Liliana by the ancient ornithopter, gaping around them with open amazement. Then the ladders were hauled in and the crew was urging *Firebrand*'s wings back into motion again.

The ship's officers saluted Amcathra as he strode toward the primary helm, assuming command. So, Taya thought, meeting Cristof's eyes. It was no coincidence that they were being picked up by the same ornithopter Amcathra had led against the Alzanan invasion.

"Belowdeck, if you please, Exalted," one of the crew said briskly. "We're clearing for battle."

"With pleasure," Cristof muttered, looking around uneasily.

Taya followed her husband and the shivering *principessa* to the mess hall located below the raked-back forecastle. They instinctively moved to the large glass casements set in the ship's bow. The Alzanan cliff was receding along their starboard side. The point around the lighthouse was covered with buildings, just as Amcathra had described, and lit up as bright as day as Alzanan soldiers scrambled to their posts.

"There," Cristof said, pointing over her shoulder. Taya nodded as she spotted two hangars, both smaller than the one they'd investigated in Demicus. Then the lighthouse slipped past and the *Firebrand* gained speed, its spotlights moving back and forth to reveal thick fog and black water.

A thunderous clap made them all start. *Cannon*, Taya thought, panicked. Several *Firebrand* aviators hurried into the galley, then stopped, confused.

"E-Exalted," one lictor stammered with a respectful bow, "if you please, we need to secure the windows."

"Go ahead." Cristof took an uncertain step backward and the crew members surged forward with their tools. Within moments, the glass windows had been pulled out of their frames and slid into narrow wooden crates while metal plates were screwed over the resulting gaps. "Thank you. I like it better that way."

"This is unbelievable," Liliana said, looking around with a combination of indignation and amazement. "How have you kept this ship hidden for so many years?"

"I guess the Council has decided to make them public now," Taya said, looking at her husband. "The decaturs must have known that the *Firebrand* would be spotted eventually."

"I wish I knew what they were thinking," he muttered. "Imperial ornithopters are going to raise a lot of old fears in our former colonies."

"Ondinium doesn't want another empire," Taya said, uncertainly.

"You and I don't want one. Let's hope the Council feels the same way."

Taya shivered, abruptly aware of the winter chill and her damp, ragged clothes. For a moment she imagined what Jayce would say about the state of her garments. She sagged against the hull.

"What's wrong?" Cristof cupped her face with his hands.

"It's just— Jayce—"

He pulled her close and said nothing. There was nothing to be said. They were escaping Alzana and leaving their friends behind to their deaths.

The Firebrands left with the packed windows, making quick, embarrassed bows to the exalted as they hurried out.

"Is there anything I can do?" Liliana whispered.

"Maybe, if your sister, the major, is still alive and we can get a message to her," Cristof replied. "Taya's worried about our staff. If we could—"

The ship unexpectedly banked. Taya and Cristof grabbed each other for support. Shouts rose over the engine noise and they felt a low rumbling through their feet.

"We must have seen the Alzanan ship." Cristof looked toward the window but was thwarted by the thick metal panels sitting in its place. Taya fought down her concern for her friends. They weren't out of danger yet themselves.

"I'm going up."

"What? Why?" Cristof grabbed her arm. "It's too dangerous."

"Stay here and keep Liliana safe. You two are the important ones."

"But I can't— *Taya*!"

She shook off his hand and fled, desperate to feel the wind on her face and pretend she was doing something useful, even if it was just watching the airfight to report to her husband later.

Anything would be better than sitting in that cramped, dark galley brooding over her friends' fates.

Taya dodged a lictor sliding down the ladder to the gun deck and scrambled up the rungs as quickly as she could, knowing that if any of the officers saw her, they'd order her back below.

The *Firebrand*'s aviators were maintaining the wing engines along the quarterdeck, running the searchlights on the forecastle, and manning volley guns mounted at the forecastle, quarterdeck, and stern. Lieutenant Imbrex, a tall, dark-haired woman, paced the length of the ship shouting orders while Captain Amcathra stood on the raised forecastle in front of the massive ondium-plated wing mounts, studying the enemy ship through field glasses. His face and light blond hair looked even paler than usual under the harsh glare of the Alzanans' spotlight.

Taya crept to the stern, where the activity was less intense. A crew member manned the binnacle and the wheels that controlled the demiwings and tailrudder, ready to adjust the ship's yaw on the primary helm's signal. Taya crouched by the rail and tucked her skirts between her knees, shivering in the icy night air.

The Alzanan ship was trying to climb over the ornithopter, striving to avoid the Ondinium vessel's fuselage-mounted gun deck and gain a superior firing angle. The foreign vessel was slow, but dirigibles could pit their engines against the wind, whereas the *Firebrand* was forced, like an icarus, to beat to windward. Amcathra ordered ballast dumped and the ornithopter rose steadily and swiftly as its buoyancy-to-weight ratio shifted in favor of ondium's lift.

Another light struck them from behind. Taya twisted, shielding her eyes with one hand. A second dirigible rose from the dense fog, its spotlights igniting. It had crept up below them, the sound of its engines drowned out by the other two ships.

The starboard cannon on the ornithopter's gunnery deck opened fire. In response, the dirigible to port began firing its repeating guns. Taya ducked, but nobody fell and she didn't hear bullets hitting the *Firebrand*'s ondium plating. Were they still out of range? No— she heard shouting from the quarterdeck as engineers reported on the condition of the port wing.

The Alzanans were trying to cripple the *Firebrand*. They wanted to capture it, not destroy it.

The *Firebrand*'s starboard cannon boomed and the entire ship gave a slight roll, swiftly compensated for by the alert helms. *We're too light*, Taya thought. The heavy weapons' recoil was affecting the ship's aerodynamics.

The dirigible to port fired again. This time bullets stitched metal and wood. Taya flinched. Why wasn't Amcathra taking them out of there?

The *Firebrand*'s port cannon gave a thunderous roar. She risked another glance through the rails.

At least some of their shot had struck the Alzanan ship— the *Firebrand*'s spotlight revealed damage to the enemy's gondola and envelope. The Alzanans returned fire. A lictor screamed, thrown overboard by the bullets' impact. Taya instinctively started to stand, then clenched her fists and crouched back down. There was nothing she could do to help him.

I want my wings, she thought fiercely, listening to the ships exchange fire. She was *useless* without her wings.

More bullets hammered into the ornithopter, this time from starboard. The *Firebrand*'s cannon answered. Taya looked over her unprotected shoulder and saw the second dirigible looming beside them, its gondola splintering under the impact of the *Firebrand*'s larger missiles. Gun barrels swung back and forth from the gondola's windows, and an Alzanan soldier fired down on them from the gunnery platform on top of the dirigible's envelope.

This is ridiculous, she thought. *If I get killed, Cris will never forgive me.*

But gunfire separated her from the nearest hatch and nobody else was fleeing the barrage. The secondary helmswoman was being protected by one of the diplomatic-staff lictors, Bright, who stood beside her firing his rifle back at the Alzanans. Taya didn't think he could hit anything at that range, but she admired his fearlessness.

Faint cheers arose, barely audible over the din of battle. Taya craned her neck and saw the ship to port fall away. The *Firebrand*'s spotlight played over its smoking engines. Its crew was, no doubt, scrambling to put out the fire before any stray sparks ignited the inflammable gas within its envelope.

The second vessel continued hammering them. Its small gondola must have been rattling with thrown brass casings, but the nonstop onslaught was having an effect. Lictors fell, bleeding, their replacements standing over their fallen bodies. Taya felt the *Firebrand* shudder as though something had gone awry with its wings. It banked and she grabbed the rail, her heart in her throat, as they began a descending spiral. Lictors plunged down the hatches, shouting. Taya breathed a prayer to the Lady, wishing she had stayed below. If they were about to die, she wanted to be with her husband when it happened.

But the deck straightened out and the lictors emerged carrying a short, stubby metal canister. They set the mortar on the deck, roping it down and pointing it overhead. Taya looked up. The *Firebrand* was pulling itself directly beneath the Alzanan ship, which was doing its slow, plodding best to escape the vulnerable position. But the *Firebrand* had greater maneuverability and maintained its relative position beneath the enemy with a gliding gyre.

Amcathra shouted an order. The lictors lit the fuse, dropped the missile into the canister, and leaped back, covering their ears.

With a deck-shaking explosion and a burst of sulfurous smoke, the shell shot into the air and splintered through the gondola's weak floor. For three heartbeats nothing happened as the *Firebrand* ceased its spiral and set its wings back into motion. As the orni- thopter pulled away, fire gouted out of the gondola's windows.

"Oh, scrap," Taya breathed, clutching the *Firebrand*'s rails with white knuckles. The ornithopter gained speed, leaving the enemy behind. Screaming Alzanan crew members leaped out of the gondola, silhouetted for a moment against the fire before vanishing into the darkness and fog.

She closed her eyes, unable to watch.

Several more heartbeats passed before it happened— a flash of light against her closed lids. Despite herself, Taya opened them in time to see the last streaks of fiery gas leap into the air while broken, burning parts of the dirigible plummeted after its ill-fated crew.

None of the Firebrands cheered. Instead, they stood for a long moment, stunned and silenced by the devastating explosion.

Then, at last, the subdued crew pulled their gazes from the falling sparks and began helping the fallen, sorting the wounded from the dead. Taya stood. This was something she could do, at least. And maybe the sight of the *Firebrand*'s casualties would alleviate the horror she felt at so many Alzanan soldiers dying alone in the endless, dark ocean below.

Chapter Five

BY THE TIME TAYA was led to the small cabin she and her husband would share, Cristof had fallen asleep in a chair, a leather folder of papers spilling from his hand. Taya picked up the papers, saw the Top Secret headings neatly typewritten over each page, and tugged the folder from his hand. He awoke, startled.

"Oh— sorry." He rubbed his eyes and straightened his glasses. "How are you? Janos told me you were safe…."

"We blew up one of the ships, after all." She sat on the edge of the lower bunk and laid the folder on the floor. She'd washed her hands, but her skirts were still stained with Ondinium blood.

"I heard the explosion." He sat beside her and pulled her into an embrace. "I'm sure he wouldn't have done it if he'd had any choice."

"I know." She buried her face in his shoulder, letting grief overwhelm her at last. Cristof held her as she mourned for her friends in the palace and the Alzanans who'd burned to death and the Ondinium corpses lined up by the ship's rails and the injured crew members being treated by the ship's physician and all of the people who were going to die when Alzana and Ondinium went to war.

By the time she'd stopped weeping, she was wrung out and half asleep. Cristof lowered her to the pillow and covered her with a blanket.

"Where's Liliana?" she whispered, her eyes closing.

"One cabin down." He kissed her cheek. "Get some rest."

"What about you?"

"In a few more minutes." He picked the folder up off the floor. "I need to finish reading the Council's contingency orders."

Taya felt a moment's curiosity, but she couldn't sustain it. Instead, she closed her eyes and let everything slip away.

· ❋ ·

Sun shining through the portals and the scent of frying bacon awoke her the next morning. After a much-needed wash, Taya changed into the plain black lictor's uniform folded at the foot of her bunk and hurried to the mess. Captain Amcathra, Lieutenant Imbrex, Cristof, and Liliana were already at a table, and a number of weary-looking crew sat around the rest of the room. Taya took a cup of hot tea and a plate of bacon and eggs to the table and squeezed in.

"Good morning," she greeted everyone.

"Good morning." Cristof's sober expression lightened. He'd also washed and changed, but the dark circles under his eyes indicated that he hadn't gotten much sleep. "Are you feeling better?"

"A little." She took a bite of eggs and realized she was starving. For a few minutes she ignored the desultory conversation as she concentrated on her meal.

"Exalted, we need to discuss our next steps," Captain Amcathra said at last. "*Principessa*, if you would...."

"Excuse me." The Alzanan girl stood. She looked as weary as the rest of them, and she'd barely touched her breakfast. "I'll be in my cabin."

"I'll find you as soon as I can," Taya promised. Liliana gave her a small, sad smile as she bade the table good-bye.

"We need to get her back to her Family," Taya murmured. "Or somewhere safe. The Agostis *must* have some allies she can trust."

"There is a problem," Amcathra replied.

"Of course there is." She finished the last mouthful and eyed the empty plate. "Give me a minute, Captain."

When she returned with another helping, she sat and picked up her fork.

"All right. I'm ready."

Amcathra nodded to Lieutenant Imbrex.

"We didn't have an opportunity to refuel in Alzana," Imbrex said bluntly.

"What about food?" Taya asked, dropping a guilty look at her refilled plate.

"Don't worry, Icarus; we are otherwise well-provisioned." Lieutenant Imbrex flashed her a smile. "And you, especially, must eat. We need you to fly for us this morning."

"I don't have an armature."

"You do now." Imbrex slid a set of keys across the table. "You'll find your wings locked in the hold."

"My wings!" Taya grabbed the keys and turned her shining eyes on Captain Amcathra. "Thank you!"

"The Council ordered me to press you into service should the *Firebrand* require an icarus," he said. "As a result, I had your personal armature released into my care."

"You don't need to press me into service— I'll do whatever I can to help!"

"Thank you, Icarus."

"Thank *you*, Captain. I can't wait to get into the air again!" She beamed and dug into her breakfast with renewed enthusiasm.

"Food and water was easy to get in Alzana," Imbrex continued. "Our agents left our supplies at predesignated drop points. But the Alzanan government is stockpiling coal for its war effort, and the supply we brought from Ondinium is running very low."

"Last night's attack damaged the *Firebrand*'s wings and engine," Amcathra added. "Our engineers are trying to make repairs, but we left the ship in a glide last night and the prevailing winds have taken us farther over the ocean. To return to Alzana — or Ondinium — we must fly against the wind, which will further deplete our limited fuel stores."

"What about going north to Demicus? No," Cristof corrected himself, "the Alzanans are probably patrolling the Demican coast, considering how many clans joined the *sheytatangri*. South to Mareaux?"

"That is a possibility."

"The Council's contingency orders are to return to Ondinium as quickly as possible and gather as much military intelligence as we can along the way, but...."

"We must address our fuel shortage first. I am also concerned about delaying *Principessa* Liliana's return to her Family. Until she testifies, the accusation that we assassinated *Il Re* Agosti will spread unchallenged. I fear that it will create diplomatic rifts between Ondinium and its allies."

"Can we send a message to the Council explaining what happened?" Taya asked.

"Not until we reach an allied country, and no explanation we could provide would carry as much weight as the *principessa*'s own testimony."

"She could write a letter, and I could carry it...."

"Not across enemy territory," Lieutenant Imbrex objected. "After the invasion failed, the Alzanans set up protective perimeters around their borders and their most important military and municipal targets. The army's looking for icarus reconnaissance teams, and they will shoot to kill."

"We should investigate our other possibilities first," Amcathra agreed. "We will be able to better evaluate our situation after the engineers' report. In the meantime, we are gliding with the prevailing winds." He looked at Taya. "We will require your assistance in maneuvering the ballast hose."

"Of course." She had no idea what maneuvering a ballast hose involved, but she'd be happy to strap on her wings for any reason.

"Also, the funeral service will be held at noon."

"How many...." Cristof's voice trailed off.

"Four, and two of our wounded have poor prospects. Our crew complement was twenty-two, so we have taken a significant loss. The six lictors on our security team are not trained in aviation."

Cristof shoved his plate aside and rubbed his temples.

"I'm sorry, Janos. This is not going to go down in history as my most successful diplomatic mission."

"You did everything you could to avoid a war," Amcathra said flatly, looking from the exalted to Taya. "If you failed in your attempt, it is because other, more powerful factions desire this conflict. We did not begin the hostilities, and it is apparent that we will not end them. Neither of you may blame yourselves for the events in Alzana or the casualties to come. It is more important that you concentrate on surviving to defend our nation. Do you understand me, Exalted? Icarus?"

"Yes, I understand." Cristof took a deep breath and nodded to his friend. "I'll try."

"Yes, Captain." Taya forced a small smile. Amcathra was trying, in his own stern way, to comfort them, and she appreciated the effort.

"Maintaining positive morale in front of the crew will be essential in the days ahead." Amcathra stood. "If you will excuse me, Exalted."

"Thank you, Janos," Cristof said, as his friend strode off, quietly trailed by Lieutenant Imbrex. He turned to Taya. "He's right, you know."

"I know. But I don't feel it here." She touched her chest.

"Neither do I. But we'll need that stubborn optimism of yours now more than ever." He reached across the table to touch her hand. "*I'll* need it."

She swallowed a lump in her throat and studied the new scars and shadows in his angular features. "How are you feeling? Are you doing all right?"

"My feet are covered in blisters, my side aches, and I'm trapped on a damaged ornithopter in the middle of the ocean, but other than that, I'm in excellent shape."

"What's wrong with your side?"

"Nothing— just too much unaccustomed exercise." He gingerly ran a hand between his coat and his shirt. "Don't worry. Nothing re-opened. I checked."

"Tell me if the pain gets worse, all right?"

"Of course." He stood, dropping his hand. "Well. Since they've cracked open the engine casing, I think I'll go take a look."

"I'm sure the crew would welcome another engineer," she said, reassured that he couldn't be in too much pain if he was ready to venture on deck to poke his nose into a machine's innards.

Taya found Liliana in her cabin and held up the purse of jewelry.

"Thank you," the girl said, taking it and lifting out one of the necklaces. "My— my brother gave this one to me. I would hate to lose it."

Taya nodded, seeing the grief the girl was trying to hide.

"We'll get you back to Alzana as soon as we can." She described their situation as the *principessa* slid on the rest of her jewels. "So I hope you'll be patient," she concluded. "Captain Amcathra is doing everything he can."

"Yes...." Liliana sat on the lower bunk, since Taya was in the only chair, and ran the last necklace through her fingers. "He was polite to me this morning."

"I expect he's more relaxed now that we're safe," Taya said, although 'relaxed' wasn't a word she normally associated with the steely lictor. "He can get brusque when there's danger."

"I thought he was going to lock me in the cabin last night." The girl's hands closed over the necklace. "I know you must be tempted to hold me hostage."

"We won't. I promise. Neither Cristof nor I will permit it."

"Then I'm glad you're with me." Liliana handed her the last necklace. "This was Lady Mazzoletti's. Maybe you can use it as evidence."

The pendant was an odd, oversized crystal that jutted out of a little brass box that had two jewels inlaid on its surface.

"It's unusual," Taya commented. "Did she wear it often?"

"I've never seen it before, but I never paid any attention to her jewelry."

"It seems a little simple for her." The design on the brass box looked foreign. Taya's eye was caught by a ring of coiled copper wire that glittered around the base of the crystal. She held the pendant up to the porthole. The wire entered the crystal, running from the pendant's base to the crystal's tip. "Look at that. It almost looks like some kind of... machine!"

"What do you mean?"

"When I saw Fosca Mazzoletti in Mareaux, she dressed to impress— she wouldn't be caught dead wearing something as cheap as copper and brass. Not unless it was a lot more important than it looked." Taya stood, slipping the pendant into the pocket of her borrowed jacket. "Let's go see what Cris thinks."

They found her husband on deck, craning his neck over the chief engineer's shoulder, and dragged him away under protest. Taya smiled at the smudge of soot and grease on his cheek and reached up to rub it off.

"What?" He defensively touched the spot with a grease-covered hand, making it worse.

"Stop that!" She rubbed his cheek with the cuff of her coat while he fidgeted. "Liliana and I have a question for you."

"Yes?"

"Do you think this is some kind of Cabisi machine?" She drew out the pendant, then pulled it away as he reached for it. "Clean your hands, first!"

He wiped his fingers on his borrowed jacket, leaving smears, and took the necklace. Propping his glasses up on his forehead, he squinted as he turned the pendant over, then held it up to the light. An ecstatic smile blossomed on his lips.

"It's a machine," Taya confirmed to Liliana.

"I think it's an abeda navigation beacon," Cristof exclaimed. "I saw an engraving in a physics article last year...."

"Is it important?"

"Very. The Cabisi use it to guide ships through the Chain reefs; the beacon draws on the abeda crystals' entangled morphic—"

"If it's a navigation device," Taya interrupted, "why would Fosca Mazzoletti be wearing it like a necklace?"

Cristof lowered the pendant and dropped his spectacles back down on his nose. "Maybe she didn't know what it was. Although didn't Alister say something about the Alzanans buying weapons from Cabiel?"

"The Mazzoletti Family owns several trade vessels," Liliana confirmed.

Cristof closed his hand around the crystal. "And Gaio was a military captain. They were probably trading with the Cabisi."

"Where is Cabiel from here? South of us?"

"South of Alzana, anyway." Her husband eyed her over the top of his glasses. "I know what you're thinking."

"No, you don't."

"Yes, I do. You've always wanted to see Cabiel."

"Well, that *is* why I joined the diplomatic corps. It wasn't fair that the Council sent us to Mareaux, instead."

"It was more worried about Mareaux's advances in aerostat technology than in opening relations with a peacefully inclined and extremely remote island empire."

"Well, that remote island empire is arming Alzana against us. That's important military intelligence, don't you think?" She gave him a speculative look. "Don't the Cabisi manufacture analytical engines, too?"

"Very advanced ones. Alister always wanted to study one, but the Council doesn't allow programmers to travel." Her husband's pale gray eyes grew thoughtful and Taya knew she'd won. "It *would* be useful to know what kind of weapons and other technologies the Alzanans have been purchasing, wouldn't it?"

"I'm sure it would be important data for the Great Engine's calculations," Taya agreed, forcing herself to look solemn.

Cristof glanced down at the crystal. "Do you mind if I borrow this?"

"No.... But remember, it's evidence linking Fosca Mazzoletti to the assassination. Don't take it apart!"

"No, of course not." He was already turning away, only half-hearing her. Taya rolled her eyes as he headed off in search of Amcathra.

"Are we going to Cabiel?" Liliana asked, puzzled.

"If we're lucky." Taya pointed at the sun, which was still on the port side of the ship. "We're drifting south already. If we can save fuel, get to a technologically advanced nation that isn't at war with us, *and* find out what the — what the Mazzolettis and their allies are up to — well, it would be hard for Captain Amcathra to reject the plan."

"But what about contacting Pietra? Or Silvio?"

"Repairing the ship is our first priority, but getting you back to Alzana is important," Taya assured her. "Think of it this way—any information we learn about what your enemies are up to will be useful to your sister, won't it?"

The girl slowly nodded, looking unconvinced.

A little later, Taya put on her flight suit and strapped herself into her ondium armature. In Ondinium she flew every day, weather permitting, but she'd been grounded for weeks in Alzana. Now she took a long warm-up flight over the ocean, sweeping under the ornithopter and exulting in the sensation of salt spray on her face. Her underused muscles would ache tomorrow, but being in the air again was worth it.

"That feels good," she said, balancing on the edge of the ship's rail a moment before hopping down to the deck. Liliana reached up to touch her silver-metal wings.

"You really *do* fly," the girl said, her concerns temporarily forgotten. "Isn't it dangerous?"

"Not over the ocean. There's nothing to hit except the ship. Flying around Ondinium Mountain— *that's* dangerous. Too many wires and cables." Taya turned to a crew member. "All right, I'm ready. What do you need?"

What they needed was for her to lower the ballast hose deep enough under the waves to provide a steady, uninterrupted stream of salt water once the aviators began to pump. If the *Firebrand* had been flying lower, they would have sent a crew member down on a ladder, but at its current altitude, calling on an icarus made more sense. Taya hooked the end of the wide, rubber-sealed canvas hose to her armature and flew it down to the ocean, feeding it several feet below the surface. When the aviators waved that it was functioning, she returned to deck.

"Taya!" Cristof gestured to her from a spot well away from the ship's rail. Taya crossed the deck, pulling off her goggles and gloves.

"What?"

"We're— um, I'm glad to see you back in your wings again," he interrupted himself. "Did you have a good flight?"

Taya smiled, acknowledging her husband's effort. He tried; he really did.

"It was refreshing, thank you."

"We're going to Cabiel! The Council might not approve, but since the Alzanans have already seen the ship, Janos and I assume it's more important to make repairs than to stay hidden. Dautry says the prevailing winds are carrying us toward Cabiel anyway, so we'll conserve fuel, and Janos agrees that it would be strategically useful to learn about the Alzanans' trade agreements while we're repairing and refueling."

Taya felt her pulse leap with anticipation, although something about what he'd said made her pause.

"Dautry?"

"The pilot who took us to Engels. She's Janos' navigator."

"Really? The Council allowed a foreigner to join the crew?"

"I suppose. I didn't ask for details." He looked disappointed by her reaction. "Going to Cabiel is more interesting, don't you think?"

Taya grabbed his hand, squeezing it reassuringly.

"Of course it is! I can't wait. You know I've wanted to visit the Cabisi Islands all my life."

He cheered up. "And I'm looking forward to seeing an abeda beacon at work and learning more about their analytical engines." He impatiently swept back the strands of his long hair that kept whipping into his face. "I'll tell Alister all about them in my next letter."

"Let's just hope the Cabisi aren't as protective of their secrets as the Council."

"Well, they're willing to sell them, aren't they?" His expression darkened. "The only thing I'm *not* looking forward to is getting heartburn at every meal."

"I'm sure they make *some* dishes that aren't spicy." Taya had dragged Cristof to her favorite Cabisi restaurant several times during the early days of their relationship, but at last he'd begged for mercy, explaining that his digestive system couldn't take it any more. Taya, by contrast, loved the burn of hot peppers and strong spices.

"You're in charge of ordering my food."

"As always." She stretched up to kiss him. "Will this be an official visit, then?"

"I think it will need to be. I don't have a mask, though. Or a clean robe." He fell silent. She wondered if he was also remembering Jayce. The young tailor had always been particular about their clothing. "We'll have to improvise."

"We'll think of something." Taya's eyes rose to the horizon, where Cabiel lay, and saw a long, dark line of clouds instead. "Looks like there's a storm building up. I hope it doesn't hit us until after the funeral service."

"A storm? Is that why Janos is bringing on more ballast? Can't we fly over it?"

"We could fly over a little drizzle, maybe, but that looks like a thunderstorm, and thunderclouds are tall. I don't think we could climb over it without getting sick."

"I don't think I'll be able to fly through it without getting sick, either," Cristof muttered, gazing at the horizon with trepidation. Taya gave his hand a sympathetic squeeze.

After the ballast tanks had been filled and the funeral service was over, the Firebrands took a collective breath and returned to their duties with a renewed sense of purpose. The ship's wings and demiwings were spread to catch the maximum amount of breeze and the *Firebrand* leaped forward, racing south with the wind, while Cristof and the engineers studied the damage to the wings' gear train.

The wind grew stronger throughout the day, heralding the oncoming storm. At last everyone was ordered to stow their loose belongings and sit down to an early dinner so the cook could secure the galley before it hit.

Taya took one last walk on deck as the sky grew dark, noting the safety lines set up across the deck and the oiled leather straps buckled to the primary and secondary helms. The crew was screwing together wooden planks in walkways that covered the ondium plating below the safety lines. One of the crew didn't wear a lictor's stripe.

"Professor?"

Cora Dautry, a Mareaux navigator and aerostat pilot, looked up.

"Taya Icarus." She straightened. "How are you? I apologize for not saying hello earlier, but I was busy...."

"Plotting a course to Cabiel?"

"Most recently, yes."

Taya leaned on the rail. Dautry had traded her conservative skirts for an oilskin coat worn over a plain gray version of a lictor's uniform. Her long brown hair was still pinned up in a bun, however, and a pair of wire-rimmed glasses hung around her neck on a thin silver chain.

"How did you end up as the *Firebrand*'s navigator?" Taya asked, curiously. "I know you're qualified, but the Oporphyr Council doesn't usually hire foreigners."

"It's Captain Amcathra's fault," Dautry said, her expression darkening. "He came to visit me several times after the invasion. At first I thought— well, I didn't realize I was being interviewed for a job. Apparently he liked what I had to say, though. He convinced your Council that since I have more navigation experience than any Ondinium pilots, I should be attached to his crew. Decatur Constante asked me if I would be interested in working on a top-secret mission involving flight...."

"And of course you said 'yes.'"

"Well, I did have some second thoughts after I saw all the confidentiality agreements, nondisclosure contracts, and state secrets acts they wanted me to sign. Tell me, are *you* under a death sentence if you talk about this ship to others?"

"Yes, although I don't know if it still matters, now that the Alzanans have seen us.... But you still signed up, obviously."

"I wanted to see what Ondinium was developing. I assumed the Council was about to throw a great deal of money and man-hours into building its own aerostat program, and I thought it would be exciting to be on the cutting edge of the project."

"But instead...."

"But instead, I discovered that your Council is full of liars and hypocrites. *And* that Captain Amcathra must have known full well that Ondinium possessed its own aerial fleet when he was lecturing me about his beloved martyr Captain Menoth and the nation's taboo against aerial warfare."

Taya's eyebrows rose. She'd almost forgotten that long-ago discussion.

"Then why did you agree to work with him?"

"I didn't have any choice after I saw the ship," Dautry said, sniffing. Then, after a moment, she relented. "I don't appreciate being interviewed under the guise of friendly conversation, and I'm not happy that your country lied about owning aerial vessels. However, I admit that I find the *Firebrand* exhilarating, and the Council gave me a generous budget for instrumentation. I've been taking copious notes— Ondinium's navigation manual is deplorably out of date, and I plan to present your Council with a thorough revision once I return."

Taya laughed.

"Has Cris seen your research instruments yet?"

"The ambassador? I spoke to him earlier about his navigation crystal, but that's all. I've been busy since then."

His navigation crystal? Taya let it pass. "You should show him. He adores new scientific instruments. You could probably get him to do most of your measurements without even asking."

"Well, perhaps tomorrow." Dautry looked up as rain began to fall on the metal deck. "Right now my instruments are locked away against the storm."

"And Cris is, too, I hope." Taya turned her face away from a sudden, wet gust of wind. "Time for us to get below."

"You go ahead. I'll be staying up here tonight to keep us on course."

· ✱ ·

Rain pounded against the *Firebrand*'s ondium deck and hull so loudly that Taya couldn't sleep. Cris had dosed himself with a sleeping draught, but Taya had set her portion aside untouched. She didn't like being helpless at the best of times, and being helpless in midair would be particularly galling.

A new sound rumbled through the ship. She rolled over, opening her pocketwatch and waiting for the next flash of lightning. 3:15. She groaned, closing the watch and slipping it back under her pillow.

Well, there's no reason to suffer alone when I could suffer in company. She unhooked her safety net and slid out of the top bunk. Cristof snored lightly in the bunk below, wrapped in his blankets and wedged in the back corner.

He won't remember any of this when he wakes up. I should have taken that draught, after all.

Too late, now. Moving quietly, she pulled on her flight suit and boots, grabbed her ship-issue oilskin coat, and slipped out of the cabin.

Principessa Liliana had taken some of the draught, too. There was no sign of movement from her cabin. Taya walked down the dark, narrow hallway, buttoning up her flight suit and pulling on her coat, until she came to the ship's ladder. Her armature had been moved up from the storage hold and locked there for her. Now it banged against the wall with each of the *Firebrand*'s lurches and rolls. Taya steadied it, frowning.

Next time I'll secure it better. But for now— she could move her wings into her bunk, but she didn't want to wake Cristof. He was an admirably brave man in most respects, but being trapped in a wind-tossed ornithopter in the middle of a thunderstorm wasn't the sort of situation he would handle well. She preferred to let him sleep through the night.

Instead, she unlocked the armature and pulled it on over her coat, keeping the wings locked tightly against her sides. The ship gave an abrupt roll to port and she yelped, grabbing the ladder. As the *Firebrand* righted, she heard shouts from above. She headed up.

The next deck was where the crew bunked, but none of them were asleep anymore. Several lictors huddled together, talking and laughing, while two — Dayvet and Helvi — vomited into chamberpots. Taya spotted Pitio, the ship's signaler they'd met on the beach, and made her unsteady way over to him.

"Icarus!" The aviators made room for her, touching her metal feathers for luck. With all the chairs put away and her armature on, Taya had no choice but to stand, grabbing one of the support beams for stability.

"You aren't going flying, are you?" asked Lucanus, a short but sturdy-looking sergeant. "Not in this weather!"

"No— I'm just keeping my wings from banging against the wall." Taya hesitated, then gave the group an embarrassed smile. "And I feel safer when I'm wearing them, to tell the truth. No offense."

"None taken. If I had wings, I'd be wearing them, too." Pitio chuckled. "This is the first real storm we've weathered, and I'll be slagged if I like it."

Taya staggered but kept her balance as the ship rocked again. "You didn't run into any storms flying to Alzana?"

"Just snow," Lucanus said.

"We never trained in a storm, either," Pitio said. "Might recommend it when we get back, though."

"The decaturs wouldn't dare risk a ship like that." Lucanus patted the deck of the *Firebrand* with affection. "Not too many of these beauties left."

"Could be hundreds, for all we know." Jager sat cross-legged with the aviation crew, apparently unfazed by the ship's motion. "It's *you* they don't dare risk. There can't be many lictors who know how to fly these things, or I would have heard rumors."

"There aren't," Pitio admitted. "Although I think the Council will have to go public and ramp up its recruiting and training if it wants to keep up with the Alzanans."

"Will only lictors be accepted, do you think, or other castes, too?" Taya asked. Her hair stood on end and she looked around, puzzled.

Pitio's reply was cut off in a burst of light and clap of thunder. The entire ship shuddered. Taya fell to her knees, felt Jager catch her arms, and clutched the lictor with raw fear as she smelled ozone and burning flesh. The ship's engine stopped.

"Lady, what was that?" she gasped. The ceiling lamps were swinging wildly, and one had burst, spilling burning oil on the floor.

"I don't know!" Jager replied, looking as confused as Taya.

"Lightning strike," Lucanus croaked, pushing himself up. "Somebody put out that fire!"

Taya forced herself to release Jager's arms. A voice was screaming over the rain's incessant pounding. She scrambled to her feet and turned toward the ladder.

"You can't—" Jager bit off her words as she saw Taya's expression. "Be careful."

On the top deck, rain blew into Taya's face and the wind threw her to one side. Her fingers brushed one of the safety lines and she grabbed it, wiping her face and squinting through the storm. Hurricane lanterns had been set up along the rails and beside the primary and secondary helms. She turned toward the primary helm and the sound of screaming.

"Back to stations!" Amcathra roared. "Mister Seius, check the engine. Miss Icilius, you have primary."

Taya heard shouted acknowledgments through the thunder and the pounding rain. The lictor at the secondary helm grabbed the safety lines and pulled herself forward. Another lictor slipped past Taya and scrambled down the stairs, on his way to the engine deck.

"I'll take secondary, Captain," a familiar voice said. Amcathra turned, rain streaming down his face as he frowned at the professor.

"I need you with me, Dautry."

"Mister Lucanus can read the compass, sir."

Amcathra's hesitation lasted only a second. His eyes swept the deck and landed on Taya. "Icarus, bring me Sergeant Lucanus."

"Yes, sir!" she replied. She was halfway down the ladder before she realized what she'd said.

"Lucanus!" she shouted. "Captain Amcathra needs you to navigate."

The lictor looked dismayed as he grabbed his coat.

"Did something happen to the prof?"

"No— she's taking the secondary helm."

Lucanus swept past her, thrusting his arms into his sleeves as he reached the deck, and Taya followed. While he headed forward, she grabbed the safety lines and worked her way back to where Dautry had strapped herself in. The professor was wiping rain off her helm's glass-covered instrument panel. Her long brown hair had fallen out of its usual strict coiffure and whipped around her face as she leaned over the panel, trying to read it in the light of a madly swinging lamp.

"Where are your glasses?" Taya shouted, grabbing the strap ring by the helm.

"I can't see through them!" Dautry looked up. "Read the numbers aloud while I listen for orders."

Taya dutifully shouted out the readings, pausing periodically to wipe the glass. The *Firebrand* kept bobbing and turning, its ondium wings and rudder powerless in the storm's strong winds. Rain struck them like pellets and worked its way beneath Taya's coat and into her flight suit. She flinched as another crack of thunder deafened them. Lightning danced around the ship, making her skin prickle.

"If you have gloves, wear them," Dautry warned. "Don't want to touch metal with your bare hands in a lightning storm."

Taya hastily yanked out her leather gloves, pulling them over her wet hands with some effort. Her eyes dropped to the wooden duckboards that kept their feet off the metal deck.

"Is that what happened up front?"

"Lightning strike." Dautry tapped the instrument panel and their discussion was momentarily suspended while Taya read the numbers again. "Mister Page was killed at once— I think the other two are alive. Keep your wings folded!"

Taya swallowed and nodded. She'd heard horror stories of icarii felled by lightning. Couriers stayed grounded in a storm, but military support and search-and-rescue teams sometimes flew through inclement weather.

More orders were relayed from the forecastle, and Dautry concentrated on keeping them stabilized. Electricity arced off the ship's tall metal tailrudder, sending sparks flying across the ondium deck. Taya regretted her claustrophobia and curiosity— she would have been much happier tucked in her bed right now, ignorant and dry.

She wasn't sure how long they'd been working before she noticed that she was able to read the instrument panel more clearly. She looked up, blinking in the still-steady rain. The sky was as dark and cloud-filled as ever. She frowned, dropping her gaze until she spotted the dim light emanating from Dautry's collar.

"Professor!" She pointed.

Dautry looked down, then lifted a chain from around her neck. Fosca Mazzoletti's abeda crystal glowed with an inner luminescence.

"What does it mean?" Taya asked, mystified.

"It means we're still on course." Dautry let the crystal drop back into her coat collar. "That is, if your husband's theory is correct."

"Should we tell Captain Amcathra?"

"We need to get through this storm first."

Getting through the storm took hours. Eventually the lightning stopped, but it was still cloudy and gray when the cook came on deck with mugs of hot tea. The winds were gusty and strong, but the rain no longer pounded as hard as it had. The crew members who'd huddled below during the storm looked haggard as they relieved the lictors who'd worked all night.

Taya smiled as she saw a tall, thin figure clutching the ropes as he headed for them through the steady drizzle.

"You were here all night!" Cristof accused as he drew near.

"I couldn't sleep, so...."

"How do you think I would have felt if you'd been lost in the storm while I was fast asleep?"

Taya's smile faded.

"I wasn't, so why are you worrying about it?"

"Because I worry about *you!*" He scowled, looking at her armature. "It doesn't matter how talented a flier you are— you shouldn't go aloft in a storm!"

"I wasn't aloft. I just wore this... for security."

"Security? Metal in a lightning storm? Taya, how can I keep you safe if you insist on putting yourself into danger without me?"

"I don't need you to keep me safe!" Taya snapped. Cristof's head jerked back and he drew in a deep breath, then let it out, slowly. His hand tightened on the safety rope.

"No, I suppose you don't," he said, tonelessly.

Before Taya could say anything else, Dautry cleared her throat. "If you'll excuse me, Ambassador...." the Mareaux professor unbuckled herself from the helm, "I need to report to the captain."

"The beacon started working last night," Taya said, hoping the news might distract her husband from his hurt feelings.

"That's good," he said, without any apparent interest.

Dautry hesitated, then reached behind her neck and unclasped the necklace, handing it to him. The crystal still glowed.

"Perhaps you can tell me more about how this is supposed to work," she said. "Will the light change in intensity as we draw closer?"

"I don't know." Despite himself, Cristof took the crystal with his free hand, nudging up his glasses as he inspected it more closely. Taya breathed a quiet sigh of relief as he fell into step next to the professor, one hand on the safety rope and the other holding the crystal. Taya trailed behind, glad to be forgotten for a change.

They found Amcathra with his back to the rain, finishing his cup of tea.

"How are you, Janos?" Cristof asked.

Amcathra handed his cup to the lictor closest to him. His pale blue eyes landed on the crystal in Cristof's hand.

"I am well, Exalted. I see the beacon is working."

"Professor Dautry said it activated a few hours ago. I think that as long as it's glowing, you're on the right course to Cabiel. You might want to keep it up here."

"I shall have it affixed beside the ship's compass." He glanced at Dautry. "Unless you would prefer to keep it?"

"Putting it next to the compass makes sense. At the moment, I can't take a sighting *or* rely on dead reckoning to determine our position, so that light will have to guide us until the storm clears."

Amcathra slipped the necklace into his overcoat pocket.

"Did we weather the storm all right?" Cristof asked.

"The engine is damaged and we have lost two crew members. Our primary helmsman and one of our engineers were electrocuted when the ship was hit by lightning."

"Can we still handle the ship? Do you need me to do something?"

"Your continuing assistance as an engineer would be appreciated, Exalted." Amcathra turned to Dautry. "And although your service as the *Firebrand*'s navigator has been invaluable, I would like you to continue serving as secondary helm until you can train a replacement."

"As if I were a real crew member?" Dautry's question held a touch of acrimony. "I'm happy to assist the ship in an emergency, Captain, but don't forget that I'm on the books as a foreign advisor. What I'm permitted to hear and do on the *Firebrand* is strictly delineated by the agreement I signed, and it doesn't include serving as one of the ship's helms."

Amcathra promptly turned to Cristof.

"We are down to sixteen skilled aviators, Exalted, of whom several have been injured. I intend to train the lictors we brought from Alzana, but we are currently undermanned. With your permission, I would like to override the Council's restrictions and enlist Professor Dautry's service as a full crew member. I have observed her navigation and piloting skills on numerous occasions, and I find her capable, clear-headed, and calm in a crisis. I believe she would serve admirably."

Color rose in the normally composed professor's cheeks.

"Permission granted," Cristof said. "Although I notice that any blame for this decision will fall on *me*."

"I will share the responsibility."

"You'd better not. The decaturs are less likely to shoot an exalted."

"Perhaps you have not correctly grasped our comparative values in the Council's eyes."

Cristof's lips twisted upward in a fleeting smile.

"Perhaps not." He turned to Dautry, whose correct posture stiffened even further. "Janos is a hard man to impress, so if he vouches for you, I'm sure you'll do fine… assuming you want the position, of course. I suppose it'll end up being a lot more work with no more pay."

"I would be delighted to accept a full-time position on the *Firebrand*'s crew," Dautry said, her color still high. "And while I can't say I approve of your government, Exalted, I assure you that I will serve this ship to the best of my ability."

"Fair enough. I don't approve of my government most of the time, either."

"Then you are relieved, Dautry," Amcathra said, ignoring Cristof's comment. "I recommend you get some sleep too, Icarus. We may require your assistance later."

The word *sleep* was enough to trigger a yawn, and Taya nodded, covering her mouth.

"I will. If you'll excuse me, Captain?"

She and Dautry headed below.

"Taya…"

"Yes?"

"Are your husband and Captain Amcathra really putting themselves into danger by appointing me to this position?"

"No, not shot-for-treason danger. They may have to undergo some more debriefings and loyalty exams when we get back, but your skills *are* needed, and the decaturs respect Amcathra's judgment…." she glanced around and lowered her voice, "more than they do Cris's."

"That reminds me. I was given to understand, the last time we traveled together, that Captain Amcathra spies on your husband for the Council. They seem to get along well despite that, though."

"They're old friends. Reporting on Cris is part of Amcathra's job, but he's selective about what he sees and hears."

"And says," the professor added, tartly. "So it doesn't bother you that he's misrepresented himself in the past— to you, to me, and to others?"

"Well… I don't always like what the Council has asked him to do, but I respect the fact that he's loyal enough to the Council to do it."

"I see." Dautry looked thoughtful. "This must be another cultural difference between Ondinium and Mareaux."

"But you just agreed to work for him," Taya pointed out. "Like Cris said, you've impressed him, and that's not easy to do."

"I agreed to work for the *Firebrand*," Dautry corrected her. "As for the captain, he still needs to impress *me*." She began pulling pins from her hair as she walked away.

Taya unbuckled her armature, considering the professor's words. She understood Dautry's reservations; she had once scolded Cristof for being a spy, too. Honesty was important in a man. But Cristof had chosen to be deceptive on his own, whereas Amcathra was under the Council's orders....

"Taya." Her husband's voice startled her. She turned to find him standing awkwardly behind her, his head nearly touching the low ceiling. "Go to bed. I'll oil your armature."

"You don't have to do that. I'm the one who wore it out in the rain."

He jammed his hands into his coat pockets.

"Fixing machines is the one thing I happen to be good at," he said, his voice strained. "You might let me do that much for you, at least."

"Oh, Cris." Taya sighed, releasing her armature and letting its wingtips float to the ceiling. "I'm sorry I didn't wake you up last night. I thought it would be better to let you sleep. But I couldn't just lie there in my bunk all night. You know how I get in tight spaces— I had to get out of bed and *do* something."

"What if you'd been swept off the deck? Or hit by lightning? I mean, first you run out in the middle of a firefight, and then you wear your armature in an electrical storm — and I can't *follow* you! I can't—"

"Cris, please." She stepped forward and touched the tight lines on his face. The scars over his eye and across his castemark were pale against his copper skin. "Stop beating yourself up about being afraid of heights. It's all right."

"It's not all right when you're married to an icarus," he said bitterly.

"You've never hesitated to fly with me when it's been necessary. Remember the time you jumped down to rescue me inside the Great Engine room, or threw us both off that exploding dirigible?"

"You're the one who usually does the rescuing."

"Do we need to sit down and make a list?" She ran a thumb over his cheek. "We could write down who's done what, when, and where. Then we could rank-order each item by frequency and danger level to figure out which one of us has saved the other more often. Would *that* satisfy your analytical, overactive brain?"

He gave her a rueful smile and pulled her closer.

"I just worry about you, love," he whispered in her ear. "The thought of losing you terrifies me."

She wrapped her arms around his waist and leaned against his rain-drenched coat. He winced and she drew back.

"Are you all right?"

"Old injuries." He pulled her close again. "The rain doesn't agree with them."

"I'm sorry. I didn't know...." No wonder he was so irritable, she thought with a pang of guilt. His arms tightened around her. Then, after a moment, he shifted.

"Everyone's gone quiet," he breathed. "I think we're being watched."

Taya laughed, gently pushing him away. The lictors around them swiftly returned to what they were doing.

"Look at how much better you've gotten at public displays of affection," she murmured, grabbing the front of his coat and standing on her toes to kiss him. He gave her a crooked grin.

"I prefer private displays of affection. But you'd need to get some sleep, first." He pointed toward the stairs. "Go on. I'll take care of your wings."

CHAPTER SIX

FOUR DAYS LATER, the *Firebrand*'s lookout spotted the first Cabisi island and they ran out Ondinium's peacetime flag: a black field speckled with silver stars. Even though Ondinium was technically at war, Cristof hoped to avoid any misunderstandings with a nation that might not be abreast of the latest continental news.

Taya abandoned Liliana and Cristof to their breakfasts and eagerly hung over the ship's rails, gazing at Cabiel through a pair of borrowed field glasses. The islands were lush and green, and small fishing boats dotted the water around them. The Cabisi working on the ships looked up, shading their eyes as they studied the silver shape glinting in the sky. One boatsman pulled out a spyglass. Taya waved at him. To her delight, he waved back.

"Should we stop to introduce ourselves?" she asked when Captain Amcathra joined her. The Demican lictor's fair skin was red with sunburn and his face glistened with sweat. He stubbornly refused to doff his heavy black lictor's uniform, although he'd allowed the rest of the crew to remove the wool jackets and roll up their shirt sleeves.

"He is not frightened by our ship," Amcathra observed, examining the fishermen through his prism binoculars. He shifted and studied the island. Taya followed his lead and saw a small village nestled close to the shore, its wood-and-thatch buildings covered with bright red and yellow patterns. Villagers gathered along the beach, squinting up at the *Firebrand*. Their skin was darker than Ondinium's copper or Alzana's bronze — it was more of a deep, black iron — and they seemed uniformly tall and handsome, with high-boned faces and thick black hair. Taya wondered if the Cabisi shared a common heritage with Ondinium's exalteds.

"Those could be aqueducts, coming from the forest," Amcathra remarked. "I see solar reflectors and copper kettles by the houses." He raised his binoculars to the forested highlands. "A signal tower on the ridge. Reflectors with some sort of arm arrangement, possibly for flags. I see no sign of cannon or other weaponry, but the forest is thick enough to hide artillery if the residents wished to keep their defenses secret."

"Do you have to be so... militant?" Taya asked, lowering her glasses.

"Yes." He continued searching the island as they glided by. "Terraced farmland, water carried by pipes. A windmill. Aerial ropeways. The villagers appear to live a low-technology but fuel-efficient lifestyle. Their windmill might power a generator."

"We know the Cabisi aren't primitive; they build analytical engines and weapons."

"Apparently they do not build them in *this* village, Icarus." He lowered his glasses and turned.

"Wait! Captain—"

"Yes?"

"What about Lieutenant Imbrex?"

He gave her a blank look. "Are you having a problem with the lieutenant?"

"No, not at all. I was just wondering— have you worked with her long?"

His expression shifted and became stony.

"Lieutenant Imbrex is a fine officer, Icarus, with a promising career ahead of her. If I understand the direction of your question correctly, I must warn you that it is not only offensive, but potentially injurious, as well."

"Right." Taya bit her lip, chagrined. "Sorry. Never mind."

He turned and walked off, giving orders to fly past the island. Taya sighed and crossed all the other lictors off her mental list of potential partners for the captain.

They passed several other islands that day, all part of the spiraling chain of island-states that constituted the sprawling Cabisi Thalassocracy. At the center of the spiral was the largest island, Os Cansai, the maritime empire's capital. The waters between the islands were full of reefs, clearly visible from above, and Taya understood why the Cabisi had developed beacons to guide sailors through the straits. However, the reefs would provide a strong defense against attacking ships without navigational aids.

Sailing ships, anyway. Taya wondered if the Cabisi feared aerial warfare as much as Ondinium. The people they'd encountered so far didn't seem very alarmed by their ship.

The *Firebrand* paused that evening over open water. Taya and Cristof joined the ship's officers to discuss how to approach the capital. Cabiel had no diplomatic representatives and a very small trading presence in Ondinium. Although the island nation had historically maintained an aloof neutrality from mainland politics, the Firebrands had no way of knowing whether it had established a political alliance with Alzana in recent months.

"We should give them time to prepare for us," Taya suggested. "We saw signal towers on the islands, so Os Cansai probably knows we're coming—"

"Yes." Captain Amcathra's reply cut her short. "We will grapple to the outer edge of the Cabisi reef tonight." He turned to Cristof. "We have made a new mask for you, Exalted."

"Really?" Cristof was unable to completely hide his dismay. "How?"

"The ship's armorer converted it from one of our cargo counter-weights." Imbrex reached under her chair to pull out a fabric-wrapped bundle. She carefully unwrapped it and offered it to him.

It was shaped like a traditional exalted's mask, a blank oval with two eye slits and a wave-shaped castemark etched over one cheek. However, instead of being made from ivory, it had been hammered out of ondium and polished to a mirrorlike shine. Imbrex turned it over to reveal metal clamps around the eyes and silk cords for tying the mask into place. She pointed to the clamps. "If you take the temples off your spectacles, Exalted, you can fasten the lenses here."

"Ondium's expensive, Janos," Cristof said, frowning. "If the mask comes loose…."

"I was unwilling to sacrifice our ammunition casings," Captain Amcathra said. "Please tie your knots carefully."

"May I?" Taya waited for her husband's nod before she took the mask from Imbrex. Its shape was more curved than normal, with narrow flanges under the chin and at the cheek and temple that would help keep the lighter-than-air ondium from floating off Cristof's face. She lowered it. "This is well-constructed."

"Our armorer does decorative metalwork as a hobby," Imbrex said, looking pleased. "He was honored to create an exalted's mask."

"I'll thank him tomorrow." Cristof made no move to take it, so Taya wrapped the mask up and slid it under her chair, settling it against the underside of her seat. "I suppose if I have to wear a mask, I'll also have to have to wear a robe...."

"We are in the process of constructing one from the limited material on board," Amcathra said. "It will not be up to your usual sartorial standards."

Cristof waved away the comment, his expression shadowed. Jayce had set those standards.

"After we make repairs, how long will it take to fly back to Ondinium?"

"Perhaps five days to reach the tip of Mareaux," Amcathra said. "If the headwinds are not too strong, another week to ten days to Ondinium."

Taya calculated. They'd been attacked almost a week ago. Assuming a week in Os Cansai, and another two to get back to Ondinium... a month would have passed since the king's murder.

"Could we make better time if we took the train from Mareaux?" she asked.

"You might cross Mareaux faster," Lieutenant Imbrex said dubiously, "but you'd lose time once you got to the border station, and it wouldn't be nearly as safe."

"I never thought I'd say this," Cristof muttered, "but I *do* prefer an ornithopter to a train."

Taya reached out and squeezed her husband's hand.

"What about dropping off the *principessa*?" she pursued. "Are we going to leave her in Mareaux or take her to Ondinium?"

She'd expected Amcathra to immediately vote for Ondinium, but he remained studiously neutral, watching Cristof.

"You think the Council will try to use her as a bargaining chip, don't you?" Cristof asked at last.

"I have said nothing of the sort."

"No, of course not." Cristof rubbed his forehead. "Liliana came with us in good faith, and she's our most valuable defense against Alzana's accusations. Taking advantage of her vulnerability would be diplomatically disastrous."

"The Council may believe that the time for diplomacy has passed."

"It probably never thought diplomacy was a realistic option in the first place." Cristof dropped his hands. "Could we drop her off in Echelles? Queen Iancais would take good care of her."

"Echelles would be a convenient place to refuel and reprovision."

"Then we'll do it," Cristof said, with finality. Taya looked from him to the lictor, wondering if the two men really believed that Liliana would let them decide her fate so easily.

· ✳ ·

Warm rain pattered over the *Firebrand* as it approached Os Cansai. The abeda beacon maintained a calm, steady glow as the reefs opened below them. The number of ships in the water increased, and Pitio identified canoes, pirogues, ngalawas, and feluccas for Taya. She called Cristof over to look at a large ship powered by a steam engine and paddlewheels, its deck piled high with barrels and crates and caged livestock. He studied it with interest but kept a death grip on the *Firebrand*'s railing.

The Cabisi ships were painted in bright, primary hues. Sailors crowded onto their decks, shielding their eyes from the drizzle as they gazed at the ornithopter above them, its hawkish wings tilted like metal sails and a silver-and-black flag hanging beneath its sealed gundeck. The *Firebrand*'s engines had been lit in anticipation of docking maneuvers and smoke trickled from the chimneys under the wings. Taya cheerfully waved at the sailors, looking forward to landing and meeting the Cabisi face-to-face at last.

With the ship moving lazily through the drizzle, the Firebrands had plenty of time to observe their destination. The island's harbor was guarded by high, fortified sea walls that protected the busy port within. Watchtowers along the walls flew long carmine banners that displayed a stylized shark, the official emblem of the Cabisi empire.

Moored atop one of the watchtowers floated an Alzanan dirigible.

"Oh, scrap," Taya breathed, lowering her field glasses and wiping droplets of rain off the lenses. She looked up to the forecastle and saw Captain Amcathra standing next to the *Firebrand*'s starboard wing mount, also studying the ship.

Taya handed the glasses to her husband, who stepped away from the rail before taking them with both hands.

"It's got the Alzanan gryphon on it," she said. "And a '10' painted on the prow. Does that mean they have ten ships?"

"They know we're here," he said, his spectacles tilted high on his forehead as he adjusted the focus on the field glasses. "Someone's looking back at us through the gondola windows."

"They wouldn't open fire in port, would they? That would be an incredible breach of etiquette."

"You'd better warn Janos, then, before he gives any undiplomatic orders."

"He wouldn't do that!"

"Are you sure?"

Swearing under her breath, Taya ran forward, dodging the lictors who had stopped in their tracks to stare at the enemy ship.

"Captain—" she halted at the wing mount.

"Yes?"

"It wouldn't be polite to fire on the Alzanans while we're in the Cabisi port."

"Thank you, Icarus. I had no intention of doing so."

She flushed. "Well, it *is* my job to prevent diplomatic incidents...."

"It is highly unlikely that the crew aboard that ship has heard about Agosti's death. Telegraphy does not operate over the ocean."

Chastened, Taya returned to find Liliana by Cristof's side. The *principessa* was looking at the dirigible with a combination of anticipation and apprehension.

"Are we going to get into another fight?" she asked.

"Apparently not." Taya joined them. "Amcathra doesn't think they've heard about your grandfather's death yet."

The girl gazed at the ship, one hand resting lightly on the *Firebrand*'s railing. "If the captain is an Agosti ally...."

"Then you could return to Alzana with him." Taya nodded. "But you'd have to be very careful once you got back. Fosca Mazzoletti can't afford to let you live to tell the truth."

Liliana nodded, looking pensive as she gazed at her countrymen's war vessel.

As they drew closer, Cabisi appeared at the top of one of the watchtowers on the opposite side of the port and began waving flags.

"They're using Alzanan signals," Pitio reported to the captain. "They want us to dock at that tower and they're asking if we need lines thrown out."

"Reply with an affirmative to both," Amcathra said, turning to Imbrex to give orders. Within minutes, the *Firebrand*'s steam engines were stoked into action. The giant wings moved and the ship made a wide arc over the busy port. Taya returned to their cabin to dress Cristof in his formal robes.

"I'd rather hoped I wouldn't have to do this," Cristof grumbled, affixing his dismantled spectacles to the ondium mask. Taya pulled his long black hair back into a simple tail tied with an embroidered silk ribbon. It wasn't anything like the ornate, bejeweled hairstyles he usually wore on official business, but she didn't know how to create an exalted's intricate loops and plaits.

The layers of silk under-robes he'd worn during his escape had been cleaned, but if any Cabisi saw their waterstained and mended hems, Ondinium's reputation would be ruined. Taya swept the robes over his borrowed boots. They didn't even have gloves to cover his hands, which would simply have to remain hidden by his long sleeves. His new outer robe had been pieced together out of black lictors' uniforms, its only color a series of bright bands cut from the ship's signal flags that ran along its collar and bottom hem.

Once her husband was dressed, Taya changed into her flight suit and unlocked her wings. They climbed on deck, Cristof holding his long outer robe out of the way and carrying his mask. The *Firebrand* had maneuvered close to the tower, its wings folding against its hull and its ballast tanks dumping water before crossing the seawall. The light drizzle had stopped, leaving the air humid and warm.

Taya strapped herself into her armature.

"Pitio..." Taya gestured to the lictor. "Those colors on Cristof's robe don't *mean* anything, do they?"

The signaler grinned.

"Fact is, they spell out *Firebrand*. Sort of an exalted's ship uniform, like." His grin suddenly faded. "That's all right, isn't it?"

"Yes... yes, it's fine." A ship's uniform, rather than an ambassador's finery; Taya liked the idea. When she turned to tell Cristof, she found Liliana unfolding the robe's extra-long sleeves over his hands.

"Spirits are rioting," Taya muttered.

"What?" Liliana looked up, puzzled. She had combed out her windblown curls and put on all of her jewelry to brighten up her borrowed dress.

"A foreigner helping an exalted get dressed violates about a half-dozen historic taboos." Taya laughed at the girl's expression. "Not that Cris cares."

"I would hate to leave any tradition unshattered," he said complacently.

"Just don't tell the Council." Taya shook her head as she gazed at him. "Look at you. All in black again."

"I prefer it, you know, to all those fancy colors and designs."

"Yes, but you look prettier in all those fancy designs." Taya fitted the metal mask over Cristof's face as he sputtered, then tied the cords in back. "How's that?"

"Not bad." He tried to adjust the mask with his sleeve-hidden hands. She brushed them aside and fixed it for him. "Digs a little under the chin, but it doesn't sit as close to my face as a regular mask. Makes it easier to breathe. And I like the fact that it doesn't weigh anything."

"I see it makes it easier for you to speak, too," Taya said with disapproval. She stepped back and gave his ensemble an evaluating look. His trailing robe was as black as Ondinium's flag, and his silver mask looked like one of its stars. Its polished, mirrorlike surface reflected her own distorted face back at her.

"You look... ominous," she said at last. "Dangerous."

"I'll do my best not to pass out and ruin the effect."

"Let me know if you feel faint." She turned to Liliana. "May I ask you to observe correct etiquette toward the exalted while we're in front of others, *Principessa*?"

"Of course." The girl hesitated. "What should I do?"

"Please refer to my husband as the ambassador, or Exalted Forlore. Don't touch him or approach him while he's masked. You can speak to him directly, but I'll answer. Don't talk to others about what he looks like or mention that you've seen his naked face."

"All right." Liliana cocked her head. "Is that how you live in Ondinium? I'd heard exalteds were strange, but you've seemed normal so far."

Taya sighed. "In Ondinium, nobody out of caste is permitted to see an exalted's bare skin or hear an exalted's voice except icarii and certain members of the exalted's household or office."

"Why?"

"Because they're—" Cristof started, beneath his mask. Taya kicked him.

"Hush. Rant when you're not masked." She glanced down to make sure her boot hadn't left a mark on his dark robe and tugged the drapery straight again.

"Well, uh, why doesn't... Exalted Forlore act like that?"

"Because he's eccentric. But just because he's willing to bare his face to strangers doesn't mean he's not an exalted, and when he's covered, we must treat him traditionally."

"I will," Liliana promised. "But I'm glad *my* Family doesn't have to wear masks and robes. It looks uncomfortable."

"It is," Cristof muttered before Taya could stop him.

The Cabisi dockhands on the tower's wooden hoarding tossed out heavy cables. The *Firebrand* had glided in low, so the lictors seized the cables and hauled the ornithopter up and into the makeshift airdock.

The workers grinned as the silver ship bumped against the open hoarding platform, bounced, and floated a few feet away. Taya only understood about half of their comments as they admired the *Firebrand*'s gleaming, spiral-etched ondium hull and sleek, predatory shape. She translated what she could for Cristof as they waited.

Captain Amcathra and Lieutenant Imbrex joined them as soon as the ship was secured. Professor Dautry stood to one side, looking around with lively interest. Several lictors swung open the ship's gate and slid out the gangplank.

Five official-looking Cabisi were assembled behind the workers, their expressions more wary than that of the dockhands. They were all tall, with dark skin, brown eyes with epicanthic folds, and thick, curly hair that ranged from black to brown to gray. Two women and one man were dressed in deep red garments and wore multiple rows of beaded, amulet-laden necklaces, bracelets, and anklets. The other two men wore light, multicolored trousers, tunics, and loose coats. They were adorned with less jewelry than their companions but enough to indicate high social status. Taya felt another pang of regret over Cristof's stark garb. *He* might not care how he looked, but she liked her husband to outshine his foreign peers. That wouldn't be easy here.

All of the Cabisi wore knives at their belts, and the two men in trousers had slender, beautifully etched pistols holstered at their waists, as well.

"The three in red are justiciars, part of the local government," Taya murmured. "The other two are probably port officials."

"Greet them for us," Amcathra ordered.

Taya stepped to the edge of the gangplank and made an Ondinium bow, her palms flat against her forehead. She followed it with a Cabisi bow, her palms pressed together at heart-height.

"May you be safe today, honored hosts," she said, in Cabisi.

"May you be safe today, honored guests," one of the port officials replied, returning her bow. The others followed suit.

"From where do you come and for what purpose do you seek entry into the Cabisi Thalassocracy?"

Taya thought she detected a guarded note in the man's voice.

"We are Ondinium, although we come most recently from Alzana. The ambassador Exalted Forlore offers Ondinium's greetings to the Impeccable Justiciary. We seek—" she hoped she'd chosen the right word— "friendship with the Cabisi Thalassocracy and supplies for our ship."

"Are you the captain of this vessel?" the official asked, his eyes moving with reluctant fascination to the bright icarus wings that rose over Taya's back. He'd used a word before "vessel" that Taya didn't recognize. *Flying,* she guessed.

"The lictor Janos Amcathra is the captain of the *Firebrand,*" she said, indicating him. "His second-in-command is Lieutenant Tacita Imbrex." She had to use the Ondinan words for *Firebrand, lictor, second-in-command,* and *lieutenant.* She didn't know if there were any Cabisi equivalents. "They do not speak Cabisi. I am their translator. I apologize for not speaking your language well."

"You must be one of the famous Ondinium icarii," said one of the justiciars, an older woman with white hair closely cropped to her head. She spoke in strongly accented Ondinan. Taya bowed again, uncertain whether it was necessary but deciding it couldn't hurt.

"I am, honored justiciar," she said, switching to Ondinan. "My name is Taya."

"Our customs agents do not speak Ondinan. Does anyone on your crew speak Alzanan?"

"Many do, yes, ma'am." She used the Ondinan word for *ma'am* and wondered whether she should use *justiciar,* instead.

The woman turned to the two port officials.

"You can speak to the crew in Alzanan," she said in Cabisi. One of the men nodded and faced Taya.

"I beg your pardon for the inconvenience," he said, still in Cabisi, "but docking and disembarking requires the completion of several forms and a customs inspection for disease and prohibited cargo. Is this acceptable under your custom?"

"Please excuse me while I tell the captain." Taya turned and outlined the situation. Amcathra nodded.

"You may come aboard," he said to the bureaucrat directly, in Alzanan.

"Thank you, Captain," replied the Cabisi in the same language. He bowed as he and his colleague stepped aboard the ship, looking around with speculative interest.

The older justiciar bowed to Cristof.

"Welcome to Os Cansai, Exalted Forlore," she said in Ondinan. "I am Xu Chausiki, a justiciar. My companions are Tu Jinian and Ra Tafar, also justiciars. The Impeccable Justiciary is honored to have a member of Ondinium's exalted caste set foot within the Cabisi Thalassocracy for the first time in recorded history."

Taya walked back to Cristof, arranging his sleeve to drape over her arm as he laid his hand on her forearm. He signaled with the traditional tapping code that she should return the greeting.

"The Exalted Forlore is honored to visit your beautiful and much-renowned empire," she replied. "We have heard much about Cabiel, and we are delighted to be here at last."

"The customs inspection takes some time," Xu said. "If it is not against your beliefs, we have a room in the tower that is out of the sun and contains food and drink. I believe it is Ondinium tradition for exalteds to hide their faces in public, so we have hung curtains to allow you to eat and drink in private, Ambassador."

"The stories we have heard of Cabisi hospitality were not exaggerated," Taya said, relieved by the offer. The sun was already warming the deck, and she was afraid Cristof's new metal mask would soon become scalding. "Exalted Forlore would appreciate the opportunity to rest out of the sun. Justiciar Xu, may I also present *Principessa* Liliana Agosti, of Alzana's royal family. She is the ambassador's guest aboard the *Firebrand*."

"We are pleased to invite you inside as well, *Principessa* Agosti," Xu said in Alzanan, offering another Cabisi bow. Liliana gracefully curtseyed in the Alzanan style.

"Thank you, Justiciar Xu," she said, following them into the tower. On the ship, Captain Amcathra was talking to the port officials while the lictors secured the wings and released steam from the engine.

"One of your country's aerostats is also in port, *Principessa*," Xu observed, still in Alzanan. "The *Indomitable*."

"I look forward to speaking to its captain," Liliana replied.

"It carries a passenger from Ondinium, as well. In Cabisi we hear stories of political tensions between Ondinium and Alzana, but it seems the tales are nothing but idle sailors' gossip."

"There is no tension between *my* Family and Ondinium," Liliana said after a moment. Taya caught the sharp look Xu shot them and knew the *principessa*'s emphasis hadn't been missed.

The justiciars stopped at the next floor down and swept aside several layers of light curtain to reveal a circular room. Inside was a low table surrounded by floor cushions and covered with bowls of fresh fruit and nuts and several sweating carafes. The tower's windows had been opened, permitting a cross-breeze that cooled the chamber.

"This looks wonderful," Taya said, sincerely. "Thank you very much."

"Please refresh yourself." Xu bowed to Cristof, then switched to Cabisi. "May we speak to you outside a moment, Taya Icarus?"

"Of course."

Xu let the curtains swing shut and they moved to the other side of the hall.

"I regret to say that we are unfamiliar with many of Ondinium's customs," Xu said, keeping her voice low. "Therefore, I wish to ensure that we do not inadvertently offer insult to your people. May I ask you several questions?"

"Of course. That's exactly what I'm here for."

"I am grateful." Xu studied her with open curiosity. "Does an icarus always wear her wings?"

"No— only on duty. Wings are the sign of my caste."

"And does the exalted always wear a mask and robes? Also, is Exalted Forlore male or female?"

"He's male," Taya said, amused. "Exalteds remove their masks and ceremonial coverings only in front of their household staff, icarii, and social peers. As an ambassador, Exalted Forlore accepts as his peers other royal families and high-ranking nobility and ambassadors. I assume that in Cabisi a justiciar is the equivalent of an exalted. However, I request that servants and people of lesser rank not attend any discussions or events where he takes off his mask."

She was pleased to have managed most of that in Cabisi, with only a few Ondinan terms mixed in.

"If you permit me…" ventured the male of the trio, Ra Tafar. He was younger than Xu, but still middle-aged, his black hair flecked with gray. He began speaking in Cabisi, but Taya was swiftly lost. Seeing her incomprehension, he switched to accented Alzanan. "I am afraid you misunderstand Cabisi governance. A justiciar is not equivalent to an exalted. Cabiel is a sociocratie, with no heritable rank or caste. Communities nominate justiciars from their own membership to interpret the Code. Each island chooses one of its justiciars as its representative in the Impeccable Judiciary, and that justiciar serves a ten-year term before ceding the position to another."

"But the Impeccable Judiciary is Cabisi's government, isn't it?" Taya asked, also switching to Alzanan.

"Not as you understand government, perhaps," Ra said. "There is no aristocracy or other ruling class here. The Impeccable Judiciary is only a government inasmuch as it interprets the Transcendent Code whenever disputes arise that cannot be resolved at a local level. Its members also serve as the adjudicators for inter-island disputes and ritual duels. But justiciars cannot issue new parts of the Code as decaturs or kings might issue new laws. The Code binds us as it does all members of the empire, and our judgments are subject to evaluation and challenge by other justiciars, which prevents any one of us from becoming more powerful than the other."

They're a little more like Demicus than Ondinium, Taya thought. Not that it mattered. The story that Cristof only unmasked before foreign equivalents was simply a polite fiction invented to hide the fact that Cristof was a walking disgrace to his caste who didn't care if he went barefaced before barbarians. No other exalted would *dream* of treating a foreigner like an equal.

"Exalted Forlore will accept the Impeccable Justiciary as his peers," she said, toeing the party line, "even if our systems of rank and governance aren't identical. The significant factor of governmental rank is the ability of a person or body to guide its nation's policies. If the Impeccable Judiciary is that body, then it is equivalent to the exalted caste."

"We do not precisely guide Cabiel's policies, but we will treat with the ambassador if it so pleases your custom," Xu said, switching back to Ondinan. "Please tell us of any other taboos that your country observes."

Taya assured them that the exalted would be pleased to accept transport to the Hall of Justice, that being housed with one of the justiciars would not be a problem, and that their diplomatic staff was small but would likely include the ship's captain and its Mareaux navigator. In turn, she was relieved to hear that the Cabisi banks would accommodate Ondinium currency exchange, that no trade restrictions would prohibit the reprovisioning and repair of their ship, and that the lictors would be permitted to carry their weapons on shore.

"I understand that Cabisi maintain a tradition of ritual dueling," she said. "Ondiniums are unfamiliar with the practice. How do we avoid giving offense?"

Xu smiled.

"It is rare for a Cabisi to challenge a foreigner. The violations that usually lead to such a challenge are, I think, offenses in any culture— direct verbal insults, physical assault, unwelcome and persistent sexual advances, theft, and similar actions. Such behavior is, I think, as rude in Ondinium as it is in Cabiel."

"Yes." Taya was relieved. "That seems reasonable."

"In addition, the most proximate justiciar must approve a challenge before it becomes legal. We always take into account a foreigner's ignorance of Cabisi ways."

"Thank you."

"But I fear we keep you here longer than good manners dictate," Xu said, standing. "Please do not allow us to delay you any further."

After an exchange of bows, the justiciars headed downstairs. Taya walked back to the curtained chamber.

Cristof had managed to throw his lengthy sleeves back and remove his mask, which floated at the end of its tethers from a table leg. He'd poured himself a drink and sampled a few of the fruits.

"This is good," he said, gesturing to the carafe of ruby-red fruit juice. "But that thick white stuff— it's not milk."

"Did you run into anything spicy?" Taya asked, piling up cushions next to Liliana. Cristof ruefully pointed to a plate of crimson nuts.

"I didn't realize the red coating was chili until I ate one."

"You need to put on your glasses, if you're not going to wear your mask." When Taya thought she had a high enough stack of cushions, she kicked up her tailset and knelt. Good enough— nothing scraped against the floor.

"Did you work out a covering protocol?" he asked.

"We'll consider the Impeccable Judiciary your peers."

"I *would* like to tour some of their factories while I'm here— that means talking to engineers."

"I'll work it out." She tried the chili-coated nuts while Liliana peeled an odd-looking green fruit. "Did you notice their clothing? We need to get you some new robes, and maybe more jewelry."

"I like the look of those trousers and tunics," he mused. "The colors are too bright, but the cut looks comfortable. In this heat, I'm going to need something lighter to wear than this damn robe."

"What about the *Indomitable*?" Liliana asked, looking worried. "Can I go aboard?"

"We have to find out more about it." Cristof frowned. "Did you hear what Xu said about an Ondinium passenger?"

"It can't be Alister," Taya protested. "And Neuillan's dead."

"They aren't the only Ondinium exiles— just the most infamous."

"If I speak to the *Indomitable*'s captain or crew," Liliana said, "I can inquire about the passenger."

"Good idea," Taya said. "Assuming they don't leave port tonight— I'm sure they were as startled to see us as we were to see them."

"Moreso," Cristof said, pensively. "They won't have heard about ornithopters yet."

They quieted as they heard steps on the stairs.

"Exalted," Captain Amcathra called out.

"Come in."

The lictor lifted the curtains and ducked inside. His sunburnt skin was damp from the heat, although his black uniform remained tightly buttoned.

"The *Firebrand*'s stay has been approved and we are cleared to conduct our business. I will leave Lieutenant Imbrex in charge of the ship while I oversee your personal security."

"Good." Cristof pushed a pillow toward him. "Take a seat. You look like you're about to pass out."

Amcathra looked around as if hoping to find a chair tucked in the corner of the small chamber. Seeing none, he reluctantly joined them on the floor. Taya poured him a glass of juice that he drained in one swallow.

"Is that a Cabisi gun?" Cristof asked, his eyes dropping to the holster on Amcathra's belt. The lictor withdrew the firearm, laying it on the table.

"I traded my rifle for it," he said.

"I don't think the Council will approve of you giving away its weapons," Cristof said, picking up the pistol and checking to make sure it was unloaded. "But I can see why you made the trade. This is beautiful."

It *was* beautiful, Taya thought, for something designed to kill people. The weapon was made out of a dark-hued wood with a beautiful grain that was inlaid with brass, ivory, and polished stone. Its barrel was covered with etchings of water, fish, and birds.

"It doesn't seem like your style, Captain," she commented.

"I do not believe that I have a 'style,' Icarus," he countered. "I do, however, respect fine craftsmanship. I have been informed that mass production does not exist in Cabiel. Every Cabisi weapon is unique to its maker."

"Then why would someone trade this for your rifle?" Cristof dragged his eyes away from the gun. "There's nothing craftsman-like about Ondinium weaponry."

"He was intrigued by the rifle's compressed-air pump. Do you object to the trade, Exalted?"

Cristof snorted, handing the weapon back.

"It's fine, as long the crew doesn't swap all of its weapons for souvenirs."

"They will not," Amcathra said firmly. "I offered the rifle after the inspection was over, to ensure that the gift would not be mistaken as a bribe, and I made it clear that it was a gift. I was not expecting him to give me his pistol in return, but I am not displeased with the exchange."

"It won't have a rifle's range," Cristof said.

"I will requisition another from the ship's stores tomorrow."

When Xu returned, Cristof put on his mask again for their departure. The small group, now joined by Professor Dautry, followed her down to the seawall, where lines of cannon guarded the port. Amcathra paused to study one, bringing the group to a straggling halt.

"Do these interest you, Captain?" Xu asked in Ondinan.

"Yes." He laid a hand on the weapon's chase, which was as ornately etched as his new pistol. "They are smaller than I would have expected."

"My son-in-law tells me that they are accurate to an effective range of over a mile," the justiciar said. "I do not know how that compares to Ondinium artillery."

"Satisfactorily. May I?" Amcathra crouched to examine the weapon more closely. Taya could have sworn that he was on the verge of some shocking emotional breakthrough— like a smile.

"That's what he'd look like if he fell in love," she murmured in Cristof's ear. Her husband gave an undignified snort and she elbowed him in the ribs before he shattered his caste mystique. Dautry shot them a puzzled look.

"Captain," Taya said, raising her voice, "perhaps you could stroke the weapons some other time."

"Of course." Amcathra rose, his stoic mask firmly in place again. "I did not intend to delay you, Exalted."

"You must meet my son-in-law, Captain," Xu said, smiling fondly at the large Demican. "I suspect you two have much in common."

A line of vehicles awaited them on shore. Each vehicle had four wheels, with a seat in front next to the steering mechanism and two seats in back under a covered, festively painted cab.

Cristof tapped Taya's arm.

"What do you call these?" she asked.

"Quadracycles," Xu replied in Cabisi, before switching to Ondinan. "We have few horses here; they are not well-suited to our islands."

"We don't have many horses in Ondinium, either. But we don't have any vehicles like this, either."

"Perhaps Ondinium's streets are too steep for 'cyclists.'"

"I'm sure they would be." Taya took her time getting Cristof into the cab, knowing that he'd be curiously examining the vehicle behind his mask. As she tucked in his robes, Captain Amcathra took the seat next to him.

"Your wings will not fit," the lictor pointed out when she raised an eyebrow.

"Let us see to that." Xu explained the problem to one of the drivers, a muscular young man in a loose tunic and short pants that showed off his thick calves. He bowed and began dismantling his quadracycle's cab.

"Oh, don't do that!" Taya protested.

"It is no trouble," Xu assured her.

Taya felt bad as she watched the colorful, jingling panels stacked up on the seat of the last vehicle. "I could have followed in the air...."

"It is very hot for such exertion, and you do not know where we are going. Please do not worry about it. May I ride with you? I enjoy describing the sights to newcomers."

Taya thanked her and they took their seats in the now-open vehicle. Behind them, Liliana sat next to the other female justiciar, Tu Jinian, a pretty, round-faced woman whose long black hair was bound back in multiple beaded braids. Ra Tafar accompanied Professor Dautry in the last quadracycle. As Taya watched, he pulled out a fan that he flipped open and used to cool himself, then handed to the professor with a smile.

"It *is* warm here," Taya admitted. At street level, she felt the oppressive heat much more than she had on the *Firebrand* or inside the sea tower.

"Temperatures in Cabiel are considerably higher than in Ondinium." Xu glanced at Taya's thick leather flight suit. "I suggest adopting our clothing while you are here to make your visit more comfortable."

"I think the ambassador and I will do that. I'm not sure you'll convince Captain Amcathra, though."

"He looks Demican."

"He's an Ondinium citizen of Demican descent."

"The Silver People often find our climate difficult."

"Demicans?"

Xu smiled. "We call ourselves the Iron People. It requires much less heat to melt silver than iron."

Taya laughed as the 'cycles started moving, their muscular drivers weaving the vehicles through the stevedores and sailors who thronged the busy Os Cansai wharfs. Many of the people they passed stopped to stare at Taya's bright ondium wings and Cristof's blank, mirrorlike mask.

"We do not see many people from Ondinium here," Xu apologized. "And never an icarus or exalted."

"It's all right. We're used to being stared at. I'm sure we'll do our own share of gawking during our visit."

Xu chuckled and leaned forward to point out features of interest in the city.

Taya was particularly struck by Cabiel's architecture. Ondinium's buildings were tall, peaked stone structures built to withstand heavy rain and snowstorms. Alzana and Mareaux enjoyed milder climates than Ondinium, but they, too, favored stone in their architecture. Os Cansai's buildings, by contrast, were plaster-covered brick, and even the shabbier buildings boasted fresh paint over crumbling walls. Most of the roofs were tiled in red clay, but some used yellow and blue tile, as well, laid in variegated stripes or triangles. A few of the larger buildings featured bright red gates, and a few had elegant roofs that swept up at the corners. Instead of Ondinium's steep, soot-covered streets, Os Cansai's streets bloomed with trees and bushes, many of them bright with scented blossoms.

The city was filled with people, carts, and 'cycles. Most of the pedestrians were Cabisi, although here and there Taya spotted the lighter complexions of Alzanan, Mareaux, and Tizieri visitors. Almost every Cabisi carried a dagger, and some bore swords and guns. Taya wondered how Cabiel's justiciars kept the peace in such a heavily armed society. Only lictors were allowed to bear arms in Ondinium.

As they moved into the upscale neighborhoods, the streets widened and the crowd thinned. Taya admired the umbrella-shaded public squares where adults drank tea brewed by gleaming brass machines that hissed and sputtered and let off puffs of steam. Cabisi children chattered and laughed outside their schools, clutching books and wooden pencil cases. At one spot, three workers surrounding a theodolite on a tripod were comparing the view through its lenses to a map in their hands, and in another, a group was repairing a wire that ran into one of the larger buildings.

"Is that for a telegraph?" Taya asked, pointing.

"Yes. Telegraph wires corrode quickly in our salty air," Xu replied. "We are experimenting with coverings and coatings, but I am not certain it is worth the effort. We have many citizens willing to run messages across the city for a small fee."

"We can't use the telegraph in Ondinium, either. It's difficult to run lines across the mountain range, and they keep getting knocked down by storms and landslides. And like you said— if telegraphy became common, icarii couriers would be out of work."

"We justiciars hear many objections to innovations that strip citizens of their jobs."

"What do you do about it?"

"We usually permit challenges. It is important for the members of each community to determine for themselves which innovations to adopt."

"But... fighting over whether to adopt a technology..." Taya had a hard time imagining it. "That doesn't sound very efficient. Wouldn't it be better for every community to adopt the same technological standards at the same time?"

"At the price of disharmony and unemployment? Does Ondinium's Council do that? I cannot imagine maintaining a stable, well-run society while simultaneously pushing new technologies forward without the public's consent."

"Well, in Ondinium we *like* new technologies." She hesitated, though, all too aware of Ondinium's problems with vandalism, terrorism, and crime— not to mention the uproar that had followed the Council's most recent responses to the Alzanan invasion. "It's a balancing act," she said, weakly, at last.

"In Cabiel, we allow communities to move at their own pace. Our system of challenges permits them to do so."

"But dueling is so violent!"

"A belief worth holding is a belief worth defending. However, very few challenges end in death. Surrender usually satisfies the combatants."

"What if one side wins and then somebody else challenges on the same grounds?"

"Nobody linked by blood or marriage to the defeated party may issue a challenge on the same issue, but independent interests are free to repeat a challenge. Sometimes debates go on for years. But usually, after several rounds, people tire of combat and decide to negotiate."

Taya fell silent. It seemed like a bizarre way to run a country. Maybe Alzanans, with their history of inter-Family feuding, understood it better.

"The air here is very clean," she said, changing the subject. "Where are your factories?"

"On the edges of the city and on small offshore islands. Zoning laws keep our heavy industry downwind, away from heavily populated areas."

"I think that's a good way to handle it." Taya thought about the dark, gritty ash that covered everything in Tertius. The people who lived there suffered numerous health complaints caused by its constant shroud of smog; Captain Amcathra had a niece with such a problem.

Taya had been lucky enough to pass her Great Examination and leave Tertius to become an icarus.

The 'cycles stopped before a complex of buildings, their drivers panting and mopping their foreheads with checkered and striped cloths. Taya hurried to her husband's side.

"Are you all right?" she murmured, draping the hem of his long ceremonial robe over the cab's edge to hide his boots as he descended.

Hot, he signaled, leaning against her.

"Tell me if you need to unmask. I'll find us someplace private."

Soon.

The justiciars led them through giant red gates to the Hall of Justice, a long building with an upswept yellow-tiled roof.

Taya helped Cristof up its shallow steps, ducked to maneuver her locked wings through its doorway, and sighed with relief as they stepped into its cool, shadowed interior.

The building's rafters were painted the same yellow as its roof, but the rest of the interior was surprisingly simple; bare white walls and a polished wooden floor. A gallery running the length of the hall held hundreds of golden statues depicting sweet-faced, androgynous figures holding different objects. Taya identified books, tools, musical instruments, weapons, scientific devices, and fishing equipment before they were ushered past the display into a second room.

Xu led them through a double line of red-robed justiciars while Ra and Tu stayed back. As Taya and Cristof passed, the justiciars bowed, their palms pressed together in front of their hearts. Taya couldn't return the bow with one arm supporting Cristof, so she kept her eyes forward and hoped she wasn't being unforgivably rude. She wondered what Amcathra, Dautry, and Liliana were doing behind them. She didn't dare look around to find out.

"Stand here," Xu murmured, gesturing to two cushions on a broad, raised dais full of them. Taya turned Cristof around to face the justiciars and saw Tu and Ra close the doors to the chamber.

"My neighbors," Xu said, in Cabisi, "this is the ambassador of Ondinium, Cristof Forlore, an exalted. This is Taya, an icarus. This is Janos Amcathra, a lictor and ship's captain. This is Cora Dautry, from Mareaux, a ship's navigator and helmswoman. This is Liliana Agosti, an Alzanan princess. Today they come borne on an ornithopter bearing the markings of the Ondinium Empire. They have the port authority's permission to stay and conduct their business."

Taya murmured a translation.

"Please welcome them as our guests," Xu finished. The justiciars smiled and stepped up, murmuring greetings one by one in Cabisi, Alzanan, Mareaux, or Ondinan. When they finished, each justiciar found a cushion on the dais and stood by it. Taya didn't know what she was supposed to do.

Unmask, Cristof signaled. Taya hesitated. When they'd visited Mareaux and Alzana, the greeting ceremonies had been long, loud, drawn-out affairs featuring throngs of onlookers, noisy bands, and marching soldiers. Feeling like she'd missed something, she turned up her husband's long sleeves and stepped behind him to untie and remove his mask.

Cristof ran a hand over his flushed and sweat-dampened brow, then pressed his palms together over his heart and returned the justiciars' bow. Taya saw a flicker of disapproval cross Amcathra's expression and felt an echo of it in her own heart. Exalteds hadn't been granted their blessed rebirths in order to bow to foreigners.

"Thank you very much for your welcome," Cristof said in Ondinan. Taya translated. "I have read much about your country, and I am honored to be here."

The justiciars smiled and nodded and settled into their seats without further discussion. Cristof lost no time in sitting down on his own cushion. Taya tugged his robes into place and stood beside him, holding his ondium mask. Was the brief ceremony normal, or was Ondinium being insulted? Nothing in the justiciars' calm expressions suggested that anything was out of the ordinary.

"Ambassador, your ship flies Ondinium's peacetime flag," one of the justiciars said. Taya dismissed her worries and began translating again. "However, we recognize it as a military orni-thopter from the height of the ancient Ondinium Empire. Do not Ondinium's own laws forbid the use of airborne war-vessels?"

"They don't waste any time, do they?" Cristof muttered before taking a deep breath to answer.

The welcoming ceremony had taken only a few minutes, but the round-circle discussion that followed lasted until dusk. Taya's only relief came when somebody brought her a stool that allowed her to sit in her armature. The justiciars' attitudes were friendly and their questions polite, but it didn't take long for her to realize that the Cabisi feared the *Firebrand* was the harbinger of a larger military force. By nightfall Cristof and Captain Amcathra had revealed more about the Alzanan invasion and the impending war than they had planned in an attempt to alleviate the justiciars' concerns. In turn, the justiciars confirmed that Cabisi merchants had sold dirigible plans, electrical engines, and heavy weapons to the Alzanans but assured the ambassador that they would be happy to sell the same technology to Ondinium.

"Then Cabiel hasn't made any sort of exclusive trade agreement with Alzana?" Cristof pressed.

"The Cabisi Thalassocracy prefers to remain neutral in all affairs relating to the continent," Ra said. "There is a great deal of land and ocean between your nations and ours."

"That's true, but this war has taken to the skies. You may not be isolated for long."

"We prefer to pursue our scientific and technological development independent of Ondinium's... influence. We value our independence very highly and intend to defend it against even the most aggressive objectors."

Cristof raised his hands in a pacifying gesture.

"Ondinium isn't going to force Cabiel to take a side. But Alzana has done a good job of dividing the clans in Demicus, pitting them against each other and against us. Be careful that they don't do the same to your island-states."

"Political alliances are a matter for each community to address individually. However, I think no community will successfully make a pact with a continental nation without first meeting numerous challenges from objectors."

"I see." Cristof shifted on his cushion. "Well, I respect your neutrality and cautious approach to the situation. In the meantime, I'd like to get to know your country better and perhaps make contacts for future trade agreements. My captain has already shown an interest in your cannon and may wish to discuss purchases for our ship, and I'm sure Professor Dautry is curious about your charts and navigational instruments. I myself have heard a great deal about Cabisi analytical engines and would like to see one, if I may. I understand they're very different from the machines we manufacture in Ondinium."

Ra settled back on his cushion and gave a pleasant nod.

"I expect our engineers look forward to inspecting your ornithopter, as well, and to learning more about your nation's famous Great Engine."

"Of course," Cristof said blithely. Taya shot a glance at Captain Amcathra. The shadow that swept over the lictor's expression vanished in an instant, but Taya was certain that he was silently preparing a heated lecture on state security to be delivered to her husband later that night. She hoped Cabisi walls were thick.

CHAPTER SEVEN

TAYA WOKE UP early the next morning and stepped out of their guest bedroom onto a wooden walkway. Xu's house was built around a central garden full of lush blossoms and brightly feathered birds.

"We should get one of these for the house," Cristof said, fiddling with his reassembled glasses as he walked out the bedroom door. He stood next to Taya and leaned his elbows on the polished wooden rail. "The garden, I mean."

"I don't think these flowers would survive an Ondinium winter." She tucked a length of his tangled hair over his shoulder. "How did you sleep?"

"The Cabisi seem inventive enough— why haven't they learned how to build a proper bed frame, instead of throwing a mat on the floor? At least I could stretch out— it's nice to be in a country full of tall people."

"Nice for you, maybe. I was going to buy some clothes today, but I suppose I'll have to have everything hemmed up." Taya frowned, thinking again of Jayce.

"Do we have any money for clothes shopping?" he asked.

"I'll have to ask Amcathra."

Captain Amcathra assured them over breakfast that he had exchanged enough money to cover the ship's repair and a few modest personal purchases.

"However," he continued, "you must not leave this compound unmasked, Exalted, and in this heat I would not recommend you engage in extended exercise while covered."

"I'll buy whatever you need," Taya offered as Cristof gave the lictor a grumpy look.

"I'll go, too," Professor Dautry said. "I'd like to look around Os Cansai."

"Me, too," Liliana chimed in. "And I can ask about the dirigible."

"You don't speak Cabisi, do you?" Cristof asked.

"The Cabisi are reasonably fluent in Mareaux and Alzanan," Dautry pointed out. "That's *one* advantage of avoiding an isolationist policy."

"Ondinium pursues a protectionist policy," Captain Amcathra corrected.

"Ondinium regulates and restricts far more than free trade," Dautry objected. The two were deep in a civil but highly abstract debate over political terminology when Xu joined them.

"May you be safe today," the justiciar said cheerfully in Ondinan.

"May you be safe today," Taya replied, echoed by the others. Struck by Dautry's observation, she added, "How did you learn to speak Ondinan so well, Justiciar Xu?"

"I am a chemist when I am not a justiciar," she said, sitting. Cristof regarded the justiciar with fresh interest. "Many of the scientific books and articles I read come from Ondinium, so it is necessary to know the language well. It is a rare pleasure to speak it aloud and correct my pronunciation.

"Ambassador," she continued, "I am arranging a private tour of our most advanced analytical engineering laboratory for you today. However, none of its engineers or programmers are justiciars, so how do I arrange for you to ask questions?"

"If there are only one or two engineers...." Cristof said, glancing at Taya.

"It's extremely irregular," she said, "but we could arrange a private, unmasked meeting with the most prestigious of your engineers."

"Your guides are the laboratory's leading designer and its top programmer."

"Are they discreet?" Amcathra pressed.

"Janos...."

"Ensuring that you do not embarrass your caste is part of my responsibility, Exalted."

"Maybe you should wear a veil," Liliana suggested. The three Ondiniums gave her blank looks. "Like Tizieri men. It would hide your face, but you could talk through it."

"A blue Tizieri free-rider's veil." Taya grinned at her husband. "Complete with spangled fringe."

"It would be more comfortable than a mask."

"*No.*" Amcathra's tone was firm. "The problem is not simply hiding his face, *Principessa*. His voice is not supposed to be heard in public, either. That is why icarii speak for exalteds when they are covered."

"That doesn't make any sense. How can exalteds rule Ondinium when they can't be seen or heard?"

"In certain cases, it is *preferable* that the exalted be neither seen nor heard," Amcathra replied. Cristof sputtered and Taya covered her smile.

"But how does it *work*? Why do Ondiniums allow themselves to be ruled by an invisible aristocracy?"

"Because an exalted is the result of a thousand fortuitous rebirths," Taya said. "Ondiniums know that the Lady has forged each member of the exalted caste to rule over them wisely and well."

"Because Ondiniums are taught from birth that everybody must find and fit into a certain caste," Dautry countered, "and they are indoctrinated by a lifetime of loyalty examinations, laws, and customs not to question the established hierarchy."

Amcathra raised an eyebrow but didn't argue. Taya opened her mouth to rebut, but Cristof forestalled her.

"The truth is," he told Liliana, "Taya and the professor are both right. A ruling class shrouded in mystery is more likely to be regarded with respect and fear than a ruling class that people can see isn't any different from themselves."

"But *you* show your face; doesn't that dispel the mystery?" Liliana asked.

"Somewhat, to the Council's chagrin. However, I find that I'm given more respect when I wear a robe and mask than when I walk around the capital barefaced. Mystery is an integral factor in maintaining my caste's power, although as Professor Dautry noted, there are other factors at play, as well."

"But what about the thousand rebirths?" Taya insisted. "You can't deny that exalteds have *earned* their caste through lifetimes of forging and purification."

"Well...." Cristof looked uncomfortable.

"You are a devout woman, Taya Icarus," Xu observed. "You must visit one of our temples to the Dancer before you leave."

"Thank you. I'd like that."

Xu turned to Cristof.

"So, Ambassador, do you intend to wear your mask during the tour?"

"Not when we're alone with the head engineer and programmer," Cristof said, casting a quelling look at Amcathra. "Not if they promise to be discreet."

"The need for discretion is understood, Exalted."

"Thank you. I apologize for the inconvenience."

"They are your customs, Ambassador. We do our best to respect and accommodate them." Xu turned to Amcathra. "Captain, my son-in-law the gunsmith invites you to his shop and to visit some of the larger munitions manufacturers."

"Thank you, Justiciar."

She turned to the others.

"Is there anything else I can arrange?"

"After we see the analytical engines, we're doing something *I* want to do," Taya warned her husband.

"I promise to sit quietly while you fly around the city."

"I was thinking more about finding some really good, spicy Cabisi cuisine for lunch."

"As long as we're in public and I can't take off my mask to eat," he agreed complaisantly.

· ❋ ·

The laboratory tour started out as tediously as Taya had feared. Her eyes glazed as they walked through cluttered workspaces and inspected innumerable half-completed engines, Cristof exchanging enthusiastic comments with the head engineer who acted as their guide. The engineer kept presenting Cristof with books and journals in Cabisi that contained the latest research on the subject, including her own treatise, and Taya was the one who had to carry them all.

"Our latest fully functional engine is for the Os Cansai customs agency," their guide said at last, opening the final door. "You are fortunate to be visiting today, before we dismantle it for transport to the Customs offices."

Taya's boredom vanished as she gasped at the beautiful statue that stood before them. Like the smaller statues in the Hall of Justice, it depicted a smooth-faced, slender Cabisi figure wearing a cloth draped around its hips to hide its sex. The figure cupped a curious brass spherical object resembling a multi-rayed sun in one hand. Its other hand hovered lightly over the object. Its calm, half-closed eyes were made of inlaid shell and sapphire, and precious stones adorned its neck, wrists, and ankles.

"This is an engine?" Cristof circled the statue and lifted his ondium mask to his face, squinting through its lenses. Taya followed, juggling his books from arm to arm. The statue's front was a façade that hid the complex workings of the analytical engine that had been built into it. Cristof studied the pistons that connected the engine to the sphere between the statue's hands. "It moves?"

"The engine writes data to a standard wax cylinder," their guide explained, "but also, if the operator desires, to paper via the writing ball in the Dancer's hands. At the moment, the operator must manually replace each sheet of paper as it is filled. Unfortunately, we find that we lose much of the statue's aesthetic value if we incorporate an automated paper feeder into its design."

"I've seen something like this in Ondinium," Taya said, looking closely at the strange, key-covered writing ball. "My friends attached a typography machine to their analytical engine, and it printed out its data on a long strip of paper— although all the print was backward."

"Interesting," the engineer said, politely. Taya got the distinct feeling that her friends' innovation was passé in Cabiel.

"Why did you put the engine into a statue?" Cristof asked. "Is it a special order?"

"You do not do this in Ondinium?"

"No— we manufacture engines in whatever shape best suits their function."

"Why?"

"Because… it would take too much time and effort to manufacture something like this. It's not cost-efficient."

"I see. In Cabiel, we do not like to purchase ugly objects. A tool must be both functional *and* beautiful, or it does not sell, and *that* is most certainly not cost-efficient."

"The Dancer is a god, isn't it?" Taya asked, gazing up at the statue's peaceful, genderless face. "Are the statues in the Hall of Justice all images of the Dancer, too?"

"Yes. I recall that your people worship a woman?"

"The Lady of the Forge. She creates new souls out of old ones and is the patron of all invention."

"The Dancer embodies eternal change, including life and death and male and female. We usually depict the Dancer like this, young and sexually ambiguous, but sometimes we depict the Dancer as a hermaphroditic adult."

"That's— unusual." Cristof looked nonplussed. "Yet you worship it— I mean, the Dancer?"

"As you worship the Lady."

Cristof glanced at Taya. "Yes. Well. The Lady is honored in Ondinium as an inspiring concept, if nothing else."

Taya frowned. Comments like that weren't going to weigh in her husband's merit when his soul returned to the Forge. Sometimes she worried about his next rebirth.

"Not everybody in Cabiel believes in a literally embodied Dancer, either," the engineer said with equanimity, "but like your Lady of the Forge, the Dancer carries significant philosophical weight as a metaphor regardless of its deific status."

"Quite." Cristof finished circling the statue. "Well, it's a stunning achievement. Do all of your engines end up in religious statuary?"

"Many, yes, although we also place our engines in tables or cabinets. Sand and salt water destroy an engine's functionality very quickly, so purchasers prefer their engines to sit within some protective case or another. If you wish to see the pinnacle of our efforts, visit the Pearl Temple and examine the Dancer on the central altar."

"It's an analytical engine?"

"An automaton." The engineer smiled. "The *kattakas* there delight in showing it off to visitors."

"We'll go as soon as we can," Taya said at once. Her husband nodded with less enthusiasm— automata interested him, but temples didn't. Taya figured he owed her one, though, after today's factory tour.

Their quadracycle driver stacked the books in a small bin behind the seat and cycled them to what he claimed was the best seafood restaurant in town, which just happened to be owned by his uncle. The small restaurant, like so many Taya had seen in Os Cansai, had an outdoor patio full of lunchtime patrons who fell silent as soon as she stepped out of the vehicle, her ondium wings arching over her head.

Taya gave them a Cabisi bow, receiving pleased looks and a flurry of bows in return. As she and the driver arranged to have screens pulled over a corner so that Cristof could unmask, she overheard her country's name and the word "icarus" being bandied about among the diners.

The food was as good as their driver had promised, and the restaurant obligingly prepared several unspiced dishes for Cristof. He spent most of the meal cheerfully discussing the differences between Cabisi and Ondinium analytical engines. Taya tried to pay the bill when they were finished, but the owner refused to take her money, protesting that the ambassador's lunch would pay for itself as soon as people heard he'd dined there.

"I don't feel comfortable not paying your uncle," Taya said to their driver in Alzanan, their common language. He turned and spoke quickly to his relative in Cabisi, then grinned.

"He says maybe you fly for him?" he suggested. "Everyone here wants to see an icarus fly."

"Are you sure...?" All of the staff and patrons who understood Alzanan nodded. Taya wished she hadn't eaten quite so much. She conferred with Cristof and settled him, masked, at a well-shaded table on the open patio.

The restaurant owner led her upstairs to the restaurant's storeroom and out onto the roof. Below her, traffic became congested as diners urged passers-by to stop and watch. Feeling an unaccustomed twinge of stage fright, Taya carefully checked her armature and wings before pulling down her goggles and backing up to the far end of the roof.

She wasn't well-counterweighted for such a low launch platform, but a crisp breeze blowing in from the ocean gave her some lift once she beat her way over the roof level. She kicked down her tailset and straightened into a comfortable glide.

The Os Cansai roofscape was surprisingly low and free from obstacles. Taya could see, in the distance, taller buildings and chimneys that were part of the city's remote industrial district. The highest buildings in her immediate vicinity, however, were the watchtowers on the seawalls, the *Firebrand* gleaming brightly over one and the *Indomitable* looming over another.

For ten minutes Taya flew in slow, lazy circles over the neighborhood. The ocean breeze and the warm air radiating off the sun-baked streets and rooftops made gliding easy, although her leather flight suit soon became hot and uncomfortable. *New clothing after this*, she decided.

At last she returned to the restaurant roof, where the staff and patrons were gathered to greet her. She locked up her wings, pulled off her goggles, and unfastened the collar of her suit. The restaurant owner handed her a glass of water, which she gratefully drained. She poured the second glass over her sweaty neck and the back of her head, shivering with relief as the water seeped inside of her suit.

"Thank you." She handed the glass back but found herself trapped as Cabisi pressed around her, asking questions. She did her best to answer, but she was grateful when the owner and her driver finally shooed everyone away and took her back down to Cristof.

He squeezed her arm as she helped him up. She smiled.

"Great flight," she said. "But I'm going to die of heatstroke if I don't find something besides this suit to wear."

Yes, he tapped. She gave him a sympathetic look, knowing he was just as uncomfortable under his metal mask and black outer robe.

"Do you want to come to the market with me or go back to Xu's house?"

Home. Acquire— he tapped out the letters individually as they walked to the quadracycle. Taya guessed what he meant at the halfway point.

"A free-rider's veil?" she objected, helping him into his seat. "How likely am I to find one of those in Os Cansai? And you don't really think you can walk around dressed like a nomad, do you? It'd scandalize Ondinium and probably offend Tizier."

Acquire, he repeated. She rolled her eyes.

"If I see one, I'll *consider* acquiring it. But I'm telling Captain Amcathra."

She thought she heard him chuckle. Shaking her head, she turned to the driver.

"Would you please take the exalted back to Justiciar Xu's house?" she asked in Alzanan. "I have some errands to run before I return."

"Of course," the driver promised. "I deliver him fast and safe. I find you after?"

"No, I'll be fine, thank you. How much do I owe you?" She reached for the pocket where she was keeping their Cabisi money, but he waved her off.

"Justiciar Xu pay me," he assured her. Then, standing on the pedals, he headed off, Cristof sitting motionless in the back like a giant doll. Taya felt sorry for him— she knew he'd much rather walk around the markets bare-faced with her. She ran her fingers through her sweaty hair and strode toward the markets. Nevertheless, a Tizieri free-rider's veil? Ridiculous.

As soon as she set foot in the complex of stalls and wagons, Taya was swamped by curious onlookers drawn to her tall silver wings. The adults maintained a polite distance, but the children were more aggressive, peppering her with questions in Cabisi and broken Alzanan. She tried not to trip over them as she gawked at the exotic wares and colorful garments displayed around her.

Cabiel! She was in Cabiel at last! For the first time, jostled on both sides by busy locals, it sank in that she was standing in the country she'd read about for so many years; a country that had never been part of the Ondinium Empire and was vastly different from the empire's former colonies of Mareaux, Demicus, and Alzana. She took a few happy dance steps and laughed with delight.

The food section of the market made her wish that she had enough appetite left to try some of the sizzling meat that was so heavily spiced it made her nose itch and her eyes water. Brightly colored sweets on shady racks beckoned her, and even the fruit looked mysterious, the knobbed and spiked and husky objects tantalizing her with their foreign secrets.

The clothing-and-textiles part of the market was equally extensive and fascinating. Taya couldn't say how much time she'd spent looking around when she heard voices arguing in Ondinan.

"Captain?" She handed the shirt she'd been holding back to a disappointed vendor and pushed her way through the crowd.

She knew she'd found him when an Alzanan soldier staggered into her, swearing. She shouldered the man aside and saw a flushed and angry-looking Captain Amcathra punching another Alzanan across the jaw while he stood over a sprawling, gray-haired woman. A third Alzanan grabbed his shoulder. The captain rammed his elbow behind him and caught the young man in the solar plexus. The Alzanan turned pale and fell down, holding his chest and fighting for air.

The gray-haired woman beside Amcathra drew a knee under her, trying to stand. With an oath, Amcathra kicked her knee back out from under her and planted his heavy lictor's boot in her side.

Taya stared, unable to believe her eyes. Had her taciturn, obsessively formal guardian really just kicked a woman?

"Captain! Stop! What are you *doing*?"

The Alzanan next to her regained his balance and said something crude about icarii. Taya threw her arms in front of her face, blocking his wild blow, and kicked him in the shin.

"Taya!" Liliana appeared next to her, holding a heavy shopping basket. She glared at the young soldier and shouted in Alzanan. "If you hit her, I'll have you court-martialed! I *told* you, I'm *Principessa* Liliana of Family Agosti!"

"Prove it," the soldier shot back in Alzanan, "or get the hell out of my way."

Taya spun to check on Amcathra. The Alzanan soldier had recovered from being punched in the face and was circling the lictor. Blood smeared the two men's faces and fists as they relentlessly traded blows. The soldier on the ground had rolled to all fours.

"Captain! Captain Amcathra, stop this!" Taya edged around the combatants. The Alzanan landed a solid blow to Amcathra's temple. The lictor staggered and dropped to one knee, shaking his head. Then, with an angry growl, he surged upward and planted his fist beneath the soldier's breast-bone. Air whooshed from the Alzanan's mouth as he doubled over. Amcathra grabbed the man's neck with his free hand and viciously drove his head into the street.

The soldier on the ground grabbed a broken cobblestone and pulled himself to his feet. Taya grabbed the man's military tunic and yanked him around. The startled Alzanan's eyes rose to her gleaming ondium wings.

"Back away, *now!*" she snapped in her sternest Alzanan. "The guards are on their way!"

The soldier looked around with confusion, dropping his stone. Someone stepped next to Taya and she jumped away, only to recognize Professor Dautry, who was holding several tubular map cases and gazing at the fight with disapproval.

"Taya, do you have any—" Dautry broke off as, on the other side of the fight, Liliana shrieked. The third soldier had impatiently hurled the girl sideways into the crowd, his eyes locked on Amcathra. Amcathra's pale blue eyes narrowed with fury as he lunged for the Alzanan.

The woman he had kicked was picking herself back up again, one arm pressed tight against her side. She shook her long gray hair over her shoulder, revealing a scraped and dirty face tattooed with a mercate's crescent.

"Corundel!" Taya abandoned the Alzanan she had been berating and ran forward to grab the lapels of the mercate's light jacket. "Patrice Corundel, you *traitor*!"

"Icarus!" Corundel grabbed Taya's hands, trying to pull away. "What are you doing here?"

"Arresting you!"

The abandoned Alzanan grabbed Taya's armature and hauled her backward. For a moment Taya dragged Corundel along, and then she let go and kicked, trying to get the soldier to drop her. He laughed with amazement as he realized she weighed next to nothing, holding her out at arm's length.

"Stop that," Dautry snapped, swatting him across the head with her map cases. His grip loosened and his laughter ended for good when Taya's heel planted itself between his legs. He dropped her and grabbed himself, looking sick.

Taya spun, feeling her metal wings clock the Alzanan across his bent head, and spotted Corundel escaping the melee.

"Oh, no you don't," she spat. The older woman turned to push through the onlookers, and Taya raced after her.

"Stop her! Stop that woman!" she shouted in Cabisi, pointing. The shoppers drew back instead. Seeing a passage clearing for her, Taya broke into a sprint, her ondium wings rattling over her head. She sprang forward and grabbed the flapping hem of Corundel's Cabisi-style jacket. The mercate stumbled and Taya scrambled on top of her, taking them both to the ground.

Her artificially lightened weight did her a disservice when it came to fighting, but she'd learned ways to compensate. She grabbed the older woman's arm and twisted it behind her. Corundel yelped as Taya tightened the arm-lock and stood, bringing the grimacing mercate upright with her.

"You can't arrest me in Cabiel," Corundel snapped, her voice strained. Taya began marching her back to Amcathra, keeping the woman's arm tightly twisted. "You don't have any authority here. It's a neutral country!"

"We'll let the justiciars sort it out," Taya growled. "When we tell them how you used your position at AME to arm your country's enemies, they might agree to an extradition. How many of those assassination attempts were your fault, back in Mareaux? Did you poison those peaches?"

"Don't be ridiculous," Corundel gasped. Taya's grip had tightened as she'd asked her questions. "That was one of your lictors."

"You *knew*?"

Corundel squeaked and couldn't answer, stiff with pain. Taya loosened the lock.

"I knew the Mazzolettis wanted to stop you," the mercate gasped, squirming to find a more comfortable position. "I saw them talking to one of the lictors. I assumed he was their spy."

Taya bit down on all the nasty things she wanted to say as they broke through the crowd. Several Cabisi had taken charge of the situation and were questioning the onlookers. Captain Amcathra stood with his feet spread and his arms folded over his chest, glaring at the Alzanan soldiers. Dautry stood next to him, a few locks of hair straggling out of her otherwise neat bun to fall over one shoulder. The Alzanans were clustered in a small group, muttering together. Liliana and a Cabisi girl stood between the two sides, a little closer to Amcathra than the Alzanans.

Taya marched Corundel up to the lictor, who unfolded his arms as they approached.

"Good job, Icarus," he said through his split and bruised lip.

"Please tell me you didn't start this."

"I regret that I cannot."

"You attacked them without any provocation whatsoever?"

"I consider eight hundred and seventy-four Ondiniums killed in the Glasgar bombing sufficient provocation. Most were lictors and support staff. Seven were military-reconnaissance icarii."

Taya sighed and Dautry grimaced.

"But you didn't start any fights while we were in Alzana."

"I despise the Alzanans' combat tactics, but I expect no better from them and will have my revenge in battle. Patrice Corundel is Ondinium, however, and I intend to see her executed for treason."

At the lictor's grim words, the mercate began struggling again. Taya locked Corundel's arm high enough to keep her from doing anything more than strain for a pain-free breath. She decided not to tell Amcathra that the mercate had known about Rikard. In his present mood, the captain might shoot Corundel then and there.

"Do any of you speak Cabisi?" one of the officials asked, approaching them. He was a middle-aged man, strongly built and wearing a stained apron that smelled like the spices in the food market.

"I do," Taya said, as Corundel hissed the same.

"I am Su Kurari, a justiciar for the market vendors. Is this a licensed combat?"

"No!" Corundel spat.

"Not… not licensed by the justiciars," Taya said. "This woman is…" she switched to Alzanan, lacking the necessary vocabulary in Cabisi. "This woman is an Ondinium citizen and a traitor. Ondinium's ruling body, the Oporphyr Council, has issued a warrant for her arrest."

"This isn't Ondinium!" Corundel protested in Cabisi. "You are a neutral country! Ondinium law means nothing here!"

Su nodded and Taya's heart sank.

"Cabiel does not wish to interfere in disputes between foreign countries," he replied in Cabisi, "but we do not permit foreign disputes to disrupt the peace of our community. Please release this woman."

Taya let Corundel go with a dissatisfied scowl.

"What is he saying?" Amcathra demanded. Taya filled him in as Corundel took several steps away, rubbing her shoulder.

"If the justiciars do not recognize foreign disputes," Amcathra said after a moment, "then please ask him what I must do to challenge Mercate Corundel to a duel under local law."

Taya and Dautry both protested at once:

"Captain— *no*. You can't!"

"Captain, this is irresponsible. Your first responsibility is to your ship."

The lictor turned to Su.

"How do I issue a challenge?" he asked in Alzanan. "I wish to fight this woman."

Su blinked, taken aback.

"He can't!" Corundel protested. "I'm under Alzanan protection!" She turned to the soldiers. "This lictor wants to register a Cabisi challenge against us."

"Sounds good to me," one of the soldiers growled. "When and where?"

"No, no, no!" Taya threw out her hands. "We're here on a diplomatic mission, *not* to bring our war with Alzana into Os Cansai!"

"I agree," Dautry said, quietly. "You have more important priorities, Captain. The *Firebrand* will be severely impaired if you are defeated in a duel."

"We aren't afraid to fight any Ondies," another of the Alzanans jeered. "The *Indomitable* will blow that cute little silver bird of yours into scrap metal."

Amcathra gave the soldiers a cold look.

"My interest is in executing this woman," he said, "but I have no objection to destroying your vessel as a means to that end."

Taya groaned. "Captain, don't do this. Think about what Cristof will say."

"Do you think he does not want to apprehend this traitor?"

"I'm sure he doesn't want to cause another diplomatic scandal!"

"I am not married to him, but I *have* worked with Exalted Forlore for many years, and I believe that in your own benevolence you underestimate his hatred of the Alzanans."

"Oh, Lady!" Taya was afraid the lictor might be right. Cristof had never liked the Alzanans, even before they'd tried to assassinate him, taken him prisoner, shot him, and bombed his country. She knew he did his best to behave diplomatically for her sake and the sake of his ambassadorial station, but when it came right down to it, he had no qualms about killing his enemies.

Dautry shook her head and folded her arms over her map cases.

"I thought you were a more rational man than this, Captain," she said.

"Complying with local traditions in order to apprehend a traitor is entirely rational."

"Under the circumstances," Su said, looking from one group to the other and switching to heavily accented Alzanan, "I send your … your question … to the Impeccable Justiciary. You wait in peace for verdict."

One of the other Cabisi, a woman in her thirties, approached him and bowed.

"Nobody reports any property damage or personal harm, Justiciar," she said in Cabisi. Su nodded to her and turned back to the two groups of foreigners.

"No fine is due to merchants or citizens," he continued in Alzanan, "but you pay fine for—" He switched to Cabisi. "For disturbing the peace."

Taya translated the phrase into Alzanan for the others.

"When will we hear about the duel?" one of the Alzanans demanded.

"Soon. If you fight before verdict, fine increases." Su shifted to Cabisi again and Taya continued translating. "The fine is double the next time you disturb the peace, triple the time after that, and so on until you stop fighting or have no more money, in which case you work for the city until you repay your public debt."

The two groups nodded, gazing sullenly at each other as they paid Su and received scribbled receipts that neither side could read.

"Are you all right?" Taya asked Liliana as Amcathra paid his half of the fine.

"Yes...." she looked wistfully at the soldiers. "I suppose I won't be able to go home with them after this, will I?"

"You didn't have to get involved."

"I couldn't let that thug hit you." The girl pushed back a lock of curling hair and gave her a proud look. "We're allies."

"We are." Taya was glad that at least one Alzanan didn't hate her. "Thank you. And you, Professor."

"This will not reflect well upon our mission," Dautry said, quietly.

"No, probably not." Taya sighed. "For what it's worth, Liliana, Patrice Corundel had trade affiliations with the Mazzolettis, so the *Indomitable* probably belongs to them. It wouldn't have been safe for you anyway."

The young *principessa* made a face, then turned to the Cabisi girl standing quietly to one side. "I'm sorry. I should introduce you. This is Xu Sankau, the justiciar's niece. She's been helping me shop. Sankau, this is Taya, an icarus from Ondinium, and Professor Cora Dautry, a navigator from Mareaux."

"May you be safe today," Sankau said in Alzanan, bowing. Taya and Dautry returned the greeting.

"Thank you for being Liliana's guide," Taya added.

"I enjoy shopping." The girl glanced behind them, her smile vanishing. "But I do not enjoy fighting."

When Amcathra returned, Taya shook her head. His lip was split, his jaw and temple red enough to bruise, and the knuckles of both of his hands were bloody. Streaks of dirt marred his usually pristine uniform.

"Are you badly hurt?" she asked.

"I have no significant injuries." He turned to Liliana. "Were you harmed, *Principessa*?"

"No." The girl blushed. "He just scared me."

Amcathra turned to Taya. "Where is the exalted?"

"Back at Justiciar Xu's house. He didn't feel like walking through the markets in full ceremonial regalia. It's a good thing, too; otherwise he'd be involved in this mess, as well."

"I will report the confrontation to him."

"I know you will, but not yet." She pointed at Liliana and Sankau. "I don't want them shopping without an escort. If you think you can refrain from starting any more fights...."

"I will await the Impeccable Justiciary's decision."

"I hope they turn you down. We do *not* need this trouble right now! Besides, think about Liliana's feelings. How is she going to feel, watching you fight her countrymen?"

Amcathra stiffened.

"I had no intention of offending you, *Principessa* Agosti," he said, turning to the girl. "My only immediate goal is to arrest Mercate Corundel. If your countrymen would be willing to turn her over to us, I will drop the challenge."

Liliana looked up at the tall lictor, her flush deepening as she clutched her shopping basket.

"I— I can tell them that," she stammered.

"We'll write a formal letter and have it delivered to the Alzanan captain tonight," Taya said. "If we're lucky, he'll be as eager to avoid an incident as we are. Well, as *I* am, anyway." She gave the lictor a dirty look.

"I would appreciate your assistance," Amcathra continued, still addressing the *principessa*. "And I will ensure that nobody disturbs you for the remainder of your shopping trip."

Liliana nodded, her cheeks red, and glanced at Sankau, who was gazing wide-eyed at the battered but imposing captain.

"Good." Taya wavered for a moment, wondering whether she should go back to warn Cristof or continue looking for something to wear. Then she saw the way Liliana's eyes shined as she gazed at Amcathra, and the guarded expression on Dautry's face as she observed Liliana, and decided she'd much rather go shopping.

CHAPTER EIGHT

THE TWO GIRLS handed their purchases to the tall lictor, who bore his burden with as much dignity as he could, considering his bruised face and the colorful nature of the Cabisi shopping baskets. Taya didn't find a Tizieri free-rider's veil, but she did find some lighter garments and a silver-and-blue silk scarf that her husband could wrap around his face if he needed to travel inconspicuously through Cabiel.

"Isn't your lictor's uniform too hot for Cabiel?" Liliana asked Amcathra, fingering a scarf without looking at him. "You aren't going to wear it all the time we're here, are you?"

"Yes."

"Professor Dautry isn't."

"She is not Ondinium, and she is not the captain of the *Firebrand*."

"She is not a bull-headed Demican lictor," Dautry muttered under her breath. Like most of the Firebrands, she had left her jacket on the ship and was wearing only her gray quasi-uniform trousers and a white shirt, the sleeves rolled up and the collar unbuttoned. She raised her voice. "I'm certain you could find a suitable replacement for your uniform here, Captain."

"She's right." Taya gestured to the stalls surrounding them. "We're surrounded by trousers and tunics that are more appropriate to the temperature than what you're wearing."

"They are not black."

"Black!" Sankau wrinkled her nose. "Cabisi weavers and dyers are the best in the world. Why do you want to wear black?"

"It is a lictor's color," Amcathra said, simply.

Sankau shrugged and turned to the merchant, speaking too rapidly for Taya to follow. The merchant replied, leaning over the counter and pointing.

"Come," Sankau said. "A man sells black clothing over there."

"Wait for us!" Taya swiftly paid for her purchases and stuffed her new bundles into the shopping basket the captain was carrying. He gave her a baleful look.

"I don't think I've ever seen you out of uniform," she said cheerfully, patting his arm.

"That is not true. You have seen me wear … robes … once."

"It wasn't the same." Although, she admitted to herself, Amcathra's expression as they'd dressed him in Cristof's ambassadorial garments had been priceless. "All you ever wear day-to-day is your uniform."

"I am proud of my uniform."

"Well, let's find you a Cabisi equivalent."

Sankau led them to a garment-maker who sold laborer's wear in black. Amcathra dourly chose a pair of trousers and a sleeveless shirt and changed behind a curtain.

"Looks good," Taya complimented him when he emerged. She was thoroughly amused by the way Liliana's eyes widened when she saw the captain's muscular frame and the snarling bear's head tattooed on his upper arm. Of course, the *principessa* was too young for him. She shot a hopeful glance at Dautry, who was studying Amcathra's tattoo with a guarded expression.

"It is too bad you must wear black," Sankau said, looking critically at the lictor. "Black is boring. But it does not look so *very* bad against your silver skin and hair."

"And all those cuts and bruises add some color to his face," Taya added. Amcathra shot her a dispassionate look.

"These garments are cooler," he begrudgingly admitted, plucking at the loose Cabisi trousers. "But they are not a uniform."

"They're close enough, and this way you won't collapse from heatstroke while you're guarding us."

"Our heat is very bad for foreigners," Sankau agreed. "Mainlanders do not drink enough water."

"And you're already sunburned and sweating," Taya pointed out, suddenly aware of her own thirst.

"As are you."

"True." She picked up the basket. "Buy that, and I'll change into my new clothes, too. Then we'll go find something to drink."

"I'm curious about your tattoo, Captain," Dautry interrupted. "It rather raises the question of which side of the war you're on."

Something like pain flickered in the lictor's eyes, quickly hidden.

"I am not *sheytatangri*, Dautry. If I were, the Council would not have entrusted me with this position."

"Then why are you wearing the *sheytatangri*'s symbol on your arm?"

The lictor hesitated.

"At one time, the Council asked me to— interact with the organization."

"You were the Council's spy?" Dautry's voice was cool.

"I did what was necessary to protect my country."

The professor pursed her lips.

"Then you'd better wrap this around your arm to hide it, Captain." She tossed him a black-dyed scarf with a dismissive air. "Most people have a problem trusting a man who spies for a living."

Amcathra's jaw tightened. Taya shot Dautry a dark look and took his arm, tugging him to one side.

"Just ignore her, Captain," she murmured. "She doesn't understand what it means to serve the Oporphyr Council."

"I have not failed to notice that within the last month the *principessa*, my navigator, and your husband have all questioned my trustworthiness," Amcathra grated, his hands clenched tightly around the scarf. "Despite my heritage and my nephew's bad choices, I have never sought to be anything but a loyal citizen of Ondinium."

"I know." Taya felt a surge of compassion for the proud lictor. "It's not your fault. The Council has put us all into some morally awkward situations, hasn't it?"

"I cannot command a crew that does not trust me."

"Your crew *does* trust you, and so do Cris and I. Dautry's just—" Taya hesitated, thinking of the things the professor had said about the captain. "She's foreign, and she's used to a different way of doing things. I honestly think she *wants* to trust you. She just doesn't understand putting duty first."

"Putting duty first is not a habit I wish to change."

"Of course not. Nobody's asking you to." She decided it was time to change the subject. "But you can't do your duty if you're about to pass out wearing a wool uniform on a tropical island, so let's get you something to wear."

It took some time, but finally Taya convinced the lictor that his health was more important than his uniform and was able to ask Liliana and Sankau to help him find several changes of clothes. While he grimly sorted through the garments the giggling girls brought over, Taya pulled Dautry aside.

"Whether you decide to trust Amcathra or not," she whispered, "*please* don't criticize his tattoo. That tattoo and his undercover work with the *sheytatangri* both contributed to his nephew's death."

Dautry blinked, her stern expression softening.

"His nephew was the young lictor— Rikard, right? I met him briefly on the trip out of Mareaux. I thought he'd died in the train wreck."

"It wasn't quite that simple." Taya still felt a deep sense of guilt for her part in Rikard's death. "And... it was an especially personal tragedy for the captain."

"Then I won't bring it up again." Dautry looked down at her armful of maps with a pensive expression. "It's none of my business what Captain Amcathra does, anyway."

· ✷ ·

"Taya!" Cristof jumped up, his gaze frankly admiring as she walked through the courtyard garden. He'd been sitting on the wooden walkway outside their bedroom, enjoying the sun and sipping from a shallow ceramic cup. "Is that your new flight suit?"

"What do you think?" She turned on the stone path, grinning as she showed off her Cabisi clothes.

"You look lovely." He leaned over the wooden railing to give her a kiss. "Will that fabric be thick enough under your armature?"

"I bought more layers to wear when I actually go flying." She raised her eyebrows as she smelled his breath. "What have you been drinking?"

"Something made out of fermented tree sap. Justiciar Xu assured me it's very light."

"Maybe," she said, climbing the steps and picking up the ceramic carafe beside his cushion, "but you've almost emptied the bottle."

"Without you by my side I have nothing better to do but drink away my solitude."

"You are definitely tipsy." She cocked her head, amused. "But somewhat more charming than usual."

"I live to delight you." He retrieved the carafe and sat down. "Where's everyone else?"

"We dropped Dautry off at the ship with her new charts and the others are getting their shopping off the 'cycle. Captain Amcathra has a new problem for us."

"Oh, no. Should I go to the kitchen and ask for another bottle?"

"Just sit there and look stern." She stepped into the bedroom and began unlatching her armature.

"Is his problem urgent?" Cristof asked, turning to watch her. "I could give you some help with that...."

"Whatever you're drinking, I'm ordering a bottle for dinner." She grinned as she tugged her armature over to a support column and padlocked it in place. "Go away. Nothing else is coming off."

"I th—" he stopped abruptly, distracted. She joined him on the walkway. The two girls were headed to Liliana's room, loaded down with baskets, and Captain Amcathra was crossing the walkway toward them, his Ondinium uniform folded under one arm.

For a moment the two men stared at each other, Cristof absorbing the lictor's fresh injuries.

"Did you win?" he asked at last.

"The Cabisi intervened."

"Alzanans?"

"With Mercate Corundel."

Cristof swore.

"Sit down, Captain." Taya pulled the second sitting cushion out of their bedroom. "I'll be back in a minute."

By the time she returned with a large carafe and several glasses, Amcathra had related the story to Cristof. She set down the tray and poured water for them all.

"What's involved in one of these duels?" Cristof asked. "Is a Cabisi duel like an Alzanan vendetta?"

"I think Cabisi duels are faster," Taya said. "Alzanan vendettas last forever, but the Cabisi meet, fight, and settle the matter."

"For good?"

"Xu said the justiciars allow new challenges on the same subject as long as the new challenger isn't related to the first. I guess that prevents the kind of Family feuding you get in Alzana. Are you going to let him fight? I think it's a bad idea."

"Maybe, but I agree with Janos that Corundel needs to be arrested. I'll write the Alzanan captain a letter, but I don't expect him to hand her over without a fight. Honor is everything to those people."

Taya drew in a deep breath.

"Whatever happens, you can't participate, Cris. You're the ambassador of Ondinium, and an exalted, and you weren't there in the first place."

"As a representative of the Oporphyr Council, I *do* have an interest in apprehending Corundel," he countered. "And I was certainly there during the invasion. In chains, as you might recall."

"You can't uncover for a duel in front of a bunch of Alzanan soldiers while you're acting as an ambassador to Cabiel."

"I don't give a damn about covering, and you know it. I want Corundel brought back to Ondinium and put on trial!"

"I agree with your wife, Exalted," Amcathra intervened. "My duty to protect you extends to keeping you safe from the repercussions of my own actions. I take full responsibility for this challenge; it is between me and Corundel."

"Listen, Janos... I've done my best to be patient with all of your 'exalted' this and 'exalted' that, but *don't* start treating me like a child."

"I am treating you like the esteemed member of Ondinium's ruling caste that you are." Amcathra didn't flinch under Cristof's glare. "I realize that you place no value on yourself or your birthright, but those of us who have dedicated our lives to you and your service do not feel the same way."

Cristof made a frustrated noise, yanking off his glasses and pinching the arch of his nose. Taya gave the lictor a grateful smile. That statement was as close as Amcathra had ever come to a declaration of friendship, and her husband knew it.

"We need to talk to Xu," Cristof growled at last, replacing his glasses.

Xu counseled patience. So, the next morning, Taya accompanied Cristof on a tour of Os Cansai's largest boatmaking factory, where her husband was intrigued by the steam-powered paddleboats used for inter-island cargo transport. That afternoon, they visited a toymaker who specialized in clockwork automata. Taya enjoyed the second visit more, remembering the little windup birds her husband had shown her the first time she'd visited his shop. Cristof seemed to enjoy it, too, spending several hours talking with the toymaker in a pidgin of Alzanan, Cabisi, and Mareaux, facilitated by lots of hand gestures and two bottles of palm wine.

The next day they took a quadracycle beyond the city borders to visit the beautiful Pearl Temple complex. White-robed novices pulling water from a well dropped their buckets and scrambled into the temple as they arrived. Minutes later, a group of priests and priestesses hurried out to greet their foreign visitors. Taya had to mention the taboo against touching an exalted when the youngest novice reached out to touch Cristof's heavy robe, but she knelt so the children could freely investigate her armature and wings. The priests and priestesses invited them into the temple and located a young man who spoke Mareaux. He bowed deeply in the Cabisi style.

"We are honored by your visit," he said, gazing at the covered and masked ambassador with open curiosity. "You are the first Ondiniums to ever enter our temple."

"We came here to see your Dancer," Taya said. "Exalted Forlore is a great admirer of automata."

"Then please, follow me." He led them through the courtyard past a number of smaller buildings to the largest structure in the back.

"Are you a priest?" Taya asked. He looked back, realized he was outpacing them, and slowed to match their exacting progress.

"No; I am a *kattaka.*" He gestured to his waist, where he wore two belts, one holding a beautiful jeweled knife and the other made of thin, flexible metal.

"What do you do here?"

"*Kattaka* are guardians. We protect the temple against invasion, bodyguard our clergy outside the temple grounds, and protect the sacred treasures when they travel from the temple for ceremonies."

"Do you fight duels?"

"Yes, if challenges arise against members of the temple who cannot fight for themselves, or against the temple as an organization. Fortunately, that seldom occurs."

As they entered the great temple, the *kattaka* pointed to the mother-of-pearl inlay that gave the building its name and drew their attention to the ornately carved screens that divided the space, each gilded and inlaid with gems. Taya was impressed. Ondinium's churches to the Lady of the Forge seemed spartan by comparison.

As they passed the last screen, she froze and stared up at the giant bronze statue that towered over them on its tall stone altar. The Dancer was easily four times the size of a human, its clothes made of silk and its jewelry rare and expensive. The statue's hinged joints were supported by narrow black rods that rose from the altar. The rods were all but invisible against the altar's dark backdrop.

Approach, Cristof signaled.

"May we draw nearer?" Taya asked. "The ambassador would like a better look."

"Of course." The *kattaka* ushered them forward. The altar was nearly as tall as Taya and covered by small candles and bowls of incense.

"Is lighting candles a devotion you follow, too?" she asked.

"It is a means of honoring the Dancer, yes."

"May I light one?"

"Of course." He left and Cristof signaled that Taya should walk him back and forth for a better look. As they paced, she heard a low click from the altar. She looked up. Had the Dancer's arm shifted? She couldn't tell for certain, but she thought it might have.

The *kattaka* returned with a candle and explained the Cabisi ritual. Taya followed his directions, then clapped her hands and added an Ondinium bow.

Lady, she prayed, *I'm sure the Dancer is one of your manifestations, so please accept my prayer while I'm here. Please protect Jayce and everyone else we left behind in Alzana, or grant them fortunate rebirths if they... if they're already dead.*

A lump rose in her throat. She returned to Cristof, sliding her arm under his hand. He squeezed her arm gently, then tapped out his next request: *Information.*

The statue, they were told, was controlled by a simple mechanism inside the altar that moved it incrementally every hour on the hour, so that over the course of a year the Dancer completed a Cabisi dance of blessing. It had been built sixty years ago and still functioned flawlessly. The temple counted several highly skilled engineers among its religious who had learned how to clean and maintain the engine without interfering with its sacred dance.

"Would it be bad luck if it stopped?" Taya asked. The *kattaka* shrugged.

"Some may believe so, but the statue is only a machine, neither holy nor eternal." His face lit as he thought of a comparison. "This statue is for Cabiel perhaps what the Great Engine is for Ondinium. You do not worship the engine, correct?"

Yes, Cristof tapped. Taya wasn't sure whether he meant yes, Ondinium did worship the Great Engine, or yes, it didn't. She decided to split the difference.

"Some people consider the Engine infallible," she said, "but the rest understand that it's only as accurate as the people who write its programs and input its data. So no, we don't worship it."

"So." The *kattaka* nodded with satisfaction. "This statue is similar."

Cristof was disappointed to learn that he wouldn't be allowed to peer into the altar to study its workings. Nevertheless, by the end of the tour he seemed enthusiastic about going back to Ondinium to tinker in his own workshop again.

When they returned to Xu's house, they learned that Amcathra had kept himself busy on the ship, overseeing repairs and consulting with Professor Dautry on the fastest return route. Liliana had explored the city with Sankau and her friends and discovered that the ship's captain was a Fiore, a traditional ally of the Mazzolettis. She resigned herself to the fact that she'd be traveling with the *Firebrand* a while longer.

On the third afternoon they were summoned to the Hall of Justice to hear the Impeccable Justiciary's verdict. Also present were Captain Fiore, his lieutenant, the three crew members who'd been involved in the brawl, and Patrice Corundel. Taya was secretly relieved that their presence meant Cristof wouldn't be able to unmask. Captain Amcathra and Lieutenant Imbrex attended with the exalted. Liliana and Professor Dautry remained on the floor, standing with the other interested spectators, both Cabisi and foreign.

"The essence of the complaint is as follows," Xu said in Cabisi. Next to her, another justiciar translated her words into Alzanan. "Janos Amcathra, a ship's captain and lictor from Ondinium, wishes to arrest and deport Patrice Corundel, a mercate from Ondinium currently in the employ of the Alzanan Family Mazzoletti. Lucco Fiore, a ship's captain from Alzana, claims Corundel is part of his ship's complement and refuses to turn her over for arrest. Are these facts correct?"

Both Amcathra and Fiore confirmed them, giving each other cool, evaluating gazes. Captain Fiore was a handsome man whose long black hair was pulled back in a thick queue. He wore a uniform adorned with masses of gold braid, numerous shiny brass buttons, and two enormous epaulettes, and he carried a smart hat tucked under one arm. By comparison, Captain Amcathra looked markedly shabby in his unornamented and hatless black lictor's uniform, his hard-edged face covered with old scars and new bruises beneath a utilitarian blond crew cut.

"The Impeccable Judiciary is in no position to evaluate whether Patrice Corundel belongs to the Ondinium contingent or the

Alzanan ship. It seems clear to us, however, that she is still an Ondinium citizen, as her castemark remains intact."

Startled, Corundel touched the crescent tattoo over her right cheek.

"Thus, the ambassador Exalted Forlore, as the official representative of his government, has a right to expect Corundel's obedience. Therefore, as we have documentation from both sides agreeing to comply with Cabisi law and abide by the ruling of the justiciars in the case of an indeterminate conclusion, the Impeccable Judiciary approves Captain Amcathra's challenge. Justiciar Ra Tafar is to observe the Ondinium faction, and Justiciar Tu Jinian the Alzanan faction, for the duration of the challenge."

The two justiciars bowed to Xu and then to the captains of their chosen sides. Each captain returned the bow in his country's individual style.

"Because neither faction is familiar with the laws of our land, the Impeccable Justiciary hereby confines this challenge to a specified time, date, and area, for the safety of the combatants and the general populace. Tomorrow morning at 6 a.m. the two captains must take their airborne vessels outside of the Os Cansai harbor but no more than three miles from the island's coast and proceed with their duel using any matter of handheld or simple projectile weapon, or the ships themselves, but abstaining from the use of chemical weaponry, serpentfire cannon, or any other weapon of mass destruction. Justiciars Ra and Tu will determine the acceptability of any weapon's usage under these guidelines in consultation with the captains and crew members."

The audience murmured.

"The victorious ship is that which first renders its opponent helpless, as the justiciars determine, or forces the other ship to leave the combat zone. Because justiciars are aboard as observers, destroying the enemy ship is not permissible. Violating these rules or ignoring a justiciar's ruling during the challenge is punishable by the automatic loss of the challenge.

"The victor wins the right to claim Patrice Corundel. The other side agrees to take no further action to rescue or retrieve her while within the boundaries of the Cabisi Thassalocracy, on land or water or in the air. In turn, the victor must treat Corundel with respect and humanity. If Ondinium wins this challenge, it agrees to abide by Cabisi requirements for the humane treatment and maintenance of a prisoner. Should the Impeccable Justiciary learn at any time that Corundel is not safe or well as a prisoner, Cabiel must cease all trade and political relations with Ondinium. Does everybody understand?"

"Just a minute, please," Taya said as Cristof painstakingly tapped out a question. She took a deep breath as she translated his brief query into something more suitably phrased.

"Does the mandate to treat Corundel with respect and humanity extend to her sentencing under Ondinium law? The possible sentences for treason include death."

"These terms extend only to the question of which faction claims and transports Corundel from Cabiel," Xu said, "and the circumstances of that transport. What happens outside the Thassalocracy is beyond the justiciary's purview."

Cristof signaled his agreement to those terms. Taya gave him a questioning look, and he repeated his signal.

"Ambassador Forlore, representing Ondinium's Oporphyr Council, agrees to the Impeccable Judiciary's terms for prisoner treatment and transport," she relayed.

"Very good. And do both sides agree to the form of the challenge?"

"May we discuss it among ourselves?" Captain Fiore asked.

"Of course."

Both groups huddled, looking suspiciously over their shoulders at each other.

"I don't like it," Taya said at once. "I thought this was supposed to be one-on-one combat, not ship-to-ship! The *Firebrand* is already damaged from its last fight with the Alzanans."

"The repairs are going swiftly," Lieutenant Imbrex said, "and we've had no trouble finding suitable fuel."

"But they could destroy the ship! And even if they don't, they could damage it even more. Why can't we insist on single combat?"

"The justiciars are using my challenge as an excuse to see what our vessels are capable of," Amcathra said, calmly. "They will undoubtedly use the information they glean from the duel to plan new defenses against airborne attack."

"We should say no."

"I would prefer to accept. Exalted?"

Cristof shifted, making sure his back was to the Alzanans, and tilted his mask up. "How's our ammunition supply?"

"Satisfactory. Cabiel uses the same calibers as the continent."

"What was that thing she mentioned— the serpentfire cannon?" Taya asked. "Do we have one of those?"

"Justiciar Xu," Amcathra said, turning, "what is a serpentfire cannon?"

Captain Fiore's mocking laugh rang through a suddenly hushed hall.

"It is one of our newest armaments," Xu said, ignoring the Alzanan. "It fires a chemical-based projectile that ignites phlogisticated atmospheric aether. Depending on the missile's size and load, the resulting firestorm may extend up to a half-mile radius from the point of ignition."

"Lady save us…" Taya whispered. That kind of destruction would make the Glasgar bombing seem trivial. Cristof grabbed her arm, but she anticipated him, speaking at the same time as Amcathra. The lictor fell silent, letting her ask the question.

"Have the Alzanans purchased this weapon from Cabiel?"

"Yes." Xu's expression was pained.

"You have one of those things aboard your ship?" Taya turned to the Alzanan captain. He gave a broad, expressive shrug, a smile dancing around his lips. She looked at Mercate Corundel. "And *you* arranged it? You're willing to see that kind of— of *abomination* used against your own country?"

"I didn't ask to be born Ondinium," Corundel said, coolly. "I'm quite happy to live in Alzana."

Cristof took a step forward and Taya turned, grabbing his arm.

"Shh," she whispered urgently. "Mind your caste!"

He snarled under his mask. She stepped closer.

"Please, Cris. You're our ambassador. She's not worth your dignity— *please*."

He hissed something vulgar under his breath, then allowed her to turn him back to their group.

"Use of the serpentfire cannon is forbidden in this challenge," Xu reminded Fiore. He gave her a sweeping Alzanan bow, complete with a crisp click of his heels.

"We understand, Justiciar," he said formally. "We would not risk our friendship with Cabiel by violating its rules of engagement."

"I suggest that all prohibited weapons be left on shore during the challenge," Taya countered. "That way we can *ensure* that the rules are followed."

The captain smirked. "Don't worry, little pigeon. The cannons are packed in our hold. We will not incinerate your ship tomorrow. But we *will* incinerate your capital soon."

Taya turned away, her heart sinking.

"Justiciar Xu," Captain Fiore continued, "although we will attempt to leave our enemy's ship crippled but intact, if your justiciar should happen to be injured in the fighting, what will happen to us?"

"The Impeccable Justiciary forbids the destruction of the other ship," Xu said, slowly, "but both observers are volunteers. They understand that ship-to-ship combat is unpredictable and that death is a possible consequence of their choice. If a justiciar dies accidentally, no member of the justiciary or of the justiciar's family may issue challenge."

Fiore inclined his head.

"Then the crew of the *Indomitable* agrees to the terms of the combat."

Taya shook her head, looking pleadingly at Cristof. He tapped his assent.

"You can't—"

Silence. Agree.

She ground her teeth together.

"Justiciar Xu," she said, stiffly, "the crew of the *Firebrand* agrees to the terms of the combat."

"Then the Impeccable Justiciary approves this challenge. Ra Tafar is to board the Ondinium ship, and Tu Jinian the Alzanan ship, immediately, and they must remain aboard for the duration of the challenge. If either side wishes to avoid fighting by ceding victory to the other, it must do so before 6 a.m. tomorrow. At 6 a.m., both ships must leave the harbor and fly a mile from shore before commencing combat. Warning buoys must be set up demarcating the combat zone and warning other boats away. Those wishing to observe the combat from a boat or ship must stay outside of the combat zone and observe at their own risk. A private observation deck is to be set up at 4 a.m. on the eastern-most seawall tower for justiciars and noncombatants belonging to each faction. Are there any further questions?"

Taya had hundreds of questions, but she bit them back. She looked at Amcathra and Imbrex. Neither indicated a desire to speak.

"No, Justiciar," she said. Captain Fiore said the same.

The session ended. Ra Tafar joined them, bowing.

"Lieutenant, please escort the justiciar to the ship and brief the crew," Amcathra said. "I will join you soon."

"Aye, sir." Imbrex saluted and left with Ra.

"We need to talk," Taya said, grimly. "Should I ask Xu to join us?"

Cristof signaled a negative.

"But I want to ask her about that cannon and why in the world they're selling weapons like that to foreigners!" Her voice was rising, but she couldn't help it.

"That information has no bearing on tomorrow's combat," Amcathra said. "Find us a room where we can converse."

Taya felt a surge of annoyance at his high-handed manner, exacerbated by Cristof's signal of confirmation. She pulled her arm away and spun around, scowling.

Xu turned to Taya as soon as she stormed up.

"Icarus. Let me say at once that I believe we should restrict the sale of the serpentfire cannon. It is an experimental weapon and the science behind it remains unclear. I regret that its sale endangers your country."

"Why do you sell weapons at *all*? Don't you know that anything you sell can be used against you? Haven't you read anything about Ondinium's Last War?"

Xu sighed, suddenly looking her age. The justiciars around them fell silent, listening, and Liliana edged up with a stricken look on her face.

"Yes," Xu said, "but Cabiel is not an authoritarian state. Several strong factions value a free market and challenge any law that limits the manufacture or export of goods. The munitions manufactory that is making the serpentfire cannon is part of that group."

"But this goes far beyond guns and bombs! A firestorm a half-mile in radius? Imagine what that would do to one of your islands!"

"I know what it can do. Believe me, Icarus Taya, there is an ongoing debate about this weapon among the most influential circles of our science and defense communities. But even if public opinion becomes strong enough for the manufacturer to accept trade restrictions, it takes time to pass such policies, and the Alzanans are here now, buying as many of the weapons as they can."

"Are they buying the plans, too?"

"I do not think the manufacturer is selling its plans."

"How many serpentfire cannon have the Alzanans bought?"

"I do not know. However, the technology is new— I do not think many are available."

Taya closed her eyes, trying to control the churning in her stomach.

"Is there anyplace here where the ambassador can unmask in private?" she asked at last. Xu led them to a back room with several cushions and a low table.

Taya turned and saw Liliana and Dautry watching them. She waved them inside and closed the door.

Amcathra helped Cristof remove his mask. The exalted wiped his face on his sleeves and sank onto the cushion, still looking angry.

Liliana stood close to the doorway.

"Should I be here?" she asked in a small voice. The three Ondiniums looked at each other and then at her. She shrank back. Dautry put a hand on the girl's shoulder, giving them a cool, challenging look.

"This discussion may distress her," Amcathra said to Cristof.

"None of this is her fault," Taya reminded them.

"I can leave."

"No— no, stay if you want." Cristof took his mask from Amcathra, not looking at the girl. "If we're allies, you have the right to sit in on this conversation."

The *principessa* meekly took a cushion on the empty side of the table. Dautry sat between her and Amcathra.

"I asked Xu about the cannon," Taya said. "She said she didn't think there were many available yet. Maybe… maybe they're all on that ship."

"Let's hope so." Her husband looked at Amcathra. "Can you sink it?" Liliana put a hand over her mouth but didn't say a word. Dautry pursed her lips.

"My crew has confirmed that it uses the same inflammable gas as the others," Amcathra replied. "Our strategy will be to ignite its engines or envelope."

"But a justiciar will be on board," Taya objected. "If we sink their ship, we'll kill her, too! What if she's married? What if she has children? You aren't going to kill an innocent bystander, are you?"

Cristof rubbed his forehead, looking unhappy.

"We must assume that the justiciars are capable of making prudent decisions regarding their participation in the challenge," Amcathra said.

"Even *you've* been known to let your emotions overwhelm your good sense," Taya snapped. "That's why we're here now, isn't it?"

"Taya," Cristof interrupted. "This challenge isn't his fault."

"That is incorrect, Exalted. I *did* initiate both the fight and the challenge." Amcathra met Taya's eyes. "I will take responsibility for any deaths that occur as a result of my actions, including Justiciar Tu's. Icarus, I will not hesitate to kill a dozen innocent people if it means I can save thousands."

Taya stared at him. Could he really consider taking human life in such a cold, calculating manner? But then again, she thought with a surge of guilt, she had killed plenty of people herself to protect her husband and her nation.

"Can't you just shoot out the engines?" Liliana asked, her voice shaking. "If the ship fell into the water, the cargo would be lost but people might survive...."

"Shooting the engines would cripple the dirigible; puncturing its envelope will sink it," Dautry corrected. "If you make stopping the ship, rather than destroying it, your primary tactic, Captain, I'll be willing to serve as your helm. Otherwise, I want no part of deliberate oath-breaking and murder."

Amcathra looked from one woman to the other and slowly nodded.

"I will do what I can to spare the crew's lives while ensuring that the serpentfire cannon cannot be used against Ondinium."

"I'm going, too," Taya said, remembering how chilled she'd felt in the last airfight when a crew member had fallen into the ocean to die. "I can try to save anyone who falls overboard from *either* ship."

"Absolutely not," Cristof snapped. "I need you next to me, not out in the middle of another airfight."

"If I can save someone's life, I will," Taya argued. "Search and rescue has *always* been part of my duties."

"You're in the diplomatic corps now. Your first duty is to me."

"You are *not* going to order me to stand back and watch people die!"

"Why not? That's what you and Janos want *me* to do."

"You're an exalted and I'm an icarus!"

"My exalted birth was a mistake and everybody knows it. My family's crazy, and the Council would have outcaste me last year if it didn't need me for this ridiculous charade." The color was high in his castemarked cheeks. "You *know* this was never my idea."

"I know," she said, struggling to rein in her temper. "But I won't be in any danger. If anyone falls out of the ship, I'll fly down and drop them a cork ring until they can be rescued. Cris, I'm the only one here who can do that. Please — I've already seen too much death — I've *caused* too much death — the nightmares keep coming no matter how many candles I light to the Lady! I have to do *something* to counterweight all the wrong I've done or I'll never be able to look at myself in the mirror again."

Cristof deflated, casting her a wretched look.

"It won't be safe, no matter how careful you are."

"I will keep her as safe as I can," Amcathra said, quietly.

"You think she should do it, too?"

"How can your spirit be well if your wife's is not?"

"My spirit sure as hell won't be well if she dies!" He looked away, frustrated. "I don't even *believe* in spirits."

Taya started to say something but Amcathra gave her an almost imperceptible shake of his head. She bit back her words.

Liliana had pulled herself into a small huddle, watching the argument with mournful eyes. Dautry was also watching with a troubled expression on her face.

"Keep her alive, Janos," Cristof said after a moment, his voice hard. "I'll hold you responsible if she dies."

"I have always sought to protect your wife as I would protect you, Exalted."

"You have," Taya whispered. Amcathra had sacrificed more to save her life than any man should be asked to do.

"All right, Taya," her husband said, each word sounding wrenched out of him. "I won't stop you. I suppose I *can't* stop you."

She waited for more, but he fell silent, as if that was all he could bring himself to say. At last, she nodded.

"Thank you."

Chapter Nine

THE SKY WAS clear, the morning breeze cool, and the rising sun made the ocean glitter like diamonds. Taya stood on the raised forecastle next to Captain Amcathra and Ra Tafar, listening to the *Firebrand*'s ondium-plated wings move back and forth as it swept the ship toward the combat zone.

Despite their uneasy agreement in the Hall of Justice, she and Cristof had argued again that night in Xu's house, until they'd both ended up lying on the thin Cabisi mattress with their backs to each other, tensely pretending to be asleep. That morning their good-bye kiss had been emotionless and perfunctory, and Taya had turned away with a heavy heart. Then Cristof had grabbed her arm, yanking her back around to face him.

"If Janos starts a suicide run, promise me you'll get off the ship," he said fiercely, his fingers digging into her leather flightsuit.

"A su— he wouldn't do that!"

"That's *exactly* what he'll do, if it's the only way he can destroy the *Indomitable*."

"But... his crew...."

"His crew's a bunch of lictors who've taken the same damn military oath that he has. But you never took that oath, so don't you *dare* die with them."

Taya stared at him, shaken.

"I won't."

"Good." He looked down at his grip on her arm and released her, stepping back. "I just— I don't—" His voice cracked and he fell silent, his face twisting.

"Cris." She swallowed the lump in her throat and touched his cheek, running her fingers over his wave-shaped castemark.

"I try, Taya," he whispered, his voice rough. "I *try* not to worry about you. I know you're brave and resourceful and smart. But if you think it's easy, staying behind while you risk your life—"

"I'll be careful," she promised, tasting salt as she kissed him. She didn't know if it came from her tears or his, and it didn't matter. They clung to each other a long time, despite his bulky ceremonial robes and her awkward ondium armature.

Now her mood was somber as she listened to the ship and crew. The *Indomitable* was flanking them in the distance, both vessels straining to beat the other to the designated area.

"When we move into the combat zone, Justiciar," Captain Amcathra said at last, "I recommend you go below to view the fight through the observation window in the mess hall. We will leave the glass windows in place for you. The hull is metal-plated, so despite the glass, you will be reasonably safe from stray bullets."

"Thank you, Captain," Ra replied. "I prefer to stay on deck to watch the maneuvers, but I appreciate your recommendation."

"Please restrict yourself to the quarterdeck, then," Amcathra said. "Icarus, would you take him there?"

"All right." Taya had already agreed to remain there during the battle. She gestured to Ra and they both headed back.

Today Taya was carrying field glasses around her neck, a long coil of rope wrapped around her waist, and a cork flotation ring secured to her armature. She was also carrying, in one flight-suit pocket, the familiar weight of a small bomb.

Amcathra had wordlessly offered it to her when she came aboard, and she'd accepted it with the same bleak silence. As an icarus, she was forbidden to carry weapons, but she'd shattered that law months ago. She wouldn't use the bomb unless she had to; she already had too much blood on her hands from bombs just like it. But she would rather blow up another dirigible — even one carrying an innocent justiciar — than watch Amcathra destroy himself and the *Firebrand* trying to do the same thing.

She might be sacrificing her happiness in the next life, but Taya knew she couldn't be happy in *this* life if she didn't do everything she could to save the people she loved.

The Cabisi had laid out a line of bright red buoys and small boats to divert water traffic and retrieve any combatants who fell into the ocean and were still afloat by the fight's end. Numerous Cabisi had volunteered for zone duty, and more had gathered on Os Cansai's docks with spyglasses and telescopes, eager to watch the fight.

The night before, the *Firebrand*'s crew had unloaded the ship's excess cargo and furniture into the mooring tower and taken on more water as ballast. The ship's load currently consisted of crew, coal, weapons, ammunition, and just enough material for emergency repairs. Taya had bundled a number of cork floats by the quarterdeck rail, but their weight was negligible.

Now the *Firebrand* dumped part of its ballast and pulled ahead, its great wings sweeping it forward and upward. Despite her misgivings, Taya felt a thrill of excitement. She glanced at Ra and saw a smile playing around his lips as he inspected the Alzanan ship through his field glasses. She lifted her own. The *Indomitable* was struggling to catch up, but the *Firebrand* would reach the combat zone first.

They crossed the line and continued gaining altitude. Amcathra was putting the *Firebrand* between the rising sun and the Alzanan ship to blind the *Indomitable*'s gunners. He ordered Ondinium's crimson war flag run out, replacing the peacetime flag they had flown over Os Cansai.

Behind them the *Indomitable* veered south, putting itself out of firing range as it sought a more advantageous position. Taya heard the lictors cheer as the Alzanan ship crossed the red line.

The duel had begun.

The *Firebrand* circled southwest, its deck tilting as its port wing and demiwing caught the wind in an aggressive swoop. Taya held the rail and the deck gunners braced, waiting for the *Indomitable* to come into sight and range. Below them the *Firebrand*'s gun deck opened with a mechanical rumble and cannon were rolled forward.

The Alzanans had put four soldiers on the *Indomitable*'s topmost firing platform. The two heavy, tripod-mounted guns would deter the *Firebrand* from flying directly over the dirigible. The rest of the Alzanans were inside the dirigible's engine and command gondolas.

"I think they've upgraded their weapons," Taya muttered uneasily.

"The *Indomitable* carries several steam-powered cannon," Ra said in Alzanan next to her. "It is likely the Alzanans are loading our thunderclap shot."

"What's that?"

"A specially prepared hollow ball that contains gunpowder and iron scraps. It explodes upon impact."

"Does Captain Amcathra know about it?"

"Yes."

"Aren't you afraid of being hit by your own weapons?"

Ra smiled, lowering his field glasses to look at her.

"If death is the price I must pay to fly like a bird, then so be it. Cabiel has hot-air balloons, but no dirigibles and certainly no ornithopters. Our engineers develop and sell many aerostat plans to continental traders, but aerostats are too resource-intensive to manufacture ourselves."

"Wouldn't aerial ships be more useful than naval ships?"

"For what?"

Taya considered and discarded several responses. At last she shrugged and raised her glasses.

Steam cannon could propel shot faster and over greater distances than powder cannon, but they were bulkier and louder. Ondinium mounted its steam cannon in bunkers at key strategic points throughout the country and in the signal stations along its border, but the *Firebrand* carried only powder cannon.

No wonder Amcathra wanted to stay high. The *Firebrand* was significantly outgunned.

As she was thinking that, the cannon below her feet fired their first deafening volley. Taya watched for a strike, but nothing happened.

"They are finding their range," Ra said conversationally. "I am impressed that the *Firebrand*'s cannon cause so little roll."

"You've fired cannon before?"

"I am a retired naval officer. The scent of gunpowder is an old friend."

"Who did you fight? Was Cabiel at war?"

"No, but there are many pirates in our waters."

The *Indomitable* was still rising and keeping its distance. The *Firebrand*'s approach, riding the wind in a gyre, was causing it to lose altitude. It fired again and Taya saw part of the *Indomitable*'s engine gondola splinter.

"A little low," Ra reported. A series of sharp cracks sounded from the *Indomitable*.

The explosive battering of the Alzanans' thunderclap shot shoved the *Firebrand* sideways, kicking up its starboard side and causing it to broach to. The wind caught the ship's hull and Taya's gloved fingertips slipped off the rail as she lost her footing. She slammed against the ondium-plated deck and rolled onto her stomach to protect her wings. Her armature dug into her flesh and she hit something hard that checked her slide. Around her, the crew was shouting and the *Firebrand* groaned and protested.

She'd landed against the secondary helm. She clutched it and stood. Professor Dautry was bound to the helm with leather safety straps and was bracing herself against the steeply tilting deck as she worked.

"Can I help?" Taya shouted.

"I have it."

Taya propped a foot against the helm to steady herself as she pulled down her goggles and thrust her arms between the armature's wingstruts. She unlocked her wings and kicked away, run-scrambling several feet down the steeply sloping deck before propelling herself off the ship's rail.

The *Firebrand* had been hit in the middle of a turn and thrown leeward. In the belly of the ship, two lictors were dragging another back onto the open gunnery platform. Taya began a circling descent, searching the ocean for anyone less fortunate. There— a dark figure flailed on the surface of the water, one hand waving wildly. She locked her wings in a glide and slipped her arms free to drop a cork rescue ring.

"Hold on and wait," she shouted as the lictor swam toward it. He grabbed it and she flew back toward the ornithopter.

The sound of repeating gunfire made her swerve. The *Indomitable* was closing on the *Firebrand* and its platform crew had fired a warning shot at her. She changed direction, keeping the ornithopter between herself and the Alzanan ship as she reached the deck. She landed hard and stumbled.

The *Firebrand*'s cannon roared. Taya locked her wings high and ran to Ra Tafar.

"Are you all right?"

"Excellent!" he replied cheerfully. "And you?"

"I saved someone," she said, allowing herself a moment of satisfaction. She pulled another cork ring off the bundle and tied it to her belt.

The *Indomitable* returned fire. Taya ducked as thunderclap shot struck the ornithopter, sending it rocking back and forth in a barrage of metal plates and wooden splinters. Bits of detritus gouged Ra Tafar's unprotected arms, leaving red streaks running down his dark skin. He remained standing, watching the Alzanan ship through his field glasses. Gunfire raked the far side of the *Firebrand*'s deck, plowing furrows into the ornithopter's gorgeously etched ondium plating. Taya stayed low, disinclined to join Ra in his bold defiance of death. She'd been shot once in the past, and that had been more than enough for her.

The *Firebrand*'s volley guns raked the *Indomitable*'s front gondola in retaliation, tearing off chunks of wood and ripping through its open windows. She hoped the *Indomitable*'s crew was as busy as the *Firebrand*'s. Any lictor who wasn't steering the ship or manning a weapon was checking wing mounts, screwing down loosened ondium plates, and assisting the injured. Captain Amcathra stood close to the fore helm, snapping orders.

The *Firebrand*'s attempt to cut off the *Indomitable* had been thwarted by the Alzanans' first explosive volley, and it had been forced to adjust its direction to stabilize itself. The *Indomitable* had gained on it during its maneuvering, and now the two ships flew nearly parallel as they ran with the wind, firing broadsides. Dautry shouted a warning: "Hold fast!"

Taya grabbed the rail as the *Firebrand*'s wings tilted and swept back. The ornithopter's prow sliced through the air as the ship simultaneously cut southeast and climbed, breaking across the Alzanans' nose. The gunners on top of the Alzanan ship swiveled their weapons and opened fire. Taya cringed as she saw lictors stagger back, hit. The *Firebrand*'s cannon boomed, pounding the dirigible's gondola, struts, and envelope.

Then they were over and across the *Indomitable*, making a wide turn for another high pass as the *Firebrand*'s volley guns pounded. One of the Alzanan platform gunners dropped.

"Do you have a first-aid kit?" Ra Tafar asked. Taya turned and saw that the justiciar had sat down, his back to the railing, and was clutching his side.

"Oh, Lady! Were you hit?"

"Perhaps wearing red on a ship full of black uniforms is unwise." His smile was strained.

"The surgeon's in the cockpit. Come on." She wrapped an arm around his waist and helped him to the nearest hatch. A lictor on maintenance-and-medic duty took him down the ladder.

Meanwhile, the *Firebrand* had completed its turn, dropping to give its gun deck a clearer shot at the *Indomitable*'s engine. The

Indomitable's steam cannon and the *Firebrand*'s powder cannon roared at the same time.

Taya was thrown off her feet again as the *Firebrand* pitched and yawed, something mechanical giving off a chilling screech. The *Firebrand*'s movement made it hard to focus on the Alzanan ship ahead, but she saw smoke rising from the *Indomitable*'s gondola. Half of the gondola's wooden skin had been torn away, revealing its naked frame and the weapons and men inside.

The ornithopter's jerking was making her nauseous. Taya struggled to her feet, stumbled, and threw herself toward the nearest railing. The *Firebrand*'s crew was shouting panicked orders as flame licked one of the wingmounts. She straddled the rail and looked over the side. Plenty of room to fall. She slipped her arms into her wings, unlocked them, and jumped overboard.

Unidirectional freefall was a relief after the *Firebrand*'s sickening lurches. Taya dived between the ships and spotted a black shape on the water. She swept around in a circle. A lictor was floating face-down in a spreading pool of red. Taya shouted, but the woman remained motionless.

Dismayed, Taya flew on. Something large whistled past her and struck the ocean to her left, startling her into a wild swerve. Steam rose in a hissing cloud— it was one of the Alzanans' steam-cannon, cast overboard and sinking in a white rush of bubbles. Taya gained altitude to see what was happening above her.

The *Indomitable* had taken grievous damage and its crew was hurling fiery chunks of machinery and furnishings out of the ripped-open gondola in an attempt to avoid an explosive conflagration. The dirigible had turned its nose east, away from Os Cansai and the crippled *Firebrand*. Taya was about to fly back to the ornithopter when she heard a loud scream. Two figures plummeted from the *Indomitable*, twisting as they grappled in midair.

They hit the water just as Taya recognized the red robes of the young justiciar who'd flown with the *Indomitable*. She swept back down. Both bodies bobbed back up to the surface, motionless. The Alzanan's neck was bent at a fatal angle. The Cabisi floated on her back.

Taya locked her wings and untied the cork ring from her belt.

"Tu! Wake up! Tu!" She dropped the ring next to the young woman's face, searching for some sign of life. The justiciar didn't move.

Taya thrust her arms back into her wings. Could she get help? The *Indomitable* was flying away, its crew busy firefighting. The *Firebrand* listed and spun in slow, wide circles, one wing frozen at an awkward angle.

No assistance there. The justiciar was sinking again— and bubbles were rising from her mouth.

"Oh, scrap." Taya realized what she had to do. "Cris is going to kill me." She flew straight up, lifted her wings over her head, and plunged feet-first into the water.

The ocean was a lot colder than the air. Taya freed her arms and grabbed Tu's robes, her ondium wings and armature providing plenty of buoyancy. She thrashed her way to the cork ring, grabbed it, and shifted her grip to keep Tu's head out of the water. Then she grabbed the Alzanan.

Dead. With regret, she shoved the body away.

"Tu! Tu, wake up! Tu Jinian!"

The woman groaned and gagged. Taya held the justiciar's head up as she convulsed with a hacking series of coughs.

"Careful, easy! Grab the ring."

Tu threw her arms over the cork ring, shooting a dark look up at the fleeing Alzanan ship. "They threw me overboard!"

"You took one of them with you." Taya pointed at the body, which hadn't slipped beneath the surface yet. "He's dead."

"Good!" Tu spat a Cabisi word that Taya hadn't learned yet. Above them, the ships were drawing further and further apart, the *Firebrand* struggling in midair and the *Indomitable* steadily heading east.

"I don't think they're going back to Os Cansai," Taya muttered. "Did they tell you anything about their plans?"

"No, but the captain's order to have me thrown overboard is not the behavior of a man who intends to return to the Impeccable Justiciary to claim his victory."

"You're lucky he didn't shoot you."

Tu glared at the retreating ship.

"I think I am alive only to distract you and your ship from giving pursuit," she growled. She tossed her long rows of braided hair over her shoulder. "Captain Fiore owes me for this insult."

Taya looked up. *The only good thing about this*, she thought, watching the ornithopter's wing shudder, move, and then freeze again, *is that Captain Amcathra can't make a last-ditch suicide run*. But that was the only bright spot in what was otherwise a complete disaster. The Alzanans had escaped with the serpentfire cannon, and the *Firebrand* was damaged again, worse than ever.

"Can you fly?" Tu asked, after a long moment.

"No— I'm not counterweighted enough to take off from the water. And before you ask, no, I don't know how to swim, either. I'm afraid we're stuck here until someone picks us up."

"Then can you signal your ship? Sharks live in these waters, and the dead body will attract them."

"Sharks— aren't those the fish on your national flag?"

"Yes." Tu gave her a grave look across the cork ring. "Very big fish with very sharp teeth for tearing into fresh meat."

Taya swallowed. "Let me see what I can do." She slipped her arms into her wings and began waving them back and forth to catch the morning sun.

Two Cabisi fishermen on rescue duty pulled them into a small boat with the other surviving lictor, who thanked Taya for the ring she'd dropped to him. The Ondinium corpse had been lost, but the Alzanan corpse was pulled aboard.

By the time they reached the harbor, the *Firebrand* was tacking back to its mooring tower, one wing frozen.

After thanking the fishermen and arranging for the body to be taken to the Os Cansai morgue, Taya, Tu Jinian, and the lictor walked across the harbor. Taya's clothes and armature were covered in dried salt and she was getting blisters where her armature had rubbed through the Cabisi garments in flight. Tu and the lictor seemed similarly uncomfortable, plucking at their salt-stiffened garments with distaste.

As they approached the *Firebrand*'s mooring tower, they saw that the observation party was already there. A young justiciar hurried to them, bowing.

"Icarus," he said in heavily accented Alzanan, "the ambassador waits for you." He indicated an enclosure made of curtains draped between several quadracycles.

"Thank you." She turned to Tu. "When will we hear the Impeccable Justiciary's verdict? Should we meet you someplace later today?"

"Does the ambassador prefer we deliver our decision here or in the Great Hall?"

"Will your deliberations take long?"

"I think no more than an hour. Perhaps less."

"Then we'll wait here. But if we could get some fresh water....?"

"Of course." Tu translated her request for the younger man, bowed to Taya, and entered the mooring tower with the *Firebrand*'s rescued lictor.

Taya headed toward the 'cycles.

"Cris, it's me." She pushed aside a curtain.

"Taya!" Her husband grabbed her hands, squinting as he scanned her from head to toe. "What happened? The *Firebrand* signaled that you needed to be picked up— were you hurt?"

"No, I'm fine. I had to jump into the water to save Tu Jinian. The Alzanans threw her overboard."

"Bastards." He pulled her close, wrapping his arms around her and her armature. She rested her forehead against his shoulder, satisfied to lean against him and feel his long hair tickle her cheek.

"So," he murmured after a long, contented silence. "You saved the justiciar you were so worried about. I'm glad."

"And a lictor, too." She reluctantly pushed away. "But at least one other lictor died, and the *Indomitable* escaped."

"We'll deal with it." He brushed her salt-stiffened hair away from her face. "I'm happy you were able to help. I'm sorry that I keep forgetting how important that is to you."

"It's just—" she felt awkward. "I joined the diplomatic corps to do something good. But it seems like everything's gone so *wrong* since then, and I don't know who to trust anymore, and I've had to kill people, and it's— it just feels like everything is falling apart around us and I need to do everything I can to hold it together."

Cristof drew in a breath. She expected his usual exhortation that she'd only done what was necessary to survive, but instead he slowly exhaled and hugged her again.

"I'm lucky you stay with me," he murmured. "Sometimes I *still* think too much like an exalted."

Puzzled, she pulled back and searched his face. He gave her a crooked smile and tapped her keel.

"Look at this mess. You know salt water will ruin your wing mechanisms, don't you?"

She smiled uncertainly back. She wasn't sure what was going through his mind, but she was relieved to be back on familiar ground again.

"If you'll get me some fresh water and your kit from the *Firebrand*, I'll clean it while we wait," he continued.

"The ambassador of Ondinium can't be seen cleaning an armature!"

"Oh, to hell with the ambassador of Ondinium. All he ever does is argue and start wars. Your *husband* is proud to keep his heroic wife's armature well-maintained and ready to use."

Taya blushed and beamed, standing on her toes to kiss him. He looked startled but gratified as she slipped off to fetch her cleaning supplies.

· ✳ ·

Later, the justiciars descended, with the *Firebrand*'s officers, to relay their decision.

"In terms of the challenge," Xu Chausiki announced, "the Impeccable Justiciary finds Alzana's *Indomitable* victorious, leaving Ondinium's *Firebrand* unable to continue the combat. The *Indomitable* has won the right to keep Patrice Corundel with its crew while it remains within the Cabisi Thalassocracy."

Taya stared at the justiciar, shocked. A ripple of protest ran through the *Firebrand* crew. Even the Cabisi in the audience seemed surprised, leaning their heads toward each other to murmur comments. Taya glanced at Cristof, but his expression was hidden behind his mirrorlike mask. Captain Amcathra might as well have been wearing a mask, too; his face was inexpressive. Behind him, Imbrex and Dautry frowned.

"However," Xu continued, "the Impeccable Justiciary finds the *Indomitable* guilty of intentionally causing harm to Justiciar Tu Jinian. Accordingly, we declare the crew of the *Indomitable* in violation of Cabisi law and subject to arrest and return to Os Cansai for a hearing. We believe the *Indomitable* is fleeing our nation and we are therefore sending signals across the Thalassocracy reporting its fugitive status and asking for updates regarding its flight path. If the *Indomitable* lands in Cabiel, its crew is subject to arrest."

Well, that's something, Taya thought, nettled.

"In gratitude for your rescue of our justiciar," Xu continued, looking at Taya, "the Os Cansai harbor agrees to help you repair your ship and see you on your way as speedily as possible. The Impeccable Justiciary also agrees to convey to the continent, on the next ship departing for Mareaux or any other destination you prefer, any message you wish to send to your Council."

"Thank you," Captain Amcathra replied.

"Finally," Xu added, "Tu Jinian, a justiciar, seeks to challenge the captain of the *Indomitable*, an Alzanan aerostat, for ordering her murder and throwing her overboard. Although Captain Fiore is not here to offer his defense or accept the challenge, after hearing witness testimony, the Impeccable Justiciary agrees that Tu Jinian's complaint is valid and approves the challenge according to the laws of the land."

Tu bowed to the justiciars, looking satisfied.

"Are there any questions about or protests against these decisions?"

Taya turned. The *Firebrand*'s crew shifted restlessly, their glances cutting toward Captain Amcathra and Lieutenant Imbrex. The two officers shook their heads.

"Thank you," Xu concluded, bowing. Taya and the Firebrands glumly followed suit. Then, as though released, the Cabisi onlookers divided into smaller groups, talking and exclaiming over the battle.

"Captain Amcathra," Tu said in Alzanan, approaching the lictor and bowing. "May I travel with your crew back to the continent?"

"Do you intend to pursue the *Indomitable*?"

"I do."

"Then I have no objection."

CHAPTER TEN

THE FIREBRANDS OBSERVED funeral services for the three lictors who had died in the battle— the one who had been lost overboard and two who had been killed on deck during the firefight. Thirteen crew members were left. Captain Amcathra, after a drawn-out consultation with Cristof, reluctantly agreed to allow a select group of Cabisi engineers and shipwrights aboard to assist with the repairs.

"The Council will hate the thought of foreigners on the ship," Cristof told Taya, "but since Ondinium's secret is out, anyway, I don't see any reason to keep them off."

"I'm still surprised the captain agreed to it."

"He doesn't have much choice. The damage is extensive. Our crew can perform simple repairs, but they're not aeronautical engineers."

"And the Cabisi are?"

"They're the ones who sold dirigible designs to the Alzanans, so they have more technical knowledge of aerostats than most of us. I'm sure they'll be able to help."

"Will we be able to leave soon, then?"

"Not for a few more days, at least."

"But that means the *Indomitable* will reach Ondinium before we do!"

"I don't think it's going straight to Ondinium, love. Remember, the ship was badly damaged, and its crew doesn't know King Agosti is dead. I expect it will return to Alzana to be repaired and to deliver its cargo. That means the Alzanans won't have a chance to use the serpentfire cannon for several more weeks." He squeezed her hand. "The Council will get our warning long before that."

She hoped he was right. Amcathra, Cristof, and Pitio had worked out a coded message to be carried by Cabisi traders to the nearest port in Mareaux. From there it would be telegraphed to Terminal, which sat on the Mareaux-Ondinium border. The lictors at Terminal would relay it by luxograph to the capital. If they were lucky, the whole process would take about a week, but Taya could imagine dozens of things that could go wrong with the plan.

In the meantime, she and Cristof had little to do. The Cabisi showed the Ondinium ambassador around their factories and laboratories, and they attended several exhibitions of dance and music and a private reception at an art gallery. Liliana attended the cultural events but skipped the industrial tours in favor of going out boating and sightseeing with Xu Sankau and her friends. She seemed to be coming to terms with her losses, although Taya still caught the young *principessa* gazing into the distance from time to time with a forlorn look on her face.

Taya wished she could skip the industrial tours, too. She was usually able to avoid the worst of her husband's gearhead enthusiasms, but whenever his fascination with machines overlapped with his activities as an ambassador, she had little choice but to accompany him.

"I do not think it is good to work too closely with your spouse," Tu Jinian mused one afternoon over lunch in the marketplace. Cristof was spending the day on the *Firebrand*, where he could chat unmasked with the Cabisi engineers who were proposing improvements to the ornithopter's engine and wing structure. "A little working together is important, or you have nothing to say to each other, but too much working together leads to numerous opportunities for argument."

"Are you married?"

"No, not me. Husbands want attention and children, and I am not yet ready to dedicate my time to either one."

"They *do* need attention, although Cri — the ambassador — doesn't want children."

"Do you?"

"Yeeeees…." Taya grimaced, thinking about everything they'd gone through recently. "Eventually. My sister's having a baby, so she's started me thinking about it, too. But not right now. Our lives are too busy and too dangerous for children, so I haven't tried to change his mind about them."

"Do you think you can?"

"I think he secretly enjoys children. He's just afraid to have any of his own. His family— wasn't the best."

"Then it is wise to wait and let him grow more comfortable with the idea." The justiciar pushed her empty plate to one side, leaning back in her chair.

"So what do you do when you aren't a justiciar, Tu?"

"Please, call me Jinian, or Jin, if you prefer. I am a *kattaka*."

Taya remembered the term. "A temple guardian?"

"Yes."

"I'd better warn you that my husband isn't very religious."

"That is not important."

"You don't think so?"

"Why should religious belief be important?"

"So that you'll do the right things to attain a better rebirth!"

"Does he do the right things, your husband, even without belief?"

Taya hesitated.

"Yes. Mostly. He's honorable and loyal and tries his hardest to be a good person. We've both had to kill people, but...."

"Killing *is* sometimes the right thing. The Dance unfolds in many ways and requires us to strike many poses over the course of our life."

That's right, Taya reminded herself, picking up her glass of palm wine. *I'm talking to a religious warrior in a country where dueling is an acceptable way of settling disputes.*

"On second thought," Taya said, "you two will probably get along just fine."

Jinian looked pleased.

The Cabisi engineers had a number of excellent suggestions for improving the ornithopter, Cristof reported that night, although some of them were impractical for the amount of time they wanted to spend in Os Cansai. Still, the work moved along quickly with their help and within a week the *Firebrand* had been repaired, refueled, and reprovisioned. Captain Amcathra took the opportunity to buy new Cabisi ammunition and to bring several Cabisi weapons on board, including new cannon to replace the heavier Ondinium weapons.

"Did you buy any serpentfire cannon?" Taya asked with trepidation.

"The manufacturer had none left that were close to completion," Amcathra replied. "The *Indomitable* bought all three working models."

Taya shivered.

The ceremony to bid them farewell was as simple as the ceremony to welcome them, with a dinner the night before and then a line of justiciars and a mob of curious townsfolk at the harbor the next morning. When the group reached the *Firebrand*, Cristof went below to change out of his mask and robes while Taya stayed on top to watch their departure.

"I liked Cabiel," Liliana said, next to her. The girl had bid tearful goodbyes to her new friends the night before, but that didn't stop her from growing teary again as she watched the harbor recede. She wore her best Cabisi dress and a number of the bright bangles her friends had given her as going-away presents. "I felt safe there."

"Are you not safe in Alzana?" Jinian asked, leaning against the rail. She had stepped down from the Impeccable Justiciary before leaving and now wore regular Cabisi garments and jewelry. However, like the *kattaka* in the Pearl Temple, she wore two belts around her waist, one metal and one supporting a long dagger.

"I always had guards and maids wherever I went," Liliana explained. "We always had to be wary of kidnappers and assassins...." She looked at Taya, her expression crumbling.

"Then it is true that the Families in Alzana fight each other without rules?" Jinian asked as Taya squeezed the girl's hand.

"My Family's enemies killed my mother," Liliana said, her voice catching. Jinian's eyes widened. "And my oldest brother, and my grandfather *Il Re*, and I don't know about Silvio and Pietra yet, but...." Her fists clenched on the ship's rail. "Taya and the ambassador rescued me and promised to help me get revenge."

"You are fighting a vendetta right now?" Tu looked astounded.

"Nobody told you?"

"No." Jinian looked at Taya.

"We fled Alzana after the rebels killed the king and framed us for the murder," Taya said, feeling uncomfortable. "We weren't in time to save Liliana's family, but we were able to take her with us when we left."

"Does Xu know about this? Or are you keeping these secrets from the justiciary?"

"Well...." Taya squirmed. "It wasn't a secret from the *justiciary*, exactly. We didn't want the Alzanans to find out their king was dead, so we forbade our crew from discussing it. I suppose we could have mentioned it to the Impeccable Justiciary after the *Indomitable* had fled, but... it didn't occur to us. We were so concerned about getting the *Firebrand* repaired that we forgot you didn't know the whole story."

"I see." Jinian gave her an evaluating look. "Even if that is true, the 'whole story' is now very important to *me*, since I am traveling with you."

"If you don't... we could drop you off at one of the islands...." Taya bit her lip.

"As it happens, I have no objection to helping a foreign princess defeat her enemies. You have my assistance, Liliana, if you wish it."

Liliana nodded, wiping away incipient tears with the back of her hand.

"Thank you, Jin."

"Good." Jinian folded her arms. "Is an Alzanan vendetta nothing but kidnappings and assassinations? I do not care for such tactics."

"Not always. Sometimes there's direct combat when the Families run into each other on the street, or one Family invades another's lands. Other times there might be ambushes." Liliana dropped her gaze from Jinian's expression. "My sister Pietra knows more about vendettas than I do. She's a major in the army."

"Excuse me," Captain Amcathra said, stepping up behind them. "Now that we have left the harbor, I would appreciate it if passengers stayed off the forecastle."

"We were telling Jinian about Liliana's vendetta," Taya explained.

"I am certain that can be done just as effectively on the quarter-deck."

"Are you also one of Liliana's allies, Captain?" Jinian asked.

"I serve the exalted, and I respect his alliances."

"Good. I need somebody to tell me more about our relative strengths and weaknesses compared to the Alzanans." Jinian looked around. "Perhaps we can begin with this ship."

"Icarus..."

"We'd better let the crew get to work," Taya said. "Maybe Captain Amcathra will show us around when he's off duty tonight."

"It would be more efficient to assign a lictor who is off-duty right now to answer your questions." He turned to the nearest crew member. "Tell Sergeant Lucanus to report to our passengers."

"Yes, sir."

"In Cabiel," Jinian said, "we expect our most respected experts and leaders to serve as guides to their facilities. They provide more insightful answers than less experienced employees."

Amcathra's eyes narrowed.

"If you wish, I will be available to answer your questions after dinner, Justiciar Tu."

"I am not serving as a justiciar anymore, Captain. Now I am a *kattaka* again."

"Thank you, Captain," Taya said quickly, leading her friends away before they could try the lictor's patience any further.

"He's always in such a bad mood." Liliana sighed. "I don't think he likes me."

"That's not it," Taya assured her. "He's just busy."

"Are you fond of the captain, Liliana?" Jinian asked. The *principessa* shot her a mortified look and the Cabisi woman laughed.

"I'm *not!*" the girl protested. "I'm worried about my Family and if I'll ever be able to go back home to Alzana— I don't have *any* time to care about some bad-tempered old Demican soldier!"

"Your worries are serious, Liliana, but they are not made less serious by taking the time to admire a man. Your bad-tempered Demican soldier is too pale for my taste, and I do not find Ondinium castemarks attractive, but he is not old and he has a very nice body. I imagine he looks quite handsome naked."

"Jinian!" Liliana was shocked.

Taya burst into laughter.

"For the Lady's sake, don't *ever* let him hear you say that!" she exclaimed. "And don't let the crew hear, either."

"Why not?" Jinian looked puzzled. "Is this another Ondinium taboo?"

"He's the *captain*. He has to maintain his dignity."

"How does admiring a man threaten his dignity? Most men are proud to be admired."

"Excuse me, ladies?" The short but sturdy-looking lictor stood to one side of their small group. "I'm Sergeant Cento Lucanus. I'm here to answer any questions you have about the *Firebrand*?"

"Oh…" Liliana looked flustered.

Lucanus gave them a conspiratorial grin. "And for the record, if you feel like admiring *me*, my dignity won't be threatened at all."

Jinian smiled. "I am glad that not everybody with a black stripe on his face lacks a sense of humor."

"It *is* a caste requirement, but the Great Examination isn't perfect. May I ask whose dignity is at risk of being over-admired?"

"*No*," Taya said, firmly. "But Tu Jinian would appreciate it if you'd give us a quick idea of how well ornithopters stand up to dirigibles in a fight."

"Happy to oblige, Justiciar Tu."

"Just Jin, please. I am not a justiciar now."

Lucanus was well into his explanation when Cristof finally joined them.

"Haven't you heard enough lectures over the last few days?" the exalted asked, sliding an arm around Taya's waist and kissing her hello. "I could have sworn you'd be sick of machines by now."

"Liliana and Jin had questions." She smiled at him. "Amcathra's going to take them on a tour of the ship this evening."

"He didn't say it was going to be a tour," Liliana protested. "Besides, Sergeant Lucanus has told us so much now...."

"Janos is giving a tour? You must have twisted his arm."

Taya nodded to the Cabisi. "Jinian did, diplomatically speaking."

"I am very interested in the ship," Jinian agreed, "but perhaps Liliana prefers to tour it alone with the captain tonight."

"What? No! Wait!" Liliana looked panicked. "I can't talk to him alone!"

"A private tour is much more intimate..."

"No— *Jin!*"

"Very well. I will be a chaperone." Jinian's eyes danced at Liliana's blush. Cristof fixed his skeptical gaze on Taya.

"What is all of this about?"

"Captain Amcathra needs to learn how to socialize with women."

"While he's commanding a ship?"

"He'll be off-duty tonight. And he needs the practice. You know, the only time he ever accepted a social invitation from us was for our wedding, and I don't think he stayed at the reception longer than ten minutes."

Cristof turned to the other two women. "Don't expect much. Janos has a very functional approach to life, and he doesn't consider most conversational topics or leisure activities to be functional. I'm afraid you won't find him very entertaining."

"I've heard him make jokes," Taya objected.

"Very rarely," Cristof retorted. Taya laughed and his smile crooked up as he realized what he'd said. "And I don't think he'll ever work his way up to 'rarely.'"

"There are other ways of getting a soldier's attention," Jinian remarked.

Cristof pushed up his glasses and cast a meaningful glance toward Liliana. "*Age*-appropriate ways?"

"My thoughts involve combat training, but I am suddenly dying to hear *your* thoughts on the best way to draw the captain's attention." Jinian gave the exalted a devilish grin. "Please share them with us."

"Combat training sounds perfectly appropriate to me," Cristof said hastily.

"Tomorrow night I teach you how to fight," Jinian said to the *principessa*. "It is useful to know, and soldiers cannot resist watching somebody else train."

The girl shook her head. "I couldn't."

"It's not a bad idea," Taya encouraged her. "I was taught some basic self-defense when I started working as a courier, but I could use a refresher course. Why don't we learn together?"

"But I wouldn't be … it's not … it's not dignified!"

Which means she doesn't want Amcathra to see her sweating, Taya thought with a sigh.

"There's nothing dignified about being a victim, either." She changed tack. "Your sister knows how to fight, doesn't she? She'll need you to fight by her side if you two are going to defend the Agosti Family from the rebels. You don't expect your little brother to fight for you, do you?"

Liliana swallowed. Taya held her gaze until the girl gave a tiny shake of her head.

"Good. Then we'll train together."

Jinian grinned and turned to Cristof. "You are welcome to join us, Ambassador."

"Me? I thought this was a girls-only conspiracy."

"There is no conspiracy. I wish to help Liliana win her vendetta. If the captain becomes involved in her training as well, that does not make the training any less important. What are your combat talents?"

"Cris is good with his fists and a pistol," Taya volunteered.

"Excellent! I have little experience with firearms," Jinian said. "Will you teach me how to shoot better?"

"I'll consult Janos about it," Cristof said, sighing.

· ❋ ·

Later that evening, Cristof looked up from the notes he'd spread across a table in the mess hall as Taya slid into a chair across from him.

"You're not going on the tour?"

"I'll let the captain handle those two on his own."

"Liliana is too young for him, you know."

"I know. Don't worry— she's just feeling a little hero-worship because he threw a punch for her in that marketplace brawl."

"And Jinian...."

"She says he's not her type."

"I see." He looked at her over the tops of his glasses. "I haven't forgotten that you intend to set him up."

"I keep trying, but he keeps resisting," she said, making a face. "So far all I know for sure is that he pays attention to women's necklines and hem lengths. I *suppose* that means he prefers women. Or at least he likes their dresses."

"Janos isn't interested in men. I worked with him for years, and he never once made a pass at me."

"As if that means anything!" Taya kicked him under the table. "You were an ill-tempered old crow back then."

Cristof raised his eyebrows. "Does that mean I'm not any more?"

"You've gotten better, but *now* you're taken, and I'm sure he wouldn't poach." Taya blew her husband a kiss, then rested her elbows on the table. "So, what are you going to tell the Council?"

"That we're lucky the Cabisi islands have such limited natural resources. If they ever forsake artisanry for mass production, we'll be in trouble." He straightened his notes. "I'm going to suggest we set up an intellectual exchange program like the one with Mareaux. Our manufacturers have grown set in their ways, while Cabiel's engineers are fresh and creative— it comes from having to do more with less, I expect. An exchange might breathe some new life into our old industries."

"If Cabiel's serpentfire cannon doesn't destroy us all, first."

"I'm sure it won't come to that." Cristof looked at her and his expression softened. "Come on, love, don't start brooding about it and upsetting yourself. There's nothing we can do until we're back on the continent."

"I'm not very good at being patient."

"You need a distraction. Jinian's lessons will be good for you."

"They don't start until tomorrow."

"You could catch up with Janos's tour."

"No, thank you."

He cleared his throat.

"We could always go back to our cabin."

"Wh— oh." Taya felt a ridiculous smile creep over her face. "In those little bunks?"

"It'll be more distracting that way."

"Not *too* distracting, I hope." She pushed her chair back and stood. "Let's find out."

Her husband swept his papers into a messy pile and bundled them under one arm, returning her grin.

The next evening, Jinian took Taya and Liliana to the ship's stern and showed them how to defend themselves against knife attacks.

"Last time I was in a knife fight, I was wearing my flight suit," Taya muttered as the short piece of wood Liliana was wielding slashed across her stomach. "*And* my armature."

"Wear them during training, if they are what you usually wear in Ondinium," Jinian advised, watching Taya counter. Taya's shard of wood grazed Liliana's corset as the girl twisted away and struck her wrist. The *principessa* had refused to put on a practical lictor's uniform, although she'd loosened her laces and hiked her skirts to mid-calf.

"Not fair," Taya complained. "Your corset's like armor."

"That's why Family women wear them." Liliana lunged and Taya jumped back, forgetting to redirect the girl's knife arm in her panicked retreat. The "knife" stabbed her in the side.

"Hey!"

"Very good," Jinian said. Liliana blushed and allowed herself a small smile.

Their slashes and stabs quickly drew the attention of the off-duty crew members, just as Jinian had predicted. The lictors gathered around to watch, offering advice and approbation. Jinian asked them what kind of training they'd received and learned that the crew had been trained primarily in hand-to-hand combat, pistol, rifle, and cannon.

"No swords or sabres?" Liliana asked, surprised. "What do you use when you duel?"

"Dueling's illegal in Ondinium," Taya said. "And only lictors and a few citizens with special licenses can carry firearms or a blade longer than a utility knife."

"Your citizens settle all of their personal disputes in the courts?" Jinian asked. "That seems very time-consuming."

"And what do you do about honor and romance?" Liliana added. "Laws don't cover everything!"

"It's not that we never get into fights," the ship's temporary navigator, Lucanus, explained. "But fights aren't duels, and they aren't usually fatal. Ondinium takes murder very seriously."

"You get more armed combat out in the countryside," Mister Pitio mused. "A lot of hunters and camp guards carry rifles...."

"And of course we're allowed to kill in war," Cadet Fidenus chimed in. The rest of the lictors fell silent and Liliana dropped her eyes. The eighteen-year-old cadet blushed. "I mean—"

"War is a matter for soldiers," Jinian said lightly. "I wish to teach my pretty friends here how to fight off men with evil intentions. What do you lictors advise icarii and princesses to do when somebody points a knife at them?"

"Scream."

"Run away."

"The princess could carry a gun and shoot the bastard."

Jinian eventually persuaded the lictors to offer more pragmatic, hand-to-hand solutions and asked them to demonstrate. Soon Taya and Liliana were only one pair in a much larger group as the lictors practiced different ways to avoid, deflect, and control an enemy's knife. Although Taya and Liliana remained paired most of the time, Jinian periodically asked some of the younger, more handsome male lictors to partner with Liliana for a few rounds, "so she can practice against a bigger opponent." The new partners were, to a man, overly cautious about attacking the pretty *principessa*, who crowed with delight every time she avoided their blades. Young Cadet Fidenus seemed to be a particularly inept knife-fighter, perhaps to make amends for his earlier undiplomatic observation.

By the time the sun set, everyone was tired and in good spirits. Taya raked back her hair and saw Cristof and Amcathra standing side-by-side, watching. Jinian spotted them at the same time.

"Will you join us tomorrow, Ambassador?" she asked.

"Thanks, but I prefer to shoot my enemies."

"Your wife says you practice fisticuffs."

"Only in a pinch— and Janos taught me most of what I know."

"Moreover, the exalted has not kept in practice," Amcathra observed.

"Then you must refresh your skills, Ambassador. If Captain Amcathra is your usual instructor, then he must be your sparring partner tomorrow, as well."

"Oh, no." Cristof raised a hand to ward her off, but Amcathra considered the invitation.

"Perhaps more training would be prudent," he said at last. "If the weather holds, we will have a considerable amount of free time before we reach Mareaux, and I purchased a surplus of powder and shot in Os Cansai. Arms and combat drills would be a productive use of the crew's free time."

"Do I get any say in this?" Cristof grumped.

"As you are not one of my crew members, Exalted, you are of course free to squander your time on less useful pursuits."

The exalted scowled.

"My time on board has been very well-spent so far."

"Of course. I would not wish you to embarrass yourself by demonstrating inferior combat skills before your wife and the crew."

Cristof shoved his wire-rimmed glasses higher on the bridge of his nose.

"Are you really lowering yourself to baiting me?"

"Such transparent tactics would never work on the divinely blessed product of a thousand fortuitous rebirths."

"Besides, even if I lose to you at fisticuffs, I'm better with a needler."

"We shall see."

"I look forward to witnessing Ondinium's legendary military prowess," Jinian said, grinning at Taya.

The Firebrands spent the rest of the journey practicing gunnery drills under Captain Amcathra's critical eye, while Jinian offered more relaxed and good-natured hand-to-hand training to anyone who was interested. Every sunset the lictors took scandalized pleasure in watching their captain spar the exalted, although they seemed torn between cheering for their castemate or their social superior. Taya was pleased to see that Cristof held his own, at least in the short term.

"You strike fast and have a longer reach, but a man as big and solid as the captain needs only to defend himself while you tire yourself out," Jinian advised the sweating exalted during a momentary break. "You must take a bigger man out of the fight quickly. Aim for his eyes, throat, solar plexus, groin, and knees. High and low, high and low."

Amcathra nodded with approval and lifted his fists as Cristof gave a weary sigh. In the end, the exalted always lost, but he shook the captain's hand with good humor.

Later, Captain Amcathra gave Jinian and Professor Dautry permission to learn how to load and fire a rifle and needler. Cristof drilled the two women until they were able to maintain a respectable speed of loading, firing, and reloading.

"Not bad," Cristof said, examining the targets. "Professor, with a little more practice, I think you could be better than Janos."

Dautry looked embarrassed, tucking her hair back into its bun. "I used to hunt with my family...."

"I need a secondary helm more than another gunner," Amcathra said, "but it is useful to know that I can call on you to take over a weapon if necessary."

Dautry stiffened. "I'm a scholar, not a soldier, Captain. Participating in your duel was quite enough excitement for me."

Amcathra met and held her gaze.

"You agreed to join the *Firebrand*'s crew."

The professor hesitated, glancing at the lictors working and sparring around her.

"I did," she said, "although I should point out that right now I'm serving without rank or compensation, Captain."

"Are you training a replacement on secondary helm?"

"Yes. Your lictor Bright shows promise."

"Have him in place by next week and resume your old duties."

"As a navigator?" Dautry couldn't quite hide the disappointment in her voice. "Under my old contract?"

Amcathra's eyes narrowed.

"I have no intention of allowing you to renege on our agreement, Dautry. I will formalize and backdate your position as a warrant officer in the ship's log as soon as I return to my cabin this evening. You will find that a ship's navigator is more highly compensated than its secondary helm."

Taya grinned at the professor's startled expression.

"That sounds reasonable," Cristof agreed. "The Council will hate it, but you're right, Professor— it's only fair that we pay you for your service, especially in combat."

"Oh." Dautry blinked, then allowed herself a small half-smile. "A warrant officer on the *Firebrand*. Thank you, Captain. That will do nicely."

"However, in exchange I will expect you to serve in whatever capacity may become necessary," Amcathra warned. "Including gunnery, if we find ourselves short-handed."

"Of course." The professor gave her target a critical look. "Then if you don't mind, I'll continue to practice."

The lookout sighted Mareaux's coast on a gray, drizzly afternoon about halfway through their tenth day out. Two hours later, the *Firebrand* was close enough to shore for its crew to see an Alzanan dirigible rising from the harbor and flying out to meet them.

CHAPTER ELEVEN

"IS IT THE *Indomitable*?" Taya ran to Lieutenant Imbrex, who'd pulled out a set of field glasses. The lieutenant lifted a hand and Taya fell silent, every muscle tense. Behind her, Cristof caught up and laid a hand on her shoulder.

"I don't believe so," Imbrex said at last. "There's no sign of any damage to the ship. The number's difficult to make out at this angle...."

"Ten? The *Indomitable*'s number was ten."

"No. Twelve? Thirteen? The last number isn't a zero."

"Alzana has thirteen ships?"

"More important, what's an Alzanan ship doing in Mareaux's harbor?" Cristof interjected.

"Well, it's left the harbor now," Imbrex said absently. "That's good — there'll be fewer diplomatic consequences if we meet in *aerus liberum*."

Cristof frowned. "Free air?"

"Under imperial law, the boundaries for territorial waters and territorial airspace were identical."

"And now?"

"Nobody updated the law after the empire collapsed. I suppose it never seemed necessary." Imbrex lowered her glasses. "If you will excuse me, Ambassador, I need to consult with the captain."

"Do you think they were waiting for us?" Taya asked her husband as the lieutenant left. The on-again, off-again drizzle started once more, raindrops pattering on the ondium-plated deck.

"It looks like it. I'm sure the Alzanans warned their troops to be on the lookout for us."

Taya leaned on the rail, studying the ship. Cristof's hand slid from her shoulder as he maintained his wary position away from the ship's rail.

"I wonder how the decaturs are explaining the *Firebrand*," she murmured.

"I hope it's causing them all sorts of discomfort."

"They must have known that they couldn't send it into foreign airspace without *somebody* seeing it."

"I expect its mission was a calculated strategy. The Council was probably hoping to reduce enemy morale by demonstrating that Ondinium's skies aren't as unprotected as everyone thought. The fact that the *Firebrand* was seen fleeing Alzana right after the king's assassination was unfortunate, though. I'm sure everybody believes we masterminded the coup."

"Our allies won't approve. What will we do if they abandon us?"

Cristof moved to one side as a lictor hurried past with a stack of ammunition boxes in her arms.

"Not much. Ondinium is reasonably self-sufficient, and other nations need our ores and technologies too much to put us under any long-lasting embargoes. I expect that as long as Ondinium remains intact, its economy can ride out a few years of diplomatic tension. The Council has always valued national security over international relations."

"That doesn't sound very friendly."

"Ondinium has *never* been very friendly, love." Cristof gave her a wry but affectionate smile. "The oldest Houses have never forgotten the lessons of the Last War, and they retain a strong presence on the Council."

"I guess we won't be able to call it the 'Last War' anymore, will we?" Taya's shoulders slumped as she watched the now-familiar burst of pre-combat activity around them.

"Let's hope this conflict never reaches Last War scale." He squared his shoulders and cast a defiant look around the open deck. "I'm going to volunteer for repair duty."

"Good. They'll need you." Taya stood on her toes and kissed him. "I'll put on my armature."

Cristof started to say something, then checked himself. "Be careful."

"Always." She reached into her pocket for the keys and headed below with him.

· ❋ ·

Captain Amcathra surprised them, however, by attempting to outrun the Alzanans. Taya and Jinian stood at the rail next to a deck gun, watching as the two ships maneuvered to take advantage of the wind while staying out of each others' firing range. Amcathra allowed the Alzanan ship to chase them inland, over Mareaux.

"This is my first time visiting the continent," Jinian said, gazing with interest at the patchwork of small agricultural plots and orchards below them, their colors washed out by the rainy weather. "It is as wide as the ocean."

"More people live on it, though." Taya didn't understand why Amcathra was taking them through Mareaux instead of hugging the coast. If a ship crashed here, it would kill everyone aboard *and* devastate the land around the crash site. Alzanan ships, in particular, were prone to fiery explosions that could wipe out miles of good farmland even on a damp, drizzly day like this. And while Taya approved of avoiding a fight, she didn't see how they were going to shake their pursuer. It wasn't as though they could hide over southern Mareaux's flat, rolling fields, and the enemy dirigible had the advantage of being able to fly against the wind.

Nevertheless, the *Firebrand* was maintaining a strong lead against "Number Twelve," as they'd dubbed it. The cook prepared a cold lunch as the chase continued throughout the day, frightening cattle and sheep and startling farmers. One herder lifted a shotgun and fired at them, even though they were well out of range.

"Your husband is unhappy about something," Jinian observed, hours later. Taya turned and spotted Cristof huddled in a long oilskin overcoat and dripping hat, shaking his head and gesturing as he spoke to Captain Amcathra.

"I hope there's nothing wrong with the engine." Taya couldn't imagine much else that would bring Cristof up top in the middle of a rainstorm. She headed toward them, pausing when she reached the forward deck. Captain Amcathra gestured her closer.

"Your wife is here, Exalted. Let us determine her opinion on the subject."

Cristof glowered and irritably tugged his coat collar higher. "Tell him you don't do nightflights, Taya. Especially in the rain."

"I don't usually," she admitted, looking from her husband to Amcathra. "Why?"

"I am planning to board the enemy ship as soon as it grows dark. I would appreciate your assistance in the endeavor."

"You mean— capture it? How?" She'd seen Amcathra capture an Alzanan dirigible during the first invasion, but in that case the *Firebrand* had dropped down from above, unexpected and unseen. They had no such advantage in this fight.

"After it is dark, I would like you to fly up to the enemy's gondola and fasten several climbing ropes to it. My lictors will wear ondium rescue harnesses and climb up the ropes to the ship. If any of my crew should fall, I would like you to retrieve them."

"I can do that," Taya said, firmly. "Just let me know where you want the ropes tied."

"And I'll wait here, as always." Her husband's expression was dark.

"You are our most valuable cargo," Amcathra pointed out.

"Liliana's your most valuable cargo."

"The Alzanan *principessa* may be politically important, Exalted, but I value your life more highly."

"Cris— I'll be all right, and think of how useful it will be to take the crew alive. If they have any idea what happened to the *Indomitable*...."

"I know, I know," he growled. "All right. Do what you need to do, Janos. Just don't expect me to like it."

"I seldom enjoy that expectation, Exalted."

An hour later, Amcathra selected the boarding party: himself and three others.

"I want to go, too," Jinian volunteered, stepping forward. "I am very good at climbing ropes and I have no fear of heights."

"You are not a lictor."

"Your caste encompasses bodyguards and other security forces, does it not? I am the equivalent of a lictor in my own country."

"Neither are you a sharpshooter. A few days of training with the exalted does not make you an expert."

"I can use a needler, and I have more skill in hand-to-hand combat than any of your soldiers. You wish to take the crew alive, do you not?"

"You would be a security risk."

"You do not trust me?"

"You have not been trained—"

"Let her go, Janos," Cristof interrupted. "She's perfectly competent, and — I apologize, Jinian, but I need to speak the captain's language here — she's not a politically significant individual or a trained crew member, which makes her more usefully expendable than you or any of your lictors. Or my *wife*."

Taya winced, but Jinian nodded, unoffended.

"Is that an order, Exalted?" Amcathra inquired.

"If you want to take it that way."

"Very well." He turned to Jinian. "You will ascend last."

"Thank you, Captain. And you, Ambassador."

Later that afternoon, Taya and Jinian stood in the mess hall, keeping dry and sipping tea.

"I don't think Captain Amcathra knows what to do with foreigners like you and Professor Dautry," Taya said. "Ondiniums respect the chain of command, but you two are always disagreeing with him about one thing or another."

The Cabisi woman shrugged.

"He is not my friend or commander, so I have no reason not to argue with him as one equal to another. Besides, it seems clear to me that he enjoys debate. I expect he considers it 'functional' to evaluate the worth of his ideas by the reactions of those around him."

"Maybe...." Taya had never considered arguments 'functional' before.

"Perhaps that is why he chooses to serve your husband, who is not afraid to disagree with him, and seeks to retain a navigator who regards his country with skepticism. He appreciates the challenge of diverse viewpoints."

Taya slowly nodded. She supposed that, for a lictor, debate could be seen as a form of combat training— a way to discover weaknesses and test strengths before split-second decisions were needed. It seemed like an uncomfortably competitive way to live though.

When the sun dropped low on the horizon, Jinian, Cristof, and Taya stood on deck, squinting through the rain.

"Are you sure you want to be up here?" Taya asked her husband, who stood with one hand locked on the rail. "How do you feel?"

"Other than weather aches, vertigo, and an intense fear for your life, I feel just fine."

"Oh, Cris...."

"Would you mind if I held on to you for a while?"

"Of course not." She stood next to him as he laced his fingers through hers.

The rainy day offered no colorful sunset; just a swift plunge into a cloudy and moonless night. Scattered lights on the ground indicated the presence of farmhouses. On deck, lictors stood poised by each of the hanging lanterns. Another lictor made adjustments to the unlit kerosene spotlight next to the ship's raked-back prow.

Amcathra studied Number Twelve, murmuring to Lieutenant Imbrex. Then, at last, he lowered his field glasses.

"Douse lights!"

The lictors sprang forward and the lanterns went out. For a moment there was still a glow of light belowdecks, and then that vanished, too.

Taya grabbed the rail and tightened her grip on her husband's hand a split-second before the *Firebrand* tilted, dropping into a tight, descending spiral.

The lights on the Alzanan ship were still lit, clearly revealing its position above and slightly behind them. Minutes passed as it continued to approach. Suddenly, a bright spotlight snapped on, its piercing beam transforming the light rain into a silvery veil.

"Carbide? No, that would be insane…." Cristof fell silent as Taya hushed him.

The breeze around them changed, and then the creaking of the ornithopter's wings stopped, leaving only the chug of its steam engine. Number Twelve continued motoring forward, its spotlight moving up, then down, to the right and to the left in a limited arc. As the dirigible drew closer, Taya heard movement on the *Firebrand*'s deck. She squeezed Cristof's hand.

"Time to go," she whispered.

"Wait." He found her face with his fingertips and kissed her in the darkness. She gave him a tight, fierce hug before heading to the foredeck.

Number Twelve was almost overhead, the illumination from its gondola and searchlight providing Taya with enough light for her mission. Amcathra handed her three coils of heavy, looped rope with grappling hooks attached to one end. The other end remained loose on the *Firebrand*'s deck. Taya fastened the coils to her armature, bounced up and down, and added another two counterweights to her belt. Captain Amcathra, the other three lictors, and Jinian were busy adjusting their ondium rescue harnesses as Taya finished her check and climbed up onto the rail. With a kick, she was in the air.

Rain streaked her goggles and the dangling ropes threatened to tangle her tailset. *Fly up to the gondola and fasten several climbing ropes to it* was easy for Amcathra to say. Cursing the rain that blinded her, Taya rose behind the dirigible and advanced until she was parallel to the vast expanse of its envelope. When she was confident nobody had seen her, she dropped, keeping pace with the dirigible until she was under the envelope's swell. She kicked up her tailset and let her legs swing down. After a few failed attempts she hooked her boot through the gondola's access ladder, locked her wings, and pulled her arms free. Grabbing a rung with one hand, she loosened the first coil of rope with the other. The noise of Number Twelve's engine and propellers was deafening.

With her flight feathers tapping the envelope over her head and the darkness and rain making it impossible to see more than a foot or two ahead, Taya crept through the supports along the length of the gondola and hooked two of the grapples where their loose ropes wouldn't drag across a window. *So far, so good.* She took a deep breath, uselessly wiped off her goggles with her wet leather sleeve, and clambered down the back of the gondola, her wings buffeted by the wind.

Captain Amcathra had asked her to attach one of the grapples to the flag line and support poles beneath the command gondola, near its trap door. Sweating despite the chilly winter drizzle, Taya swung beneath the gondola, hooking her legs around the braces and struts, and released her grip. Hanging upside down, she swung the grappling hook up. A miss. She tried again. One of the metal tines caught the flag line. She wrapped the line around her wrist, freed her legs and fell, swinging wildly beneath the enemy ship.

The rope pulled tight and the flag line bent. Taya pulled herself up, grabbed the flag line's support pole, and secured the grappling hook around a stronger metal support.

Done. She wrapped her legs around the rope and slid down as she thrust her arms into her wings. With a twist, she kicked the rope aside and let herself fall into the night.

The *Firebrand* was still hidden somewhere in the darkness below, so Taya quickly straightened, afraid that she might end up flattened on the ornithopter's deck. She flew away from the dirigible on a horizontal, turning only when she was sure she was clear of both ships.

Number Twelve's searchlight was her only reference point in the rainy night. Taya strained for a glimpse of the *Firebrand*. There— a glint of reflected light on one of its silver-plated wings. She flew closer until she spotted dark shapes clambering up the ropes.

The first lictor reached the control gondola; that would be Captain Amcathra, who'd chosen the most dangerous entrance for himself. As Taya circled, the other boarders reached the gondola. Two crept over its top to the access ladder leading to the envelope's inner framework. Jinian and a lictor would use that accessway to reach the engine gondola. The other two lictors found secure places to wait, readying their needlers.

The sound of the Alzanan engines changed as Number Twelve began to turn, its searchlight still scanning for the lost *Firebrand*. Taya dropped lower.

Minutes passed like hours. Finally the trap door over the engine gondola opened and two figures lowered themselves onto the top of the gondola.

Taya shot forward, flying as close to the three lictors on the command gondola as she could. As they looked up, startled, she rocked her wings. One of the lictors waved acknowledgement. She turned, returning to the engine gondola and repeating the signal.

Trap doors were thrown open and a heavy boot shattered a gondola window as the Firebrands attacked.

Taya swept around in a tight arc. The engines, the rain, and her leather flying cap made it impossible to hear what was going on inside the Alzanan ship, but she saw that the soldier manning the spotlight had withdrawn. She kicked up her tailset, threw back her wings, and hit the searchlight's metal support bracket boots-first, backbeating to stay aloft. Bracing one foot on the searchlight bracket and the other on the open windowsill, she slid an arm out of her wings to grab the searchlight and peer into the gondola. Heat radiated from the searchlight's metal canister and warmed the side of her face.

Now she could hear the shouting and gunfire. The lictor who'd entered from the top was on the stairs, firing down at the gunners and crew, while Captain Amcathra had rolled into the doorway of the control cabin with a needler in each hand, one pointed out at the crew and the other covering whoever was at the controls. The third lictor had broken through a window and was braced on the outside of the gondola, firing inside.

A stray bullet buried itself in the windowsill close to Taya's shoulder. Folding her wings, she climbed over the hot searchlight to the top of the gondola.

The *Firebrand* was on the move, sweeping forward and rising with all its lanterns lit once more. The ornithopter's gunnery deck was open and lictors manned the deck guns. Taya dangled one leg over the side of the gondola and used her foot to torque the searchlight as high as possible to keep its beam from blinding the *Firebrand*'s crew.

Behind her, Number Twelve's engine coughed and died, its propellers slowing, then coming to a full stop. Jinian leaned out the engine gondola's window and waved.

The Firebrands had taken the dirigible.

"Close your eyes," Taya directed, steadying her husband as he gingerly edged onto the horizontal rope ladder strung between the *Firebrand* and the dirigible's engine gondola. Inside the gondola, Jinian and the *Firebrand*'s chief engineer reached out and took Cristof's arms from her, steadying him until he was inside. He opened his eyes with a sigh of relief and gave her a grateful wave.

The *Firebrand*'s wings were docked as the ship floated next to the *Resolute*, secured to it with a network of ropes and grappling hooks. Lictors swung back and forth between the ships, scavenging the Alzanan vessel's weapons, fuel, and supplies. The surviving captives — eight of the ship's ten crew members — were being questioned by Captain Amcathra, with Liliana's assistance.

The *Firebrand*'s boarding party had escaped relatively unscathed; one lictor had sprained an ankle in her leap through the trap door and Amcathra had taken a bullet graze across his ribs, but the others bore only minor cuts, scrapes, and burns. The Alzanans, caught by surprise, had been quickly demoralized after the first soldier had been killed, and when their engines had sputtered out, they'd surrendered with weary resignation. Much to Amcathra's annoyance, the *Resolute*'s captain had promptly put a bullet through his head rather than fall into enemy hands.

Seeing that her husband was safe, Taya joined the chain of crew members passing goods from the Alzanan ship to the *Firebrand*'s deck. She was tired and the rain hadn't stopped, but nobody was going to get any sleep that night. Amcathra wanted the captured vessel stripped and destroyed by dawn.

At last there was nothing left in the command gondola worth keeping; they'd even pried off the searchlight and hauled it back to the *Firebrand* for inspection. Lieutenant Imbrex and the quartermaster began inventorying the pile of loot, evaluating each item's weight against its utility.

"Lieutenant Imbrex wants to know how much of this we need to take with us," Taya said, returning to the group inside the Alzanan engine room.

"All of it," Cristof said, looking up with shining eyes. "Can we bring the entire engine on board?"

"We don't have enough counterweight," the chief engineer said, reluctantly.

"Nonsense. If this flimsy bag of gas can carry it *and* the steam cannon—"

"We can't do it, Exalted, not without losing something of equal weight. The captain won't want to pitch his new Cabisi cannon overboard."

Cristof scowled.

"Ondinium already has a dirigible engine to study," Taya pointed out.

"But this engine would be *mine*," he said, plaintively.

Taya laughed.

"You don't understand— it's *electromagnetic*. Ondinium doesn't even manufacture electromagnetic engines yet!"

"We manufacture them in Cabiel," Jinian said from the corner, where she had perched on a tool chest. "But this one is ugly, so it must have been built in Alzana."

"More second-hand technology," the engineer said with a dismissive snort. "Figures. The Alzanans couldn't invent their way out of a burlap sack."

"Well...." Cristof straightened, the top of his head almost brushing the gondola's ceiling. "If we can't take the engine, what *can* we take?"

Taya and Jinian carried the designated plunder to Lieutenant Imbrex, who would make the final decision. By the time Taya returned, Cristof had already crossed the ladder to the *Firebrand*.

He looked pleased with himself as he unbuckled his ondium rescue harness and handed it to the chief engineer to take below. "Next thing you know, you'll be asking for your own armature," she teased him. He smiled, then reached out and pulled her in for a hug.

"I guess Janos was right about taking the ship," he whispered in her ear. "But don't tell him I said so."

"I wouldn't dream of it." She closed her eyes, leaning on him. "I'm exhausted."

"Why don't you go below and take a nap?"

"No point in trying to sleep before they blow up the ship." She sighed. "It's too bad we can't keep it. Destroying it seems like such a waste of resources."

"Believe me, I'd like nothing more than to paint an Ondinium warflag over the gryphon-and-bear and fly it to the Alzanan border. But we don't have enough lictors to crew it, and the ridiculous things burn up too easily, anyway."

Taya nodded, still leaning against him, already half-asleep.

"Oh, look, they dismantled the searchlight— was it carbide, after all?" Cristof perked up, looking over her shoulder. With a groan, Taya pushed herself away.

"I can't imagine why anybody would take such a risk, but...." He nudged up his glasses and made a beeline for the piece of equipment. Taya sighed and wondered if the cook had prepared any tea.

Chapter Twelve

THE SKY WAS starting to brighten when the gutted *Resolute* was towed over a lake and long, crackling fuses were lit. The *Firebrand* sped away as the lictors stood on deck counting in unison. When the bombs exploded and the giant envelope burst into a ball of billowing fire, they gave a ragged cheer. Burning detritus showered across the lake, hitting the surface with a hiss of steam.

Taya leaned on the *Firebrand*'s rail with a borrowed set of field glasses, watching. She couldn't guess how badly the burning dirigible would pollute the lake, but she didn't think it was going to be a high point in Ondinium/Mareaux diplomatic relations.

Still, she was relieved that Alzana had one less ship to pit against Ondinium. And she couldn't blame her crew-mates too much for cheering— they'd worked all night in the rain and were scraping by on little more than strong tea and willpower.

Once the *Resolute* was nothing more than hissing steam and bobbing scrap, every lictor who was off-duty stumbled below to catch a few hours of sleep.

Taya headed to the mess hall, where Captain Amcathra had called a meeting.

"It has been over a month since we fled Alzana," Amcathra stated after everyone had settled down. Cristof, Lieutenant Imbrex, Professor Dautry, and Liliana had joined them. The *principessa*'s eyes were red, and Taya had a bad feeling about what the captain was about to say. "According to the Resolutes, Alzana has stated that Exalted Forlore and his staff came to the palace under the pretense of negotiating for peace in order to assassinate the royal family. The ambassador and his icarus shot and killed *Il Re*, his daughter, and his grandson, and kidnapped his youngest granddaughter as a hostage. Meanwhile, Ondinium's lictors broke into the royal family's wing of the palace while they were dressing for dinner and went from room to room, killing everyone."

"No…" Taya reached across the table to grip Liliana's hand, stricken. The girl clenched her fist, her shoulders tight with grief, but didn't move her hand aside.

"Two members of the immediate royal family survived the attack," Amcathra continued. "*Principe* Silvio was shot in the arm but escaped through a secret panel and *Principessa* Pietra was with her army unit in another part of the country. Most Alzanans assume we have killed *Principessa* Liliana. One of their major newspapers is offering a reward to anyone who finds her body and brings it back to the palace for burial."

"What did they say when they found out who you were?" Taya asked, her heart aching for the girl.

"They think you're forcing me to help you," Liliana whispered.

"What about our staff?" Cristof asked.

"*Principe* Silvio stated that his attackers wore black uniforms and caste stripes," Amcathra said, his expression stony. "Our staff was promptly arrested and the lictors executed. The crew said that when they left Alzana, about two weeks ago, the non-lictate staff members were still alive."

Taya released Liliana's hand to rub her eyes, feeling utterly exhausted.

"Is the prince an accomplice, or does he really think he saw lictors killing his family?" Cristof asked, looking from Amcathra to Liliana. "How old is he?"

"Fourteen," Liliana whispered.

"The rebels who attacked us were also wearing black uniforms and painted stripes," Captain Amcathra pointed out.

"True, but that doesn't mean he wasn't in on the conspiracy. I'm sorry, Janos, but we've already seen how easily the Mazzolettis can turn idealistic young men against the people who trust them."

"Silvio wouldn't be the next king, though, Exalted." Lieutenant Imbrex seemed unaware of the sudden tension around the table. "His older sister Pietra is first in line to inherit."

"Yes," Liliana said. She swallowed. "She is now the acting queen, although the Resolutes said she's still in the field."

"Doesn't she need to go back to the capital to take the throne?" Taya asked.

"Not during a war. We're not— Alzanan rulers *lead* their armies. They don't stay at home giving orders. Pietra probably swore a vendetta against your country." Liliana sounded despondent. "She won't rest until she's avenged our Family."

"Then we need to take you to her as soon as we can," Taya said. "She needs to know that we aren't her enemies."

"Did we learn anything else?" Cristof asked. Amcathra nodded.

"Yes. Alzana has spread the news that Ondinium has a secret military aerial force. They claim that we had been mobilizing a secret fleet against them and that their invasion from Demicus was intended as a pre-emptive strike."

"Ridiculous," Cristof scoffed.

"The accusation has widely discredited Ondinium's claims of innocence. Demicus and Alzana have already invaded Ondinium to little international criticism. Foreign observers have reported seeing ornithopters patrolling Ondinium's borders, which has apparently given more credence to the secret fleet story."

"Invaded— how far are they?"

"Unknown."

"So Ondinium's ornithopters are public now," Dautry mused. "I hope that means we won't be executed for flying openly into Os Cansai."

"We didn't have any choice," Lieutenant Imbrex countered.

"Finally," Amcathra said, shooting the two a quelling look, "the prisoners said that Queen Iancais is allowing Alzana to move military materiel, troops, and vessels across Mareaux's borders. She has censured Ondinium's actions against Alzana and set up aerostat and balloon patrols throughout the country."

"But— we'd never attack Mareaux!" Taya felt a surge of indignation. "She knows that! We were just there!"

"And we told her in good faith that Ondinium was concerned about Mareaux's aerostats because it believed in war-free skies," Cristof said, heavily. "What is she supposed to believe now? For all she knows, everything we said during our visit was a lie."

"But I *promised*." Taya pushed her chair back. "I promised that constable — Chief Inspector Gifford, remember? — I *promised* him Ondinium wasn't going to war with Mareaux!"

"And we won't," Cristof said, soothingly. "Taya, the queen's patrols can look both ways. She's protecting herself from Ondinium *and* Alzana. It's a prudent move, under the circumstances."

"The Council turned us into liars!"

"It didn't—"

"It manipulated you into becoming an ambassador, it lied to everybody about having aerial ships, it put us under a death penalty if we said anything about them, and then it sent us on a diplomatic mission it knew we would fail!" Taya stood, her nerves frayed from exhaustion and stress. Amcathra started to say something and she turned on him. "And *you* knew all about these ships when we were in Mareaux! You'd already *trained* on them, and you still let us babble away about the importance of ethical warfare and weapons-free skies!"

Amcathra fell silent.

"Taya!" Cristof stood and grabbed her arms. "I'm not going to defend the Council's actions, but this outburst isn't helping."

"I *trusted* them!"

"I know." He gently pulled her toward him. She resisted a moment, still angry, but he looked so unhappy that she finally gave in and leaned her head against his chest. "I know you did. I'm sorry."

She took a deep breath, feeling his arms wrapping protectively around her. He was right. She needed to calm down. But the news about their staff, about Liliana's family, about the tension between Mareaux and Ondinium— it was too much. She felt betrayed on all sides.

No, not quite all sides. Cristof had never trusted the Council, even in the days when she had. He'd always done his best to protect her from it. And Captain Amcathra would never betray them, even if he was bound by duty to keep the Council's dirty secrets. His scrupulous sense of honor angered and frustrated her, but it had also saved her life, and Cristof's, more than once.

At last she pushed away, nodding to indicate that she was feeling better. She wiped her eyes with her shirt cuff.

"I'm sorry," she said, taking another deep breath and sitting down. "I apologize, Captain. I didn't mean it. I'm just— I'm just *angry*. I'm angry for all of us and the situation we're in."

"Understood," Amcathra said, without rancor.

"It's understandable that we're tired and upset." Lieutenant Imbrex looked around the table. "But to make matters worse, we had to run with the wind to stay ahead of the *Resolute*, which means we're farther west than we'd intended. We need to get to the border as soon as possible, but we can't cross Mareaux by day without being seen. On the other hand, there isn't anyplace to hide in the middle of all this flat farmland. We can't simply anchor the *Firebrand* behind someone's barn and hope they don't notice."

"And in the meantime, our presence in Mareaux airspace can be considered an act of war," Cristof filled in, wearily. "I'm sure the Alzanans will be happy to use that fact against us."

"Yes," Amcathra agreed. "They have already alerted Mareaux to expect our presence. The *Resolute* had heard that we might be returning to the continent from the *Indomitable*, which crossed their path a few days before. The *Indomitable* continued to Alzana while the *Resolute* diverted to Mareaux to warn the queen and patrol the coast."

"Do we know whether our warning about the serpentfire cannon got through?" Cristof asked.

"The Resolutes knew nothing about it. However, if Mareaux is no longer our ally, its authorities may have intercepted and blocked the message at any point."

"Then we have no choice." Cristof sounded grim. "We need to fly across Mareaux as quickly as possible."

"Our path will be noted," Amcathra warned. "Mareaux will undoubtedly gather its ground and air forces along the border to stop us from crossing."

Taya closed her eyes, visualizing a map of the continent. Mountains formed a natural, protective border around Ondinium on almost all sides. When the empire had collapsed, Ondinium had been driven back to its most defensible core.

"What if we cut west, where the Mareaux wouldn't expect us to go, and approached Ondinium from Samaras?" she suggested.

Professor Dautry shook her head. "I'm not certain we have enough fuel to get to the Mareaux border, much less Tizier or Samaras. We *could* shave a day or two from the journey if you're willing to cross over Alzana, however."

"Sounds dangerous," Cristof said. "But if we install the *Resolute*'s steam cannon, we should be able to fight off most Alzanan dirigibles, at least one-on-one."

"However, we will be traveling through Alzanan mountain territory," Amcathra reminded him. "It is difficult to dodge a mortar or cannon in a narrow pass."

"We'll just have to hope that the Alzanans never spent as much time studying aerial warfare and tactics as you did, Janos."

"What about me?" Liliana asked, tensely. "If you dropped me off in Alzana, I could send a message to my sister."

"We shall have to see if the opportunity arises, *Principessa*. In the meantime, it would be useful if you would continue to try to convince the Resolutes of the truth."

"What *is* the truth? Am I really free to go, or are you planning to keep me as your hostage?"

The lictor turned to Cristof, and Taya saw a flash of disappointment in Liliana's expression. *That's that*, she reflected. *He's just lost her affection.* Liliana wanted a dashing hero who would defy all odds to protect her, not a methodical soldier who respected hierarchy and put duty before emotion.

"Of course you're not a hostage," Cristof said. "We're allies, and as soon as we warn Ondinium about those damn cannon, I promise that we'll turn our attention to putting the Agostis back on the throne."

"But you won't let me go until then."

Cristof gave the girl a sharp look over the frames of his glasses.

"Your safety is of paramount importance to us, Liliana. You are very likely the only person who can stop this war without bloodshed. Forgive us if we want to keep you out of the hands of your — of *our* — enemies as long as possible."

Liliana held his gaze a moment, then sighed and slumped back into her chair.

"And forgive me if I just want to go home again," she said softly. "I just want to go home."

The *Firebrand* sped across Mareaux's skies as fast as the wind and its wings could carry it, flying one thousand to three thousand feet from the ground. Several times its lookout spotted what could have been reconnaissance balloons floating next to military encampments and the ornithopter veered to avoid them. The captain had agreed to the shorter Mareaux-Alzana-Ondinium route in an attempt to conserve fuel, and now everybody was preparing for war.

Liliana was taking Jinian's hand-to-hand training seriously now. Grief, Taya thought, and fear, and anger. The girl had been able to push her problems aside in Cabiel, but now the reality of her situation was sinking in.

Jinian had, in turn, asked for more pistol and rifle lessons. Professor Dautry joined her whenever she was off-duty, quietly intent on beating Captain Amcathra's scores in what had become a nightly shooting competition between the captain, Cristof, Jinian, and Dautry.

When he wasn't overseeing shooting lessons, Cristof helped the ship's chief engineer mount the *Resolute*'s steam cannon into the *Firebrand*'s gun deck, an experiment that had Lieutenant Imbrex and the quartermaster fretting about weight and recoil and the rest of the lictors enthusiastically shifting the other cannon around to compensate. Captain Amcathra insisted on testing it, a noisy endeavor that resulted in the destruction of a small copse of trees on a hillside. The lictor seemed pleased, although Taya didn't think it would do anything to enhance future Mareaux-Ondinium diplomatic relations, either.

Taya was practicing her own knife-fighting drills one evening when Cadet Fidenus asked Jinian to show him some Cabisi fighting techniques.

"Fighting with a knife *is* a Cabisi technique."

"But it's not much different from how we fight in Ondinium," Fidenus protested.

Jinian grinned. "There is only so much a human can do with two hands, two feet, and one head."

"Well, Alzanans use sabres, and Ondiniums don't...."

"Oh, you want different *weapons*." She rested a hand on her metal belt. "Are you familiar with the whip sword?"

"No." Fidenus perked up. "What is it?"

The other lictors paused and Liliana lowered her knife as Jinian shook out her belt into a long, flexible metal strip.

"That's a sword?" Liliana looked skeptical. "How can you stab someone with *that*?"

"It does not stab." Jinian walked to an open spot on deck and glanced down. "I do not wish to scuff these nice designs...."

"Ondium's hard," the lictor Pitio said. "You can't hurt it."

"You are certain?"

A chorus of agreement urged her on, so Jinian shrugged and began to swing the blade around her, gaining speed until the sword was a blur of moving metal shifting from side to side and front to back, raising sparks as its tip struck the deck and the rails. Taya held her breath, watching the *kattaka* swivel and leap, deflecting unseen blows and swinging the whip over her head and under her feet. At last Jinian spun and wrapped the whip around the muzzle of the nearest deck gun, yanking the muzzle downward as she ended on one knee, panting, her dark skin shining with sweat.

Applause filled the air. Jinian stood with an abashed smile, shaking her sword loose from the gun and wiping her face with her forearm. She was immediately swamped by lictors who passed the flexible sword from hand to hand, peppering her with questions. Taya grinned as her husband pressed forward, holding the weapon close to his spectacles as he flexed it back and forth.

"Interesting. I don't suppose you know how it's made?" he asked Jinian.

"I am sorry, Ambassador. I do not."

"You might be able to make one out of ondium," Taya suggested. "The primary feathers on my wings are almost that flexible."

"True, but it would be prohibitively expensive. I'd rather figure out how Cabiel manufactured a strip of metal that flexible out of steel...."

"Gearhead."

"Well, I'll need *something* to do after the Council fires me. I've been thinking about that Dancer statue, too. I could build programmed automata like that. Smaller, of course. And more practical. What do you think?"

"I think it's too early to worry about a career change," Taya said, twining her fingers through his. She didn't add the rest of her thought: *We have too many other things to worry about, first.*

Lieutenant Imbrex developed a new set of frown lines as she checked and rechecked the *Firebrand*'s fuel consumption and tried to convince the captain to jettison the ship's cannon and ammunition, an option he refused to entertain. He did, however, abandon their Alzanan captives in the middle of a rolling vineyard, agreeing that they were an unnecessary tax on the ship's resources. Taya thanked him for his mercy, suspecting that if Amcathra had been on his own, he would have simply shot them and thrown them overboard. Cristof helped the chief engineer monitor the ship's engine and brainstorm ways to eke out a few more miles, from rearranging the ship's stowage to adjusting the wings' tilt. Professor Dautry kept a close eye on her maps and the horizon, making sure they didn't deviate from their carefully plotted route.

Their new course would take them out of Mareaux and over Alzana for two days before they reached Ondinium. Their goal was the Alzana-Ondinium Terminal station. After the initial Alzanan invasion, both nations had closed down their rail lines and evacuated their support personnel and citizens, leaving only two heavily armed military camps to glare at each other over newly constructed barriers. With luck, the Ondinium troops would be able to cover the *Firebrand* as it swept over the Alzanan encampment. But whether they could reach A-O station would depend on their fuel reserves, the prevailing winds, and the Alzanans' military preparation.

The crew gathered on the *Firebrand*'s deck when it finally reached the Mareaux-Alzana border. Even the cook abandoned the mess hall's observation window to get a 360-degree view up top. The flat, rolling agricultural plains of southern and central Mareaux had gradually turned into higher terrain over the last few days, and as they neared the northern border the hills had grown steeper and more thickly forested, with rising mountain passes visible in the distance.

Signs of a military presence had also increased as they'd neared the border— they'd seen more encampments, more trains carrying covered loads, and more armed patrols. Now the *Firebrand* sped over the forested land dividing the two countries as a group of red-coated Mareaux soldiers bivouacking around a farmhouse took wild shots at the ship.

"We're in Alzana now, Captain," Dautry announced, less than an hour later. She pointed to a winding river that gleamed silver in the early afternoon light. "That's our landmark."

"Thank you, Dautry." Amcathra's tone was dry, perhaps because of the telltale group of blue-coated Alzanan soldiers camped on the border beside the river. The *Firebrand* swept over them as they scrambled for their weapons. He looked around at the lictors leaning over the rails. "Does nobody here have any work to do?"

The lictors hurried back to their stations.

That evening, as they drew closer to the mountains, Lieutenant Imbrex reported that their fuel situation was grave. The winds over the last three days hadn't been as steady and strong as she'd hoped.

"We're going to end up stalled on the wrong side of the border," she warned, as if she hadn't been fretting about the same thing since they'd fought the *Resolute.* "Unless the wind suddenly picks up, we'll soon be dead in the air."

"Strip the ship of as much excess as you can," Amcathra ordered. "Burn anything that can be used as fuel."

"That won't buy us more than a few hours."

"Hours are miles, Lieutenant."

"Can we sail on wind alone?" Cristof asked.

"A few imperial captains were said to have rigged their vessels for emergency sail," Amcathra said, "but we have no masts or sails in the hold, and neither I nor my crew know how to rig a ship."

"What if you just raised the wings like sails?" Taya inquired.

"We would have extremely limited maneuverability."

"So what do we do if we stall?"

"We evacuate, destroy the ship, and proceed on foot."

Taya opened her mouth to object, then closed it again. Of *course* the Council had ordered Amcathra to destroy this beautiful, remarkable ancient artifact instead of letting it fall into Alzanan hands.

"How many ornithopters do we have?" Cristof asked.

"I do not know." Amcathra hesitated. "Perhaps many. The access tunnels beneath Ondinium are extensive, and I believe a great deal of imperial technology was hidden within them during the Reclamation. However, the more relevant question is how many lictors have been trained to fly an ornithopter. I believe there are only thirty or forty of us, and at least half of that number were assigned to this ship."

"While the Alzanans have at least twelve dirigibles."

"Of which at least five have been destroyed and one captured."

"We only destroyed three in the invasion," Taya objected. "And the *Resolute.* That's four."

"One of the invading dirigibles was forced to descend. It was too damaged to repair, so the crew burned it."

"Either way," Cristof said, "we can't spare the *Firebrand.*"

"I have no choice, Exalted. We must destroy the ship if it runs out of fuel. Lieutenant, would you please attend to making that occurrence as unlikely as possible?"

"Yes, Captain." Imbrex looked unhappy as she left.

Cristof waited until they were alone in the mess hall before sighing and pulling off his glasses.

"What is it?" Taya asked, resting a hand on his shoulder. "Are you worried about losing the ship?"

"I'd hate to see such a magnificent machine destroyed," he said, studying his lenses with a frown, "but I'm more worried about how the loss will affect Janos's career. What a slagging disaster all of this has been!"

"The Council can't be too hard on him— he's done everything he can to get us back to Ondinium."

"I know. Taya, would you hate me if I retired?"

"Retired… as ambassador?"

"Yes." He looked up, sliding his glasses back on. "If the Council doesn't fire me, first."

"This isn't your fault."

"I don't know about that," he said, wearily. "I can barely sleep at night anymore, wondering what I should have done differently."

Taya brushed his long hair back over his shoulder. Not for the first time, she noticed the new worry lines and scars that creased his sharp-featured face.

"I feel like I haven't done a thing to help Ondinium since I left my old shop," he continued. "I was more useful as a clockwright than I am as an exalted."

"You're a very good clockwright," she murmured, her heart aching for him. "But you're an excellent exalted, too. And you *did* help Ondinium— you tracked those illegal shipments to Demicus and helped stop the invasion."

"You were more instrumental in all that than I was."

She shook her head.

"You're the one who made the plans, who convinced me to stick with the investigation to the end, who identified the steam cannon parts, and who told me everything about the ships that I reported back to Ondinium. And you let yourself get captured so I could escape. We're a *team*, Cris. You're the one who thinks things through and figures out what's going on— I'm the one who runs the messages back and forth."

"You do a lot more than that." But his lips quirked up, just a bit. "Do you still want to be a diplomatic envoy after all of this?"

"I think I'll *have* to be, after all this," she said, seriously. "You're right. This *is* a disaster. It's not *our* disaster, but we got caught up in it, and we'll have to deal with the aftermath. Just because the decaturs are a bunch of bastards doesn't mean we don't have a responsibility to Ondinium."

The quirk became a crooked smile.

"Does that mean you aren't going to let me quit?"

She studied his face, trying to decide if his self-mocking tone indicated bitterness or amusement.

"I'll support you either way," she said at last. "But will you wait until we're back in Ondinium to decide?"

He sighed and pressed her hand against his scarred cheek a moment.

"Of course," he agreed. "We'll talk about it again when we get home."

The rest of his sentence — *if we get home* — hung unspoken between them.

CHAPTER THIRTEEN

THE FIRST EXPLOSION hit the *Firebrand* directly under its starboard wing, sending the entire ship spinning wildly. Its juddering roll knocked everyone off their feet and sent one screaming crew member overboard.

Taya, who was below dismantling the ship's interior for firewood, was thrown against the hull and sent sprawling; the hatchet flew from her hand. Broken furniture and splintered planks pelted her as she curled into a ball, protecting her head. Flashbacks from the train crash made her heart hammer with fear.

"Cris!" Her panicked shout was lost in the shrieking of strained mechanisms, the thumping of the steam engine, and the alarmed voices of the crew. "Cris, where are you?"

She uncurled and staggered to her feet. A second mortar hit the ship with a cacophony of bending metal and splintering wood. The ship shuddered again. A thundering rumble shook the floor as the *Firebrand*'s gunnery deck opened.

"Taya!" Cristof appeared in the doorway. She pulled herself up and they met in the center of the tiny cabin, clutching each other as much for balance as relief. "Are you all right?"

"I'm fine," she said, unconcerned about her bruises and sore wrist. "You?"

"I think—"

Staccato gunfire cut him off— the *Firebrand* was returning fire. They plunged out the door, pressing close to the half-demolished wall as lictors ran to their stations.

"Where's the ship?" Taya shouted, raising her voice over the clamor.

"Don't know," one of the lictors shouted back as he scrambled up a ladder.

The *Firebrand*'s steam cannon boomed and the mountainsides and valley below tilted as the ornithopter struggled to maintain its equilibrium.

"I'm going up to go help the engineers," Cristof said, visibly bracing himself. Taya nodded, following him.

The top deck was chaos as the primary and secondary helms fought to steady the ship and repair teams swarmed over the starboard wing mount. Captain Amcathra and Lieutenant Imbrex were shouting orders and lictors manned the volley guns, firing them downward at a steep angle. Jinian and Liliana were on one, too, the *kattaka* firing and the *principessa* struggling to reload the extra breech block. Taya searched the skies but didn't see any sign of a dirigible. A moment later she realized why the guns were pointed down— their attackers were Alzanan infantry bivouacked in the mountain pass. Once she knew where to look, she saw soldiers moving on the mountainside and puffs of smoke rising as their cannon and mortars fired.

Cristof joined the wing mount crew, nearly falling as the ship was jolted upward by another blast. Taya threw open the nearest rescue harness chest and yanked one of the harnesses off its restraining cable. She grabbed a lead-filled weight belt and slammed the chest shut.

"Cris!" He was unscrewing the protective metal skin over the wing servomechanism. She dropped to her knees next to him. "Put this on."

"What?" He gave her a distracted look, then blinked as she thrust the harness at him. "I don't—"

"Yes, you do," she said firmly. "When you're on deck during a firefight, you do. You're an *exalted*."

"Then you should wear your wings," he complained, sliding his arms through the harness and then leaning over to work again. Exasperated, Taya reached around him to snap the chest straps closed, then wrapped the lead belt around his waist and buckled it. "Taya, would you please—"

A second mortar hit the stern. Metal shrieked and crumpled, the ornithopter pitching sharply forward. Cristof grabbed Taya as she tumbled backward and they both clutched the wing mount. Screams filled the air and gears gave off horrible metallic grating sounds, stripping their metal teeth before freezing. The ship's engineer swore as he tried to cling to the wing-mount with one hand. At last he dropped his wrench. It clattered away from him as he used both hands to grip the mechanism.

Another mortar slammed into the ship, shaking it.

Holding on tightly to avoid sliding down the steeply tilted deck like the engineer's wrench, Taya looked up. The ornithopter's broken tailrudder floated vertically over the ship, still attached by a few strained wooden struts. Captain Amcathra bellowed orders and shouts answered from the primary and secondary helms, but the *Firebrand*'s port wing kept moving, pulling the ship down toward the ground.

The steam cannon gave another roar, jolting the ship. At least one lictor intended to fight until the end.

"Taya..." Cristof was breathing hard, his eyes wide as he looked down the length of the deck to the ground far below.

"You'll be all right," she reminded him. "You're counter-weighted. If you fall overboard, you'll float to the ground. If you think you're descending too fast, just drop a lead weight out of your belt."

He swallowed.

"I think," he said, shakily, "that this would be a good time for me to apologize for objecting to a rescue harness."

"Apology accepted."

The wings and demiwings stopped moving as the helms resumed control. The *Firebrand* rocked back a little from its previous sharp pitch, but not enough for Taya to want to try standing. Someone shouted the captain's name. Both she and Cris looked up to see Captain Amcathra pulling himself hand-over-hand up the rail toward the floating rudder.

Cristof swore under his breath. "I should go help him."

"No!" The thought of her awkward husband trying to follow Amcathra's lead made Taya's heart rise in her throat. "He'll be fine."

"He's not wearing a harness."

"He knows what he's doing." *And he won't seize with panic if he looks over the edge.*

Around them, lictors were struggling to get back to their stations, but few were in any position to succeed. Taya heard distant gunfire—the Alzanans were shooting at them, but nobody on board could shoot back except the lictor manning the steam cannon. Taya could only imagine that the cannon had a perfect shot toward the ground now.

Amcathra reached the empennage and straddled what little of the tail assembly remained intact. Moving carefully, he grabbed the twisted wooden strut that still held the floating rudder in place. Holding it with one hand, he pulled out his boot dagger with the other and began hacking at the splintering wood.

Another shot hit the *Firebrand*. A lictor screamed and Taya jerked her head around, but the receding sound of his horrified wail told her what had happened. Her fingers tightened on the wing mount as she prayed for him.

Amcathra gouged and chopped at the wood until, with an aching creak, it gave way. The broken rudder snapped up into the sky and the *Firebrand*'s deck dropped, roughly level again.

Everybody scrambled to their feet. The helms shouted to each other, but only the port wing began moving. Cristof spun and began working on the starboard wing with the chief engineer. Lieutenant Imbrex ran to the hatch, ordering the crew to cast off all excess weight. Professor Dautry secured her navigational instruments and followed the lieutenant below. Captain Amcathra was climbing back on deck and a very pale Liliana was dashing tears from her eyes as she leaned against the volley gun she'd been clutching. Jinian began checking the wounded.

Guns fired, and the steam cannon went off once more, even though it must have lost its ground target when the ornithopter had stabilized.

"Are you all right?" Taya asked, hurrying to Liliana's side. The *principessa* nodded, looking sick and shaken. Several feet away, the deck had been torn apart by the attack, its broken railing dangling from a few ondium plates that hadn't wrenched loose yet.

"I just— we were hit, and Cadet Fidenus was thrown off the side," she said, fresh tears welling in her eyes. "And Mister Pitio was shot— I think he's dead!"

Taya crouched and put an arm around her, heartbroken as she saw Amcathra straighten up over the signaler's body and shake his head.

"I'm sorry," she said, uselessly. "I'm sorry."

Both wings started moving again. The *Firebrand* flew unsteadily away from the battle, its course angling badly to starboard as that wing periodically stuttered and seized.

"Wait here." Taya crossed the deck and pulled out another rescue harness, carrying it and a weight belt back to Liliana. "Put these on."

Liliana's hands shook as she buckled the harness and fastened the belt around her waist. They worked to the sound of receding gunfire.

"Don't take off the belt," Taya warned, yanking on the harness. It had been counterweighted for an adult lictor, not a slight sixteen-year-old girl. If Liliana removed the belt, she'd be blown away in a gust of wind. "This will keep you safe if you go overboard."

Jinian returned.

"I'm going below to help Lieutenant Imbrex," Taya told her.

"Go," Jinian said, dropping a hand on Liliana's shoulder. "We are safe."

Taya smelled smoke as she climbed down the ladder to the gunnery deck.

"Lieutenant Imbrex? Professor Dautry?"

Two lictors were trying to put out a fire by one of the cannon, scooping water from the ballast tank into a bucket and running across the deck to douse the flames. As Taya's boots hit the deck, she saw Lieutenant Imbrex and Professor Dautry heaving a cannon through the open firing bay. It tilted and dropped out of sight.

Two lictors— less than half of the gunnery crew. Taya wondered where the other three had gone. She glanced fearfully at the open bay.

"What can I do?" she asked, dragging her eyes away from the empty sky. Imbrex pointed to the steam cannon, now silent.

"Cut the ropes and heave it overboard," she ordered. "Watch the barrel— it's hot."

"Oh, the captain's going to hate that," Dautry said.

"He can dock the replacement cost from my slagging salary," Imbrex growled, shoving a case of shot overboard. "Assuming any of us live to pick up our next paycheck."

Taya looked around for something to use on the thick cables and remembered the hatchet she'd dropped one deck above. She had picked it up and was heading back down when the ship jolted again. A second later something exploded overhead. The cries and screams made Taya change her mind and scramble to the top deck, her heart in her mouth as she searched for her husband.

Cristof was kneeling on the deck, turning over a fallen lictor. Black, oily black smoke rolled from the ship's engine. Taya hesitated, torn. She wanted to help Cristof, but if the engine was dying, they needed to jettison all the excess weight they could.

She searched the deck, saw that Jinian and Liliana were all right, and raced back down to gunnery.

"The engine's been damaged," she shouted.

"Throw *all* the cannon and shot over," Imbrex ordered, spinning and heading up the ladder. The fire had been put out, so Taya started using her hatchet on the cables while the other crew members discarded the shot. They were shoving the giant steam cannon overboard when Lieutenant Imbrex came flying back down the ladder.

"Rifles and ammo to deck," she ordered. "Ship at seven o'clock low!"

Taya instinctively reached for the steam cannon's cables, but it was too late. The giant weapon was gone.

The sound of gunfire was deafening as Taya hurried across the deck with the last box of volley-gun ammunition. She dropped the crate next to Liliana and Jinian and fell to one knee, gasping for breath.

The *Firebrand* was in full, careening retreat, riding the wind and losing altitude as the ship behind it picked it to pieces with cannonfire. Groans and cries filled the air. The lictor who doubled as ship's physician was gone — he'd been one of the gunnery crew lost overboard — and everyone else was too busy trying to save the *Firebrand* to tend to the wounded. Blood ran through the etched spiral grooves in the ondium plates that covered the deck, spilling over the edges each time the broken ornithopter jerked and heaved under another attack.

Blood also soaked the sleeve of Jinian's bright yellow Cabisi jacket, but she continued firing the volley gun with narrowed eyes and grit teeth, and Liliana stayed by her side, reloading, any remaining loyalty to her countrymen forgotten in the mindless fight for survival. Taya left them to it and scuttled down the deck to Cristof, who knelt at the stern rail firing his rifle side-by-side with Captain Amcathra and Professor Dautry. The pursuing dirigible was close enough now for Taya to read its name and number: the *Formidable*, Number Nine, holding at a dangerous seven o'clock low and blasting away at the *Firebrand*'s damaged stern.

Abruptly Captain Amcathra rose, slinging his rifle over his shoulder and bellowing, "Prepare to evacuate!"

So, the time had come at last. Taya grimly dug into her pocket for her armature keys.

"Cris, I'm going—"

A round hit the deck next to her and threw her off her feet. Jagged pieces of wood and metal filled the air and pierced her clothing. Taya felt herself sliding, and suddenly there was nothing at all beneath her legs.

"Taya!"

Half-blinded by the blood in her eyes, she reached for Cristof as she dangled from the wreckage that was all that was left of the ornithopter's stern. Their hands clasped, jerking Cristof toward her. He was spread-eagled on the deck, but his ondium harness made him too light to anchor her. She gave an involuntary shriek as her hips dropped over the edge.

"Taya, hold on!" Cristof's fingers tightened, but Taya felt her hand slipping, blood and sweat working their treacherous way on their mutual grip. He gave her a panicked look.

Then Captain Amcathra threw himself over Cristof's back and closed a fist around the exalted's rescue harness strap. Like the two of them, his face and pale blond hair was streaked with blood from exploding metal and wood. "I have you, Exalted."

"Come on, Taya, you can do it." Cristof stretched out his other hand, trusting his friend to secure him. Taya lunged. Her fingers touched his and slid past. Their eyes met in a moment of crystal-clear comprehension.

She was going to fall.

"Taya! Taya, no!" Liliana shouted.

Taya's stomach had slid over the edge and her hand was slipping from Cristof's grip. Horror filled his gray eyes as their fingers began to part. She lunged again with her free hand. This time her fingers closed around his thin wrist just as their clasped hands slid apart. Taya gasped as she dropped, dangling in midair with only their mutual grip to support her. Bullets from the Alzanans' guns pinged on the broken wood and rang off the bent ondium plates around her. She looked up. Cristof was half-over the shattered deck himself, his long, soot-stained fingers plucking at her sleeve for a grip while Amcathra strained to keep him in place.

"Janos, let me go! She's falling!"

"Taya!" Liliana knelt on the edge of the broken deck, her long hair whipping around her and her fingers working at the buckles on her rescue harness. "Don't let go!"

"*Principessa*, be careful!" Amcathra snapped. "*Kattaka*, grab her!"

Taya's blood-covered fingers slipped down Cristof's wrist. She looked up and fought for a smile to make him feel better.

Falling to death wasn't such an unusual fate for an icarus. She hoped she'd meet him again in her next life.

"No!" Cristof roared, twisting fiercely against Amcathra's iron grip.

Liliana yanked off her harness and swung it downward as Taya's fingers slipped over Cristof's wrist. The harness's flying straps and loose buckles struck her face and she instinctively grabbed it.

The *Firebrand* hurtled away in a trail of smoke and debris. Taya's hands tightened around the floating ondium harness, her heart battering her ribs. For a moment she saw Cristof's pale face and heard his despairing shout, and then the *Formidable* was thundering beneath her, its guns continuing to pound the hapless ornithopter to pieces.

Sobbing, Taya thrust an arm through one of the harness straps, watching as the two ships vanished around an angle of the mountain pass. The sound of their engines and gunfire gradually faded into the distance.

For a few minutes she simply floated, bobbing a little, pushed by the wind. She was suspended almost a thousand feet over the forest that carpeted the mountain pass and almost equally as far horizontally from the nearest mountainside on her left.

After what had seemed like hours of weapons fire, engine roar, and shouting, the mountains' silence was almost frightening.

At last, slowly, she began to discern the smaller noises around her— her own ragged breathing, the wind shushing through the trees, a hawk's plaintive cry.

No crash. Not yet.

She took a deep, shuddering breath.

"Lady, keep them safe," she whispered. Her voice sounded small and lonely in the vast, empty space around her.

After taking another minute to gather her strength, she pulled herself up and into the harness, her midair gymnastics causing her to spin and wobble. Finally she secured the latches around her chest and waist, cinching them as tightly as possible.

She was floating, but she was helpless without her wings. The wind would probably blow her toward the mountainside, but that could take hours, maybe even days. She pulled out the pocketwatch Cristof had made her, cradling it with both hands.

3:30 p.m. She closed it and thrust it deep into her pocket for safety. She reached into her other pocket and felt her armature keys.

No food, no water, no matches, no compass— nothing to protect her from the cold of a mountain pass on a winter's night.

"I never learn," she said ruefully.

She listened again, wondering what had happened to the *Firebrand* and when the *Formidable* would return.

Only a few more hours until nightfall. If she didn't want to be blown into sharp rocks or tall pines in the dark, she'd have to descend.

She reached into one of the harness pockets and pulled out a small bar of ondium. The silver metal tugged upward in her hand. The tiny object was worth a year of her salary, at least.

With the greatest reluctance, she let it go. It flew up into the air and she sank.

She'd released two-thirds of the precious ondium bars before her feet brushed the tops of the tall pines. She curled and spun around in midair, pulling herself down into the prickly branches, her eyes closed and her face tucked into her chest.

At last she righted herself, wrapping her legs around a thick branch and leaning against the tree trunk. She ran her hands over her face. Dried blood crumbled under her fingers and scratches ached as they threatened to re-open. She probed a gash along the side of her face that felt larger and more painful than the others and wished she had a mirror.

Her blood-spotted clothes had been torn ragged by flying wood and metal. None of the scratches on her body seemed too bad, although she'd be black and blue for a while. One of the gouges along the top of her left leg could have used a bandage. She peeled up her pants, tearing scabs, and let the fresh blood seep.

A distant shout carried through the forest. She froze, holding her breath. Voices called back and forth in the distance.

Alzanan soldiers.

She looked up. Her descent had taken about twenty minutes, and although it was shady between the trees, night was still several hours away. She pulled her borrowed lictor's jacket closed over her brightly patterned blue-and-white Cabisi shirt and rummaged through her pockets one more time.

She wasn't carrying any identification— her papers had been left behind in the Alzanan palace. She unfastened the gold icarus pin from the front of her jacket, hesitated, and pinned it to the inside cuff of her trousers, rolling her pants back down to her boots. She jammed her armature keys and pocketwatch into one of her boots between her sock and the leather.

Her trousers weren't remarkable, but her uniform jacket was obviously Ondinium. She could take it off, but she was reluctant to lose what little protection it offered against the winter chill. She wriggled out of the rescue harness.

Let it go or buckle it to a tree branch? She was loathe to lose more of the precious metal, but if the Alzanans found it, she'd be breaking yet another of Ondinium's strict prohibitions— the prohibition against letting ondium fall into the hands of foreigners.

With a groan, she opened her hands before she could talk herself out of it. The harness shot upward through the narrow tree branches and into the sky.

More shouts. Somebody had seen it.

Taya yelped as the branch she was sitting on suddenly bent under her weight. She scrambled down to a stronger branch, hugging the tree trunk with both arms. The soldiers drew nearer, shouting directions to each other in Alzanan.

"There! You, come down here!"

Taya peered around the trunk. A blue-coated soldier pointed a rifle at her as others ran forward.

"Please, don't shoot!" she cried out in Mareaux. "Do you speak Mareaux?" It was a gamble, but with luck the Alzanans wouldn't detect an Ondinium accent in another language. With her auburn hair and light skin, she could pass as Mareaux, and the soldiers might be reluctant to hurt a citizen from an allied country.

"She's Mareaux," one of the soldiers told the rest. He shouted up in the same language. "You, come down here!"

"Yes, yes, I'm coming." Taya awkwardly descended, slipping and scraping against the trunk and clutching at branches. At last her boots hit the forest floor and she straightened, holding her hands in front of her in a placating gesture.

"Turn around and keep your hands up," one of the soldiers ordered.

With deep misgivings, Taya turned toward the tree, raising her hands. A soldier grabbed her arms, twisting them behind her back and tying them. Then he spun her around again, throwing her back against the tree trunk.

"Who are you?"

"Tatienne Gifford," she lied, then gave them her best worried, fawning smile. "Tatia, sir."

"What are you doing here?"

"I was on the ship...." she let herself cringe as they stiffened, glaring at her. "The flying ship, they made me go with them. The Ondiniums— they kidnapped me from Os Cansai."

"Os Cansai? Where's that?"

"In Cabiel?" She let herself sound frightened and uncertain, which wasn't hard. "I was studying Cabisi religious practices.... The Ondinium's ornithopter came and fought an Alzanan dirigible...."

Murmurs and exchanged looks. They had heard about the duel, then.

"Why did they take *you*?"

Taya fought for tears. She needed tears. She thought about Jayce and the rest of their staff, some executed, others still in prison. She conjured up her husband's expression as she lost her grip on his wrist. She imagined him dead in a terrible crash.

The last did it. She squeezed her eyes shut as tears ran down her face. They threatened to become uncontrollable. She fought to banish the horrible, all too easily conjured image of a battered and broken Cristof and concentrated on her story.

"They wanted to go through Mareaux— they needed to get to Ondinium." She drew a shaking breath, wiping her cheeks on her shoulders. "They grabbed me and told me I had to guide them. What could I do? They were soldiers, lictors, with guns and those horrid black stripes on their faces...."

More murmurs, angrier this time.

"How did you get off the ship, then?" The speaker looked unconvinced.

Taya steadied herself. Pretending to cry had affected her more than she'd expected. The tears threatened to release a deep well of pent-up grief and fear that she couldn't afford right now.

"They— they have rescue harnesses that float. I saw them being used, so when the ship was hit and nobody was looking, I grabbed one and jumped. I— I— the ship was being blown to pieces and I didn't want to die."

"That's what we saw," a soldier muttered in Alzanan. "The harness must have had ondium in it."

The others nodded. Her interrogator jerked his head and two soldiers fell back with him, conferring in low tones. Taya slumped against the tree trunk, not needing to pretend to look exhausted and fearful.

"Those clothes you're wearing—?" one asked.

"They didn't give me any time to pack. When they forced me on board, I was wearing this shirt, and a skirt and sandals."

Back to the murmured conference.

"Please," she ventured. "I'll tell you everything I know about the ship. Please don't shoot me. I just want to go home to Echelles."

The leader seemed to reach a decision.

"We're not going to shoot you— not yet, anyway." He raised his rifle and slung it over his shoulder. The rest of the soldiers relaxed, putting their weapons away. "I'll take you back to the main camp and let the captain decide what to do with you."

"Thank you," Taya said in a deliberately small voice. She caught herself starting to bow and turned the movement into a shifting of her weight. The Alzanans, like the Mareaux, reserved bows for men and curtseys for women. *Be careful*, she warned herself.

This wasn't going to be easy, but as long as she was alive, she had some hope of seeing Cristof again. She prayed he'd gotten off the *Firebrand* alive.

CHAPTER FOURTEEN

THE SOLDIERS STARTED up through the pass that evening toward the Ondinium border. Their progress was slow and Taya found the climb especially difficult with her hands tied behind her back and hidden objects digging into her ankles. That night, after she'd been allowed a small bowl of soup and some water, they bound her hands together again and tied her ankle to an iron stake driven deep into the ground inside their tent. Taya barely slept, surrounded by enemies, but none of them bothered her.

The trip took three days. On the second day, they passed a long train of riders and wagons hauling more mortars up higher into the pass. The soldiers lingered for some time trading stories about fighting the *Firebrand* as it had passed overhead and cursing the Ondinium "invaders." Taya pretended not to understand as she strained to hear. Nothing was said about a crash— if the *Firebrand* had been driven down, it had happened elsewhere.

On the third day she spotted the dirigible first, moored on an open plateau near a encampment of tents and cannon large enough to resemble a small city. The *Formidable* looked unharmed, its giant number nine unscathed. Taya's chest tightened. There was no reason why it should be damaged — the *Firebrand* had thrown its cannon overboard — but she'd still harbored a tiny hope that the ship might have been miraculously defeated.

The Alzanans were using the encampment as a staging point; hundreds, maybe even a thousand soldiers were there, both cavalry and infantry, as well as countless drivers and carters and grooms and cooks and other support staff. Long lines of carts and wagons filled with food, supplies, and weapons flanked the camp. Taya kept her head down as her guards passed the checkpoints.

She had never seen an army before. About a hundred lictors lined up each year for the annual Great Examination processional, and whenever new decaturs were inducted into the Oporphyr Council or — as she knew too well — sent into exile. She'd seen several hundred lictors in Glasgar, but they'd been scattered throughout the city, and now they were dead.

Taya stole another furtive glance around her and wondered if there were enough lictors in Ondinium to fight such a force.

Her captors marched her into a larger, cleaner part of the encampment. Taya answered questions as meekly and briefly as possible as she was handed from one Alzanan soldier to the next, until she finally found herself standing inside one of the fanciest tents before a harried-looking captain.

"What part of Mareaux are you from?" he demanded, in Mareaux.

"Echelles," she said, keeping her eyes cast down. "But I was in Os Cansai when I was taken."

"That's in Cabiel?"

"Yes, sir."

"What were you doing there?"

"Studying their religion, sir. I'm a university student."

"Hmm." The captain frowned, studying her. "Why in the Great Father's name would Ondinium soldiers abduct a *religion* student?"

"They needed someone to guide them across the country. There aren't many other Mareaux in Cabiel." She had concocted an entire tale of her meeting, abduction, captivity, and escape during the three days' hike to camp, but she preferred not to say any more than was necessary.

"You escaped during the firefight."

"Yes, sir." She finally risked a question. "Did you capture their ship? Its crew could tell you…."

"No." The captain fished out a watch and glanced at it. "How much of the enemy vessel did you see?"

"Most of it, sir. I was a prisoner on it for more than a week."

"All right. Good." He closed the watch and tucked it away. "I'm sorry to treat you so poorly, Miss Gifford, but I'm sure you understand our situation. I'm afraid we're going to have to inconvenience you for a few more days, but then I think we'll be able to send you on your way."

"Thank you, sir."

"The *Formidable* leaves in an hour, and I'm going to put you on it. Colonel Agosti will want to hear everything you can tell her about the Ondinium ship, but then I'm sure she'll put you on a train back to Centro. You'll be able to book passage from there to Echelles."

Colonel Agosti. Liliana had said that her older sister, Pietra, was a major, but that had been before the royal family had been slaughtered. Maybe the Alzanan army thought that its new commander-in-chief deserved a higher rank.

"Thank you, sir," she repeated, trying to hide her sudden apprehension.

At the captain's orders, she was given a scarf and gloves and her hands were tied more comfortably in front of her. She was taken to the *Formidable*, where she was cuffed to a pole on the second floor of the command gondola. *Just like Cristof*, she thought sadly, wedging herself between the boxes for warmth. She tried to eavesdrop on the soldiers below, but they seemed more interested in discussing a brawl between two of the crew the night before than analyzing their upcoming mission or the fate of the *Firebrand*.

Some time later the engines were started. One of the *Formidable*'s crew members walked up the stairs, a blanket folded over one arm.

"How do you do, Miss Gifford," he said in stilted Mareaux. "Captain Sciarra conveys his respects. He regrets treating a member of an allied country with such suspicion, but he hopes you will understand the need for caution. He has sent a blanket to help against the cold of flight."

"Thank you," Taya said, meaning it. The air was already chilly, and she knew from experience that it would only get colder as the ship rose. The soldier draped the blanket over her shoulders. "How long will the trip take?"

"No more than an hour, ma'am. I should warn you that we will be flying over contested area, and you may hear sounds of combat. We will be perfectly safe, however."

"You're fighting the Ondiniums?"

"We have taken Terminal," he said proudly, "and we are pushing the Ondies deeper into the mountains, despite all their tricks and clever machines."

"Tricks? Do they have more flying ships?" If there were others, maybe—

"So far we have only seen the one, and it crashed." He shrugged. "Their other machines seem just as easy to break. Ondinium technology is not as impressive as we had been led to believe."

"Other machines?" Taya was mystified.

"More of their ancient weapons," he said with disapproval. "But they are all old and slow. Ondinium technology may have been impressive a thousand years ago, but *our* weapons have moved on and *their* weapons haven't."

Taya nodded, afraid to say anything, and pulled the blanket closer. The ship jerked as it began to rise.

"You do not need to worry," the soldier said. "We will keep you safe." He gave her a reassuring smile and headed back down the stairs.

Once he was gone, Taya stood and shoved the crates aside. She had to stretch her chained arm out to full length and crane her neck, but she was able to watch through one of the gondola's tiny portholes as the military camp slid out of sight.

As the ship traveled onward, Taya spotted military forces moving on well-beaten trails and, at times, saw flashes of metal that could have been the train tracks to A-O Terminal. Her muscles began to ache from holding the awkward position, but just as she was thinking about giving up and sitting down, she saw a deep black gash in the earth. She stood on her toes, wishing for a better angle as it drew closer. It was a long, gaping hole in the ground, the earth and trees thrown to either side as though something had exploded. Had the *Firebrand* crashed there? Wouldn't there be some non-ondium-plated wreckage left behind if it had? Taya's stomach churned. *If the* Firebrand *had crashed there, the Alzanans would have taken the crew prisoner*, she told herself, fiercely. *It must have crashed farther away.*

The *Formidable* continued implacably onward. As they drew closer to Terminal, the signs of combat grew more obvious—torn-up earth and fire-scorched lines of trees. Taya saw another deep gash in one of the mountainsides, but this time she could tell that the explosion had come from *within*, blowing earth and rocks outward and away. A twisted, fire-blackened machine lay half-buried in the scattered rubble. She squirmed, trying to get a closer look, but the object was too mangled to be identified. She didn't think it was part of the *Firebrand*, but she couldn't be certain.

"They're all right," she whispered, frustrated and frightened. Captain Amcathra would have done everything he could to bring the *Firebrand* down safely, and he would have thrown Cristof overboard in his rescue harness if a safe landing had been impossible. And as for her husband, as long as he had his wits and a gun, he'd be fine. He might be socially awkward and physically gawky, but he was an exalted at heart— determined and resourceful and far more ruthless in the pursuit of his goals than she liked to admit. She was sure that as long as there was a breath in his body, he'd get a warning to Ondinium.

Unless, of course, he was foolishly romantic enough to try to find her instead of the nearest Ondinium military force.

She backed away from the window to roll her aching shoulder and adjust her blanket. Then she slid her fingers into her boot top to touch the heavy golden watch he'd made for her, reassured by its steady, rhythmic ticking.

He would be all right. She had to have as much faith in him as he had in her.

After she'd shaken the kinks out of her arm, she looked out the window again. They were traveling parallel to the train tracks now. Camps sat at regular intervals along the tracks, perhaps protecting them from vandalism. Taya had heard that Ondinium had buried explosives at key points along its own tracks so that it could blow them up if it were ever invaded. Hidden mine fields were one of the rumors her conspiracist friends Pyke and Victor liked to bruit about, along with stories of secret Council weapons-research labs, lictor assassins, hypnotically programmed sleeper agents, and deep-mining death camps. Of course, the more she learned about the Council's secrets, the more reasonable some of those conspiracy theories started to sound. Underground pneumatic railroads, ancient imperial ornithopters, and now these new imperial weapons, whatever they were— maybe the idea of mined railroad tracks wasn't so far-fetched.

A column of smoke punctuated her first sight of A-O Terminal. As the ship drew nearer, Taya covered her mouth.

Glasgar must have looked like this, after the attack— full of broken or blackened buildings, torn up streets, and upended and twisted train cars and loading equipment. She couldn't tell what was being burned in one of the trainyards, sending up a long plume of smoke, but she was afraid it might be corpses.

The *Formidable* began maneuvering lower for a landing. Taya moved the crates back into place and sat, her stomach clenching. What was she going to say to Major — Colonel — Agosti?

After the ship docked, a soldier escorted her outside. Taya rubbed her wrists as she looked around, not needing to hide her dismay. She'd never visited Alzana-Ondinium Terminal before, but she'd seen its sister on the Mareaux-Ondinium border. This ruin was nothing like that lively border city and, as far as she could tell, it had never been so. What remained of the shelled-out buildings suggested a sterile, fortresslike architecture, with no sign of the friendly little shopfronts and welcoming hotels that existed on Mareaux's border. The high but shattered wall that ran down the center of the city suggested that the Alzanans and Ondiniums who'd lived in Terminal had enjoyed very little interaction.

"If you will follow me, Miss Gifford?"

Taya nodded, glad that the aviator made no attempt to tie her up again as he led her through the occupied city. He didn't need to; the streets were filled with Alzanan soldiers.

The abrupt, staccato sound of gunfire made her freeze.

"It's outside of town," her escort said. "Nothing to worry about."

"The Ondiniums are that close?" She tried to hide her leap of hope behind what she hoped was a suitably fretful expression.

"They're just harrying our scouts. Terminal is well-guarded, and we'll have another sentry watching from the *Formidable* now that we're in dock."

Taya hoped the Ondiniums knew that.

Colonel Agosti had set up office in one of the buildings that was still more or less intact; a few windows were broken and boarded up and its walls were pocked with bullet holes. An Alzanan flag hung from a pole in the wall, and a regimental banner had been pinned over the doorway. The *Formidable*'s crew member handed Taya and a letter over to the guards, then nodded amiably to her and left. Taya shivered in the cold as the letter was taken inside, her nervousness growing. At last she was ushered inside and led through several rooms of busy-looking soldiers to the colonel's office in the back. A knock, a shout, and she was allowed in.

The office was dim and filled with bluish smoke. Colonel Agosti pushed back her chair and gave Taya a cool, assessing once-over that reminded her of the colonel's dead grandfather.

Pietra's Agosti heritage showed in her dark, well-arched brows, curling black hair, and strong features. She was a slender woman in her mid to late thirties, her uniform elaborate and well-tailored with fresh-looking creases and golden braid. A slender cigarillo burned between her fingers. Taya coughed. Smoking was uncommon in Ondinium.

"I understand you're here to spy on me," Agosti said in fluent Ondinan.

Taya blinked, realized she'd betrayed her understanding of the language, and shook her head.

"They gave this to me," she said, touching her jacket as she sought to inflect her Ondinan with a Mareaux accent. "I am not a lictor."

Agosti gestured to a basin and pitcher in one corner of the room.

"Perhaps you would care to wash your face to refresh yourself."

Careful, Taya thought as she nodded and pulled off her scarf and gloves. *This one's no fool.* She walked to the basin and scrubbed her hands and face. It felt good to clean up, and she fleetingly wished for a bath. She hadn't been really clean since she'd left Os Cansai. She made a point of vigorously drying her face before turning back to the colonel.

"Take a seat," Agosti said, still speaking Ondinan. Taya wondered if the Alzanan knew Mareaux or was simply playing some sort of game. "What's your name?"

Taya perched on the hard chair by the desk and glanced down. Yes, the letter laid there, open.

"Tatienne Gifford."

"What do you do?"

"I am a religion student studying the Cabisi Dancer."

"The Dancer is a goddess?"

"Goddess and god."

"Sounds confusing. How can it be both?"

Taya hesitated.

"Because it represents the entire universe at once."

"Do you think that makes the Dancer more powerful than the Mother of Earth and the Father of Sky?"

"I think... it is easier to love and respect a mother and a father than a deity as strange and remote as the Dancer."

"Yes, you're probably right." A pained expression crossed the colonel's face, and Taya was abruptly reminded that the soldier had recently lost most of her family. "Maybe that's why Alzana and Mareaux care more about people and the Cabisi and Ondiniums care more about things. We venerate the divine creators as our parents, whereas they have turned the divine creators into strangers— the Ondies' masculine Lady of the Forge and the Cabisi's two-sexed Dancer. What kind of twisted societies could misinterpret nature's essential truth so profoundly?"

"You are a philosopher," Taya ventured. She disagreed with the colonel — there was nothing masculine about the Lady of the Forge — but she was impressed that a soldier, a king's granddaughter, had considered such matters at all.

"War turns soldiers into philosophers or butchers. I think we have enough butchers already." Agosti contemplatively nursed her cigarillo. "The lictors on the Ondinium ship; were they philosophers or butchers?"

Taya wasn't sure how to answer. What did Agosti want to hear? What would a Mareaux prisoner say?

"They were not cruel to me," she said at last. "They forced me to come, but they were not abusive."

"Yet you leaped off the ship, anyway."

"I was afraid. The rudder was gone, the engine was damaged, and they were throwing their cannon overboard." She swallowed. "Many of the crew were dead."

"Was there an exalted on board? A man in a mask?"

Her heart stuttered and she forced herself to nod.

"He did not wear a mask," she said, unsteadily. "But they called him exalted."

"No mask?" The colonel looked surprised. "What was his castemark?"

Taya touched her cheekbone.

"A wave on both cheekbones."

"Hmm. I was told that exalteds always wore masks, but I suppose it's too ridiculous to be true." Agosti fixed her with a steely gaze. "That man killed my grandfather, the king."

Taya shivered.

"I heard him say he was framed," she said, quietly. "He said an Alzanan woman did it."

"Who— my sister? Liliana?"

"No. The *principessa* was on the ship with him."

The colonel straightened, setting her cigarillo on the edge of a metal ashtray.

"She was? How did she look?"

"She was well," Taya said, quickly. "She looks like you, with long curling black hair and dark eyes. She had a necklace that she said her brother had given to her— a yellow stone, a birth-stone, maybe?"

"Was she a prisoner?"

"No. She seemed to be friends with the Ondiniums."

"Sweet Mother of Earth." Agosti slowly sat back into her chair. "The ship crashed behind Ondinium lines, so we left it alone. If I'd known she was on board...."

Taya remained silent. She wanted to tell the colonel that Liliana had bravely torn off her rescue harness and thrown it to Taya, saving her life, but it wouldn't fit her story, and it would provide cold comfort if the *principessa* had died as a result of her sacrifice.

Someone knocked on the door. Agosti sighed, shaking her head slightly.

"Who is it?"

"Lady Mazzoletti is here to see you, sir."

"No!" With a burst of fear, Taya lunged forward, grabbing the colonel's arm. "No— she's the one who killed the king!"

"What?" Agosti shook her off. "Who?"

"Fosca Mazzoletti shot the king— well, she ordered another man to do it, but—"

Pietra Agosti seized Taya's shoulder, dragging her up out of the chair.

"Send her in," the colonel barked.

Taya tried to escape, but the Alzanan officer held her fast as the door opened and Lady Mazzoletti swept in, looking as beautiful and well-groomed as ever. Her eyes landed on Taya and widened. Then she threw back her head with a trill of delighted laughter.

"Congratulations, your majesty! You've arrested one of the Ondinium assassins. I suggest you execute her at once."

CHAPTER FIFTEEN

"THAT'S NOT TRUE!" Taya bust out in Alzanan. It didn't matter what language she spoke anymore— her ruse was blown. "Fosca Mazzoletti gave the orders— I was there, I saw it! And so did Liliana. Just find her and ask her!"

Fosca's palm cracked across her face. Taya staggered, only held upright by the colonel's relentless grip.

"I would *never* harm *Il Re*," Lady Mazzoletti hissed, her face inches from Taya's. She straightened, the color high in her cheeks. "This is Cristof Forlore's icarus wife, your majesty. She helped him kill the king and kidnap *Principessa* Liliana; she was on the vessel that destroyed one of our dirigibles during their escape, and her ship attacked and crippled the *Indomitable*. Executing her will send a clear message to Ondinium's government that Alzana does not tolerate lies and betrayal."

"You're the liar," Taya protested. "Colonel, she wants me dead because I'm one of the few people still alive who knows what she did!"

"Is Liliana really alive?" Agosti demanded.

"*Yes!* Yes, if she survived the crash, she's alive. She was on the *Firebrand* and she swore a vendetta against Fosca Mazzoletti!"

"*If* your sister is still alive, she's undoubtedly been tortured and brainwashed—"

"Find her and ask her yourself! Please, Colonel, she wants to see you again; if you go out there and search for her, you'll find out that I'm telling the truth!"

"All right, enough!" Colonel Agosti shoved Taya back into her chair. "Sergeant!"

"Yes, ma'am!" The door opened and a soldier appeared, at attention.

"This woman is an Ondinium spy. I want her shackled and locked up with a guard at the door. No visitors and no interference; nobody touches her or speaks to her without my permission. Understood?"

"Yes, ma'am!"

"Be careful, Colonel," Taya said as the soldier hauled her back out of the chair. "Mazzoletti killed your family, and she's probably here to kill you, too. Don't let her or her allies stand behind you in a firefight."

"You—" Fosca Mazzoletti started forward but was stopped when Colonel Agosti stepped between them. Taya was yanked toward the door where another soldier covered her with his pistol.

"That's enough," the colonel snapped. "I said that *nobody* touches her without my permission."

"Your majesty," Fosca argued, "she's a trained Council spy and assassin! She's trying to turn us against each other!"

"I'm not—"

The door shut and Taya's face was pressed against the corridor wall while the sergeant fastened iron manacles around her wrists.

"*Principessa* Liliana was on the Ondinium ornithopter that crashed," she said, keeping her voice as controlled as she could. "If any of your soldiers find her, she'll tell you the truth about what happened to the king."

"Quiet," the sergeant growled, pulling her back upright with a rough shake. "I don't want to hear it."

"Fosca Mazzoletti is going to kill the colonel. You shouldn't leave them alone together."

The sergeant swept his foot forward, knocking her ankles out from beneath her. Taya wasn't expecting it and was sent sprawling, banging her head against the floor. She instinctively rolled aside, her shoulders slamming against the wall.

"Careful," the sergeant sneered, grabbing her jacket and hauling her back to her feet. "It's hard to keep your balance in irons."

Taya glared but kept her mouth shut.

The Alzanans locked her in what must have been A-O Terminal's jail before the occupation. It hadn't come through the fighting with all of its walls intact, but three of the small, windowless cells in the back were still functional. Fetters ran from her right ankle to a ring in the floor. The heavy cell door was locked behind her, the iron cover over its viewing grate firmly shut. She was given no bedding and no pot to piss in.

"At least I'm not chained to the wall this time," she muttered in a forlorn attempt to look on the bright side.

If she was lucky, she'd planted enough doubts in Pietra Agosti's mind to buy time while the colonel looked for Liliana, but Fosca Mazzoletti would argue strongly for her execution... or she might simply get rid of the colonel. Taya couldn't think of any other reason for the head of the Mazzoletti Family to have come out to the front line.

If Fosca killed the colonel, Taya would be next. She wondered how much Fosca suspected about her brother's disappearance. If she had access to the Ondinium rumor mill, she might guess that Taya and Cristof had been involved in stopping the Alzanans. But she wouldn't know whether Gaio was alive or dead. The Council had announced that several Alzanan dirigible crews were being held prisoner, but it hadn't identified them or the ships that had been taken. That information had been one of the bargaining chips in their peace negotiations.

Hours passed. Nobody bothered her. At some point, the door opened long enough for a soldier to bring in a cup of water, some bread and cheese, and — at last — a chipped chamberpot.

"Could I please have a blanket?" she asked, staying well away from the door. "It's freezing in here."

The man didn't say anything; the door closed.

The food wasn't much. Taya left the empty plate and cup next to the door and moved the chamberpot to a corner where it would be difficult for someone peering through the grate to watch her use it.

After what seemed like a long time later, the grate slid open, and then the door was unlocked. A soldier threw in a wool blanket and removed the cup and plate.

"Thank you!" she called out as the door shut and the grate cover was replaced. Hoping that it was a good sign, she curled up in a corner with the blanket wrapped around herself and tried to sleep.

She awoke when the door opened and a lamp shined in. She blinked and squinted, pulling her blanket closer around her.

"Here we are."

"Taya?"

Taya drew in a sharp breath as she recognized the voices. Patrice Corundel— and Alister!

The mercate held the lantern in gloved hands as she stepped inside. Alister entered behind her, his blindfolded head held high and his chestnut cane lightly rasping across the floor in front of him.

Behind them, in the lamplight, Taya saw the guard sprawled on the floor.

"What do you want?" she asked, swallowing.

"Ah, good, it *is* you." Alister's lips turned up in a small smile. He reached into the heavy winter coat he was wearing and dug out a handkerchief, which he offered in one hand. "Here. It wouldn't do to have her cry for help."

"If we just *killed* her—" Patrice set down the lantern.

"Then I wouldn't enjoy myself nearly as much and you would have a murder on your soul. The handkerchief, if you please."

"I don't like this," the mercate mumbled, taking it. "You're putting us all into danger."

"Before she screams?"

Taya suddenly made sense of their conversation and drew in a breath to do exactly that. Patrice leaped on her, yanking her hair back and cramming the handkerchief into her mouth. Taya reached out and clawed the mercate's face, raking her nails across the older woman's eyes and cheekbones. Patrice jerked her face away and slammed Taya's head against the prison wall, swearing.

Taya's eyes watered with pain as she tried to spit out the handkerchief. She attempted to strangle the woman with the length of chain that draped between her cuffs. Standing behind the mercate, Alister dropped a hand on Corundel's shoulder, orienting himself. He reached into his coat pocket and pulled out a needle gun.

Taya's eyes widened. Patrice tore the chain away from her neck, yanking Taya's hands down.

"Exalted, we need to use the chlor—"

The needlegun spat its deadly staccato.

Patrice collapsed against Taya, who stared in shock at the long steel needles jutting out of the back of the mercate's skull.

Alister's hand tightened on the woman's shoulder. He pulled her back, dropping her carelessly at his feet.

"Taya? Are you all right?"

Taya tore the handkerchief out of her mouth.

"You killed her!"

"Excellent." He stepped back, lowering the gun. "I would have been quite chagrined had I murdered the wrong woman. For one thing, it would have put an irreparable strain on my relationship with my brother."

Her heart leaped. "Is he here?"

"Cris? No, I'm afraid you're stuck with the *bad* Forlore brother." His smile was strained. "Even so, don't I get a 'thank you'?"

"Why? I mean, what are you doing here?"

"Engaging in what is quite likely to be a pointless and ill-fated attempt to redeem myself in your eyes." He cocked his head. "And perhaps in the Lady's, although I still think She would have approved of my plan to improve the caste system."

"But— you're *here*? With the *Alzanans*?"

He tucked his cane under his arm, reached into his coat pocket, and pulled out a small ring of keys.

"Well, yes. After I left you, I decided to stick around the capital a little longer, speaking quite loudly against Ondinium and my bastard of a brother. As I'd expected, Lady Mazzoletti quickly brought me in and asked me whether I'd like to avenge myself on both. Since then, I've been earning my keep by briefing Alzana's military — well, Lady Mazzoletti, although as I understand it, they're essentially identical — on Ondinium's various internal defenses." He held out the keys. "The mercate said these were the guard's keys. Let's find out if she was telling the truth."

Taya snatched them away and tried them on her manacles. Her eyes drifted to Corundel's corpse. A lock of graying hair fell from the woman's knit cap.

"And Patrice—" she said, thinking, *murder doesn't even bother me anymore. That's not good.*

"Was on the train from the capital with the rest of us and the Cabisi weapons she'd brought back on the *Indomitable*. But she came *here* to help me kill you. She was trying to nerve herself up to do it on her own when I offered to do it for her in exchange for a little private time with you first. I think she was relieved to pass the burden to me, although she didn't precisely approve of my motives."

"That's disgusting!" Taya freed her wrists and leaned over to unlock her ankle.

"It is, but if I hadn't provided her with a reason to keep you alive, my little hawk, I wouldn't have been able to distract her long enough to kill her. It isn't easy for a blind man to commit murder, you know; it requires proximity and surprise. And as invaluable as Florianne has been to me over the last few years, there are *some* things I simply can't ask her to do for me."

Taya stood. Alister was still holding his needler, but he wasn't making any threatening gestures with it.

"What are you going to do now?"

"*You* are going to put the mercate into your place and cover her with the blanket. If she has any weapons, you might want to take them. Oh, yes, and please don't forget to retrieve my handkerchief. Somebody might recognize it."

Taya looked down at the body with a mixture of regret and distaste. She didn't want to touch it, but she understood Alister's plan. She grit her teeth and dragged Patrice's dead weight into the corner. The woman's flesh was still warm. She curled the body up and covered it with the blanket. There wasn't much blood. She wiped her hands on Alister's handkerchief, anyway.

"I didn't see any weapons."

"There should be a phial."

Taya searched Patrice's coat pockets and pulled out a small brown bottle wrapped in a stained, stinking rag.

"I have it. And your handkerchief."

"Good. Be sure to confiscate the guard's gun when we leave, as well."

Taya slid the bottle into her jacket pocket, then pulled out her armature keys and pocketwatch and put them into her pockets, too. She had bruises where they'd been digging into her ankle for the last three days. At last she picked up the lantern and stepped outside.

The jail was empty and cold. Canvas had been tacked over the holes in the walls and windows to keep out the wind. The guard lay on the ground. To Taya's surprise, he was alive.

"You drugged him?" she asked, puzzled, as she took his pistol.

"The phial contains chloroform. Florianne bought it from the camp physician. One wonders what he thought she was going to do with it, but I suppose she paid him well to keep his questions to himself. I hear he does a little side trade in laudanum, too."

"How long will he be unconscious?"

"Not long enough. I suggest you use my needler; Alzanan soldiers carry percussion weapons, and they're too noisy for this sort of work."

"I— I don't want to kill him." Taya drew back from the body. "Let's just leave him here."

"My dear, he may have seen me. I did my best to stay behind while Patrice carried out the dirty work, but that doesn't mean he couldn't have caught a glimpse of me as he struggled."

"They'll know you did it anyway, once they see the needles."

"It's Patrice's gun; she killed the guard, and you killed her." He sighed and swept his cane forward until it hit the soldier, then tapped around the man's contours. His blindfolded face was turned down as though he could see the body. "Really, Taya, I would have thought you'd be more pragmatic by now. Hasn't Cris explained that every Alzanan you leave alive is an Alzanan who will kill your countrymen?"

"Alister, *no.*" She grabbed his wrist. "The Alzanans haven't treated me badly, and I'm sure he didn't see you. Please, just help me escape. How are we going to get out of camp?"

"With some effort. Which reminds me, Florianne is outside; would you please let her in before she freezes? I told her to stay around the corner."

Taya started to walk off, then spun, catching Alister in the act of raising his needler. She seized his wrist again.

"Don't. Give me the gun."

"I don't suppose you intend to shoot him for me, do you?"

"No."

He sighed and relinquished the weapon with the slightest of smiles.

"Are you this headstrong with my brother?"

"Yes." She set the gun's safety and held out her arm, placing Alister's hand on it. "Come on."

He slid his hand down until his fingers rested lightly on her elbow and followed as she headed for the door.

Florianne was waiting for them in the cold and dark, just as Alister had described. The young woman handed Taya a bundle of clothes, and Taya gave her Alister's needler in return. She pulled on the heavy blue Alzanan coat and winter hat with relief and found gloves in the coat's pocket.

"Thank you," she said with genuine gratitude.

"You could pass as an Alzanan soldier now," Florianne murmured.

"I thought a bit about the feasibility of arranging your escape by train or dirigible, but I'm afraid neither is practical," Alister said as Florianne handed him the needler and set a soldier's hat on his head. "For one thing, the engines take too long to heat up. So I'm afraid you'll have to escape by foot, and to make matters worse, we will need to backtrack several miles to get past the patrols. They're paying close attention to the border side of Terminal, but not as much to the Alzanan side. Since you don't like shooting people, I hope you won't object to chloroforming anyone who gets in our way."

"How?"

"Soak a rag in the chemical, clap it over your opponent's nose and mouth, and hold him still until he passes out."

Taya fingered Alister's handkerchief and nodded. "I can do that."

"I have no idea how much of the chemical is necessary," he continued. "I recommend using a considerable amount, just in case. There's no point in saving the stuff."

"All right." She looked at Florianne. "Are you coming with us?"

The girl shrugged.

"He needs me. I am his eyes."

"And you don't mind the danger he's putting you into?"

"It's more interesting than running a boarding house with my mother."

"All right. I hope he's worth it. Where do we go now?"

"Follow me." The girl picked up the lantern. Alister put a hand on Florianne's arm.

"Would you hide this under your coat for me?" he asked, thrusting his cane in Taya's direction. She tucked it under her arm and folded her coat flap over it. Alister pulled down his blindfold, letting it hang loosely around his neck as they began to walk. The sight of the hollowed eyelids under his hat brim made Taya cringe. She'd been a witness at his blinding.

"*I* told her that the ornithopter's main weakness is its unprotected deck," Alister said stridently in Alzanan as they stepped out into the dark, unlit street. He pulled a steel flask from his coat pocket and adroitly flipped the lid to one side, gesturing with the flask. "It doesn't have anything to do with speed or maneuverability — it's all about altitude and angle of fire. The Ondies are used to being *above* everyone else, you see. They never thought to protect themselves from another flying ship, not until the enemy started using floaters in the Last War, and by then it was too late to change the ornithopters' design. But floaters couldn't carry much weight, so even then the problem was negligible. But now, you see, *now* our flying ships have changed *all* the rules, and the Ondies haven't realized that yet."

Taya looked around as Alister continued his loud monologue, punctuating it by taking showy swigs from his flask. Several armed Alzanan soldiers shot them curious looks as they passed but didn't question their presence. Once somebody roared at them to shut up and get lost, but Alister's discourse never faltered as they continued down the street.

On the western side of town they encountered groups of soldiers sitting around trash fires drinking and arguing just as vociferously as Alister. Between the night, the hat, and the fact that he was tucked between Taya and Florianne, nobody noticed that Alister's eyes were scarred shut or that his cheeks bore crudely broken castemarks. He was just another loud, inebriated soldier being carried back to camp by his friends, and as buildings gave way to tents and they wound their way through the frozen, muddy streets, Taya started to appreciate his ruse. Who was going to be suspicious of three people making themselves so obnoxious? It was a brash, nervy strategy; just the kind she would expect from a man like Alister.

"Quiet a little," Florianne said at last. "People are sleeping."

"Are we still in camp?" Alister asked, his voice low.

"Yes, but we are reaching the edge. Perhaps it is time for you to be sick now."

Alister sagged in their arms, groaning. Taya adjusted his arm over her shoulder, flinching as the pungent liquor in his flask spilled down the shoulder of her new coat. She hoped he wasn't actually drinking the stuff; it smelled like it would eat through ondium plating.

"This way," Florianne said, turning them onto a narrower path. The scent of Alister's liquor was quickly overcome by the reek of the camp latrines as he begged to be put down before he spewed. He played the role of an obnoxious drunkard remarkably well, Taya thought, but then again, he'd been quite the actor when she'd first met him, too. He'd fooled her into thinking he loved her.

"Don't let him fall in," one of the soldiers joked as they passed. Alister groaned more loudly and the soldier laughed.

Suddenly, a burst of gunfire rattled through camp and the sky lit up behind them in a booming explosion.

Taya and Florianne both grabbed Alister's arms and yanked him down. Flames erupted between the buildings behind them.

"They're attacking the other side of Terminal!" Taya exclaimed.

"Well, that ought to distract the guards," Alister said calmly. He cocked his head, listening. "The lictors are probably trying to destroy the *Formidable*. That's what I would do, if I were in charge. A train pulls in and then, a day later, a dirigible lands — they *must* know that the Alzanans are planning something."

Taya handed him his cane as they stood. He recapped his flask and slid it into his pocket. Nobody was paying them any attention anymore; everybody was running toward the firefight.

"The train was carrying the serpentfire cannons?" she asked.

"Yes, it was loaded with a number of weapons bearing fanciful names. I never realized the Cabisi were so poetic." He reached out and Florianne guided his hand to her arm. "Shall we go?"

They walked quickly along the edge of the town, Alister holding his cane off the ground and trusting Florianne to lead him. Taya caught herself waiting to steady him if he stumbled over the uneven ground. *Well, he is my brother-in-law*, she thought, ruefully.

"The train's cargo included thunderclap rounds, laceration shells, serpentfire cannons, and a holocaust bomb," Florianne said, calmly.

"A holocaust bomb?" Taya didn't like the sound of that. "What does *that* do?"

"I don't know, but Corundel spent a great deal of time discussing its placement with Lady Mazzoletti." Alister grimaced. "At the risk of bringing back unfortunate memories, Taya, I should probably mention that they hoped to detonate it inside the Great Engine's chamber."

Taya nearly tripped over a hummock. "Impossible! They'll never be able to reach it!"

"Mercate Corundel knows where it is. Allied Metals & Extraction manufactured replacement parts for the Engine."

Another explosion went off.

"We're headed for one of the imperial tunnel entrances," Alister said. "The Alzanans put a guard over it, so I'm afraid you may need to shoot someone, after all. I don't suppose we'll be able to take them by surprise anymore."

"There's a tunnel here? For a—" she remembered Florianne and cut herself off. "You know about the tunnels?"

"I *was* a decatur, you know. Florianne, my dear, what do you see?"

"Everyone's running to the east of town," she reported. "It looks like they're setting up a defensive perimeter around the ship and train yard."

"Are we going to raise any suspicions by going in the opposite direction?"

"It might look better if we were jogging. At least then we'd appear to have a purpose."

"Lady save me. Can we get away with it?"

"Maybe. Mrs. Taya should go first to clear the way and you and I will follow behind her."

"Are you really his landlady's daughter?" Taya asked, staring at the girl. She seemed awfully calm for a civilian.

"Yes. Will you take the lead? Alister needs as clear and level a path as you can find."

"All right." Taya pulled her collar higher and tugged down on her hat.

"Carry the pistol," Florianne suggested. "That way you'll be mistaken for another soldier."

Taya made a face and pulled out the Alzanan firearm, checking its safety before beginning her jog. She wasn't sure where she was going, but she assumed the surprisingly competent Florianne would let her know if and when she needed to turn. They soon became one of a crowd of people rushing this way and that. Most were headed toward the firefight, but everybody was so intent on getting to their posts that nobody paid attention to anyone else.

"Left," Florianne sang out. Taya turned down the next alley between two ruined buildings, slowing as they left the larger flow of soldiery.

"This way," the young woman said.

"How do you know the route so well?" Taya inquired.

"I walked through the camp last night, when we arrived."

"Just once?"

"I have a very good memory."

Taya fell silent as the girl moved into the lead. They heard more gunfire, sounding closer, and shouts, and a great mechanical grinding that made Taya freeze a moment before hurrying after her guides.

"There." Florianne stopped and pointed. They stood at the edge of Terminal, between a row of demolished buildings and charred foundations. A makeshift fence had been erected around a hole in the ground, and two Alzanan soldiers stood tensely by the entrance, clutching their rifles and staring in the direction of the noise and fighting.

"We'll never sneak past them," Taya breathed. At her side, Florianne was whispering a description of the setup in Alister's ear.

"I think you'll need to use your gun," Alister agreed. Taya looked down at the pistol and felt her gut clench.

"I can't."

"Well, *I* certainly can't," Alister said, dryly. "I have a reasonable chance of hitting someone at point-blank range, but otherwise I shoot like a blind man. And I certainly hope you aren't planning to ask *Florianne* to commit murder for you."

Taya gave a heavy sigh, but then, to her surprise, Florianne set down the hooded lantern and held out her hand.

"I will kill them if you cannot."

"Have you ever used a gun before, my dear?" Alister asked, gently.

"Of course; my father taught me how to shoot when I was just a little girl."

Something exploded, much closer than before, and rubble pattered down in the street two blocks away. Taya swallowed. The soldiers were headed in this direction. If they didn't act quickly, they'd be caught.

"I'll do it," she said with despair. She'd never shot a gun in her life, but she'd watched Cristof numerous times and she'd paid attention while he was teaching Jinian and Dautry. Now his instructions ran through her mind as she lifted the pistol, carefully sighted on the first guard's chest, took a deep breath, let it half out, and tightened her finger on the trigger.

It didn't move. She lifted her finger, confused.

The safety was still on.

"Oh, Lady," she gasped, gripped by the shakes. Was that a sign? It couldn't be a sign. Icarus or not, she *had* to use the gun. She flipped the safety off with shaking hands, lifted the pistol again, and then lowered it. Her hands were too unsteady; the sight was wobbling back and forth. She took a deep breath. *Be like Captain Amcathra*, she counseled herself. *Be a rock. You've killed people before, to save yourself and your country. This is no different.*

Fire burst from the tunnel, sending both guards flying. Taya jerked backward, into Alister and Florianne, and yelped as her gun went off with a loud retort, burying a bullet in one of the walls beside her.

"What is it? What's happening?" Alister demanded. Florianne dragged him backward and Taya dropped the pistol before she could accidentally fire it again.

Black-uniformed lictors burst out the dark tunnel behind the guards, shooting them as they tried to scramble back to their feet. Then, from around the corner, Alzanan soldiers poured into the streets, firing back at the lictors. Noise and the scent of blood and gunpowder filled the air.

"Oh, scrap." Taya flattened herself on the ground as Florianne pulled Alister down. "What now?"

Alister held up a finger until Florianne finished telling him what was happening, her eyes fixed on the firefight in front of them.

"Don't run out and try to talk to them," he said, tightly.

"I wasn't going to!" Taya's heart pounded as one of the lictors screamed and fell, blood gouting from a bullet wound in his neck. More mechanical grinding sounded and the lictors fell back, shouting and firing, as a giant machine lurched out of the tunnel. Taya's jaw dropped as it moved forward, swaying back and forth as it moved on six gear-driven metal legs. It turned ponderously toward the Alzanans and froze. Flame and bullets burst from the array of gun barrels running across the front of its chassis. Taya heard screams and swearing and shouts for a mortar.

Then, with a puff of steam and a growl of gears and chains, the machine rotated again and strode forward, surrounded by lictors, until it vanished out of sight beyond the alley.

"What was that?" Taya breathed, grabbing Alister's arm. "It was a huge walking machine with three legs on each side."

"It seems the decaturs have dusted off their collection of mecharachnids. I wish I could have seen it."

"Those aren't supposed to exist anymore!"

"Neither are ornithopters."

"But—" she stared at him. "What *other* weapons do we have?"

"The passage is clear," Florianne observed.

"Alister, what else is down those tunnels?"

"More lictors and ancient machinery, from the sound of it. I recommend—" He broke off as someone shouted behind them in Alzanan.

"You! Identify yourselves!"

"Lady Mazzoletti's staff!" Alister shouted back at once.

"We arrived yesterday on the train," Florianne added, rising from the ground with her hands up. Taya tugged Alister around and they both raised their hands.

The three soldiers covering them with rifles looked jumpy.

"What's your name? Why are you here?"

"We—"

A shot rang out and one of the soldiers jerked. His gun went off as he fell, and the other two soldiers spun and began firing back at their unseen assailant. Taya ducked as bullets whined past her and struck the walls, sending chips of stone flying. Something burned against her jaw and she clapped a hand against it. Alister shouted and she whipped around. He was on his knees, his cane lost, blindly reaching for Florianne. The young woman had collapsed.

"Florianne!" Taya pushed Alister aside as the soldiers at the mouth of the alley ran away, still shooting at their unseen foe. A bullet had struck the girl's temple, plowing a deep, blood-welling furrow into her skull, and another had pierced her coat. Taya tugged the fabric aside and saw an entry wound over the girl's lung.

"How is she?" Alister demanded. Taya pulled him forward and put his hand on the young woman's face.

"She's dying," she said, honestly. "She's been shot in the head and the chest."

"No!" His agony seemed real and Taya felt a burst of pity as he leaned over the girl, his permanently closed eyes seeming to strain for some glimpse of her face. "Florianne, wait, hold on. I'll take you to the infirmary— you're strong, you can do this."

Florianne twitched, one hand rising an inch, before falling limp. Alister drew in a sharp breath as if he could feel her spirit passing through his hands.

"I'm sorry." Taya laid a hand on his shoulder. "She's gone."

He breathed out, half sigh, half protest, and leaned over the girl's body.

"Florianne? Florianne?"

The corpse didn't answer, her dull eyes staring into the night sky.

"Do you want to stay with her?" Taya asked, swallowing the lump in her throat. "I'm sure somebody will find you soon."

His fingers slid over the blood on Florianne's face. He pulled himself upright. Tears glistened on his cheeks, and Taya was struck by the realization that she'd never seen Alister cry before— not even during his blinding and exile.

"No," he said roughly, reaching out with his bloody hand. "Where's my cane?"

She picked it up and handed it to him. He laid it across his knees and reached around his neck, pulling up his blindfold. His fingers left wet streaks that glistened across the black fabric as he smoothed it over his eyes like a mask.

"Are you sure?"

"Let's go."

"We'll have to leave her here."

"She's dead; it doesn't matter to her anymore."

"You cared about her, didn't you?"

"I'm sure she was a spy, reporting my activities to the Mareaux government." He coughed, grabbed his cane, and climbed to his feet. "But when you're blind and in exile, you cherish whatever friends you can make, and you don't ask too many questions."

"I'm sorry, Alister." Taya felt her heart being wrenched, and the feeling angered her. It wasn't *her* fault he'd made bad choices. Still, she couldn't help feeling sorry for him and the poor girl lying dead at their feet. She took a deep breath. "Are you ready to run?"

"Yes." He held out a hand and Taya placed it on her arm. She glanced at the gun lying on the ground, then deliberately looked away.

No. She hadn't shot anyone yet, and she didn't intend to start now. She picked up the hooded lantern, instead.

"Let's go." She looked up and down the street. The fight had moved on, soldiers swarming around the mecharachnid three blocks away.

She ran toward the tunnel, zig-zagging around the fallen bodies and forcing herself to keep moving even when she heard one of the soldiers groan. Alzanan or Ondinium, she couldn't tell, and she couldn't afford to stop and find out as stray bullets from the firefight up the street struck the walls around them.

They passed through the shattered fence and Taya slowed to help Alister negotiate the rubble and uneven ground. The air smelled like fresh blood, turned earth, gunpowder, and machine oil. She gagged as she saw the guards' shattered bodies.

"Hey, you! Stop!"

The words were in Alzanan, not Ondinan, so Taya grabbed Alister's arm and yanked him into the dark, broken tunnel entrance.

The drop was steep and they stumbled as they half-ran, half-tumbled down the dirt slope. Taya lost her grip on Alister but held the lantern tightly, keeping it up and out of the way as she staggered, dropped to one knee, pulled herself back up, and finally felt her boots strike stone instead of soil. She threw her free hand in front of her face and took several blind, unsteady steps forward. Nothing.

"Taya?" Alister's voice. She heard him take a step and draw in a sharp breath.

"I'm here. Shhh." She heard gunfire and shouting and a distant mechanical sound that had to be the mecharachnid's engine, but she didn't hear anyone scrambling down the slope after them.

After a long moment, she unhooded the lantern and peered around.

They were deeper underground than she'd expected. The sides of the tunnel had collapsed here and there, leaving large chunks of rock to skirt around or climb over, but otherwise the tunnel walls were smooth and finished. This passage wasn't as wide as the tunnels she'd seen in Ondinium, but like those it seemed to have been carved out of solid stone. About twenty feet in, she saw a symbol etched deeply into the wall— a word or number in Ondinium's old, long-abandoned imperial script.

"I think we're alone," she said, returning to Alister. He was leaning over and gingerly probing his right ankle. Dirt covered his coat and trousers; he had stumbled on the way down.

"Are you all right?"

"I may have twisted something." He lifted his head and coughed. "Do you see my cane?"

"Just a minute." Taya scrambled back up the dirt slope a few yards and grabbed it, bringing it back down to him. He closed his hand on it with an air of relief.

"Good. Where are we?"

Taya described the tunnel.

"Are there tracks in the dirt?"

Surprised, she looked down.

"Not railway tracks." She walked farther down the corridor, holding the lantern close to the floor. Alister followed, the tip of his cane scraping lightly across the ground as he advanced. "Footprints and something big and circular— the machine, I'll bet. Oh, wait."

"What?"

"There are some wheel marks, like a cart, maybe." She crouched. "But the wheels are about twice as wide as my hand."

"Does the tunnel extend past Terminal?"

"It looks like it, although I can't tell how far it goes."

"Do the wheel tracks extend past the hole to Terminal?"

"You're guessing something— what?" She backtracked, leaving Alister in the darkness as she checked. "Yes, the tracks continue on."

"I think they are using an augercar to drill their holes in the tunnel," Alister said, with another cough and a wince. "The explosives are probably only being used to break through the walls."

"That makes sense." Taya had never visited Ondinium's mines, but she'd seen augercars, mobile drilling machines, being driven out of Tertius to Safira O-Base-0 for shipment.

"No doubt the lictors are clearing a passage deeper into Alzana. However, we should head toward Ondinium, instead."

Taya retraced her steps and laid Alister's hand on her arm. They began walking, the sounds of war fading as they moved farther from the opening. Taya was worried about her brother-in-law's limp, but he didn't complain, using her arm and his cane to support himself.

"The Alzanans didn't know about the tunnels, did they?" she asked at last.

"I doubt it, or they would have collapsed them long ago."

"Why did the empire dig them?"

"Mining. Trade. Storage. Spying. I really don't know for certain. A number of military records were lost in the Last War, and more were destroyed or sequestered during the Virtuous Reclamation."

"Who *would* know?"

"Does Evadare Constante still sit on Council?"

"Yes." Decatur Constante was the conservative System Analyst who had orchestrated much of the invasion's cover-up and ordered Cristof and Taya into Alzana.

"Eva's in charge of national defense and security. She may not know *all* of Ondinium's secrets, but I'm certain she knows more than the rest of the Council."

"She doesn't trust us— Cristof and me."

He coughed.

"I expect that's my fault. She and I used to work together developing war scenarios for the Great Engine. I think she would have voted for Clockwork Heart."

"If you hadn't taken matters into your own hands first."

He didn't answer. She looked at him and couldn't see anything in his blindfolded face to reveal whether he'd ever had second thoughts about making the precipitous decision to commit murder in order to influence the Council's vote.

"Did you know about the ornithopters?" she asked.

"No."

"Why not?"

"The Council is like the Labyrinth Code, Taya; each decatur commands a piece of Ondinium, but none of us command it all. Military secrets weren't my area of expertise."

"You stole the Labyrinth Code," she pointed out.

"Yes, well, I didn't steal Evadare's secrets. Anyway, the Alzanans aren't trying to *steal* Ondinium; they're trying to *hack* it, and both the Council and the Code are very resistant to hacking."

"What's the difference?"

"The Alzanans are attacking us from the outside— trying to hack their way through our defenses and into our nation. They won't find that easy to do. The Demicans, however, could have stolen Ondinium from within long ago, if they'd been the least bit organized. They've already made significant changes to our culture and physique. Just look at our skin color. The lower castes, which interbreed with Demicans quite often, have grown progressively lighter, whereas exalteds, who rarely breed out of caste, have remained dark. Tell me, my hawk, do you and Cristof intend to have children?"

Taya scowled at the reminder of Alister's fixation on social engineering and eugenics. "I don't have any Demican in me."

"No, but you have the light skin of Mareaux, which will inevitably lighten the skin of your children."

"I don't see why that matters. It's the soul that's born to a caste, not the skin."

"Skin reflects soul. The purer the color, the purer the spirit."

Taya's scowl deepened. Alister was wrong, she knew it, but she wasn't sure how to argue with him when she'd spent years of her childhood wishing for dark copper skin and straight black hair herself. Passing the Great Exam had allowed her to move from the famulate caste to the icarus caste, but it hadn't transformed her from an immigrant's daughter to a pureblood Ondinium. That would only happen if she lived well and earned an auspicious rebirth.

Which reminded her of something he'd said in the cell.

"You're worried about your rebirth, aren't you? That's why you're helping me."

Her words hung in the air for several minutes. They were far from the entrance now, and the only sounds in the tunnel were their own.

"I have a death or two that weighs on my soul," Alister admitted at last, his tone studiously casual. "My work was always intended for the greater benefit of Ondinium, but the deaths became problematic. It seems wise to counterweight them while I still can."

"Do you think the colonel would have killed me?"

"Mazzoletti would have, if Agosti didn't."

"Are you going to come back to Ondinium with me, then?"

He fell silent again. Taya didn't remember him thinking so long before he spoke, before. It was another thing that had changed since his exile.

"I wasn't intending to come this far with you in the first place," he said at last. "However, I don't think I have a choice anymore."

She bit her lip, thinking of Florianne, left dead in the snow.

"I'll vouch for you," she promised.

"I would appreciate that."

Something boomed and the tunnel shook, stone and dirt falling from the roof. They ducked, holding their arms over their heads. Taya widened the lantern's aperture to see what was happening through the cloud of dirt and dust. Gunfire rattled, not too far behind.

"Come on!" She grabbed Alister's arm and pulled him forward.

"What's happening?" he shouted, stumbling as he held his cane high. A loud mechanical sound accompanied the next crumble of rocks. Taya looked over her shoulder and saw lights bobbing along the side of the tunnel. More shots. One of the lights fell and went out.

"I think the firefight just broke back into the tunnel."

"Do you have your identification papers with you?"

"Of course not! And I'm wearing the Alzanan coat you gave me!"

"Get rid of it."

That sounded like a bad idea in the middle of winter, but Alister had a point— being spotted in a soldier's coat would likely get her shot before anyone thought to ask questions. She grabbed his hand and wrapped his fingers around the lantern's ring.

"Hold this."

The noise behind them was growing louder: shouts and shots and the mechanical clank and wheeze of a walking war machine. Taya tore off her coat and threw it into a corner. Lictors looked for castemarks before they looked at clothes, but she hoped her lictor's jacket would be recognizable enough to make them hesitate before they fired.

Assuming it was the Ondiniums who caught them. A bullet pinged down the hallway. The Alzanans were following the lictors into the tunnel.

"Hurry!"

Alister stumbled and bent over, coughing again. He thrust out the hand holding the lantern.

"I *can't!* Take this back!"

Taya grabbed it, then took Alister's hand and began running full tilt. The last thing she wanted was for one of them to be killed like Florianne by a stray bullet.

The tunnel split.

"Scrap!" She stopped, steadying Alister as he stumbled against her. "Which way?"

"The way that wasn't used by the mecharachnid."

"Right." She pulled him into the narrower tunnel, checking the ground with her lantern. No sign of the machine's heavy circular prints or an augercar's wheels. She retreated several yards from the branch and then stopped to hood the lantern.

"We'll let them pass," she said.

"Make sure they don't see your light."

"Already done."

"I'm going to sit down and rest, then."

She decided to join him. The tunnel floor was cold. She set the lantern by her boot and reached out until her gloved fingers touched his coat. He shifted and his hand touched hers. She didn't say anything as he clasped it.

They sat wordlessly in the dark, holding hands, as the lictors and mecharachnid were pushed backward, firing and shouting. Then she heard the Alzanans shouting, "fall back, fall back!" A few seconds later, a ball of flame lit the passageway and an explosion shook the tunnels. Taya threw her free arm over her face, twisting toward Alister as a blast of hot air swept over them. The lictors' screams and cries of agony were barely audible over the ringing in her ears. Something else exploded, sending scraps of metal spinning and clattering down the tunnel.

Only gradually was Taya able to make out the orders being shouted. The Alzanans were heading back to Terminal.

"Bring back any Ondies who can walk!" a commander shouted. "Kill the rest!"

Taya shuddered as shots rang out, fewer this time, deliberate and well-spaced.

The Alzanans drew closer, their lanterns bobbing in the darkness. She scooted back against the wall, pulling Alister with her. The soldiers raised their lanterns and glanced down the tunnel, but their light didn't extend all the way to where Taya and Alister were hiding. The soldiers kicked chunks of broken mecharachnid aside and continued past the tunnel mouth for a few minutes before returning.

"Nobody down here," one shouted. "Looks like we got them all."

"Good; take their weapons and fall back. We'll round up some reinforcements before we go any deeper."

Taya waited, her heart pounding, as the Alzanans marched away. Silence and darkness fell, but she didn't dare move. The smell of blood, burnt flesh, and seared metal stung her nose. Periodically she heard a metallic creak or pop, and small stones pattered down from the roof.

"Are they gone?" Alister whispered at last.

"I think so."

"We should move on, then." He squeezed her hand. "How are you holding up?"

"I'm fine." She pulled her hand out of his and picked up the lantern. Something rattled and she froze. "Did you hear that?"

"The icarus caste reports a disproportionately high incidence of claustrophobia," he murmured. She heard the scrape of his cane tip as he stood and checked around him for obstacles. "Do you suffer from it, too, Taya? If so, allow me to remind you that these tunnels have stood for over a thousand years."

"Probably not with people setting off explosives inside of them, though," she retorted, guiding his hand to her arm.

"Are you using the lantern?"

"Not until I find out whether they posted a guard."

"Then let me lead."

She paused, confused, before she understood and laid her hand on his arm, instead. He walked forward, his cane lightly scraping the ground in front of them.

At last he stopped, his cane striking something that returned a metallic clink. Rubble from the broken walking machine, she guessed. She lifted her face and thought she felt a waft of fresher air. They'd reached the big tunnel.

"Anyone here?" he asked softly.

"No." The tunnel was pitch black. *This is what it's like for Alister all the time*, she thought with a guilty shiver.

"Then you had better unhood the lantern. I believe the passage may be a bit cluttered around here."

She opened the aperture into a narrow slit. He was right; parts of the Ondinium walking machine had been hurled yards down the tunnel. She looked around, then swiftly yanked her eyes away from a bleeding, disembodied arm in the wreckage.

She didn't want to look any closer.

"Let's go," she said shakily. Alister laid a hand on her elbow as she guided them beyond the range of the explosion.

She wasn't certain how far they'd gone when she heard a scraping sound and was blinded by a bright light that caught her and Alister in the center of the tunnel. She gave an alarmed cry and raised her free hand to cover her eyes, squinting.

"We're friends!" she shouted in Ondinium. "Don't shoot!"

"What happened?" Alister asked, dropping his free hand into his coat pocket. "What's going on?"

As Taya's eyes adjusted, she saw that the light came from a lantern mounted in front of a mirrored parabolic reflector much farther down the tunnel. She blinked. Both were part of a giant steel mecharachnid that squatted in the center of the passage, its multiple gun barrels aimed directly at them.

"It's a mecharachnid," she hissed. "Don't move!"

A grating, scraping sound came from within the machine. A side door swung open and a black-uniformed figure squirmed out and dropped several feet to the ground. He straightened and pulled a grimy scarf away from his face.

"*Taya?*"

She dropped the lantern and ran forward to throw herself into Cristof's arms.

CHAPTER SIXTEEN

CRISTOF HELD HER so tightly that she could barely breathe, but she didn't care, standing on her toes, her arms wrapped around his neck and her face buried in his shoulder. His embrace felt like a shelter she'd been seeking for days.

"Oh, Lady, Taya, it *is* you. I was so afraid I had lost you for good," he said, his voice shaking. "I was so afraid I'd lost you!"

"Taya?" Alister's voice rose behind them. "Hello? What's happening?"

Taya squeezed her husband tighter, reassuring herself that he was there, tall, solid, and reeking of machine oil and coal smoke. Only now could she let the tears burn her eyes as she admitted to herself how frightened she'd been for him.

It was a long time before he lowered her back to the ground, and then only to cover her face in kisses. She brushed back his long black hair and returned them, tasting tears and soot.

Alister coughed.

"Cris? Can I assume that's you?"

Her husband made a meaningless noise in reply, then reluctantly drew back, his eyes still fixed on her face and his arms still wrapped around her. Taya smiled, ridiculously happy to see his sharp features smudged with grease and streaked with tears. His wire-rimmed glasses were fogged up and knocked askew. She straightened them, then ran her hands over his dirty cheeks.

"I'm so glad to see you," she said, taking in his filthy lictor's uniform and the soot-smudged scarf wrapped around his neck. His right wrist was bandaged in grimy strips of fabric. "I was afraid I'd lost you, too."

He mustered his own helpless, crooked smile.

"Sorry. Got you dirty." He rubbed at something on her cheek. "Tell me you're all right. Tell me those bastards didn't hurt you."

"Is there *anybody* here who will talk to me?" Alister asked, sounding exasperated.

"Nobody hurt me," she said. "Did the ship crash? What happened to your wrist?"

"Sprained— we had a rough landing." He pulled her close and looked at Alister, standing alone in the spotlight. "What are you doing here, Al?"

"Rescuing your wife." The blind exalted coughed. "I don't suppose there's an army of lictors behind you."

"*Far* behind me. I'm rear guard for the assault team; they wouldn't let me go in with them." He looked down at Taya. "Jinian's out there, looking for you. If she didn't find you in camp, we were going to leave the team and search for you on our own."

"Really?" Taya bit her lip. "Cris, a lot of lictors have been killed already. The Alzanans blew up the other mecharachnid, and they're pulling together another group to head down the tunnel."

He tightened his embrace, looking grim.

"All right. We knew they might try to find us." He held her another few seconds, then let go and stepped away. "Take Alister and keep walking down the tunnel. The main camp's about an hour away, but you'll run into perimeter guards before you get there. I'll join you as soon as I can."

"No!" Taya grabbed his arms, careful of his bandaged wrist. "The Alzanans have *bombs*, Cris. They blew the other mecharachnid to pieces!"

"It probably ran out of ammunition. I'll keep them too far away to throw bombs."

"Then I'm staying here with you."

"There's only room for one person in that thing, and I'm *not* leaving you out in the open."

"Well, I'm not leaving you now that I've found you again!"

"Oh, please, I can't stand to listen to any more of this." Alister stepped forward, aiming the needler at them. "*I* will take the machine, if you please."

"Alister, no!" Taya was horrified. Had he planned this all along?

"Don't be an idiot." Cristof walked up and grabbed Alister's gun wrist, twisting the needler out of his hand. "You'd crash the slagging thing into a wall."

"That's not the point, Brother." Alister didn't struggle, turning his blindfolded face toward Cristof. "*I'm* staying and you two are going."

"I can't do that."

"Lictor Gryngoth fights the enemy; Imperate Viridinion stays safely behind."

"We're not playing games anymore," Cristof said, his voice rough with emotion. He released his brother's wrist. "Besides, you've already been a hero tonight. I'll never be able to repay you for saving Taya."

"Well, I rather hope you get the chance to try." Alister touched the front of his coat, to the left. "There's a bullet lodged somewhere right about here, Cris. Under a rib, I think. I don't have an hour of walking left in me."

"Alister!" Taya gasped as Cristof grabbed his brother's coat and yanked it open. "Why didn't you tell me?"

"I wouldn't be any better off in Terminal with Florianne, would I?" He smiled tightly and put the needler back into his pocket while his brother swore at the sight of his bloody shirt. "I figured that I had a much better chance of getting decent medical assistance from the Ondiniums than the Alzanans. It's too bad the main force is still so far away."

Cris looked up at the mecharachnid, and Taya could see the calculations running through his head.

"The top of the machine is too close to the tunnel roof for someone to ride it," he began, uncertainly, "but if we made some kind of sling...."

"Are the mecharachnids significantly faster than a walking human? I seem to recall reading that the imperial strategists always needed to take their lack of speed into account when planning military actions."

"At least you'd be off your feet!" Cris snapped, the pain audible in his voice.

"I have a better idea." Alister reached out and found his brother's arm, resting his fingers on it. "Show me the gun controls and leave me here to shoot at Alzanans. Then you and Taya head to camp as quickly as you can and send back reinforcements— with a competent physician, if you don't mind."

"I could stay..." Taya ventured. She loathed the thought of sitting in a metal machine shooting helpless soldiers, but she couldn't just stand there and let her husband and brother-in-law debate who was going to do the job without volunteering herself.

"No," Cristof said firmly.

"It's not an icarus's job," Alister demurred, simultaneously. "It's a lictor's job, actually, but since we don't have one handy… give the job to the fallen exalted, Cris. Allow me this chance to redeem myself in the Council's eyes. I don't expect to be welcomed back to Ondinium, but at least they might add a footnote to my name saying that I wasn't a complete embarrassment to my caste."

"He's counterweighting," Taya said, swallowing a lump in her throat. "That's why he saved me. He's trying to do something good before he faces the Forge."

"Al… you don't believe any of that scrap, do you?"

"Weren't *you* invoking the Lady just a few minutes ago?"

"Rhetorical convention."

"Don't tell me that you weren't praying for your wife to be alive and well." Alister cocked his head. "And she is, isn't she? Maybe the Lady sent me to Terminal with Mazzoletti to give us *both* a chance."

Cristof let out an impatient, frustrated breath.

"I'm not going to stand here and have a religious debate with you while you're dying!"

"What better time? This is the second time I've come face-to-face with my own mortality. I'd say it's an eye-opening experience, but…." he gestured wryly.

"Don't do that."

"Show me how to operate the guns and make sure they're pointed in the right direction."

"You won't be able to see the soldiers coming!"

"In my experience, the Alzanan military seldom travels quietly. I assume there's some sort of hatch or door I can leave open to listen."

"Yes…."

"And the engine is off, and I certainly don't need any lights. I'll surprise them as you surprised us."

"Assuming you don't bleed to death, first."

"I intend to do everything I can to stay alive until your lictors return for me." Alister paused. "I promise, Cris. This is not a suicide stand; it's a pragmatic solution to a strategic problem."

"Don't try to tell me you aren't hoping to come out of this a hero."

Alister smiled. "I wouldn't mind that, of course."

Cristof looked from his brother to Taya, clearly torn. Taya started to say something, then closed her mouth. She couldn't force Cris to choose between his wife and his brother. That was something he had to do on his own.

"All right," he said at last, his shoulders slumping. "Damn you, Al, if you get yourself killed after all I've done for you...."

"You've always known me to be a thankless bastard."

"You are," Cristof replied, but he stepped forward and gave his brother a hard hug at the same time. "But I'm not. Thank you for bringing Taya back."

"You're welcome," Alister said, bending over and coughing as his brother released him. Cristof immediately looked alarmed.

"I'm sorry— I didn't think—"

"It's all right." Alister's smile lingered on his lips as he straightened. "I think our feisty little icarus has been a good influence on that clockwork heart of yours."

Cristof scowled and grabbed his brother's sleeve.

"Get in. I'll show you the controls."

They helped Alister up into the machine. Taya wrinkled her nose when she saw the tight quarters; it was little more than a hard chair with operating controls around it, everything covered with soot and smelling of smoke.

"It has a ventilation problem," Cristof said, grimacing. "I had to travel with the door ajar."

"I was wondering why you smelled so bad." Alister wedged his cane next to him. "Fortunately, dirt doesn't bother me as much as it used to. How do I operate this thing?"

Cristof moved his hands to the various controls, explaining the guns at some length.

"Everything here and here," he put Alister's hands on the levers to his left and right, "controls the legs, but don't try it. This thing is almost impossible to maneuver; I've had two days of practice and I can still barely keep it moving in a straight line."

"How many mecharachnids do we have?"

"I don't know, but we'd better hope our victory doesn't rely on them. The ornithopters work surprisingly well for a bunch of thousand-year-old machines, but these things are in desperate need of a design overhaul."

"Which I assume you have already worked out in your head."

"I've had a few ideas," Cristof admitted.

"I look forward to hearing your plans." Alister rested his hands lightly on the gun controls. "Now, you'd better get going. I'd like to get this bullet out of me soon."

"Al...." Cristof reached in and squeezed his brother's shoulder before dropping down to the ground. "Someone will be here for you in two hours. Stay alive for me."

"I'll do my best."

"Wait." Taya pulled herself up to the driver's cabin and lightly kissed Alister's cheek. "Thank you, Alister. Take care of yourself." She jumped back down and turned away. *Lady, keep him,* she prayed, squeezing her eyes shut a moment. *He's a bad man, but he's trying, and that has to count for something.*

Cristof unhooked the lantern from the front of the machine, pulling it out of its mirrored niche. He looked at Alister.

"We're leaving now."

Alister lifted a hand to wave, and then carefully set it back down on the firing controls.

They talked quietly as they walked through the dark tunnels. Taya told Cristof everything that had happened since he'd seen her floating in midair, clutching Liliana's rescue harness. He wasn't happy to hear that she'd been held captive, but she assured him that the Alzanans had treated her respectfully. She chose, upon seeing Cristof's dark expression, not to tell him about the soldier who'd tripped her in the hallway or about Alister's rationale to Patrice Corundel for breaking into her cell.

"I'm sorry the Mareaux girl died," Cristof said, when she'd finished. "Do you think she was really Al's minder?"

"Maybe. She seemed too self-possessed for a civilian, but I think she genuinely liked him, too." Taya braced herself. "So, tell me about the *Firebrand.*"

"Janos is alive, but he lost most of his crew, including Lieutenant Imbrex."

"Oh, no!" Taya was stricken. "What happened?"

"She was shot manning a volley gun." Cristof sighed. "The *Formidable* tore us apart. If there hadn't been an Ondinium weapons platoon guarding the border with mortars and ondium-tipped missiles, we might have all died, but when they started firing, the Alzanans turned back. Janos brought the ship down to a sliding stop in a narrow U-shaped valley not far from the platoon and anchored it. We were retrieved by a patrol that patched us up, covered the ship, and took us into the tunnels."

"Is Liliana all right?"

"Yes...."

"What?" Taya felt a spike of panic. "What happened?"

"The commander in charge is Decatur Constante, who arrested her. I tried to talk her out of it, but she's holding Liliana until she hears from Ondinium." Cristof made an impatient sound. "She sent a lictor to the nearest signal station two days ago; she refused to send her only icarus, so it could be another two or three days before we get the Council's reply."

"They're treating her well, though, aren't they?"

"Oh, yes, don't worry. Constante's a System Analyst— she understands how important Liliana's testimony will be for our nation."

"And Jinian's out there fighting with our lictors?"

"She insisted on it." He frowned. "I hope she's all right."

"Me, too. Where's Captain Amcathra?"

"Back in the valley with Professor Dautry and some of Decatur Constante's military engineers, trying to get the *Firebrand* back into the air. Apparently I'm to be sent back to Ondinium as soon as possible." He snorted. "Which is why I was going to escape with Jinian as soon as the assault team returned. I couldn't leave without finding you, first."

"But you didn't even know I was alive."

"Of course you were alive." He pulled her into a tight, one-armed hug. "You're the toughest woman I know. And I wasn't going to let anyone drag me out of these mountains until I'd found you again."

She squeezed him back, certain that everything would be all right as long as they were together.

They had walked a long time before they were finally confronted by two armed lictors calling out a challenge. Taya raised her hands at once, but Cristof took a moment to tug his scarf up over the bottom half of his face before he lifted his. It was the scarf she'd bought for him in Os Cansai, she saw, its blue silk and silver embroidery smudged with soot. The fact that he'd retrieved it from the crash brought a lump to her throat.

"Taya Icarus and Exalted Forlore," she said, meeting the lictors' eyes. "The Alzanans are gathering a force to enter and explore the tunnels. You need to send a force back there to stop them."

"With a physician," Cristof added. Taya shot him a scandalized look. He wasn't supposed to speak when he was covered.

"With a physician for Alister Forlore, who's holding off the Alzanans in a mecharachnid," she elaborated. "He was shot in the chest. He still seemed strong when we left him, but he needs medical attention."

"I'm sorry, but first... Exalted....?" the older lictor sounded apologetic. Cristof pulled down the scarf enough to reveal the wave-shaped castemark tattooed over his right cheekbone. The lictor sketched a bow, looking relieved when Cristof pulled his scarf back up again. "Thank you, sir. I apologize for the necessity." She turned to Taya. "Do you have any identification?"

"Of course not! I was— no, wait, I do." She bent over, then froze as the rifle shifted to cover her. "I'm just going to roll up my pants cuff, all right?"

"Slowly, please."

She carefully unpinned her golden feather and held it out. The lictor's stern expression lightened at last.

"Welcome back, Icarus," she said, kindly. "Your friends have been worried about you."

"I've been worried about them, too," she said, pinning the feather to the front of her jacket. "May we pass?"

"Go ahead. Lasse, run ahead with the report."

The younger of the two lictors nodded and raced off.

"We'll send another platoon out as soon as we can, Exalted," the older lictor said. Cristof started to answer and Taya put a hand on his arm. He stopped, looking at her.

"Thank you," she said for him. "The man in the mecharachnid is the exalted's brother. He was injured rescuing me from the Alzanans and he's down there now guarding our backs. Please take good care of him."

"We will," the lictor promised. Taya thanked her one last time and drew her husband away.

He was silent until they lost sight of the guard, and then he sighed, pulling down the scarf.

"Decatur Constante asked me to cover my face to avoid offending the troops, but I haven't bothered observing the rest of the rules."

"What happened to your mask?"

"Janos needed the ondium, so I gave it back." He smiled. "He didn't have to twist my arm."

"No, I don't suppose he did." She stopped and touched his cheek, running her thumb over the scar that broke his castemark. "I know you don't like being covered, and you didn't have much choice about speaking for yourself before this, but now that I'm back, please let me do my job."

"I wasn't going to go looking for you because I wanted my *icarus*," he objected, forcefully.

"I know." She held his face and his gaze. "But I'm proud to represent my husband properly before the rest of the world."

"You know it makes me uncomfortable."

"Then don't wear a mask at all."

"Apparently that makes the *lictors* uncomfortable."

"You've never worried about making them uncomfortable in the past."

"That's true, but… this time they're risking their lives to defend our border. I don't want to add to their stress."

"That's very sweet of you."

He grimaced. "I thought we were past 'sweet.'"

"But I so seldom get a chance to say it." She smiled at his expression and they started walking again, their hands slipping comfortably together.

They passed another guard who didn't demand to see Cristof's castemark and entered the Ondinium encampment, which had been set up inside a vast, cavernous chamber lit by a multitude of lanterns. The room's rock walls were ornately carved with ancient images and its floor was crowded with soldiers, camp gear, weapons, two more mecharachnids, barrels, crates, and bags. A small group of lictors was assembling by the doorway, checking their weapons. Taya looked around, but this chamber had never been converted for the pneumatic rail.

"Exalted!" A famulate wearing the uniform of a Constante house servant stepped up and bowed, his palm against his forehead. "Decatur Constante is waiting for you." They followed him to a large tent set up against one of the walls. He stopped outside and waved them through the tent's double-flap entrance.

Decatur Constante sat at a small wooden desk, her ivory mask close to hand as she studied a map. She was a solidly built woman in her seventies with strong features and a piercing gaze. Her robes, including the heavily embroidered outer robe draped over the back of her chair, were conservative in their design and color, and her long white hair had been pulled back into a series of old-fashioned braids and knots.

Taya gave a deep, respectful bow as the decatur looked up. Cristof tugged down his scarf.

"Icarus." Constante's eyebrows rose. "Welcome. I'm glad to see that you are alive."

"Thank you, Exalted."

"I understand the Alzanans plan to investigate the tunnel?" the decatur asked, turning her attention to Cristof.

"Yes. You're sending a group to meet them, aren't you?"

"You passed them coming in." Constante gestured to the folding camp chair in front of her portable desk. "Report."

"Go ahead," Cristof said, nudging Taya toward the chair, instead. She eyed it wistfully but shook her head.

"Decatur...." He frowned at Constante.

"Please be seated, Icarus," Constante said politely, as if that's what she'd intended from the start. Taya wavered a moment before sinking into the chair with relief. The decatur wrote out a note and handed it to Cristof. "Give this to Romaeus; he'll bring us some tea. You both look chilled."

"Thank you," Taya said again. "I would like that."

Cristof nodded and pulled up his scarf, ducking outside.

"Just the highlights," the decatur said, turning back to her. "I'll want a detailed report later, but for now tell me only what's important."

Resisting an urge to stand again, Taya related what little she knew about the camp at A-O Terminal, the *Formidable*, and the train's shipment of weapons. She described the armaments of the soldiers who'd blown up the first mecharachnid. Cristof returned as she mentioned that they'd left the man who'd rescued her in Cristof's machine, guarding the tunnel. She didn't mention his name to Constante, who didn't ask. Cristof didn't seem inclined to volunteer the information, either.

The tea came, along with a large plate of sausage and cheese that made Taya's stomach growl. Constante encouraged her to eat as she asked several follow-up questions, paying particular attention to the train and dirigible.

"I have already been briefed about most of those items," she said as Taya repeated Florianne's list of weaponry, "but what is a holocaust bomb?"

"I don't know, but apparently Mazzoletti and Corundel were talking about planting it by the Great Engine."

Constante's expression darkened.

"How would they get to it?"

"Well, Corundel probably knows all of the secret entrances and exits," Taya said, repeating Alister's speculation.

"They'd have to get the bomb into the capital in the first place...." Cristof mused.

"They have the *Formidable*," she reminded him.

"One ship against all our defenses?" He looked at Constante. "I assume we have more operative ornithopters by now."

"Yes, and most of them are guarding the capital. Moreover, we have assigned guards to every city gate and established patrols throughout the capital security zone. Nobody is permitted on or off a train at O-Base-0 without an identification check."

Taya approved. She'd flown over Ondinium's security zone numerous times as a courier— the artificially cleared twenty-five mile stretch between the station and the city would be all but impossible for anyone to cross unseen.

"Well, the main goals for tonight's raid were to destroy the train and the *Formidable*— either would be good, and both would be ideal." Cristof ran a hand through his long hair. "If we're lucky, they'll never get the holocaust bomb out of A-O Terminal."

"The team should return in a few more hours." Constante looked at the pocketwatch next to her mask. It wasn't one of Cristof's pieces. "I recommend you two go refresh yourselves. I will call a meeting as soon as we get a report, and I'll expect you both to attend."

"Yes, Exalted." Taya sprang out of her seat and bowed. Cristof frowned.

"Very well," he said, ungraciously. "We'll be in my tent."

Cristof's tent was the same size as the lictors', although someone had draped an extra piece of fabric over the entrance to provide him with more privacy. It contained those few possessions he'd scavenged from the *Firebrand*, including a handful of his Cabisi-language technical books and journals, Taya saw with amusement. They had to maneuver around each other in the confined space, but she was happy to undress and scrub too many days' worth of accumulated dirt and sweat off her skin with the help of a washrag, a scrap of soap, and a bowl of lukewarm water. While she washed, Cristof dug out her Cabisi clothes from a duffel bag.

"You brought them with you?" she exclaimed, surprised.

"I thought you might want them, once I found you." He smiled at her pleasure and would have gotten her all dirty again if she hadn't ordered him to wash himself off first. As it was, she didn't change into her clean clothes for some time afterward.

CHAPTER SEVENTEEN

TAYA WAS HALF-ASLEEP in front of Cristof's tent, waiting for the water in his small metal teapot to boil, when she heard a familiar voice.

"Icarus. Well met in time of war."

She spun around, catching Captain Amcathra with an expression on his face that she thought she'd never see— a small, relieved smile.

"Captain!" She leaped up. His smile vanished as he endured her embrace with the long-suffering air of a man who'd learned to stop fighting the inevitable.

"There you go again," Cristof muttered, crawling out of the tent half-awake and giving them a quizzical look. "You're the only man she hugs like that, Janos. Well, except me, of course. I don't understand it."

"I do not, either," Amcathra said, sounding pained. "Unless your wife has finally given up thrusting other women at me and has decided that we should become romantically involved, instead."

Taya released him with a startled gasp, then flushed as Cristof laughed.

"You are *not* allowed to make jokes!" she ordered, pointing a finger at the poker-faced lictor. "And I am definitely not done thrusting women at you!"

"I have no interest in the *principessa*, Icarus."

"Of course you don't! And I didn't thrust her at you, anyway."

"I believe it is called aiding and abetting."

"Don't be silly. I just thought it would do you some good to practice being nice to women. Lady knows, you need the help."

"Not from where I'm sitting," Cristof observed.

"Cover your face while you're outside," Taya scolded, giving him a stern look before turning back to the captain. He had several scrapes and ripening bruises visible on his face and a bandage wrapped around his right hand. "Is your hand all right?"

"It is a shallow wound. An ondium plate slipped while I was cutting it."

"Cris says you're fixing the ornithopter?"

"We are modifying it. The *Firebrand* will not be able to carry cannon anymore, but I believe it will bear five or six people back to the capital with reasonable speed."

"You're done, then?" The teapot whistled and Cristof reached for the lid, then snatched his hand back with an oath.

"I'll get it." Taya used one of her gloves as a kitchen mitt.

"Dautry and I will take it on a test flight tomorrow." Amcathra sat across from them. "You have not yet told me how it is that your wife has returned, Exalted. Were you and the *kattaka* successful?"

"Huh? What makes you think we were looking for her?"

"My many years of familiarity with your thought processes."

"You're guessing, aren't you?"

Amcathra took the cup Taya handed him. "Thank you, Icarus."

"Don't spill it," she warned. "Alister rescued me."

Amcathra's pale blue eyes widened, and he shot Cristof a suspicious look. Her husband raised a hand.

"I had no idea my brother was here!"

"He arrived with Lady Mazzoletti— it's a long story," she said. "I'll probably tell it at the briefing— you'll be there, won't you?"

"It is why I have returned."

"The short version is that Alister killed Patrice Corundel and rescued me. Florianne's dead, and Alister was shot." She indicated the area, looking at the lictor's face for some reaction. "He was walking and talking, but his shirt was covered in blood and he said he was too tired to walk another hour back to camp, so he stayed in the mecharachnid to guard the tunnel instead."

Amcathra looked from her to Cristof.

"It is difficult to gauge the severity of such a wound," he said, answering their unspoken question. "If he was able to walk and talk, then he is probably not in any immediate danger. Infection is the most likely risk."

"We understand infection," Cristof said flatly. Taya handed him a cup of tea.

"May I ask why you left a blind man to guard the tunnel?"

"I wanted to get Taya back to camp and warn Constante about the Alzanan advance. Alister volunteered to stay behind."

"I hope he does not shoot our troops."

"He won't as long as they're not speaking Alzanan."

"Would he recognize Cabisi?"

"Jinian wouldn't have anyone to talk to in Cabisi, anyway," Cristof said, looking uncomfortable.

"That is true." The lictor sipped his tea and eyed the exalted over the top of the cup. "The *kattaka* told me you were planning to look for your wife."

"You're welcome to call me Taya," Taya interrupted, a little tartly. "I'm more than just his wife, you know."

"I apologize, Icarus."

She rolled her eyes.

"Why in the world did Jinian tell you our plan?" Cristof looked nettled.

"She knew what I would do if I found you missing. Or perhaps you thought I would travel to Ondinium by myself after you had vanished?"

Cristof sighed.

"If you had no way of knowing where I was, then yes, I assumed you'd proceed to Ondinium to take a report to Council."

"Clearly you have learned little from your many years of familiarity with *my* thought processes."

"I also left you a letter explaining what I was doing and asking you not to come after me."

"Asking or ordering?"

"I prefer not to give you orders, Janos."

"I am pleased to hear that." Amcathra gave him an impassive look. "As it was, I gave her a map and compass to ensure that you did not get lost."

"I'm surprised you didn't try to stop us."

"I am satisfied with the *kattaka*'s combat ability and overall common sense."

"So," Taya said innocently, nestling her cup of tea close to her chest, "is *that* the kind of woman you like?"

"Icarus...." The lictor closed his eyes a moment, as if searching for internal restraint. "There are many women whose talents I appreciate without any amorous undercurrents."

"Fine. What about Professor Dautry?"

"She is in good health and has been instrumental in rebuilding the *Firebrand*."

That wasn't quite what Taya had meant, and she had a feeling Amcathra knew it, but she let the moment go and became more serious.

"Then tell me about the firefight, Captain. I was so sorry to hear that Lieutenant Imbrex didn't make it...."

· ✽ ·

The last time Taya had been to a military briefing had been in Glasgar, during the initial Alzanan invasion. She looked around, half-hoping to see General Kammel at the table, but of course she wasn't there. The general had died in the bombing, like almost every other lictor Taya had met there.

Feeling solemn, she bowed to the lictor in charge of this meeting, Major Leppala, who instructed her to sit in the front. Cristof hung back with coat collar pulled high and his soot-stained, silver-and-blue Cabisi scarf wrapped over the lower half of his face.

A few minutes later the decatur entered, masked and robed, with her long sleeves spilling over an icarus's proffered arm. Everyone stood and bowed as she sat at the head of the table, her icarus efficiently straightening her robes and perching on a stool beside her, the decatur's hand on his arm. Leppala introduced Decatur Constante and the icarus Keman, mostly for her benefit, Taya assumed.

Keman was an older icarus with graying hair and a kind but careworn face. It was unusual for an icarus his age to still wear wings; most icarii retired early, grounded by the damage that years of long flights and hard landings wrought on their muscles and joints. His ease around Decatur Constante suggested that they'd worked together for a long time.

Leppala nodded to one of the men sitting in the front with Taya. "Corporal Getha. Your report?"

"Sir." Getha stood and faced the group. "My team has just returned from investigating reports of an Alzanan incursion into the tunnels." He drew their attention to the contour map on the table. Someone had drawn in A-O Terminal and the underground tunnels. He dropped a finger about halfway between their current camp and Terminal. "The tunnel has collapsed here."

Taya gasped.

"We attempted to dig through, but the collapse is too extensive. I sent a fireteam around to the Epsilon door to recon from the outside and intercept our returning troops. The team hasn't returned yet."

"What caused the collapse?" someone asked.

"We think the Alzanans set off explosives to block our access to Terminal."

"Then they don't know about the Epsilon door."

"No, sir."

"What—" Taya stopped and looked around. Nobody objected to her speaking, so she continued. "What about the mecharachnid that C—Exalted Forlore had been driving? Did you find it?"

"No, ma'am. It was beyond the area of collapse."

She bit her lip. "Beyond it, or... or beneath it?"

"We don't know, ma'am. Our team will attempt to determine that during their reconnaissance."

Taya swallowed hard.

A brief discussion followed concerning whether the troops stranded by the collapse would find the Epsilon door and whether it would be safe to use an augercar to clear the path again. Taya had nothing to contribute, her stomach filled with acid.

Her report was next. Over the next hour, she told the group everything she could about the Alzanan camps and armaments and explained how she'd escaped with Alister Forlore. The shock and discomfort around the table was palpable as she described how the blind outcaste had killed Patrice Corundel to rescue her, and how he'd stayed behind in the mecharachnid to guard the tunnel. Nobody dared look at Cristof openly, but numerous sidelong glances were cast his way. To Taya's relief, Decatur Constante, through Keman, was more interested in Corundel's plans for the holocaust bomb and the Great Engine.

At last Major Leppala thanked her and said they were done.

"Just one last thing, if you please, Decatur," Taya said, turning to Decatur Constante. "My impression of the colonel — Queen Pietra Agosti — was that she's a reasonable woman who's very concerned about her sister's welfare. If you could arrange a meeting between her and *Principessa* Liliana, I think we might be able to work out an end to these hostilities."

The gray-haired icarus at the decatur's side gave her a benevolent look.

"The decatur thanks you for your suggestion, Icarus," he said.

Taya bowed to the masked exalted and sat. She knew the tap code didn't allow for lengthy responses, so Keman's brief reply didn't mean the decatur was ignoring her suggestion.

Captain Amcathra was the next to give his report. He briefly described the modifications his team had made to the ornithopter and confirmed that if the test run was successful, he'd take Exalted Forlore back to Ondinium to report their progress to the Oporphyr Council.

"Are you going, too, Icarus?" Major Leppala asked, looking at Taya. "We could always use another set of wings on the line."

Taya hesitated. She didn't want to leave Cristof's side, but serving in times of emergency was an integral part of an icarus's duties.

"I'd like to escort Exalted Forlore back to the capital," she said after a moment. "Once he's safe, I'll be happy to go wherever the Council sends me."

Out of the corner of her eye, she saw Keman give her a brief, approving nod.

"Then—" the major was interrupted by a commotion at the door. Everyone turned. Taya slipped away from the table to join her husband. Cristof was standing at the edge of the group, his gloved hands jammed into his coat pockets and his shoulders high. His expression was hidden by the scarf, but when she wrapped an arm around him, she felt the tension in his bearing.

The officers around the table moved aside to let in a new group of lictors, several of them bandaged and limping. Taya held her breath until she saw a familiar face among them.

"It's Jinian!" She sighed with relief, then realized that Cristof was still searching the small group for a face that wasn't there.

"Sir." One of the lictors saluted the major. He had an angry red streak across his face and blood matted his light brown hair. "Private Eret reporting, sir."

"Go on."

"Sir, we took two Alzanan prisoners."

The enemy soldiers were brought forward. They carried themselves with brave defiance, although both wilted a little when their eyes fell on the regal, ornately robed and masked figure of Decatur Constante and the stern icarus in full armature who stood beside her.

"Take them away; we'll question them later," Major Leppala directed. Two lower-ranked lictors at the fringe of the gathering took the prisoners' arms and marched them off.

"Continue, Private."

Eret crisply described what Taya could only consider to be a failed mission— one mecharachnid and driver down, one missing in action, twelve lictors dead, and four wounded. The explosives team hadn't been able to get close enough to the train or dirigible to blow either up, although it had managed to destroy the tracks. They'd retreated to the tunnels only to encounter a platoon of Alzanan soldiers fleeing through the entrance after a ceiling collapse. The two prisoners were what remained of that platoon.

"From what we could figure out, sir, the Alzanans ran into Exalted Forlore's mecharachnid and were driven back by its guns. I don't know if it was the gunfire that collapsed the tunnel or an Alzanan bomb, but we didn't see any sign of the vehicle or the exalted on the Terminal side of the tunnel." The private swallowed. "Did... did he make it back?"

Cristof's knees collapsed. Taya grabbed his arms and the lictors around them burst into motion, one of them leaping off a chair and passing it back, the others jostling each other aside in an attempt to give the exalted more room. He sat heavily on the chair, leaning over. Taya interposed herself between him and the assembly.

"The exalted's brother was in the mecharachnid," she told the private, who was looking confused. Her throat tightened. "He never came back."

The young lictor gave her a stricken look.

"Excuse me." Keman pushed through the crowd and lowered his voice as he reached Taya. "Let me help you get the exalted out of here."

They flanked Cristof, one icarus on each arm, and led him away from the table. When they reached his tent, he staggered inside and collapsed on the cot, yanking the scarf from his face.

Keman stood outside, holding open the tent flap. "Tea or something stronger?"

"Something stronger, I think," Taya said, kneeling next to her husband. "Thank you."

"Take care of him," he said gently, closing the flap. Taya pulled off her gloves and scarf and wrapped her arms around her husband, pulling him close.

"I'm sorry," she whispered.

He nodded, holding her. Neither of them said anything else. Neither of them needed to.

They had both grieved for Alister before.

· ✱ ·

Taya left Cristof asleep in the tent. Outside, the vast chamber was as dark as ever, although the noise level had fallen off. She checked her pocketwatch. Almost seven in the morning. She wearily ran her fingers through her hair.

"Taya."

Jinian and Liliana were sitting cross-legged in front of the neighboring tent. They stood and hugged her, and Taya felt suddenly, fiercely grateful to have her two new friends with her again.

"Do you want some tea?" Jinian asked as they settled back down again.

"Yes, please."

They sat in silence until the tea was served.

"How are you?" Taya asked at last, taking her cup.

"I am well." Jinian cocked her head. "I am sorry to hear about your husband's brother."

"Thank you." Taya pulled her legs up and rested her chin on her knees. Liliana gave her arm a quick, comforting pat.

"You know, we thought he'd died once before, back in Ondinium. It turned out he'd faked his death to commit a crime. Now I keep thinking, 'what if he faked this death, too?' But I don't think he did. He was wounded; I saw the blood. And he was blind, and he'd twisted his ankle. There's no way he could have escaped…." A lump rose in her throat.

"You never know," Liliana said, straining to sound encouraging.

"I do not wish to seem insensitive, but I think it is better to avoid clinging to false hope," Jinian said, gently. "However, it is appropriate to honor him for his heroism— for holding back enemy soldiers in an ancient war machine, blind and alone, in order to protect his loved ones and his nation."

Taya nodded, blinking back tears.

"He said he was trying to redeem himself before he died," she said, her voice shaking.

"I'm sure the Mother of Earth and the Father of Sky will honor all the truths he held in his heart," Liliana said, comfortingly.

Taya wasn't sure what truths, if any, had ever been held in Alister's heart, but she certainly couldn't find it in her own to loathe him anymore. She sighed and held out her cup for Jinian to refill. The three of them gradually brought each other up to date.

"Did Captain Amcathra leave again?" she asked, when the conversation lulled. "He's testing the ship today, isn't he?"

"Yes. He stopped by before he left." Liliana sighed. "I wish I could go outside, too. Decatur Constante won't let me leave. And she won't unmask for me, either. Her icarus does all the talking and she just sits there like a statue. It's creepy. I like working with your husband better, Taya."

"Lil— did Amcathra tell you I met your sister?"

"*What?*" Liliana's face lit up. "Pietra?"

"She's a colonel now." Taya described her brief encounter with Pietra Agosti and Fosca Mazzoletti. Liliana squealed and hugged her, then immediately began to worry about her sister's safety with the murderous Mazzoletti at her side.

"I'm not sure Lady Mazzoletti will dare do anything now," Taya said. "I mean, she'll be the first person the colonel's staff interrogates if anything happens to the colonel."

"Do you think I could talk to her? Pietra, I mean?"

"I suggested it to Decatur Constante. We'll see what she decides."

After they'd finished the tea she checked on Cristof. He was still asleep, so she took a tour through the camp with her two friends. Lucanus and one of the helmswomen, Strand, had survived, although Strand had suffered a broken leg in the crash. She was in good spirits, though, and both Firebrands were relieved that Taya was alive and well. By the time Taya returned, carrying breakfast, Cristof was up and cleaning a rifle in front of the tent. The bottle of whiskey that Keman had left there remained unopened.

"I brought you something to eat." Taya set down the crate lid she was using as a tray and sat beside him. He tugged down his scarf to kiss her. He looked tired, and his pale gray eyes were shadowed with sorrow.

"I'm not hungry."

"Try to eat something, anyway." She offered him a bowl of stew. It wasn't her idea of breakfast, but she supposed fresh eggs and bacon might be asking too much of an army camp. "Take a few mouthfuls, at least, for strength."

He ran a rag through the barrel of the rifle and set the parts aside, wiping his hands on his trousers before taking the bowl.

"You're not going to use that rifle on anyone in particular, are you?" she asked. He looked up at her over the edges of his spectacles.

"No, nobody in particular."

He resumed cleaning his weapon once they'd finished eating. Taya returned the dishes.

"How is the exalted doing?" Keman asked, catching up with her as she left the mess tent. He was out of armature and, like her, wore a golden feather pinned to his lapel.

"He's up, and he ate a little."

"That's good." The icarus smiled and made a polite bow. "Allow me to introduce myself. I'm Keman, military corps, on long-term assignment to Decatur Evadare Constante."

"I'm Taya," she said, returning the bow. "Diplomatic corps, on long-term assignment to Exalted Cristof Forlore."

"Of course you are. You're the caste's most famous icarus, Taya. Or maybe the most infamous, right now."

She blushed, looking around the cavern, but nobody was paying attention to them. "Do people really think we assassinated *Il Re* Quintilio?"

"To be honest, nobody was sure what to think. You and your husband *have* developed something of a reputation over the last year."

"But the real story is being 'graphed back to Ondinium, right?"

"Yes. The report includes a summary of Princess Agosti's testimony."

"Good. I don't want my family and friends thinking I'm a murderer." Her mood darkened. "Even though I *have* killed some people."

"I'm sorry." Keman drew her aside as a group of lictors brushed past them to enter the mess tent. They began walking through the support-services tents. "Killing isn't easy even when you've been trained for it."

"Do you get nightmares, too?"

"I do. And I've known many lictors who've had nightmares too, although they don't like to admit it."

"How long have you worked for the military?"

"Thirty-one years. I joined as soon as I was eligible and spent my first twenty years on regular duty and the rest assigned to House Constante." He gave her a rueful smile. "I was planning to retire last month."

"The decatur wouldn't let you?"

"I requested an extension. I didn't want her distracted by a new icarus while she was on the front line."

"That was thoughtful of you."

"She's a good leader. I know some people think she's cold and conservative, but you have to remember that the safety of the nation rests on her shoulders. She weighs everything she says and does in the context of Ondinium's long-term survival."

"How does she feel about last night's attack?"

"It could have gone better," Keman admitted. "She's been up since the briefing, working on her next move."

"What will that be?"

"I can't say. But she wants to send Exalted Forlore back, if your captain can get his ship in the air. Your husband isn't going to charge out and avenge himself on the Alzanans who collapsed that tunnel on his brother, is he?"

Taya gave the question serious consideration, thinking about the rifle Cristof had been cleaning.

"I don't think so," she said at last. "Although he'd probably enjoy killing some Alzanans if he got the chance."

"Let's make sure he doesn't." Keman gave her an avuncular pat on the back as they reached the lines of sleeping tents. "Go keep him company. I'll see that you're notified if anything important happens."

The morning passed slowly and the lictors gave the exalted as much privacy as they could in such tight quarters. It was a little after noon by Taya's watch when they were invited back to the decatur's tent. Captain Amcathra stood beside it.

"How did it fly?" Taya inquired.

"Adequately." He inclined his head toward the tent. "When you are finished with the decatur we will discuss our departure."

Decatur Constante and Keman were waiting inside. The decatur was unmasked.

"Two reports have come in," Constante said, looking grim. "We have a reply from Council, but also, the *Formidable* has departed camp."

"Which way did it go?" Cristof demanded.

"Over the border. Toward the capital."

"Lady help us," Taya whispered. They must have loaded the serpentfire cannon.

Constante handed Cristof a strip of paper. Taya leaned over his arm to read it.

destroy weapons hold border peace optional do not risk royal witness return ambassador reinforcements coming

"Would setting up a meeting between Liliana and her sister be a risk?" Taya asked.

"The meeting would have to be private," Constante said, glancing at Keman. "A public meeting would be too dangerous for both of them."

"Because Lady Mazzoletti might have them assassinated?" Cristof nodded. "Right. Put some snipers in the bushes and call it an Ondinium double-cross. She'd get rid of two more Agostis that way. Then there'd only be a fourteen-year-old boy between her and the throne."

"You said Queen Agosti seemed reasonable." Constante looked at Taya. "Would she call off this war if her sister convinced her we didn't kill her family?"

"I think so," Taya said. "At least, I'm sure she'd turn her vendetta on the Mazzolettis and their allies, and it's unlikely she'd want to pursue a foreign war while simultaneously fighting a civil one."

Constante tapped her fingers on the desk, her eyes narrowed as she gazed into the distance. "Perhaps you're right, Keman. Perhaps we *do* need to extract her."

"Extract her!" Taya exclaimed.

"To a private conference," Keman elaborated. "Without Lady Mazzoletti knowing."

Cristof frowned. "That won't be easy, now that the camp's on alert."

"Give me a rescue harness and I could do it," the icarus replied with confidence.

Taya understood his plan at once. "Not by yourself!"

"It would have to be a nightflight, of course, but I've made hundreds of them. I've even carried out one or two extractions in the past."

"Alone?" Cristof inquired.

"Well— no."

"Right. You'll need backup. Someone who can carry a gun. But since you can only carry one person at a time...." Cristof suddenly scowled and snapped his mouth shut.

"Then you'd need two icarii to carry two people!" Taya said, understanding. "*I* could carry a lictor."

"No! We just got you out of that camp— you are *not* going back in again."

"But Keman can't do it alone." She looked from her husband to the decatur, then back again. "If it works and Colonel Agosti believes her sister, we could end this war tomorrow."

"Besides, you don't have an armature," Cristof said with finality.

Taya looked at Keman, who shook his head. No spares.

Someone cleared his throat outside. Taya froze, then turned and pushed aside the double flaps.

"Captain?"

Amcathra studiously gazed into the distance.

"It occurs to me that in our previous conversation I may have neglected to mention that your armature was locked securely in the *Firebrand*'s hold. It suffered some damage in the crash, but the decatur's engineers were able to repair it. I could have your flight suit and wings delivered here by nightfall, should you happen to have any need of them."

Taya's heart leaped. Amcathra took a guarded step back.

"Icarus...."

Taya checked her impulsive advance, beamed at him, and bounced back into the tent.

"Cris! Amcathra fixed my—"

"Wings, yes, I heard," Cristof said, vexed. He raised his voice. "It's taboo to eavesdrop on exalteds, *lictor*."

"It wasn't his fault," Taya defended him. "We're in a *tent*."

"Extracting Colonel Agosti could be construed as an act of aggression, of course," Decatur Constante said, apparently deciding to ignore the episode with as much dignity as possible. "If she does not believe her sister's story, we will have no choice but to hold her."

"But then Ondinium would have Alzana's queen and princess in captivity," Keman pointed out. "All the Mazzolettis would have left would be a pawn."

"Unless Lady Mazzoletti kills the boy and crowns herself." Cristof folded his arms over his chest. "For the record, I object to either of our icarii entering the enemy camp."

"But as Taya said, we could bring in a lictor that way," Keman pointed out. "The chances of our success would be much higher."

"We were just driven back by the Alzanan troops a few hours ago. Twelve, no, *thirteen* people died and four were wounded, and one of the dead was my brother." Cristof looked at Taya, his face pale. "You aren't going to do this to me, are you?"

Taya's enthusiasm for the plan sputtered out like a wet fuse. With a rush of contrition, she reached out and took his hand.

"Cris...."

"Perhaps this plan needs more work," Keman said softly.

"This is *war*, Exalted Forlore," Constante snapped. Cristof straightened, his expression hardening. "I understand why you don't want to put your wife at risk, but you *must* put your personal feelings aside and let the icarus do her duty."

"I don't want to hear *anything* from you about the two of us doing our duty," Cristof retorted, flushing with anger. "Taya and I did our duty when we ventured into that Alzanan snake pit to buy you time to uncrate your war machines, and we've been running for our lives ever since. We've done more than our share of *duty* over the whole last slagging year, and I am sick and *tired* of losing everything I care about to it!"

"This is war. People die," Constante shot back. "Do you think those eight hundred and seventy-four Ondiniums in Glasgar weren't doing *their* duty? Or those twelve lictors last night, or even your outcaste brother, criminal though he was?"

"Cris!" Taya grabbed her husband's arm to keep him from lunging at the woman in his fury. Keman stepped protectively in front of the decatur. Taya's fingers dug into Cristof's sleeve. "Don't! Please— don't."

"My brother died a hero," Cristof shouted.

"He was still a traitor," Constante spat back. "He killed Caster Octavus, who happened to be an old friend of mine, and he betrayed the Council just to put a *breeding program* onto the Great Engine!"

Taya cringed and Cristof pulled away from her grasp, nearly tearing the door flaps off as he strode outside.

"I'm sorry, Decatur!" Taya spun and dropped to her knees, one palm pressed to her forehead. "I'm sorry— please forgive him. He's mad with grief—"

"Get out, Icarus," Constante grated. Mortified, Taya scrambled to her feet and backed out of the tent, still bowing. Outside, she paused only long enough to give Amcathra a pleading look before she turned and plunged through the camp, looking for her husband.

CHAPTER EIGHTEEN

THE NIGHT WAS bitterly cold and the heavy clouds that obscured the stars and moon threatened imminent snowfall. Taya crouched on the edge of the much-altered *Firebrand*, looking down at the distant lights of A-O Terminal. Her bright silver wings had been painted a dull black, matching Keman's, and all of her visible skin had been smudged with soot. Cristof stood next to Captain Amcathra and Liliana, holding a rifle and looking grim.

It had taken hours of heated discussion between her husband, the captain, Keman, and her before they'd finally agreed to the plan, and they'd ended up dragging in Dautry, Liliana, Jinian, and Lucanus to thrash out the details.

The extraction would be a risky endeavor, and much of it had depended on Liliana's consent, but she'd finally been persuaded to help. They had one chance to snatch the colonel. If it didn't work, they would leave the letter that Liliana had written, explaining everything.

Either way, whether the colonel was on board or remained in Terminal, the *Firebrand* would head back to Ondinium next and Keman would return to the camp.

Cristof hadn't liked the idea of taking Colonel Agosti with them, but Decatur Constante had brushed off his concern. They had no time to waste— the *Formidable* was already a day ahead of them, bearing its devastating weapon deeper into Ondinium. Only the slim chance that having Colonel Agosti with them would help them stop the *Formidable* before it reached the capital made this attempt worth the delay.

Cristof had also wanted to be the one to venture into camp with them, despite his fear of heights. Amcathra had objected that the exalted was too valuable to lose and had volunteered to go himself. Lucanus had observed that the captain was needed aboard the ship and put himself forward as the best choice. Jinian had pointed out that both were trained aviators and that, since she didn't know how to fly the ship, she should be the one to go into camp. Dautry had countered that Jinian would be automatically recognized as a foreigner, whereas only she and the two icarii had any chance of passing themselves off as Alzanan in a pinch. After much discussion, and despite Amcathra's argument that he needed his pilot and navigator in one piece, Dautry had been chosen for the mission. Cristof had later muttered to Taya that it was probably because Decatur Constante considered a Mareaux citizen the most expendable of the group.

Major Leppala had a map of A-O Terminal as it had looked before the bombing, and they'd located the building where Colonel Agosti had interviewed Taya. According to their prisoners, Agosti bunked on the second floor of the same building.

"Stop here," Dautry murmured, lowering her field glasses. The *Firebrand* was flying high and dark, its new and much smaller engine looted from a mecharachnid. Cristof had cut the power when they'd seen Terminal's lights on the horizon, and they'd floated in over the city in silence. Now Amcathra and Lucanus threw their shoulders against the manual levers that had been jury-rigged to the wings, sweeping them forward. The ornithopter slowed and came to a standstill.

Dautry handed Taya the field glasses. Taya found the train station and followed the streets back, getting a fix on the colonel's building. With a nod, she passed the glasses along to Keman.

Keman had rigged makeshift loops to Taya's tailset for Dautry's feet— unnecessary for an emergency rescue but preferable for "passenger flight," as he called it. Dautry wore a rescue harness over the Alzanan uniform they'd taken from one of the prisoners, and Keman had wrapped a small counterweight around each of her ankles. She and Taya had practiced flying together most of the day before. The professor wasn't a natural athlete, but she understood flight. By evening, she and Taya were working reasonably well in tandem.

Now they balanced on the railing, Keman supporting them, and hooked themselves together. Taya waited for Dautry's nod and rolled off the rail.

The *Firebrand* hadn't stopped perfectly over their target, but it had come close. Taya maintained a tight, spiraling descent, just as Keman had instructed. He would follow her down. The Alzanan guards were unlikely to spot two black-clad icarii dropping straight down from above, but it wasn't impossible— speed and accuracy were paramount.

As they dropped lower, Taya adjusted her trajectory to approach the steeply peaked roof from the rear. As she got closer, she felt Dautry pull her feet loose and unsnap her rescue harness from the armature. Then Taya was skimming over the roof and Dautry released her, floating softly down to the building.

Taya tilted and circled. The next landing was hers. She kicked her legs out of the tailset and swung them forward, her boots hitting the spine of the roof with a thump that made her wince. She backbeat and shuffled her feet until she stabilized, one foot planted on either side of the roof's ridge. She crouched lower, both wings spread horizontally for balance.

To the side, Dautry slid down the slope of the roof to the eave. The navigator's greatest danger now was being blown away by a gust of wind as she maneuvered herself through a second-story window.

Taya locked her wings close to her body and slid her arms free, then kicked her tailset up out of the way. Keman landed several feet away with practiced ease, joining her moments later.

They waited. Dautry's job was to get inside the building and make certain no guards were stationed by the colonel's room. She was dressed as an Alzanan soldier, and if she ran into any trouble, she was armed with a needler loaded with a set of sedative-bearing needles, Corundel's bottle of chloroform, and an Alzanan percussion pistol.

Earlier that day, back at the Ondinium camp, Dautry had tried on the Alzanan uniform with an introspective air.

"It seems I owe you an apology, Captain," she had said at last, pinning up her long hair. Taya handed her the soldier's cap and she tried it on. "I may have judged you too quickly when I condemned you for your undercover work."

"If you are morally opposed to carrying out this mission, I am still willing to take your place," Amcathra said, stiffly.

"No; it makes more sense for me to go, and it doesn't hurt me to re-evaluate my opinions from time to time," she said, turning. She shot a glance at Taya. "Besides, the exalted will need you safely on the *Firebrand* to take him home."

"You have piloted numerous aerostats, and you have as thorough an understanding as I concerning the steps that will be necessary to keep the *Firebrand* aloft over the next few days. I believe you could get the exalted home in my absence."

"But I don't know anything about aerial combat—"

"I am offering you a choice, Dautry, so that you will not be obliged to compromise your principles on behalf of my nation."

The professor tilted her head and considered him a moment. Taya held her breath.

"Thank you, Captain," Dautry said at last. "However, I'm content to wear this uniform as long as the deception is restricted to my enemies. My friends and colleagues know that I'm not really an Alzanan soldier."

Amcathra's jaw tightened.

"As I am sure *your* friends and colleagues know that you are not *sheytatangri*," she continued, turning away to inspect the Alzanan's pistol. To Taya's amusement, Amcathra had blinked, looking disconcerted.

Now Taya shifted, her knees aching. Snowflakes drifted out of the night sky, brushing her face. She wondered how Keman was holding up in the cold. She wondered what Dautry was doing inside the building. She felt completely helpless, standing outside and waiting. *This must be what Cristof feels like when he's left behind,* she thought with a flash of empathy.

Hours seemed to pass before she heard the front door of the building open.

"Not shift time already, is it?" the sentry asked, his voice low.

"Could you come in here a moment?" Dautry asked, in impeccable Alzanan.

The sentry just had time for a puzzled "What—" before Taya heard the swift, sharp hiss of a needler.

A minute passed, and Dautry whispered an all-clear.

Keman and Taya dropped down from the roof and slid inside the open door. Dautry quietly closed and locked it behind them.

The front room was dimly lit by the embers of a fire. Three soldiers were unconscious around them, one of them half out of his sleeping roll. Dautry had pulled the door sentry inside and laid him on the floor as if he were sleeping. Taya checked them and gave Dautry a thumbs-up. They'd all been chloroformed or shot with sedated needles. None of them were dead.

Dautry, who was buckling her rescue harness back over her uniform, pointed to herself and the stairs. Keman nodded and pulled out a long knife that was a far cry from the short utility blade issued to courier icarii in Ondinium. They slid upstairs first and Taya followed. Unlike Keman, she'd chosen not to carry any weapons.

Four doors lined the short hallway, but light only glowed beneath one of them. Dautry and Keman pressed to the wall on either side and Keman reached for the door handle.

Dautry nodded.

The gray-haired icarus threw the door open and Dautry hurled herself around the corner just as a shot fired from inside the room. Keman dashed in after her and Taya followed with a prayer on her lips.

Colonel Agosti stood behind her desk, her gun aimed at Dautry's head. Dautry's needle gun, in turn, was aimed at the colonel's heart.

"Wait!" Taya exclaimed in Alzanan. "This isn't what it seems!"

"You mean it's not another assassination attempt?" The colonel sounded calm, despite her predicament. "Decided to pick off the rest of the Family, did you?"

"No." She reached into her flight suit and withdrew Liliana's letter, holding it out. "This is from your sister. She's waiting for you just a few minutes away. She wants to talk."

"Taya...." Keman's voice was low. "Somebody might have heard that shot."

"Read it." Taya thrust the letter toward the colonel.

"Liliana's your prisoner?"

"She's our *guest*. She fled with us from Fosca Mazzoletti." Taya stepped closer, still offering the letter. "We want to take you to her. Please— let's end this war before anyone else has to die."

"Ending a war isn't that easy," Agosti said, but she lowered the gun.

"Please," Taya repeated. "Read it."

Agosti plucked the letter from her hand and shook it open one-handed. Her expression grew even more grim as she read her sister's words. She looked up.

"Why didn't you bring Lil here, to the office?"

"We couldn't take the chance that she'd fall into Lady Mazzoletti's hands."

"Mazzoletti isn't in camp anymore."

"Scrap! Is she on the *Formidable*?"

The colonel raised her eyebrows.

"Does she have the holocaust bomb?" Taya pressed, certain she knew the answer.

Agosti looked away, mutely confirming her fears.

"What do you intend to do now?" the colonel inquired.

"Come with us," Taya urged, feeling sick to her stomach. "Talk to Liliana and help us stop the *Formidable* before it reaches Ondinium."

"You want me to go *with* you?"

"Unless you have some means of signaling the *Formidable* from here."

"Do I get to bring my guards?"

"No. I'm sorry, but— no. We can only carry one."

Agosti gave her a bitter, knowing smile. "In other words, you want me to voluntarily hand myself over to my enemy."

Dautry promptly shot her in the shoulder.

"Professor!" Taya watched, horrified, as the colonel staggered back, tried to raise her pistol, and then collapsed. Dautry holstered the gun and knelt next to the woman.

"Let's go," she said, pulling out the drug-coated needles. Keman unhooked the rescue harness from his armature.

"What are you doing?" Taya demanded. "She'll *never* trust us now!"

"I agree with Captain Amcathra and your decatur that Queen Agosti is safer with us than in camp," Dautry said, helping Keman buckle the colonel into the harness. "This way Princess Liliana will have another chance to convince her to end the war. By the way, don't leave her letter behind."

Taya picked up the fallen sheet of paper, aghast at what they were doing. Keman stood, hoisting the counterweighted colonel over one shoulder.

Someone knocked on the front door downstairs and all three froze.

"Scrap." Taya ran to the window facing the back of the building and threw it open. "You'll have to squeeze through, Keman."

"I can't."

"Yes, you can. You go through first, and I'll hand the colonel through."

He swore and threw a leg over the sill. Sliding his arms into his wings, he unlocked them and twisted them through the opening one at a time. His armature creaked as he freed one arm and wrenched himself outside, leaving gouges in the windowsill.

Dautry jammed the colonel's pistol into her waistband and turned toward the office door, covering it with the needler.

Keman hung outside the window, his boots on the sill and his free hand holding the window frame. Taya hauled the nearly weightless colonel forward and buckled her harness to Keman's armature. It wouldn't be easy for him to fly with Agosti dangling motionless in the harness, even if her weight was almost zeroed out.

"Ready?" she asked. "I'll brace you from inside."

"Don't get captured again," he said, twisting around. She grabbed the back of his armature and held him in place as he slid his free arm into its wing. "Your husband would kill me."

"I'll be right behind you. Hurry!"

"On the count of three."

Shouts sounded from below. The unconscious soldiers had been found.

"One— two— *three*." Taya released him and Keman sprang from the windowsill, beating fast to keep himself aloft. As soon as he rose over the building across the alley, she began squirming through the window, herself.

"Dautry! Meet me on the roof!"

"I will!"

Taya winced as her wings scraped against the sill. Without anyone to hold her armature for her, she straddled the window and insinuated her arms into her wings. Furniture scraped. She glanced over her shoulder. Dautry was shoving the colonel's desk against the doorway.

"Professor! Come on!"

"As soon as you're out of my way!"

Swearing under her breath, Taya jammed her feet against the sill. This wasn't going to be even close to graceful, but at least she didn't have an unconscious body to carry. She kicked off, arms spread wide, and flapped like a dying duck. At last she cupped air and rose, overshooting the roof. She kicked down her tailset and circled. Soldiers carrying lanterns and guns were converging on the colonel's barracks.

Someone shouted and fired. Taya circled, uncertain whether they were firing at her, Keman, or shadows. Then Dautry clambered over the eaves. Taya made a wide circle, came in low, and flew directly at the roof.

As she passed over Dautry's head, the navigator's hands locked onto the struts of her armature. Taya swept them both into the air, hearing more gunfire. Bullets whined past, too close for comfort. Dautry awkwardly snapped her harness to Taya's armature, chest-to-chest, and hooked her legs over Taya's. Taya struggled upward, searching for the *Firebrand* through flight goggles that were quickly caked with snow. She gave her head a sharp shake, dislodging some of it, and adjusted her position. If the *Firebrand* hadn't drifted too far off, she should—

A glimmer of light broke the darkness. She angled toward it.

"Professor! Ready to drop?"

"One minute!" The professor fumbled with the hooks.

Taya swept over the ship, circled, and returned. As she glided past a second time, Dautry dropped backwards into Amcathra's and Lucanus's waiting arms. Taya circled one more time and came in for her own landing.

Her boots hit the snow-covered, metal-plated deck and slipped out from under her. She threw out her wing-covered arms to steady herself, cracking Lucanus across the head. Captain Amcathra ducked beneath her sweeping metal feathers and grabbed uselessly for her armature as she slid into Cristof. They went down in an awkward pile with her on top.

"Sorry! I'm sorry!" she exclaimed, holding her arms over her head to keep her wings out of the way.

"Are you all right?" Cristof grabbed her armature to steady her.

"Ouch. Yes. No." She winced as something pointed dug into her rear. "I may have broken my tailset."

"Literally or metaphorically?" he asked, gazing owlishly at her through glasses that had been knocked askew. She stared at him a moment and then laughed.

Behind them, Lucanus gingerly rubbed his forehead and moved forward to help.

"If you two would take a moment to untangle yourselves, we would be in a significantly better position to assess any damage, literal or not," Captain Amcathra said, straightening from his crouch. He gave Dautry a quick, assessing look. "You are well."

"Yes, Captain." Dautry was already helping Keman unhook the colonel's harness. "I'm sorry, Liliana, but your sister refused to accompany us."

"You shot her!" Liliana gasped, running forward to support her sister's head as Keman lowered her to the floor. She pushed open Agosti's coat to inspect the needle wound. "How *could* you? She was supposed to make up her own mind!"

Dautry and Amcathra exchanged a look, and Taya suddenly wondered if they had planned the colonel's abduction beforehand.

"Mazzoletti's on the *Formidable*," the professor continued, briskly. "Agosti wouldn't confirm that the holocaust bomb is aboard, but I think we need to assume that Mazzoletti is carrying out her plan to blow up the Engine."

Cristof swore. Keman muttered something under his breath as he adjusted his armature.

"Your sister may be the only one who can help us avert a disaster," Dautry added, looking at Liliana. The *principessa* glared at her, then turned a dark look on Cristof.

"So now we're *both* your hostages."

"*Principessa* Agosti," Keman said sternly, before Cristof could reply. "*Now* you are both safe from the rebel Families who killed your grandfather and in the perfect position to end this treacherously engineered war. Captain, I assume you will attempt to overtake the *Formidable*. Exalted, do you wish to return to camp or travel with the ship?"

"I'll remain with the *Firebrand*," Cristof said firmly. "Janos needs another engineer. We'll also require Colonel Agosti's assistance to stop the *Formidable*. Liliana, do you want to be dropped off at camp?"

"I'm staying with Pietra!"

"Very well," Keman said. "Ambassador, the decatur will expect you to work with Colonel Agosti to end this war."

"I'll do my best." Cristof turned to Liliana. "And *neither* of you is a hostage."

The girl stubbornly set her jaw, still clutching her sister.

"Icarus, *Kattaka*, take the Agostis below," Amcathra snapped, cutting through the moment of tension. "Exalted, would you please secure our weapons against the colonel's awakening? Sergeant Lucanus, stoke the engine. Dautry, plot the fastest course to the capital." The lictor looked toward the horizon, his eyes narrowed. "We cannot afford to waste any more time."

❋

The *Firebrand* had been grievously damaged in its fight across the Alzanan-Ondinium border, and the modifications needed to get it back into the air had been ruthless. Captain Amcathra, Professor Dautry, and the army engineers had stripped away the entire lower gun deck, the ship's hold, and the ballast tanks. They'd reinforced the berth deck with salvaged wood and covered it with the gun deck's ondium plating, its etching no longer creating an elegant design that flowed across the hull. The *Firebrand*'s stern had been so badly damaged that they'd shortened the entire vessel by five feet and jury-rigged a set of controls for the dorsal fins and a new rudder connected to the primary helm. The secondary helm and the volley guns had been removed. The ship's old broken wings had been cut down into shorter, lighter wings, and the smaller steam engine that now controlled them had been secured over the blasted remains of the old one.

Down below, the berth deck had been stripped to its bare wooden bones, an open space that stretched from port to starboard and stem to stern. It contained bedrolls, casks of water and bags of bread, cheese, and sausage, a crate of tools, and several racks of weapons— rifles, bombs, ondium-tipped missiles, and ammunition. The boiler stood to one side of the long window where the mess hall used to be, and a very large bin of coke had been set up next to it, along with several shovels.

The *Firebrand* had been transformed from a proud war vessel to a stunted cargo ship, but it still flew.

They were three days from Ondinium's capital and one day behind the *Formidable*. By necessity, everyone but the two Alzanans took turns stoking the engine, oiling the wings, running the helm, and checking their course. The makeshift crew snatched food and naps whenever they could, driving themselves to keep the ship moving day and night.

Liliana stayed with her sister until she awoke. Colonel Agosti was coldly furious at her kidnapping, and her mood didn't change even after a long talk with her sister.

"I agree that Fosca Mazzoletti must be stopped and her Family punished," Agosti said stiffly as she sat in conference with Cristof, Captain Amcathra, and Taya. Liliana hovered by her sister's side in silent support. Lucanus was busy manning the boiler while Dautry and Jinian remained above to run the ship. "However, this war began before my Family was killed, and it encompasses far more than a desire for revenge."

"Did your grandfather order the invasion?" Cristof asked, bluntly.

"He said that he did not."

"Then it was a rogue assault led by a revolutionary force and you have no reason to perpetuate their bad decision. Your grandfather was suing for peace."

"But now the Alzanans aren't the only country at war with Ondinium. Demicus has also turned against you."

"The *sheytatangri*'s strength lies primarily in the support it has received from Alzana," Captain Amcathra said. "If Alzana stops supplying the *tangri* with weapons and transportation, its influence over the clans will be significantly weakened."

"But we have trade agreements with several Demican clans."

"You?" Cristof asked. "Or your grandfather?"

"I intend to uphold my grandfather's political agreements and treaties."

"I'm not asking you to break them. But I *am* asking you to carefully consider the best interests of your Family and Alzana. Tell me, what do you hope to get out of this war?"

Agosti considered her answer.

"The war has already revealed quite a bit of valuable information about Ondinium," she said at last. "We now know that your country lied to its neighbors for centuries about its capacity for aerial warfare and that many of the imperial war machines it claimed were destroyed are still intact. That is the sort of information that could entirely reshape the diplomatic landscape of our continent."

"Perhaps, but what price have you paid for that information? How many dirigibles and crew members have you lost so far? What *else* do you expect to get out of this war?"

"If Fosca Mazzoletti's plan works, we will have crippled Ondinium and opened it for occupation."

"You won't get all that just by destroying the Great Engine. The Engine's important to us, but it's only a tool."

"Mazzoletti will do more than simply destroy your Engine," Agosti said. "She also has the serpentfire cannon. With that, she can raze the entire city."

"Pietra, no!" Liliana gasped.

"That would be an extremely short-sighted strategy," Cristof grated. "What's the point of occupying a country you've turned into charcoal?"

"I imagine we will only need to use the weapon once or twice before your Council surrenders."

"And it doesn't worry you that the person wielding that weapon is the same one who slaughtered your family?"

The Alzanan colonel tensed. "I have heard my sister's testimony, but I will wait until I hear Lady Mazzoletti's side before I decide she is guilty."

"We're chasing the *Formidable* now," Cristof said. "If you help us stop it, I'll return the ship *and* Lady Mazzoletti to you."

"And its cargo?"

"The weapons will stay with us."

"Unacceptable." Agosti gestured to the empty space around them. "I will not help you on those terms, and you don't have enough heavy weapons to take the ship on your own."

"We have already boarded and taken one of your ships with nothing more than rifles and needle guns," Captain Amcathra said without emotion. "However, I have no objection to setting down my non-military passengers and ramming the *Formidable* myself. The *Firebrand*'s boiler will ignite the *Formidable*'s envelope and destroy everything and everyone on board."

"That would be suicide," Agosti protested.

"Not entirely." Amcathra fixed the colonel with his pale blue gaze. "Since you are *not* a civilian, I would keep you on board during the maneuver."

"Captain!" Liliana recoiled. "You wouldn't!"

Taya forced herself to remain silent, although she wanted to protest, too.

"*Or* you can work with us, take the *Formidable*, Lady Mazzoletti, and your sister, and leave," Cristof said, his voice hard.

"But you would keep the Cabisi weapons," Agosti said.

"Yes, we would."

"Would you destroy them?"

"That's my ultimate goal, yes. But I don't know how quickly or safely they can be neutralized, so if I need to take them with me rather than leave them in your hands, I will."

"I see." Agosti reached into her coat, removing the case of cigarillos that they'd returned to her. She struck a match and lit up, ignoring Cristof's poorly hidden impatience.

"It occurs to me," she said after a moment of contemplative puffing, "that if your captain kills me in a suicide run on the *Formidable*, you will lose any chance you have at negotiating a peace with my sister." Her dark eyes met Cristof's. "Or would you kill Liliana, too, and try to convince Silvio that we were both casualties of war?"

For a moment they both stared at each other, impassive. Then, at last, his shoulders slumping, Cristof looked away. Taya breathed a silent sigh of relief, feeling the knots in her stomach uncoil.

"I am not a murderer, Colonel," Cristof said, his voice pained.

"I had hoped not, Exalted. Overtake the *Formidable* and I will signal its captain to stop," Agosti said, flicking her ash onto the berth deck. "I will take command of the ship and question Lady Mazzoletti about her role in the rebellion. Liliana will come with me, of course. You may do what you can to disable the serpent-fire cannon and holocaust bomb; the *Formidable*'s engineers will assist. After the weapons have been dealt with to our mutual satisfaction, we will have your promise of safe passage on the *Formidable* back to the border. After that, you and I will both take stock of the situation and decide what to do next."

"Exalted...." Amcathra growled. Cristof shook his head.

"We're not monsters, Janos." He dragged his eyes up to meet the colonel's. "We are Family Agosti's allies, and our first goal is to save Ondinium. Your terms are acceptable, Colonel."

They encountered their first conflagration zone late in the afternoon on the second day of their flight.

First the Firebrands noticed gray ash carried on gusting flurries of snow, and then they smelled burnt wood. Soon a dark swath of scorched land came into view, a long black scar that cut through the forest, still too hot for snow to cover.

"Lady save us," Taya breathed, leaning over the rail. "That's from serpentfire, isn't it?"

"There." Captain Amcathra, studying the damage through his field glasses, pointed. "Look at the ship."

Cristof took the glasses from him, looked a minute, and then passed them to Taya. One by one, each crew member examined the twisted, melted remains of the ornithopter that lay in the center of the burn.

"It's not floating," Taya murmured.

Amcathra's voice was flat. "Dephlogistication."

"What's that?" Taya asked.

"In *theory*," Cristof said, "enough heat could combust ondium's phlogiston deposits, creating a vacuum that would immediately be filled with regular atmospheric gases. The process would transform ondium into a normally weighted ore."

"It looks like serpentfire generates enough heat to induce such combustion," Dautry observed quietly.

"The holocaust bomb...." Cristof turned to Jinian. "Does it have the same effects as serpentfire?"

"I do not know— I am only a *kattaka*, not a military artillerist. You need someone like Ra Tafar to answer that question."

"Call Colonel Agosti to deck," Cristof said. "I want her to see this. But *nobody* say a word about dephlogistication to her."

Sober nods greeted his words.

"Jinian." He turned to the Cabisi woman. "Will you keep this secret, too?"

"I will." Jinian's lips tightened as she surveyed the devastation. "I do not care for this weapon. Sometimes, I think, we Cabisi are so carried away by our enthusiasm for invention that we do not think carefully enough about the consequences of the things we manufacture."

They waited as Colonel Agosti and Liliana climbed up the ladder and joined them at the railing.

"Lady Mazzoletti used the serpentfire cannon here," Cristof said, gesturing. "I thought you might want to see its effects."

Pietra Agosti surveyed the blasted area.

"She told me that the weapon would create a firestorm," the colonel said quietly. "I thought she was exaggerating."

"We were told it's capable of scorching the land in a half-mile radius."

"This fire burned farther than that," Taya murmured. "Even though it's winter."

"We need to go faster," Amcathra announced. "Dautry, are we still on course? Sergeant Lucanus, monitor the engine. Icarus, *Kattaka*, would you see to the boiler?"

"I will shovel coal, Captain, but I prefer you call me Jinian," Jinian said as she headed below with Taya. "*Kattaka* is a job, not a title."

"He'll never do it," Taya predicted as she took her place next to the boiler and pulled on a pair of leather work gloves.

"Do you notice that he uses Professor Dautry's name, but not her title?" Jinian asked, picking up a shovel.

"She's crew."

"No, he uses titles and last names when he addresses his crew members, and titles when he addresses strangers and social superiors. But he only uses Dautry's last name."

"Well, they've worked together a lot recently, and I know he respects her opinion. Maybe it means he regards her as an equal." The fire in the boiler turned Taya's thoughts back to what they'd just seen. "When you go back to Cabiel, will you tell them about the serpentfire?"

"Yes. I am here pursuing a challenge, but I am also gathering information for the Impeccable Justiciary. They wish to know more about the ways in which Cabisi technology is being used in foreign lands."

"Not well, I'm afraid."

They shoveled in silence for a few moments, each lost in her own thoughts.

"It is difficult to control a technology once it exists," Jinian mused at last, "but it is not impossible. I intend to recommend the destruction of these cannon and their plans when I return to Cabiel."

Taya nodded, although she couldn't help but think of all the ancient weapons Ondinium's Council had claimed to have destroyed. Would Cabiel's Impeccable Justiciary do the same?

For the rest of the evening Amcathra kept the *Firebrand* flying at full speed, but by nightfall he eased back on the throttle. Stars and a half-moon shined through the broken clouds.

"Still no sign of the *Formidable*'s searchlight," Dautry reported, scanning the sky.

"Dinner?" Cristof asked, joining Taya. "I hear we're having bread and sausage tonight."

"My favorite," she said, wryly. "I hope there's some cheese, too."

"I think we can arrange that."

They headed down to the communal deck, where Jinian already had the teapot resting on the boiler.

"Jinian, Janos wants you and I to wear our rescue harnesses," Cristof said, rummaging through the food supplies to pull out a loaf of bread and a knife. "Taya, he'd like you to wear your armature, too."

"Is that so he can throw us overboard if he decides to ram the *Formidable*?" she asked. Her husband paused, holding the knife in midair.

"I *hope* it's because he plans to board the *Formidable* and doesn't trust us to climb a rope," he said, after a moment. He set the knife down, frowning. "But I'm probably too optimistic."

Jinian raised an eyebrow. "Is your captain suicidal?"

"No, but he's not afraid to make hard choices."

"Does that include letting Professor Dautry die with him?" Cristof frowned.

"Or Liliana? This ship only has two rescue harnesses."

"Then he's probably not thinking about throwing us over-board," Cristof said. He picked up the knife again and began slicing the bread. "Besides, he wouldn't find it easy to toss me off the ship. I have a strong aversion to falling."

They didn't encounter the *Formidable* that night. The sun was rising over the peaks when Taya awoke. She was still half-asleep as she took her turn at the helm. Dautry stood by the engine, keeping one eye on the gauges and one eye on the horizon.

"Taya, are those icarii?"

Taya squinted at the dark spots in the air in front of them, then reached for the set of field glasses that hung on a hook by the helm.

"They're too big for icarii," she said, twisting the focus ring. The figures grew clearer and sharper. "No— those are aerostats!"

"Alzanan or Ondinium?"

"Both, I think. Are we close to Safira?"

Dautry spun to check the charts. Taya stuck her head through the hatch and shouted for the captain.

"Report," he snapped as soon as he climbed up the ladder, Cristof right behind him.

"Dirigibles and ornithopters at twelve o'clock," Dautry said. "Looks like a skirmish over Safira."

Taya handed Amcathra the field glasses.

"Change course?" Dautry asked.

"No," he said, studying the ships. "Take us as close as you can, but keep us low and out of sight."

"Yes, sir."

"What if the *Formidable* uses the cannon on Safira?" Taya fretted. "A lot of people live there...."

"Most of the civilians will have been evacuated already. Exalted, will you take the helm from your wife? Icarus, a word."

"You're not sending her into a firefight by herself," Cristof protested, buttoning up his coat.

"No, I am not," Amcathra agreed. Taya paused long enough to exchange a quick kiss with her husband before following the captain below. Liliana had put the teapot on.

"Is this a private meeting?" the *principessa* asked.

"No." Amcathra began setting out breakfast— which was the same as dinner, which had been the same as lunch, which had been the same as every other meal since they'd gotten on the ship. He sliced off a large hunk of cheese and handed it to Taya.

"Thank you," she said, startled. Then her tired brain caught up. "You need me to fly reconnaissance, don't you?"

"Yes. I would like to know whether any of those ships is the *Formidable*."

"Why wouldn't it— oh, you think the fight might be a distraction, and the *Formidable*'s sneaking in around the edges?"

"I was surprised that we did not catch up to the *Formidable* last night. However, it may have taken a different pass, especially if it had a prearranged rendezvous with other dirigibles. Our charts indicate those routes through the Yeovil Range that are best suited for icarii and ornithopters, but dirigibles do not need to pay as much attention to wind currents as we do."

Taya nodded, chewing on the hard cheese. Amcathra filled a plate with sausage and bread and set it next to her, then began cutting more.

"Do you think the Alzanans plan to use the serpentfire cannon on Ondinium?" Jinian asked, joining them. Taya's mouth went dry and she swallowed, hard.

"It is unlikely but not impossible," Amcathra replied. "I believe Alzana would prefer to take the capital with minimal damage to its resources. Explosions are more directional than fire."

"But it's not Alzana in that ship," Liliana protested. "It's Lady Mazzoletti."

"Then the question is whether her goal is to conquer or destroy," Jinian said.

"Alister said she and Corundel were planning to use the bomb to blow up the Great Engine." Taya caught Amcathra's quick, sidelong glance. She lowered her voice. "Alister may not be cremated, but I'm sure he's buried. I think it's safe to use his name."

The lictor set the second plate to one side and started a third.

"Decatur Constante said she would attempt to retrieve his body as a courtesy to Exalted Forlore," he said, "but I do not think it is high on her list of priorities."

"Well." Taya looked down. "Cris would appreciate it, if she did."

"This is important in your culture?" Jinian asked. "To have a body?"

"Yes," Liliana said, looking at the other two. "We bury our dead in Alzana, but Ondinium and Demicus cremate them. What does your country do?"

"We give them to the sea, to feed the sharks."

Taya had to fight to hide her disgust. Consigning your loved ones to a cold, wet grave was bad enough— how could you allow them to be eaten by fish?

"Whether the Alzanans intend to burn the capital or simply destroy the Great Engine," Amcathra said, firmly changing the subject, "I wish to stop them. If you locate the *Formidable* for us, Icarus, we will take steps to intercept it."

"This reminds me." Jinian unhooked her rescue harness. "I believe Professor Dautry needs this more than I do, especially if you plan to wreck the ship."

Amcathra paused in his food preparation.

"I will not ram the *Formidable* while civilians are aboard."

"Dautry is a member of your crew, is she not? I believe she is in your records as a warrant officer."

"Yes…. I meant to say that she is not a member of the lictate."

"Do you expect her to voluntarily abandon you if you make a suicide run?"

"That is precisely what I expect, *Kattaka*."

"Please call me Jinian." She held out the harness. "And Professor Dautry's name is Cora. She is not as athletic as I am, so she needs this harness in case her captain throws her overboard once she refuses to leave of her own volition."

Amcathra looked like he was making an effort to be patient as he took the harness from her.

"If you do not want to wear it, then I will give it to Dautry."

"But you will not call her Cora?"

"It would be inappropriate to appear overly familiar with a member of my crew."

"But you do not use my name, and I am not a member of your crew."

"I do not know you well enough to use your given name."

"You know Taya and her husband very well, however."

"It is also inappropriate to use a social superior's name."

"Do you think if you call him Cristof, he will believe you are flirting with him?"

Amcathra's knife slipped and he gave Jinian a dour look.

"Be careful." She smiled. "Do not cut off a finger."

"These plates are for Dautry and the exalted," he growled, picking them up. "Icarus, please be ready to fly soon."

"I will...." Taya struggled with herself, then finally sighed. "Captain."

She gave Liliana and Jinian a rueful smile after he left.

"I'm as bad as he is," she admitted. "As long as he's being so formal, I can't bring myself to call him 'Janos.'"

Jinian looked thoughtful. "Perhaps he measures his manners against yours as he does his ideas."

"Life isn't one giant competition!"

"If you are not comfortable with that image, then think of it as a game. You and the captain are playing a game of relationship. He wins if he demonstrates respect for others' ranks, and you win if you confirm a mutual friendship. Is there a way for both of you to win the game at once?"

After Taya had finished her tea, she brought up a cup and plate for Captain Amcathra as a peace gesture. He took it with a distracted nod and she sighed, wondering where that left them in their "game." Cristof gave her back the helm and went below to warm up.

Professor Dautry, now wearing the rescue harness, was keeping their flight low, approaching the conflict at an indirect angle, which made it impossible to watch the firefight. After half an hour, they slowed, hiding within Capital Pass. Beyond the pass laid Safira and Ondinium Mountain.

Taya surrendered the helm to Lucanus and took off, a set of field glasses tucked into her courier pouch. The train track glittered brightly below her, empty, as she worked her way through the breezy pass. As she reached its far end, she smelled smoke.

Gripped by apprehension, Taya continued forward until she saw O-Base-0 — Safira — spread before her in flames.

She landed on a big, broken rock at the edge of the pass and pulled out the field glasses with trembling hands.

The entire city was burning, and in its center whipped a thin, twisting, dancing tornado of fire that threw sparks and smoke in every direction. Buildings crumbled and something beside the tracks exploded. A tiny figure stumbled into view, then fell, engulfed in flame.

Taya lowered her field glasses and leaned over, losing the breakfast Amcathra had made for her. Tears burned her eyes as she coughed and spat, then gagged again as a fresh gust of wind carried the sounds and smells of the burning city to her.

I don't have time for this, she thought angrily, wiping her face on an ash-covered sleeve. The heavy smoke covering Safira obscured Ondinium Mountain beyond. She put the glasses away and took a series of short, panting breaths to control her sickness. Then, slipping her arms into her wings, she launched herself off the side of the pass and flew east, skirting the city for a clearer look at Ondinium.

She spotted the ships as she circled the worst of the smoke— a swarm of ornithopters and dirigibles in full battle, maneuvering over the twenty-five mile security zone toward the smoggy, crowded, three-tiered city sprawl that covered the face of Ondinium Mountain. More ornithopters hovered over the city like vultures— *no, bad analogy,* she thought. Like guardian angels.

And below — below, in the cleared foothills and valleys of the security zone —Demican and Alzanan troops pushed their way toward the city against a protective line of lictors shooting at them with rifles and cannon. Here and there she spotted a lone mecharachnid squatting on a higher vantage point, firing its guns at the invading army.

The *Formidable* could be one of the ships over the security zone, but she couldn't get a clear look at their numbers through the smoke and maneuvers of battle. Rather than waste precious time trying to ascertain its position, Taya swept around and headed back to the *Firebrand* at full speed.

The *Firebrand*'s wood-and-metal wings creaked and groaned as it sped past the smoking earth where Safira had once stood. They were flying low to the ground, even though it meant staying away from the sides of the ship as Alzanan and Demican troops fired up at them. Guns and cannon boomed above and below the ornithopter as armies clashed on the ground and in the air.

Dautry and Cristof were wearing their rescue harnesses and Taya her wings. Everyone on board except Taya and the two Alzanans carried a rifle. The mortar had been set up on deck, ondium-tipped missiles in a crate beside it, and all of the Ondiniums' coat pockets — including Taya's — contained a small bomb and a waxed packet of lucifer matches.

Colonel Agosti and Liliana stood on the quarterdeck to watch the fighting. Agosti's eyes were hooded as she gazed at the conflict below.

"Shoulders ache?" Cristof asked, coming up behind Taya as she rubbed her neck. She nodded and grimaced as he dug his thumbs under her armature struts and into her muscles. "Too hard?"

"No." She leaned back into his kneading grip. She'd pushed herself hard to return to the *Firebrand*, and her body was feeling the stress of the flight and the tension of their predicament. Cristof's massage hurt, but the soreness felt right, a distraction from the sick feeling in her stomach and the tightness in her chest.

"How did all those armies get close to the capital?" she asked, closing her eyes.

"They marched in from the Demican border, I imagine. Or were carried over the border on dirigibles."

"Then the *ating* didn't work."

"We knew it wasn't going to stop all the clans. The *sheytatangri* had already committed itself to this war."

"But for them to get past all our patrols...." Taya's voice trailed off as she remembered drunken, defeated Nayan. If he was representative of the rest of the government misfits exiled to the Demican border, then an army could have slipped through with no problem at all. Ondinium had never expected Demicus to turn against it.

"It's not that big of an invading force," Cristof added. "It only looks like a lot because... because we lost so many lictors in Glasgar, and because most of the troops assigned to protect Ondinium would have been stationed in Safira."

Taya shuddered.

Bullets rang off the ondium plates on their hull and something thundered overhead. One of Ondinium's ornithopters had maneuvered beneath a dirigible and hit it with an ondium-tipped explosive missile. But even as the dirigible started to burn, its bay opened and bombs dropped onto the ornithopter's open deck. Someone on the ornithopter screamed.

"Oh, Lady—" Taya couldn't tear her eyes away from the horror. Cristof pulled her down, covering both of their heads with his arms as the bombs went off. The *Firebrand* veered aside as the dirigible's wreckage rained down and the ornithopter's wreckage flew toward the clouds.

When Taya looked up again, they'd left the ships behind, the dirigible's remains burning in the snow-covered, empty sector below.

"Look!" Jinian, who'd been studying the city ahead through a pair of field glasses, pointed. "Look at that."

"Oh, no...!" Taya scrambled next to her, peering through the ship's rails. A huge column of smoke rose in the distance, bright tongues of flame occasionally appearing within it.

"The *Formidable* must have circled around to attack," Cristof said tersely.

"There *must* be ornithopters guarding that side of the city, too," Taya said, hopelessly.

"Not if they are all defending this side. Your ships are not organized as well as the Alzanan ships," Jinian observed, "and they are not fighting as well, either."

"I don't think they have trained crews. You can say what you want about our having ornithopters— I don't think the Council *ever* expected to have to use them!"

"I feel some responsibility for this." Jinian lowered the glasses and rubbed her eyes. "Much of the technology the Alzanans are using against you is from Cabiel."

"After the Last War, Ondinium decided not to sell any more of its ondium, weapons, or analytical engines," Taya said, staring out at the city. "We were afraid our enemies would use our technology against us again. But a Demican told me that's why so many northern clans decided to join the Alzanans. The Alzanans trade with them like equals."

"I think both of our countries have much to consider after this war."

"If Ondinium *survives* this war."

"The dance is not over yet, Taya."

Captain Amcathra kept the *Firebrand* speeding forward. Ondinium Mountain towered before them, not the highest peak in the Yeovil Range, but the only one that had been stripped down to bare rock and transformed into a tightly packed industrial city. Manufactory and household smoke hung like a gritty shroud over the capital's lowest levels; wireferry cables and flight towers glittered as they ascended the mountainside over peaked roofs and tall smokestacks; and stark, vertical cliffs stretched up to the mountain's summit, where the old imperial fortress, Oporphyr Tower, overlooked the rest of the range.

Two more ornithopters flew out of the city, their silver, hawk-like shapes flashing whenever the sun caught their moving wings. The Alzanan dirigibles were outnumbered, but they'd managed to cripple another ornithopter, breaking one of its wings to stall it in midair. The two arriving ornithopters opened fire, even though they were out of range, to distract the Alzanans from the helpless ship.

"They are not flying well," Jinian reported. "I appreciate our crew much more now."

Taya nodded, although the comparison wasn't fair. Captain Amcathra and Lucanus had years of formal training, and Professor Dautry had years of hands-on experience, whereas the lictors out there had probably only been given a few days of practice before being sent out to fight.

Cristof stepped up beside them, anxiously closing one hand around Taya's armature.

"Janos wants to get into the city as fast as possible, which means cutting over some of the heaviest fighting along the north-west. He says we should all brace ourselves against the helm." He pointed at the city with his free hand. "As soon as we're past the fighting, we'll climb straight to the tower."

"He'll need to gain more altitude," Taya exclaimed. "The wireferries—"

"He knows." Cristof met her gaze, his gray eyes serious. "And he says that if we crash, it'll be up to you to protect Ondinium from the *Formidable*."

"Oh, Lady." Taya leaned forward to rest her forehead on his shoulder. She knew what Amcathra was asking her to do. Again.

Something exploded next to the ship, close enough for Taya to feel a wave of heat. She opened her eyes and straightened.

"All right," she said. "If it's the only way."

He leaned forward and kissed her, his expression sad. Then he headed toward Colonel Agosti and Liliana while Taya and Jinian hurried to the helm.

Amcathra had lashed a cable around the helm to provide them with something to grip. Taya wrapped her hand around it as she knelt, her tailset scraping the ondium deck and her wings vibrating from the ship's movement. Professor Dautry had wound another cable around the helm and her waist to hold herself in place. Lucanus had climbed up from the boiler to kneel next to the professor, one hand on the line and the other holding his rifle. Taya guessed his presence meant this was their last-ditch approach— the boiler wasn't going to get any hotter before they reached the city.

Captain Amcathra crouched before the creaking wings, his eyes fixed on the city ahead as he shouted orders to the helm.

Colonel Agosti and Liliana joined them, crouching and grabbing the ropes.

"Your captain is insane," Agosti snapped.

"Any time you want to stand on the prow and signal your army to stand down, go right ahead," Taya shot back. The colonel looked away, the color high in her cheeks.

The Alzanan and Demican forces shouted and raised their weapons as the *Firebrand* passed overhead. A cannon boomed and something large struck the side of the ship, rocking it to starboard. Bullets began to chew up the wooden rails, sending splinters flying everywhere. Several bullets ricocheted off the ship's ondium plates.

"Hold fast!" Amcathra bellowed. Taya cringed, grabbing the rope with both hands, as a ragged artillery barrage struck the ship. Something large hit her armature, and she saw a chunk of unplated railing spin across the deck and fall off the other side.

"Are you all right?" Cristof shouted, grabbing one of her arm-struts to get her attention. She twisted to face him and was alarmed to see a smear of blood across his face.

"Wha—"

Another explosive hit the ship and Professor Dautry swore in Mareaux as the *Firebrand* careened in a half-circle.

"Straighten us out and bring us up!" Amcathra's roar carried over the gunfire. Lucanus sprang up to help as Dautry wrestled the vessel back under control.

"Look! It is the *Indomitable*!" Jinian crowed, standing and staring at the dirigible they were approaching. She grinned as she tightened the strap of her rifle and checked her *kattaka* belts. "Thank you very much for the ride, Captain— this is where I get off!"

"Jin, no!" Taya half-rose, but the *kattaka* was already running across the deck as the *Firebrand* raced toward the *Indomitable*, the ornithopter battered by the dirigible's gunfire.

"Captain—" Lucanus gave Amcathra a questioning look. Amcathra scowled, then nodded. With a whoop, the young lictor ran after Jinian, grabbing the ship's rail and climbing over. They jumped.

Taya twisted, trying to spot them as the *Firebrand* skimmed over the top of the *Indomitable*'s envelope, but she couldn't see anything as the ornithopter hurtled over the sprawling industrial section of the city, bypassing the Great Gates. Gunsmoke gave way to coal smoke, gritty and dark, as Dautry wrestled the ship into a climb. The *Firebrand*'s starboard wing barely slipped past one of the manufactories' towering chimneys. Below them, Tertius' streets seemed uncannily empty— the citizenry had either been evacuated or were hiding in their homes.

"The rudder's been knocked askew," Dautry called out, "and the port wing's got a nasty hitch."

Amcathra edged to the port wing, which was making an alarming knocking sound. Cristof let go of the helm cable and scuttled over to him.

"I've got it, Janos," the exalted said, looking askance at the ship's bullet-riddled rails. "*You* keep us from crashing into a clocktower."

Amcathra nodded, resuming his position on the forecastle and shouting orders. The *Firebrand* swept over a wireferry tower stop, its dedicate operator throwing open a window to stare at them.

"The enemy's closing in!" Taya shouted. The Alzanan vessels were giving chase, leaving the less agilely piloted ornithopters lurching behind to fire at their sterns. Lictors guarding the city walls fired mortars at the dirigibles.

"Do you have any signaling devices on board?" Colonel Agosti demanded.

"No," Dautry replied grimly. Agosti swore, staring behind her with a set jaw.

The *Firebrand* swept over the sector wall between Tertius and Secundus. Lictors waved in acknowledgement or support as the ship passed, then turned to fire their rifles at the pursuing Alzanan ships. Taya didn't think rifles were going to do any good, but the sector walls weren't protected with cannon. The *Firebrand* swept past a startled icarus, buffeting him aside and making him struggle not to stall in their wake.

"Port wing's going," Cristof shouted. Dautry cursed.

"Hold on tight!" she cried. Taya tightened her grip and Cristof threw himself flat, grabbing the ropes that secured the mecharachnid engine over the old one.

The *Firebrand*'s bow rose and the ship began a sharp ascent, throwing Amcathra backward. He grabbed the same rope Cristof was holding, then locked his other hand around Cristof's rescue harness. Taya held her breath, listening to the engine's rumble and the port wing's ugly, mechanical knock.

Dautry straightened them out. A terrible grating sound came from the port wing and something snapped, flinging one end of a long steel connecting rod into the air. Amcathra threw himself to one side, pulling Cristof with him, as the rod came crashing back down, its end gouging a deep furrow into the ondium hull. Cristof's rifle strap slid off his arm and the weapon clattered across the deck, then slipped over the edge.

"Cris!" Taya started to stand. Her husband rolled over and pulled himself back to the engine, grabbing a rope. Taya relaxed, her heart pounding.

Both wings froze and Dautry sagged against the ropes holding her in place, wiping the sweat off her forehead and knocking her glasses askew. Her long hair had fallen out of its once-neat bun and she impatiently yanked it back over her shoulder.

Amcathra checked to make sure Cristof was secure and sat up, looking forward. Taya followed his gaze.

Dautry had brought them on a level with Oporphyr Tower and aimed them straight at it. Propelled by nothing but its own momentum, the *Firebrand* was hurtling directly toward the ancient stone fortress.

And now, level with the Tower at last, Taya saw the Alzanan vessel moored by the Tower's door, a large number nine painted on its side.

"It's the *Formidable*!" she shouted, at the same time that Amcathra leaped to his feet and ran back to the helm, grabbing Professor Dautry's shoulder.

"Can we adjust the angle of approach?"

"Rudder's no good," Dautry reported, straightening. "I can control our roll with the demiwings, but if we overshoot the Tower, we'll be flattened on the outcrops behind it."

"Slow us down and release the steam pressure before the engine blows!"

"Aye, sir!" The professor reached for the throttle.

"Icarus, grab the exalted and abandon ship."

"What?"

"Now!" His bark was accompanied by a fierce glare. Taya scrambled up and forward. Cristof had already sat up and was giving his friend a disbelieving look.

If Dautry was doing anything at the helm, it wasn't helping—they were still heading toward the tower at high speed. Taya grabbed her husband and dragged him to his feet.

"Time to go!"

"Janos— you can't—" Cristof was sputtering as she pulled him to the rail.

"And you," Amcathra ordered, reaching for the helm. Dautry slapped his hands away.

"You do your job and I'll do mine," she snapped.

The captain hesitated a second before turning to Colonel Agosti and Liliana. "You two, off the ship!"

"I can't!" Liliana wailed. "Pietra!"

"Come on!" her older sister shouted in Alzanan, grabbing her hand.

Taya climbed up to the rail, tugging her husband after her and snapping a line from his harness to her armature.

"He's going to kill himself," Cris muttered.

"We can't stop him."

"I hate this."

She pushed her arms into her wings. The *Firebrand* passed over the cliffs. Rocks and small buildings flashed beneath them.

"Jump!" Amcathra shouted as the *Firebrand* passed over the Tower's outer walls.

"Hold tight!" Taya shoved herself off and at an angle, hearing Cristof's panicked gasp. Out of the corner of her eye, she saw Colonel Agosti hurl Liliana over the rail and follow after her.

Cristof's light, counterweighted body caught the wind and twisted Taya around in midair. She threw out her wings and tried to steer them toward the center of the courtyard, away from the walls. Then Cristof's feet hit the ground and Taya tumbled into him and the *Firebrand* slammed into the base of Oporphyr Tower with a splintering crash, a great bellow of steam, and a chorus of very human screams.

CHAPTER NINETEEN

ONDIUM WRECKAGE TORE loose and flew up into the air as Taya ran to what was left of the *Firebrand*, her heart in her mouth.

"Captain! Captain!"

The ship had hit the Tower at a scraping angle that had torn off a wing and crumpled one side of the hull, leaving the vessel tilted up against the fortress wall, its pointed prow just yards away from the *Formidable*. Flames licked up the hull from the broken boiler inside.

Taya found Amcathra sprawled amidst a pile of broken wood, blood covering his face and one leg twisted around at an unnatural angle. Dautry lay several feet away, untangling herself from the ropes that had tied her to the shattered helm.

Taya dropped to the lictor's side.

"Oh, Lady, please...." She pressed a hand against his chest, panicked. A few seconds later Cristof dropped to his knees next to her.

"Taya—"

"His heart's beating." She dropped her head against the lictor's chest, listening for the steady sound. "Thank the Lady. He's alive."

Cristof wiped blood from his friend's face, revealing a broken nose and a wide, bloody gash on his forehead.

"He hit the helm when we crashed," Dautry said tersely, joining them. She was in better shape than the captain, her mass counterweighted by her rescue harness.

"He may have broken some ribs, too," Taya added, running her hands over Amcathra's body. "And his leg...."

Dautry knelt by the lictor as Cristof gently untangled the rifle strap from Amcathra's shoulder. "I'll guard him," she said as she unslung her rifle. "You look for the others."

"We need to get him away from the ship," Taya warned. "If that fire reaches the *Formidable,* it'll blow up."

Cristof pointed to a broken plank of wood.

"Use that."

They eased their friend on the makeshift stretcher and dragged him away. Liliana and Colonel Agosti joined them as they pulled the captain around a corner of the building. Liliana was supporting her sister, whose right arm was in a sling and whose side was crudely bandaged. She sank next to the captain when Liliana released her.

"Piece of metal went through my side," Agosti said tightly at Cristof's silent query. She looked at Amcathra. "How is your captain?"

"Alive."

"He must have the Father's own luck."

"Dautry, guard Janos and the Agostis. I'm going in."

"The bomb...." All five of them looked at Amcathra, whose face was whiter than normal. He tried to sit up, then fell back, coughing.

"I know," Cristof assured him. "We'll find it."

"Warn the city."

"We don't have time," Taya protested.

"I can do it. From the Tower. Help me up."

"Be careful— you may be bleeding inside," Cristof warned.

Amcathra growled and tried to sit up again. Dautry slid an arm around his back, supporting him. He hissed with pain.

"Your stubborn sense of duty is going to get you killed," the professor said, scowling at him. He didn't say anything, his teeth clenched as he leaned on her shoulder.

"I will help you carry him inside," Colonel Agosti said, tightly. "But only if you let me signal my ships, too."

"Why?" Cristof sounded suspicious.

"I know our military codes. I'll order the army to fall back and await further orders." Agosti met and held his gaze. "Go stop Lady Mazzoletti, Exalted. Bring her back to me alive, if you can. I swear to call a truce until I can question her about the invasion and the attack on my family. I swear it by the Divine Mother and the Celestial Father."

"Pietra!" Liliana hugged her sister, who winced and clutched her side.

"Then we'll go in together." Dautry slowly began working her way out of the ondium rescue harness, trying not to jostle Amcathra too much. "Put this on, Captain. Liliana and Colonel Agosti will support you, and I'll take point."

Amcathra's jaw twitched, but he nodded and let her slide the harness over his arms.

"All right," Cristof said, turning. "Taya— we have to go."

Taya crouched and poked a finger into Amcathra's sternum. "You'd better stay alive for us— *Janos*," she hissed.

He gave her a strained look as Dautry buckled the straps around his chest.

"Keep the exalted safe, Taya Icarus."

"Hmph. Well, I guess it's a start." Taya stood and ran after her husband.

The Alzanans had broken down the Tower's doors next to the *Formidable*. Taya and Cristof advanced with one eye on the fire that was consuming the shattered remnants of the *Firebrand* and one eye on the *Formidable*.

"There's someone inside," Cristof said. An Alzanan soldier was looking out the window at the burning *Firebrand* with an expression of concern.

Taya scanned the dead bodies around the ship. Most were lictors, but she saw a few men and women wearing a dedicate's clothing, too, and a single icarus hanging in midair, suspended by his silver wings. Only two of the dead were Alzanan.

"We could wait for the colonel to catch up," she suggested. "She could order him away."

"No— I don't trust her with that ship." Cristof scowled, indicating the ornately etched, snake-mouthed barrel of what could only be a Cabisi serpentfire cannon jutting out from one window. "In fact, the sooner we get rid of it, the better."

"What—"

He slung his rifle back over his shoulder and plunged his free hand into his pocket. It emerged with a bomb.

Taya took a deep breath. "Do you want me to do it?"

"No. Never again." He touched her face with affection. "Go warn the others."

"All right." She grabbed his coat front and kissed him. "Be careful!"

He smiled, straightening his glasses, and began easing toward the *Formidable*. Taya ran back to the small group and ushered them into the shadow of the tower. The colonel arched an eyebrow but Taya held her tongue; there was no time for an argument.

When she returned, she saw that Cristof had reached the ship without being noticed, ducking under the engine gondola. No engineers inside, Taya thought, which explained why the Alzanans weren't moving the dirigible away from the fire. The soldier up front must be getting nervous, if he was the only one left aboard.

Cristof crouched, angling his shoulders to protect his matches from the breeze. Then, with a surge, he stood and raised his rifle one-handed, jamming its butt against his shoulder as he fired at a gondola window. Glass shattered as he staggered backward, having forgotten the effect of recoil on a nearly weightless man. He regained his footing and lobbed the bomb inside. The Alzanan soldier up front was looking backward, startled. When he saw Taya and Cristof, he reached for his pistol.

"It's a bomb!" Taya shouted in Alzanan as she raced toward him and the blown-out Tower door beyond. "Get out— it's a bomb!"

The soldier vanished back inside the window. Taya was almost beside the command gondola's door when it swung open. The Alzanan stepped out, holding his gun. Taya put on a burst of speed and threw herself past him and through the Tower's broken door. Her boots skidded on a polished tile floor as she spun to look for her husband.

Cristof swung his rifle around as he ran, but the Alzanan fired first. Dirt plumed up next to the exalted, who veered away and took a wild shot. The Alzanan flinched, then lifted his pistol again.

"Stop!" Taya screamed. "Don't shoot!"

Then the bomb exploded, bursting out the glass windows in the engine gondola. The Alzanan soldier ducked and Cristof vaulted over him, half-propelled by the explosion. He staggered inside the Tower, sparks smoldering on his coat. Taya pounded on his back to put them out.

"Just a minute." He turned and raised his rifle, bracing one foot behind him. Outside, the Alzanan soldier was desperately beating out the flames in his hair and uniform.

"Don't kill him!" Taya begged. Her husband grimaced, then shifted his aim and shot. The soldier yelped, grabbing his shoulder.

"He can still shoot off-handed," Cristof complained, lowering the rifle.

"He won't." Taya tugged on his sleeve and they turned, surveying the damage.

The Tower hadn't been taken by surprise. Armed lictors and dedicates lay sprawled around them, along with a number of Alzanan soldiers. An icarus had been killed halfway down the stairs, her back arched over her floating armature. Taya whispered a prayer, recognizing a member of her eyrie.

"Dammit...." Cristof's expression darkened and his hands tightened on the rifle. He started to turn back to the door and the wounded Alzanan.

"Do you think Lady Mazzoletti went through the Council chamber?" Taya asked, hoping to distract him. It worked.

"She must have," he said, spinning around again. "Let's go."

They were stepping into the chamber when a thunderous boom shook the entire Tower. Cristof gave Taya a humorless smile.

"One serpentfire cannon down," he said.

"Thank the Lady." Taya reached out to touch his arm. No matter what else happened, they'd accomplished that much.

She felt a dizzying sense of deja vu as they descended the stairs past the Council's secret door. The Great Engine's mechanical rumble grew louder as they moved deeper into the heart of the mountain.

Cristof motioned for caution as he pushed the last door open and peered inside.

A tall woman whirled, pointing a pistol at Cristof's face. Cristof knocked the gun aside with the barrel of his rifle and the pistol went off, a bullet pinging off the stone wall over the door.

"Shit!" The woman recoiled, her blue eyes wide.

"Isobel!" Taya blocked Cristof's arm before he could bring his rifle back down. "What are you doing?"

"Taya? Exalted!" Isobel looked incredulous as she sketched a belated bow. "I thought you were dead!"

"Where are the Alzanans? How many are down here?" Cristof pushed past the programmer and looked over the metal railing, then blanched and took a hasty step backward.

Beyond the railing lay the vast hollow chamber that was the core of Ondinium Mountain. Floating in its center was the Great Engine, an analytical machine constructed of house-sized ondium gears and springs, pistons and cylinders, cables and engines, each shifting and rotating in a haze of steam and grease.

"Six or seven, maybe? They rappelled down about an hour ago," Isobel said, joining him at the rail. "I think they killed all the lictors — nobody's come down to help — it's just been us engineers and programmers trying to pick them all off."

"Where did you get a gun?" Cristof demanded.

"The Council issued weapons to everyone in the Tower two days ago, when we spotted the armies. We've been living down here for weeks— nobody's been allowed in or out. Has the city been taken?"

"No," Taya said. "Not yet. Where's the rest of your team?"

"Lars and Kyle are protecting the card vaults and Victor's down there with some of the engineers, trying to pick off the soldiers. Taya, they brought something big down with them— Victor thinks it's a bomb."

"He's right. They call it a holocaust bomb."

"That sounds bad."

"Why aren't you down there fighting the Alzanans, too?" Cristof asked, a note of suspicion in his voice. Isobel bridled.

"I'm not *sheytatangri*, Exalted! I'm fourth-generation Ondinium, and I've aced every loyalty test I've ever taken, *including* the extra one they issued for everyone of Demican descent."

"I'm sorry." He held up a hand. "I'm sorry— I had to ask."

"No, you didn't." Isobel wasn't appeased. "I was going up to the main Tower to see if anyone was still alive."

"Nobody that we saw," Taya said. "Look, Captain Amcathra went up there to send a warning signal out to the city. Will you go help him? He's with a Mareaux and two Alzanans, but they're allies."

"If I don't find them, I'll send the signal myself."

"Thank you," Taya said, gratefully. Isobel nodded, hesitated, sketched a bow to Cristof, and then headed out the door.

"I had to ask," Cristof repeated stubbornly, as Taya shot him a reproving look. "After Rikard...."

"You hurt her feelings." She turned to the catwalk's metal rail. "We've got to go down."

"I know." He set the safety on his air rifle and slung the strap across his chest. "If you can land us on a gear or a catwalk above the Alzanans, it'll be easier for me to shoot them."

"Do you have enough ammunition?"

"Yes. I put a handful of cartridges in my pocket." He cast her a look. "Although that's not the comment I expected to hear from you."

Taya stared down into the rumbling, hazy abyss and heard a distant gunshot.

"I don't like it when you kill people," she said unhappily, "but right now I don't think we have a choice."

"No, I don't think we do." He took off his silver-rimmed glasses and tucked them into his pocket. "All right. I'm ready."

She patted the railing.

"Stand up here so I can secure your harness."

"I'm going to close my eyes," he warned, edging toward her with his gaze averted. She smiled, despite herself, and took his hand. He instantly squeezed his eyes shut.

"All right. I've got you," she said. "You know, you were doing so well on the ship...."

"It's better when I don't have any time to think about what I'm doing." His hand tightened on hers as she helped him swing his legs around to dangle over the void. She knelt behind him on the rail, straddling his back.

"Okay, hold on to my armature," she directed. "I need both hands to do this."

"Are you tired of carrying me around yet?"

"Life *would* be easier if you had your own set of wings. Do you remember the last time we were here?"

"Only every fifth or sixth nightmare."

"I don't think you're nearly as afraid of heights as you pretend to be," she scolded. "You only do this to amuse me, don't you?"

"Taya, I love amusing you, but not enough to throw myself off ships, cliffs, and catwalks unless it's absolutely unavoidable."

She finished buckling him close, then gave him a quick hug from behind.

"You'll be fine. Keep your eyes closed if you want. I'll warn you when it's time to pull your knees up for the landing."

Another quick staccato of gunshots echoed up from below, and someone yelled.

"Taya, if this doesn't—" he sounded serious.

"Sshh." She wrapped her arms around his chest and rested her forehead on the back of his neck, feeling the tension in his shoulders. She didn't want to hear whatever he had to say. "It's my turn to tell you that I love you."

He hesitated, then relaxed, covering her hands where they clasped over his heart.

"Is it? I lose track."

"I don't say it often enough. After this, let's stay home for a while."

"I agree."

She straightened, looking over his shoulder and down at the giant Engine.

"Ready?"

His shoulders tightened again. "No."

"On the count of three, pull up your knees and hold them to your chest." She slid her arms into her wings.

He crossed his hands over his chest, grabbing the harness.

"One— two— *three*."

Taya pushed them off, spreading her arms.

The Great Engine's colossal ondium gears and pistons, carriages and cams, rods and recording drums floated in the center of the hollowed-out chamber in the heart of Ondinium Mountain. The vast stone cavern was ringed with metal catwalks that spanned the chasm at regular intervals, providing access to the Engine. Clouds of steam and oil droplets moved like rainstorms on currents of warmer and cooler air. Here and there broad banks of carbon-filament incandescent lighting illuminated the chamber and reflected off the Engine's ondium components, but in other places, the chamber remained dim and shadowed.

Taya descended through the Engine's chamber as quickly and steeply as she dared, cognizant of the irregular sounds of gunfire below. At one point she passed two Ondinium women, one half-carrying the other, who were limping along a catwalk. They gave her startled looks, then waved frantically as they registered her wings. She tilted in acknowledgement but didn't call out.

"What's wrong?" Cristof whispered.

"Nothing. Halfway there."

"My back is killing me."

"Sorry."

The sound of shots and shouts made her slow down as she dropped closer to the bottom of the chamber. As the haze cleared, she got her first good view of the Engine Room floor.

The bottom of the far-reaching chamber was as wide as several villages tucked together, most of it divided into roofless, cubicle-partitioned offices. From her vantage point, Taya could see into all of the cubicles, noting desks and filing cabinets, bookshelves and toolcases— and a handful of Alzanan soldiers and Ondinium engineers who were dodging from office to office in a deadly game of hide-and-seek.

Directly beneath the Great Engine stood another bank of steam engines and water tanks and a complicated array of bins and conveyer belts that carried fuel and water across the complex. Thick metal struts rose from the floor, bolted to the ondium framework that formed the bottom casing for the Great Engine and moored it inside the mountain. The struts had climbing rungs on them, and elsewhere beneath the engine ondium-runged floating ladders waited to be dragged wherever they were needed. Two Alzanan soldiers lay in a crumped heap near one of the support struts.

Taya located an ondium girder on the housing that looked wide and sturdy enough to support two people.

"Get ready to land," she warned. Cristof grabbed his harness and uncurled his legs with a grimace. She swept over the strut and backbeat as he planted his feet on the girder and grabbed a crossbar to steady himself.

"Here." He reached out with his free hand and caught the keel of her armature, pulling her down to him. Taya waited until her feet touched the girder before locking her wings and releasing her arms. He unhooked his harness from the armature.

"Thanks," she said. She sat on the girder as he slid on his glasses and unslung his rifle. "Can you see the soldiers down there?"

"Yes." He edged around to another girder to get a better angle. Taya watched, worried that one of the Alzanans would spot him and shoot. However, the soldiers and engineers were focused on each other— none of them even glanced at the gigantic engine that floated over their heads.

"I only see three Alzanans left," Cristof reported, kneeling and shouldering the rifle.

"Watch the recoil!"

"Right…." He dropped flat and squirmed up to the girder's edge. With a hard swallow, he pushed his glasses higher and leaned over to take aim.

Two quick shots jarred him backward. One of the Alzanans fell and everyone — Alzanan and Ondinium — looked up, searching for the shooter. Taya shrank back, glad that her wings were still painted black.

"Isobel? Is that you?" someone shouted.

Her husband crawled to the edge, pointing his rifle over again.

"Victor Kiernan?" he shouted.

"Who the hell are you?"

Cristof fired again and Taya bit her lip as another Alzanan fell. *Firing from above is like dropping bombs from above*, she decided. *It doesn't feel fair.*

"The last Alzanan is two offices to your left, Victor," he shouted in reply.

"Not quite," a calm voice replied. Taya gasped and looked up. Fosca Mazzoletti knelt on top of a slowly rotating gear above them, her military pistol aimed at Cristof.

"Cris, *move!*"

A bullet pinged off the metal girder as her husband threw himself to one side, his legs sliding off the edge. He grabbed the girder, stopping his fall as his rifle dangled from its strap on one arm.

Taya surged to her feet and jumped. Her fingers closed on a narrow support strut overhead, and she pulled herself up, grateful for her ondium armature. The tips of her wings scraped against the teeth of a rotating megawheel as she vaulted from the strut to a fixed axis a few feet below the Alzanan aristocrat.

Fosca Mazzoletti swung the pistol around.

"You...." she hissed, her finger tightening on the trigger.

Taya leaped for the gear. A bullet seared across the back of her shoulder as her hands closed around one of the giant teeth. She grit her teeth and looked up. Fosca stood over her, the barrel of her pistol pointed directly at Taya's face.

"Your lictors told me that you and your husband killed my brother," she said, her beautiful face twisted into a sneer. "I found them surprisingly ill-equipped to handle torture."

"Bitch!" Taya pulled herself up, grabbing a handful of Fosca Mazzoletti's skirts in one fist, and yanked down as hard as she could.

The gun went off, its bullet ricocheting uselessly off a camshaft as Fosca screamed and tumbled off the edge of the gear. The thick skirt ripped and another burst of pain shot up Taya's grazed shoulder. She opened her hand and let herself drop back against the axis, clutching her injured shoulder. Her fingers dug under her armature's struts and came back bloody.

Below her, Fosca Mazzoletti had grabbed a camshaft and was struggling to maintain her grip as the ondium rod slowly rotated.

"Taya, are you all right?" Cristof had dragged himself back on top of the girder and was aiming his rifle at the Alzanan woman.

"I'm fine," she shouted back, not entirely truthfully. "Don't shoot her!"

"I'm aiming for her leg."

"She'll fall— let *me* get her!"

"Fosca Mazzoletti— if you try *anything* while Taya is saving you, I'm going to shoot your damned head off!" he roared. The Alzanan aristocrat didn't pay any attention to him, busy keeping her grip on the rotating camshaft.

"Cris— I have to drop straight down." Taya looked over her shoulder past her wing, gauging the maneuver.

"I'll cover you." He dropped to his stomach, his rifle aimed at the Alzanan.

Taya jumped, her thick boots landing on the irregularly shaped cams, and wobbled a moment before catching her balance. Her shoulder burned as she leaned down and wrapped her hands around Fosca's wrists.

"Let go!" Taya ordered.

"No!" The woman shifted her grip again, her face white. "No— you'll let me fall!"

Taya took an awkward step to avoid one of the cam's lobes. Her grazed shoulder didn't appreciate her doubled-over position. She tightened her grip.

"I won't let you fall. I promised Colonel Agosti I'd hand you over for questioning," she said, flatly.

"You'll never—" Fosca Mazzoletti shrieked as her wrists were jerked out of Taya's grasp. Taya staggered, nearly losing her balance. The Alzanan's torn skirt had been caught between a cam and a valve head. Fosca dangled head-down beneath the giant ondium mechanism, her skirt slowly dragging her upward to the rotating cam. She screamed.

Taya grabbed her short utility knife with one hand and jumped off the cam, stopping her fall by clutching her enemy's skirt. As the Alzanan woman wailed and squirmed, Taya began sawing at the fabric.

"No, stop, let go!" Fosca panicked, her eyes fixed on the floor fifty feet below.

"Stop kicking!" Taya snapped as a foot hit her in the back of the head. The skirt's fabric was too thick; she was running out of time. Counting on the fabric to hold her weight, she swung herself around, head-down like the aristocrat, and wrapped her legs around the woman's stomach.

"What are you *doing?*"

"Trying to save you for your trial," Taya grated, wincing as she slid her arms into her wings. She locked her ankles. "Unbutton your skirt."

"*What?*"

"Take off your skirt or you'll be dragged into the machine! I've got you!"

Fosca hung motionless a long moment, her heart pounding so hard that Taya could feel it against her knees. Then, with a sound that was half-curse, half-sob, the aristocrat tore at her waistband. The skirt slid off and both women dropped. Fosca Mazzoletti screamed again, terrified.

"Taya!" Cristof shouted.

Taya pulled down on her wings as hard as she could, scooping air beneath the feathers, and beat hard to slow their descent. Forty feet— thirty— twenty— she veered toward the corpses below the Engine — ten — she unlocked her ankles and let Fosca Mazzoletti fall as she shot back into the air.

Fosca's scream stopped abruptly as she landed on the bodies of her dead countrymen. Taya swept around into a perfect running landing, locking her wings up and releasing her arms as soon as she stopped.

"Taya Icarus!"

She spun. Victor Kiernan grinned through his beard as he jogged up, rifle in hand. Two of his five similarly armed companions broke away to inspect Fosca Mazzoletti as Taya caught her breath.

"Are you all right?" The programmer tucked his rifle into the crook of his arm and clasped her hand in a fierce welcome. "We thought you were dead! Was that Exalted Forlore earlier?"

"Yes." She retrieved her hand and hurried over to Fosca Mazzoletti's motionless body. "Is she alive?"

"Unconscious, and maybe she broke her wrist?" A woman in a pair of gray coveralls straightened. Unlike the rest of the group, she wore a famulate's circle on her face instead of a dedicate's spiral.

"All right, good. Keep her alive but tied up— she's incredibly important and incredibly dangerous," Taya said, with feeling. "Did you find the bomb?"

"The bomb?"

"I was afraid of that." Victor pointed up. "They were working on something up there, on the Engine's main frame."

Taya craned her neck. Her husband was gingerly working his way across the girders toward her.

"Cris!"

"What?"

"Victor says the bomb's up there!"

She didn't catch his reply, but he dropped to all fours and began moving faster.

"It's called a holocaust bomb," she told the programmer. "Cabisi-made. We don't know exactly what it does."

"Holocaust... that sounds ominous."

"Another Cabisi weapon on the same ship caused tornadoes of fire in a half-mile radius," she said, soberly. Gasps and whistles greeted her remark.

"You saw it used...?" Victor asked.

"On Safira." Taya swallowed. "And here. I don't know how bad the damage is, but I saw smoke over Secundus."

"We'd better sound an evacuation alarm," one of the engineers suggested. Victor nodded and the man shouldered his rifle and ran off, vanishing into the maze of offices.

"The rest of you take the prisoner and go, all right?" The famulate jumped up onto the access rungs of the strut they were standing under. "I'll help the exalted."

"Maybe they didn't have time to arm the bomb," a dedicate said, hopefully.

"I'll let you know, won't I?" The famulate climbed the rungs with the ease of long experience.

"Antonia, could you find some wire to tie up our prisoner?" Victor asked.

"Sure." The dedicate who'd just spoken hurried off.

"I'm going up, too," Taya said, grabbing the rungs. "Victor— we ran into Isobel on top and told her to warn the city."

"Good." He turned to the remaining men. "You two head to the archives and get the master cards. We're not leaving the Engine Room without them."

"Got it." They headed for the nearest set of metal stairs.

"I'll watch your prisoner," Victor said, as Taya climbed. "Tell Skip to shout if she needs me. I know a few things about bombs."

"I don't want to hear that!" Taya shouted back.

Cristof and the famulate, Skip, had found what looked like a fancy standing clock bolted to the Engine's frame. Its polished brass case was etched with images of curling flames and its ornate shell clockface had two hands, the hour hand pointing at twelve and the minute hand pointing at four.

Taya fished out her pocketwatch and checked it.

"The clock's off," she said. "It's actually a quarter to eleven."

"It's not a clock," Cristof said, tensely. "It's a timer."

"Well, they did an excellent job of securing it, didn't they, Exalted?" Skip kept her eyes averted from Cristof's face. "If I had a few hours, I might be able to cut through the bolts with a hacksaw, but I surely can't do it in forty minutes."

Taya's eyes fell on the hand pointing to the four and her mouth went dry.

"Forty minutes? That's all the time we have?"

"Unless I can figure out how to defuse it, but…" Cristof peered behind the bomb. "Getting in there to unscrew the plate is going to be difficult. I need some very small screwdrivers and an angled mirror."

"We got tools below, Exalted, if you like." Skip said. "Do you want me to go get them for you?"

"Victor says he knows something about bombs, too," Taya ventured. Cristof pursed his lips, then lifted an angular shoulder.

"Send him up, then. I'm a clockwright, not a bomb expert."

A deafening air horn went off and they all started, then covered their ears.

"Evacuation alert," Skip said after it stopped, giving Taya an embarrassed smile. "It needs to be loud, right?"

Taya nodded, her ears ringing. "How much damage do you think the bomb will do?"

"Impossible to say without knowing more about how it works," Cristof replied, straightening up.

"Actually…." Skip scratched her head and looked up. "You know, Exalted, I'm thinking it ain't the bomb that's the real threat, begging your pardon, sir."

"What do you mean?"

"It's where they put it, ain't it, Exalted? Right here on the corner of the mooring framework."

"Forgefire…." Cristof looked up.

"What is it?" Taya demanded.

"Ondium's effectiveness increases by volume," Skip said, tapping Taya's wings. "The more counterweights you slip into a flight belt or rescue harness, the lighter you are, right?"

"Yes...."

Skip pointed to the titanic machine floating above them.

"The Great Engine's so buoyant that the mooring piles for its support framework are sunk seventy-five feet deep into solid stone at four different points to keep it from tearing them out of the ground. The Engine is secured to the framework — this framework we're standing on here — by hundreds of support struts and cables, right? But if a bomb blew apart the framework—"

"The whole Engine would fly straight up." Taya's eyes widened as she imagined a small mountain's worth of ondium hurtling into the air.

"Oporphyr Tower's built right over the Engine Room, ain't it?" Skip continued, relentlessly. "The Engine'll tear through the fortress floor like a volcano. Rubble will be thrown all across the city, and the Engine— well, I'm thinking we ain't ever going to see it again, will we?"

Taya stared.

"This framework is the Engine's only anchor point?" Cristof pressed.

"We got maintenance rings sunk into the walls all the way up to anchor individual components for repair and replacement." Skip grimaced. "If we turn off the Engine we can try cabling it down, but in forty minutes—"

"How many people do you have?"

"Evacuation alert brings all hands down to the maintenance tunnels, so we'll know soon, won't we?" Skip stood and swung herself over, heading down. "I'll find you them tools, Exalted."

"Thank you." Cristof sat on the framework and raked his fingers through his hair, then looked at Taya. "What happened?"

"What do you mean?" Taya sat next to him, not knowing what else to do.

"You're wincing every time you move your arm."

"Oh. A bullet grazed me. Again."

"Sit still." He shifted around her. "Yes, the leather's been ripped. Unbutton your suit."

"Not the time or the place, Exalted," she joked.

"I should be so lucky." He tugged her suit down. She flinched as the fabric pulled. "Sorry. You're right; it's a graze. Not as bad as last time. We need to clean it, though."

"This is all sounding very familiar."

He dropped a kiss on her neck and straightened her suit.

"Could you fly up to warn Janos?"

"I could, but I'm not going to let you get rid of me that easily." She buttoned the neck of her suit. "How bad is it going to be?"

"If we can't defuse the bomb in… twenty-nine minutes, we'll have to leave through the maintenance tunnels. *I'll* leave through the maintenance tunnels." He moved next to her and took her hand. "I want *you* to fly up ten minutes before then to get our friends out of the Tower."

"How? The ships—"

"Take the wireferry. There's an emergency release over the door. Taya, if the Engine tears through the Tower, it'll be almost as bad as Glasgar. You need to get Janos and Isobel and everyone else off the peak as quickly as possible. You… you might want to just fly straight out, as far away from the Tower as you can. The farther you are from the Tower, the safer you'll be."

Taya squeezed his hand, frightened.

The evacuation alarm brought down eight programmers and nineteen engineers. As soon as Skip explained the situation, the programmers shut down the Great Engine. Kyle, Lars, and two other dedicates emerged from the archives carrying metal boxes filled with large tin master cards, and several other programmers dashed from office to office gathering the latest data reports.

As soon as the Great Engine's pistons slowed, enveloped in a cloud of steam, the engineers swarmed over the machine. Thick cables were locked around major components and anchored to the mountain walls. The engineers' goal was to try to secure as much of the Engine as possible— they knew they wouldn't be able to keep the entire Engine intact, but anything that might reduce the final loss was worth trying.

In the meantime, Cristof, Victor, and two other engineers interrogated Lady Mazzoletti, who'd regained consciousness. She said she knew nothing about disarming the bomb, and Taya didn't have any reason to doubt her. Cristof removed the bomb's brass backplate and studied its interior.

"I've never seen anything like it," he confessed, sitting back on his heels. "I can't even read the labels."

"Taya?" Victor looked at her, but she shook her head.

"I can speak Cabisi, but I can't read it. It uses an entirely different alphabet. If Jinian were here...."

"I'm going to guess that the detonator will set off some kind of chemical reaction," Cristof speculated, "but I don't see any way to pull the cylinders out without triggering the mechanism."

"Can you stop the clock?"

"Most bombs have some kind of failsafe built in." He checked the clockface. "Taya, you need to go."

"Then *you* need to get to the maintenance tunnels." Taya looked at Victor. "Where are they?"

He pointed.

"About seven minutes in that direction. She's right, Exalted; it's time to call people off the Engine."

"How do I get to the tunnels from outside?"

"They open onto Primus through one of the Economics and Finance vaults," one of the engineers said. "You'll have to get through building security...."

"I'll meet you there, then." Taya stood. "Victor, keep my husband safe."

"Yes, ma'am," the programmer said, grinning. Cristof shot him a cool look, then turned to her.

"I'll keep *them* safe," he corrected.

"Just be there when I get to the vault." She kissed him and he held her tight, ignoring the cleared throats and uncomfortable shifting around them.

"Fly safely," he said, at last. She mustered a brave smile as she turned away and slid her arms into her wings.

CHAPTER TWENTY

TAYA LANDED ON the top catwalk and locked her wings close in order to run through the security corridors to the Council chamber.

"Dautry! Isobel! Somebody!" she bellowed, racing through the empty chamber and into the Tower halls. "Is anyone here? We need to evacuate!"

"Here!"

She spun and saw an icarus descending the stairs. He was wearing the bright red armband of a search-and-rescue team.

"There's a bomb in the Great Engine!" she said. "We need to get everyone out of the Tower, *now!*"

"Hey, you're Taya, aren't you?"

"Yes, and Exalted Forlore is below, and he says everyone has to get out before the Oporphyr Tower is destroyed!"

The icarus's eyes widened.

"Got it. There's five of us in the S&R team. We're evacuating the wounded, but there's a group in the signal room that won't go. They told me you were down here—"

"Where's the signal room?"

"Down the hall and to the left, but one of them—"

"I'll get them. Get everyone else off the peak and as far away as possible. *Don't come back.*"

"But one of them—"

"Shut up!" Taya shouted. "And *go!*"

He turned and ran in one direction while she took the other.

"Time to go!" Taya shouted, throwing open the signal room door. Dautry was supporting Captain Amcathra while Isobel ran a card through the control panel. Colonel Agosti was scribbling a message on a piece of paper while Liliana looked over her shoulder. "We're taking the wireferry down!"

Isobel grabbed Agosti's message and another card and thrust it into a punch machine.

"Go ahead; I'll catch up in a minute."

"Isobel, we have to leave *now*— the bomb's going off in ten minutes!"

"Go, go— take the lictor, he can barely move."

"We're leaving," Dautry said firmly, sliding her shoulder under Amcathra's arm. Taya rushed in and took his other arm. The rescue harness made moving him easier, but no amount of ondium could make a broken rib and leg less painful— the lictor's face was pallored and covered with sweat.

Colonel Agosti stood, hesitated, and turned toward Isobel.

"Thank you," she said. The blond woman nodded, still punching.

"Which way to the wireferry?" Taya demanded. "We're taking the emergency route."

"Usual station," Amcathra said faintly. "There's a lever over the door."

"This way, then." Taya guided them out the door. She and Dautry began to jog, the captain stumbling between them with his teeth clenched against the pain. Liliana and her sister followed, the colonel keeping her arm pressed against her side.

"Strap in," Taya commanded as soon as they reached the wireferry. She threw open the metal door and helped Dautry maneuver Amcathra into a seat. She yanked out her watch. Five minutes left. Dautry fastened the captain's safety straps as Liliana and Agosti found seats for themselves.

As the professor buckled herself in, Taya turned back to the building. She was debating whether to leave the ferry car or not when Isobel burst through the doorway.

"I'm here!" The programmer threw herself into the car, grabbing the safety straps. Taya followed her, ducking to get her wings through the entrance, and slammed the door shut.

"Ready?" Without waiting for an answer, she tore off the safety wire that held the emergency escape lever up and yanked it down.

A giant piston drove out from the station wall and slammed into the car, hurling it forward with a neck-snapping jar. Taya was thrown into one of the benches, her wings bending behind her. Dautry shouted something profane in Mareaux and Liliana and Isobel screamed.

Taya fumbled with her safety straps as the car plunged off the edge of the mountain cliff. Gears screeched as it shot down the cable toward the terrace below. She yanked a strap through her armature and buckled it. For an endless moment, she was aware of nothing but the car rattling down the cable toward Primus and her own pounding heart.

Then the top of Ondinium Mountain burst open with a bone-rattling tremor and a windstorm of fire and metal machine parts shot into the sky.

Taya barely had time for a scream of her own when the wireferry car slammed into the Primus station and snapped the restraining cable. It tore through the safety nets beyond the cable and smashed into the heavy rubber bumpers on the station's far wall, bending their metal arms. Its supporting cable went limp as the wireferry tower on top of the mountain was blown off the cliff. The car jerked backward and dropped seven feet to the station's metal floor, bounced, skidded to the far wall, and came to a shuddering halt in the corner. With a screeching zip, the wireferry cable whipped through its pulley and snapped, whip-cracking against the top of the station before it was yanked down by the wreckage plummeting into the city streets below.

Taya clung to her safety strap, gagging. She'd been slammed into the car's sides several times, but her counterweighting had helped her avoid the worst of the damage. Now she fumbled the strap buckle open and dropped to her knees, heaving.

Still alive. That was something. She grabbed the wooden bench and pulled herself up, her neck and back protesting. Isobel wasn't moving. Liliana sobbed as she clung to her sister, and Captain Amcathra and Dautry were both motionless.

Taya watched Amcathra and Dautry until she saw their chests move, then she pried open the wireferry door. Her head was splitting and her neck was stiff. Every muscle in her body ached and her left knee felt like it had been wrenched off. She wiped blood out of her eyes and limped to the edge of the car platform, looking up toward Oporphyr Tower.

The Tower was gone. The top of Ondinium mountain was covered in a brown haze, and rocks crashed off the sheer cliffs into the buildings below. Glass from hundreds of broken windows glittered in the streets of Primus, and exalteds and their household staff shrieked for help from inside half-collapsed mansions.

Taya pushed her arms into her wings and spread them. Everything hurt, but everything moved. She took an unsteady step and dropped off the tower.

Her survival instincts kicked in and, despite her dazed, incoherent state of mind, she managed to keep herself aloft. Other icarii were in the air, too, but she ignored their calls and wing-tilts as she weaved through the streets toward the civic offices.

The Economics and Finance building had been built flush against the mountain cliff. Its ornate facade had collapsed when the mountain had shaken, and giant slabs of stone lay scattered and broken on its roof and the streets around it.

Taya landed badly, staggering and skidding on her knees, then falling over with one wing caught under her. She lay prone in the street, tasting blood and catching her breath.

"Hey, Icarus! Hey, are you— Forgefire, is that you, Taya?" She felt hands on her face. "Cassi, come here!"

"Pyke..." Taya groaned as he helped her sit up, easing her arms out of her wings.

"Is your arm broken? You're covered in blood! What happened?"

"Cris." She tried to get up, collapsed, and tried again.

"Scrap, wait! Cassi!"

"Oh, Lady, is that Taya?"

"I think she's hurt."

"Taya, Taya, sweetie, look at me. Are you all right?"

Taya blinked and focused, her friends' faces swimming before her. They were both wearing bright red armbands. Search and rescue.

"Cris," she said again, getting her feet underneath her. "The tunnels."

"What tunnels?" Cassi slid an arm around her waist. "Pyke, lock her wings up for her."

"In the building. Maintenance. From the Engine." Taya tried to push away. "Cris is down there."

"Okay— okay, we'll get him. Which building?"

Taya pointed, flinching at the pain in her arm. Cassi led her to it.

"That building is *not* safe to enter," Pyke protested.

"It's a search-and-rescue mission, isn't it? We're searching for the exalted." Cassi brushed hair back from Taya's face. "I'm not letting her go in there alone, Pyke. I thought— I thought I'd lost her *and* Jayce."

Pyke swore and hurried to catch up.

The Economics and Finance building had been evacuated as soon as the enemy armies had been sighted. Taya pulled herself together as they ventured into its dark hallways, summarizing the situation for her two friends.

"The vaults will be cut directly into the cliff," Pyke said, "so they must be this way." They walked deeper into the building before reaching a heavy, steel-reinforced door. Pyke rattled the handle.

"Locked." Cassi bit her lip. "We need to find someone who works here."

Taya staggered to the door and yanked on it, tears burning her eyes. "Cris! Cris, are you there?"

Nothing.

"Taya…" Cassi took her arm. Taya shook her off, plunging her hand into her pocket.

"Get back," she said.

"Whoa!" Pyke's eyes widened. "Is that a *bomb*?"

"Taya, no! You are *not* setting off a bomb to open that door!"

"Yes, I am." Taya placed it at the base of the doorframe and pulled out her waxed package of lucifer matches. Her hands were shaking so hard she nearly dropped them. She had no idea if the explosive would be strong enough to blow down the door, but she had to do *something*. "Go hide around the corner."

She struck a match, which promptly fizzled out. Clenching her fist, she tried to calm her nerves.

Cris was in the tunnels. He was safe. She only needed to get to him.

She pulled out a second match.

Pyke squatted next to her and took it.

"Let me do it, Taya. I've always wanted to set off a bomb inside a government building."

She stared at him, struggling to make sense of his words.

"You'll never pass your next loyalty test," she said at last.

"It'll be worth it." He grinned and gently tugged the packet from her fingers. "Go on, calm Cassi down before she passes out."

"You'll have to run."

"Oh, don't worry about that."

"Promise me you'll light it."

"I promise. Go on."

She painfully staggered to her feet and limped down the hall, still trembling. Cassi dragged her around the corner and into an unlocked office, forcing her to kneel.

Moments later they heard Pyke's whoop. He raced down the hall and spun around the corner, laughing like a madman. The bomb went off just as he dived through the office door.

Taya was on her feet before Cassi had even uncovered her ears.

The bomb hadn't destroyed the door, but it had blown it far enough off its hinges for Pyke to haul it aside and let all three slip through.

"Hello?" Taya shouted, looking down a long hall lined with similarly heavy doors. "Cris? Are you there?"

One of the doors swung open and a red-faced, soot-covered dedicate staggered out, coughing. He looked up with relief.

"We're here!" he shouted, turning. "We made it!"

A ragged cheer rose as more dedicates tumbled out, nursing burns and laughing with a touch of hysteria. Taya threw herself into the crowd of strangers, shouting for her husband, until at last he wrapped his arms around her, armature and all.

The rest of the day was chaos as emergency crews rescued the trapped and injured. The Oporphyr Council had lost four out the six decaturs who had been in the Tower during the Alzanan assault. Three other decaturs had been stationed elsewhere in Ondinium, Constante included, and one had been home sick. Thus only three decaturs were left in Ondinium to sit down with Cristof to figure out what to do next while the Alzanan and Ondinium armies waited tensely for further instructions.

After being bandaged by emergency workers, Taya had asked Cassi and Pyke to look after Captain Amcathra and Professor Dautry, both of whom had been knocked unconscious in the wireferry crash. Fosca Mazzoletti, who'd escaped the explosion under Cristof's guard, was taken to prison and Liliana accompanied her sister to the emergency Council meeting that had been set up at the University just an hour after the explosion. Among the many tasks before the remaining three decaturs was deciding what to do about the enemy ships that still circled Ondinium waiting for orders.

Taya, of course, stood in the meeting next to Cristof. They were both bruised, battered, and bandaged, but so was everyone else in the room.

"I am willing to maintain a cease-fire while we investigate the possibility of peace," Colonel Pietra Agosti said to the trio of masked and robed decaturs. "However, I wish to have time to talk in private with Lady Mazzoletti about her actions and to decide the best course of action before we open formal negotiations."

An icarus leaned close to his exalted, then nodded.

"It seems to the Council that you are not in a strong bargaining position, Queen Agosti," he said on the decatur's behalf. "Why shouldn't the Council simply hold you and your sister hostage to your nation's good behavior?"

"Because if you do, my enemies will claim the throne for themselves." Despite her injuries, the colonel remained calm and confident. "I know you do not consider the Agosti Family your allies, but I assure you that if you support my return to the throne, your assistance will not be forgotten. And if you do *not* support me, some other Family will take command of the armies standing at your doorstep, and you will lose much more than you already have."

The icarus waited a long time before looking up. Taya knew that meant he had a difficult message to convey. She crossed her fingers.

"The decatur is willing to return you to your country if you will sign an armistice agreement with the Council," he relayed. "However, we would like your sister to stay in Ondinium as the Council's guest and a guarantee of your good behavior. We will return her when our ambassadors return to Alzana with a new peace treaty."

"Unacceptable. I will not allow you to use my sister as a hostage."

"You may have our ambassador in exchange." The icarus inclined his head in Cristof's direction.

"Wait a minute!" Taya objected. "Don't we have any say in this?"

Cristof laid a hand over hers, frowning at the decaturs, then leaned toward her. "If I go, will you stay here to look after Liliana?" he asked, softly.

"You *aren't* going to agree to this, are you?"

"I might as well do something right before I retire."

"If you go, I go, too."

"Is there any chance you'll listen to reason?"

"I do *not* consider leaving you on your own in Alzana to be reasonable!"

He sighed.

"I agree to go to Alzana as the Council's representative," he said, straightening up and addressing the decaturs. "Taya will go with me." He turned to Agosti. "Your sister can stay in our estate while we're gone. Our dedicates will take good care of her."

Agosti gave him a long look, then inclined her head.

"I regret that Lady Mazzoletti's conspiracy ended in your lictors' deaths, Ambassador," she said. "But to the best of my knowledge, the rest of your staff is still being held in prison. As a gesture of goodwill, I will arrange for their freedom as soon as we arrive."

Taya gripped Cristof's hand, a lump in her throat.

"Thank you," Cristof said, squeezing her hand. "My wife and I would deeply appreciate that."

The discussion went on for hours, but Taya finally excused herself and reclaimed her armature. She needed to reassure her father and sister that she was alive and well, and she wanted to tell Cassi that Jayce might still be alive.

Days later, the war's toll on Ondinium was still being calculated. Five separate serpentfire conflagration zones had devasted the land around the capital, and the Safira rail terminus had been utterly annihilated. The inferno over Secundus had consumed hundreds of homes and offices and took twenty-four hours to bring under control. Rescue teams were still calculating the human losses. Oporphyr Tower was gone and the top of Ondinium mountain had collapsed in on itself. Rocks periodically tumbled down onto Primus as the cliffs shuddered and shifted under the pressure. The Great Engine had been gutted by the explosive eruption, along with the offices and data archives that had surrounded it. Taya's programmer friends predicted that the vast amount of information that had been lost would be sending shudders through Ondinium's social and economic infrastructures for years to come.

It had taken two days for the three absent decaturs to return to Ondinium. Constante had assumed leadership of the Council with enviable ease and swiftly arranged the signing of an Alzanan-Ondinium Armistice. The Demican *sheytatangri* weren't included in the armistice, but they sullenly agreed to meet with their clan elders in a new *ating*. Several ornithopters were dispatched to bring all of the previous *ating* members together in the capital. Taya was glad to see that the icarus Nayan seemed to have sobered up under his new responsibilities, and she was delighted to introduce Cristof to Edvin Talus, who had accompanied his mother, an elder, on the trip. They soon had an invitation to visit the clan the next time they returned to Demicus. Taya hoped they could accept the invitation soon. She still hadn't given up her hope of seeing a white bear.

In the end, the *sheytatangri* and the clans who had joined it agreed to a peaceful return to Demicus, although quite a bit of the loot they'd scavenged during the invasion vanished across the border with them. The *ating*'s Ondinium facilitators stoically looked the other way.

Jinian and Lucanus had successfully crippled the *Indomitable* before Agosti's signal to stand down had been received, and for nearly twenty-four hours they had held its engine gondola while Captain Fiore and the surviving crew waited for further orders. At last they accepted the captain's offer to disembark over a neutral zone and returned to Ondinium. Jinian declared her challenge satisfactorily resolved and Lucanus returned to duty. Jinian joined Liliana in the Forlore estate as a guest while Cristof, Taya, and Colonel Agosti returned to Alzana.

Captain Amcathra had been unhappy about being left behind, but he had been in no shape to follow them. To his great displeasure, Cristof and Taya had been quick to sing his praises to anyone who'd listen, and the Ondinium press jumped at the chance to laud the Demican-descended ornithopter captain who'd rescued an exalted from Alzana's capital, fought aerial battles over four nations, and delivered an enemy queen to the Council. Ondinium needed a hero to defuse the social tensions that had arisen during the war, and the wounded Captain Amcathra and his loyal Mareaux navigator — the first foreigner to be formally confirmed as a warrant officer in Ondinium's new aerial force — were made to order.

When Taya and Cristof arrived at the Alzanan palace, they found six members of their diplomatic staff waiting for them, thin but clean and well-dressed.

"Jayce!" Taya hugged her friend with tears in her eyes. "Oh, Jayce, I was so worried about you!"

"Lady help us," Jayce said, returning her embrace, "we thought you were dead, too! Everyone told us you were dead."

"When did they let you out?"

"A week ago." He swallowed and mustered an unsteady smile for her. "That was when we finally heard the truth."

"Did they treat you badly?"

He looked over her shoulder at the Alzanan entourage and lowered his voice.

"At first I thought we were going to be killed in our cells. But after the first week or two they left us alone. I heard the prince was protecting us, but I don't know why."

"Silvio Agosti?"

He nodded, then touched her sleeve. "Taya... they said the fighting reached Ondinium. Is the Great Engine really gone?"

"A lot of it, although the Council says it'll be rebuilt bigger and better than ever." Taya squeezed his arm. "I have letters for you from Cassi and your parents— they're in my trunk."

He smiled and Taya hugged him and the rest of the staff again before rejoining Cristof, who was waiting patiently for her in his new robe and ivory mask.

A week passed before the official peace negotiations began, a week during which Queen Pietra Agosti presided over Fosca Mazzoletti's public trial. Much to Taya's surprise, Lady Mazzoletti confessed to her crimes and named her co-conspirators. Later she learned that Fosca had agreed to cooperate if Liliana dropped her vendetta against the Mazzolettis. As a result, although many of the adult members of the Mazzoletti Family were executed, the younger and more distant Family members remained alive under much reduced circumstances.

The young *principe* Silvio was never implicated in the slaughter. He had been lucky enough to escape the initial attack, and Fosca Mazzoletti had decided to keep him alive to garner the nation's sympathy. What she had not counted on, however, was that the apparently bitter Ondinium exile she'd taken under her wing — the "assassin's" own estranged brother, Alister Forlore — had given Silvio his older sister's golden bracelet with the news that she was alive and well and wanted him to keep the Ondinium prisoners safe. The fourteen-year-old had believed Alister and put the prisoners under his personal protection. Taya made a point of thanking him for looking after her staff, and he thanked her in turn for saving his sister's life.

Despite this strong start, the peace treaty took more time to hammer out than Taya had expected. Neither Pietra nor Cristof were forgiving souls, and they had years of rancor between the two countries to work through. At last, however, an agreement was reached and signed in a lavish public ceremony. A few days later Taya and Cristof were on a train back to A-O Terminal, their copy of the treaty secured in a metal case locked to Taya's armature.

"I'm sorry, Exalted," Major Leppala said as they stood on the Ondinium side of the city, where their locomotive was taking on water and fuel. "We found your brother's body inside the mecharachnid under the collapse. I know you would have preferred to be here for the service, but... I thought it would be better to send him onward sooner than later."

Cristof nodded, his lips tight. Taya wrapped her arm through his with a pang. Despite everything, she'd harbored the tiniest hope that maybe, just maybe, Alister had faked his death one more time.

"We gave him a military cremation, with honors. His ashes were spread with everyone else's."

"Thank you. Where....?"

"Over the ridge." Major Leppala pointed. "You have time to pay your respects, if you want. It will be another half-hour before your train's ready to go."

Taya accompanied her husband out of the station. The path to the ridge was marked with a wooden arrow and had been walked often enough to wear the snow and dead grass down to dirt.

"This isn't too bad," she murmured when they reached the top and gazed at the valley below and the mountains beyond. A wooden sign on the ridge bore a long list of names. Alister Forlore's was inserted alphabetically with the rest, with no title or caste indicator next to it. Taya couldn't find Florianne's name anywhere on the sign. She hoped the girl had some kind of marker, somewhere.

"Well, it's just me, now," Cristof said at last, pulling off his glasses and cleaning them with the end of his scarf. "The end of the line."

"Not if I have anything to say about it." Taya gave him a sideways look. "Now that you're retiring and I'm taking a vacation, it's the perfect time to start a family. You wouldn't mind staying home to watch a baby or two once I'm back on duty, would you?"

"Taya, my family—"

"I'm not having children with your family; just you. Although I *am* hoping our children will end up with your looks and my disposition."

He gave her a sour look.

"In other words, you want them to be gawky crows who ignore everything their father tells them and leap off tables and rooftops whenever our backs are turned."

She smiled and hooked her arm through his.

"Exactly, although I also expect them to be able to fix everything they break," she said, tugging him away from the ridge.

"You know I don't like children."

"They seem to like you."

"My father—"

"Has nothing to do with this. You're a better man than he was, and I'm expecting you to pass that along to our children."

"I don't have any choice in this, do I?"

"Well, you *do*, but I don't think you'll enjoy abstinence." She grinned at his resigned expression.

"All right. One."

"Two. I distinctly heard you say 'their' father."

They debated numbers all the way back to the train.

"Congratulations," Captain Amcathra said. He was still using a crutch, but his ribs had healed and the bruises and cuts that had covered his face had faded over the last two months.

"That is a great honor," Dautry agreed. Unlike Amcathra, she wasn't wearing her military uniform, although her conservative garments still gave her a serious mien. She'd been temporarily assigned to the University to teach a course on aviation while she finished the military's new navigation manual.

"I didn't accept." Cristof refilled their wineglasses. It was just the four of them; Liliana had left the day before with Jinian, who wanted to see Alzana before she returned to Cabiel.

"Why not?" the professor asked. "You would make a good decatur, Exalted. The Council needs more free-thinkers like you."

"Thank you, but Taya and I have other plans, and I've never been interested in serving on the Council. You may have noticed that I'm not very comfortable with rules."

Amcathra gave Cristof a stern look. "I think you should reconsider, Exalted. The most efficient way to change the Council will be to do so from inside."

"I agree, which is why I nominated you for the position."

Amcathra blinked. "I am a lictor."

"As it happens, nothing prohibits a lictor from serving on the Council. Nobody's ever suggested it before, but I couldn't find any bylaw that specifically forbade it."

"I'm sure your imperial ancestors would riot at the thought," Dautry commented.

"Probably." Cristof kept his eyes on Amcathra. "You'd need to take the usual Tower oaths about seeing an exalted's bare face, and you'd probably have to endure your share of prejudice, but your practical experience and public popularity make you a good choice. The Council is suffering from a public relations crisis, and you're a national hero. You're exactly the kind of man the Council needs as its representative now that I'm retiring, and not even the most conservative decatur could question your loyalty to the nation."

Amcathra's pale complexion flushed. "The Council would never accept me."

"It's *already* accepted you, Janos. The decaturs wanted to make the offer in a formal session, but I insisted they let me do it in private so you wouldn't feel obliged to accept." Cristof gave him a crooked smile. "But I hope you do. It would be a significant new direction in Ondinium's governance, and it would put a man I trust to make the right decisions exactly where the country needs him."

"Please say yes," Taya pleaded, fixing her eyes on the lictor. "Decatur Constante's going to retire soon. You'd be the perfect man to take her position as head of national defense and security."

"Ondinium would never trust anyone but an exalted in that position."

"You already know Ondinium's military secrets," Cristof argued, "and unlike any of the other decaturs, you have years of real experience in the military."

"Most of my service has been in civic defense—"

"Except for when you've been the most successful aerial commander in the nation," Cristof said, dismissively. "Your practical experience surpasses that of everyone else on the Council, including the candidates for the three other open positions."

"But you also have practical experience."

"I'm retiring."

"He's promised to settle down, build automata, and father children," Taya elaborated as Amcathra drew in a breath to argue. The lictor's eyes widened and he left his protest unspoken.

"Two children," Cristof said, firmly. "*Maximum*. I'm hoping she'll change her mind after one."

"I... I am surprised to hear that." Amcathra looked at Taya. "Congratulations, Icarus. I am sure that was not a battle easily won. I look forward to seeing children in this house."

"If you feel like contributing any of your own, Cris says he'll be happy to babysit," Taya said, blithely.

"I *never* said—"

"We do not—"

The two men stopped. Cristof looked startled and Amcathra uncomfortably cleared his throat.

"There's a 'we,' Janos?" Cristof raised his eyebrows. "Well. Congratulations to you, too. But let me make it clear that Taya has completely misrepresented my stance on babysitting."

"You have nothing to fear on that count," Dautry said calmly.

"I think," Amcathra said through grit teeth, "that we were discussing *your* plans for the future, Exalted, and not mine."

"No, I'm certain it was your future we were addressing. What do you think, Dautry? Should Janos become a decatur?"

"I think *somebody* needs to keep your Council honest," Dautry replied, seriously. "And Jani's knowledge of aerial warfare will be indispensible now that Ondinium's not the only country with an airborne fleet."

Amcathra still looked unconvinced. Taya remembered Jinian's description of him— competitive, comparative, and ever aware of hierarchy.

"It won't be easy to be the first lictor to be made a decatur," she said, thoughtfully. "You'll need to constantly prove yourself an equal to the exalteds. But you'd be an inspiring role model for every other caste in Ondinium, and Cris and I would be proud to see our friend serving on the Council."

"You'll end up outranking me, of course, but it's not like I've never worked for you before," Cristof added wryly.

Amcathra looked at Dautry, who nodded.

"Very well," he said, reluctantly. "I will accept the position if you feel it is that important."

Taya cheered and jumped around the table. The lictor stoically endured her hug, looking mildly relieved when she released him to turn and embrace Dautry.

"Excellent. I'll tell the Council the good news," Cristof said, shaking his friend's hand. "I expect you'll get the formal invitation by tomorrow evening— the Council needs something positive to feed the press."

"Please do not assume that your retirement will be permanent, Exalted," Amcathra said, pushing himself to his feet. Dautry handed him his crutch and the group walked slowly toward the front door. "While I respect your wife's plans for your future, if we are to rebuild Ondinium and re-establish strong diplomatic ties with the rest of the continent, an exalted ambassador and his envoy will be required."

"You're going to be just as bad as the rest of the decaturs, aren't you?" Cristof asked as their guests pulled on their coats.

"Don't worry, Exalted," Dautry said. "I'll make sure political power doesn't go to his head."

Cristof smiled.

"I'm sure you'll keep him honest, Professor. And anybody who can get away with calling him 'Jani' in public is allowed to call me Cristof," he said, giving her a quick embrace. She blushed.

"Then you must call me Cora," she replied, self-consciously. The small group stepped out onto the front porch and Amcathra paused.

"Nevertheless, Exalted, I trust that you will make every attempt to father your children soon, so that I may call you both back to service within a reasonable time frame." He turned to Taya. "Please ensure that your husband does not shirk his duties on that account, Taya Icarus."

Taya shot Dautry an exasperated look. "Tell me, has he gotten around to using *your* first name yet?"

"Well— occasionally," Dautry admitted.

Amcathra leaned on his crutch, his blue eyes narrowed. "Are you going to become any easier to work with once I have been sworn in as a member of the Council, Taya?"

"I wouldn't count on it, Jani," she said brightly. The lictor closed his eyes a moment in weary resignation.

"I was afraid that might be the case." He inclined his head and turned, allowing Dautry to steady him as he limped down the steps.

Taya closed the door behind them, then turned to her husband, grinning.

"Well, I think we've been given our orders," she said, holding out her hand. With a crooked smile, Cristof twined his fingers in hers and let her pull him up the stairs.

**Our titles are available at major book stores
and local independent resellers who support
Science Fiction and Fantasy readers like you.**

EDGE Science Fiction
and Fantasy Publishing

www.edgewebsite.com

Our titles are available at major book stores and local independent resellers who support Science Fiction and Fantasy readers like you.

Necromancer Candle, The by Randy McCharles (tp) - ISBN: 978-1-77053-066-9

Of Wind and Sand by Sylvie Bérard (translated by Sheryl Curtis) (tp)
  - ISBN: 978-1-894063-19-7
On Spec: The First Five Years edited by On Spec (pb)
  - ISBN: 978-1-895836-08-0
On Spec: The First Five Years edited by On Spec (hb)
  - ISBN: 978-1-895836-12-7
Orbital Burn by K. A. Bedford (tp) - ISBN: 978-1-894063-10-4
Orbital Burn by K. A. Bedford (hb) - ISBN: 978-1-894063-12-8

Pallahaxi Tide by Michael Coney (pb) - ISBN: 978-0-88878-293-9
Paradox Resolution by K. A. Bedford (tp) - ISBN:978-1-894063-88-3
Passion Play by Sean Stewart (pb) - ISBN: 978-0-88878-314-1
Petrified World (Determine Your Destiny #1) by Piotr Brynczka (pb)
  - ISBN: 978-1-894063-11-1
Plague Saint, The by Rita Donovan (tp) - ISBN: 978-1-895836-28-8
Plague Saint, The by Rita Donovan (hb) - ISBN: 978-1-895836-29-5
Pock's World by Dave Duncan (tp) - ISBN: 978-1-894063-47-0
Puzzle Box, The by Randy McCharles, Billie Millholland, Eileen Bell, and Ryan
  McFadden (tp) - ISBN: 978-1-77053-040-9

Reluctant Voyagers by Élisabeth Vonarburg (pb) - ISBN: 978-1-895836-09-7
Reluctant Voyagers by Élisabeth Vonarburg (hb) - ISBN: 978-1-895836-15-8
Resisting Adonis by Timothy J. Anderson (tp) - ISBN: 978-1-895836-84-4
Resisting Adonis by Timothy J. Anderson (hb) - ISBN: 978-1-895836-83-7
Rigor Amortis edited by Jaym Gates and Erika Holt (tp)
  - ISBN: 978-1-894063-63-0

Shadow Academy, The by Adrian Cole (tp) - ISBN: 978-1-77053-064-5
Silent City, The by Élisabeth Vonarburg (tp) - ISBN: 978-1-894063-07-4
Slow Engines of Time, The by Élisabeth Vonarburg (tp)
  - ISBN: 978-1-895836-30-1
Slow Engines of Time, The by Élisabeth Vonarburg (hb)
  - ISBN: 978-1-895836-31-8
Stealing Magic by Tanya Huff (tp) - ISBN: 978-1-894063-34-0
Stolen Children (Children of the Panther Part Three)
  by Amber Hayward (tp) - ISBN: 978-1-894063-66-1
Strange Attractors by Tom Henighan (pb) - ISBN: 978-0-88878-312-7

Taming, The by Heather Spears (pb) - ISBN: 978-1-895836-23-3
Taming, The by Heather Spears (hb) - ISBN: 978-1-895836-24-0
Technicolor Ultra Mall by Ryan Oakley (tp) - ISBN: 978-1-894063-54-8
Ten Monkeys, Ten Minutes by Peter Watts (tp) - ISBN: 978-1-895836-74-5
Ten Monkeys, Ten Minutes by Peter Watts (hb) - ISBN: 978-1-895836-76-9
Tesseracts 1 edited by Judith Merril (pb) - ISBN: 978-0-88878-279-3
Tesseracts 2 edited by Phyllis Gotlieb & Douglas Barbour (pb)
  - ISBN: 978-0-88878-270-0
Tesseracts 3 edited by Candas Jane Dorsey & Gerry Truscott (pb)
  - ISBN: 978-0-88878-290-8
Tesseracts 4 edited by Lorna Toolis & Michael Skeet (pb)
  - ISBN: 978-0-88878-322-6
Tesseracts 5 edited by Robert Runté & Yves Maynard (pb)
  - ISBN: 978-1-895836-25-7

Vampyric Variations by Nancy Kilpatrick (tp)- ISBN: 978-1-894063-94-4
Vyrkarion: The Talisman of Anor (Part Three of The Chronicles of the Karionin)
by J. A. Cullum (tp) ISBN: 978-1-77053-028-7

Warriors by Barbara Galler-Smith and Josh Langston (tp)
-ISBN: 978-1-77053-030-0
Wildcatter by Dave Duncan (tp) - ISBN: 978-1-894063-90-6